PAPER DOLLS

A Christian Novel

Kara R. Hunt

ISBN: 978-1-956654-26-4

CAST OF CHARACTERS

The Dolls:

Kite Tanner

Priscilla Martin

Lydia Dooley

Eve Stockton

Mary Rabin

Others:

Windy Jordan – Kite's Tanner's twin sister

Jack Eagle – owner of Eagle Eye Investigative Services

Lauren DeMint – Prosecuting Attorney

Diamond Liz – Priscilla Martin's best friend

Lola – Priscilla Martin's best friend

Barry King – Real estate mogul

Mabel Martin – Priscilla's mother

Ada, Bethany, Claudia, and Dinah – Lydia Dooley's daughters

Philip Stockton – Eve Stockton's husband

Kay Locke – Eve's mother

Roger Roarke – Eve's music producer

Three-Sixteen – Christian music band

John & Donna Melson – Mary Rabin's biological parents

Ezra & Aviva Isaac – Mary's adoptive parents

Paul Melson – Mary's biological brother

Christianna Saxton – Mary's biological sister

Ethan Rabin – Mary's husband

Lloyd Greene – Pastor of Resurrection Church

Kite Tanner leaned forward to get a better look at the small crowd that had gathered across the road from her. She was a good distance away and the windshield needed a good cleaning, but the target was easy to spot.

Five-foot-ten. Lanky build. Untamed black curls. Boyish good looks. The client profile listed his age as forty-one. She squinted and leaned in a bit more. The guy in her line of sight could easily pass for half that age. That was also in the profile.

She grabbed the Canon Mark III from her lap and double-checked to make sure it was still in silent mode. She tossed her purse on the van floor and began rapid shooting just as the target jogged toward a group of kids, who were running toward him. He lifted a young blond boy about the age of seven before the rest of the kids collided with his long legs.

An Asian girl stomped to the side, folded her arms, and pouted. Without letting go of the boy, he scooped her up with his free arm. She flung her arms around his neck and smiled.

The kids ranging in age from about five to twelve, wore dark green T-shirts with the name Gideon's Club emblazoned in white across the front. They followed the subject down the street to a small red brick building with a steeple but no name on the outside. The man set the boy on the wooden railing that lined the walkway, then turned to open the door. The kids filed in, one after the other, a few stopping the line to talk with him. After the last one stepped inside, the boy jumped off the railing and ran into the church. The target continued to hold the door open, chatting with the girl in his right arm until four other adults—three women and one man—approached from the side of the church wearing the same style T-shirts. He handed the girl to one of the women.

Kite zoomed in on the women to see if any of them fit the "Botoxed bottle blonde" description the client gave. None of the women even came close.

She lowered the camera and sat back. From the looks of it, her client's husband wasn't cheating on her. Apparently, the four hours every Tuesday night that he disappeared were not spent with another woman but with a group of kids. A group of kids who were excited to see him.

The question was, why was he keeping this from his wife?

Kite retrieved her phone from the dashboard mount. A quick internet search described The Gideon's Club as a local Christian organization that reached out to kids in crisis. That explained it. She'd had the unfortunate privilege of meeting his wife, the outspoken assistant district attorney, Lauren DeMint, at the office a few days back. Not only was Mrs. DeMint a proud atheist, she also didn't hide her disdain for children.

Kite flicked her eyes from her phone back to the windshield and wondered why a guy who obviously loved working with children—and from the way they reacted, the feeling was mutual—would stay married to a woman like that?

She tossed her phone onto the passenger seat and laid her head against the headrest. Working for Jack Eagle and Eagle Eye Investigative Services the past eighteen months had her asking questions she'd never before thought to ask. Wasn't her business to ask. She glanced at her opened purse on the floor. Her recently delivered P.I. license stared back at her and reminded her that now it was.

She placed the camera next to her purse and started the ignition while more T-shirt wearing adults entered the building. She knew Jack would want her to stay longer, to make sure that, when the meeting was over, the target didn't leave with a Botoxed blonde, but her gut told her that Mr. DeMint was just taking the coward's way out. By not disclosing his Tuesday night activities, he was avoiding what was sure to become one heck of an argument. Kite had seen his wife in action on the local news. She wasn't the type one looked forward to getting into a cage with.

As the last person entered the building, her cell phone rang. She didn't recognize the number, but she also knew that J.S., their office intern, sometimes called from a phone at his high school. She pulled out of the parking space then tapped the answer button.

"This is Kite."

"Come and get me."

Kite eased her foot off the accelerator. The voice on the

other end sounded like it belonged to her twin sister, but Windy always called her personal cell, never the agency mobile.

"Wind, is that you?"

"I need your help."

Her sister's definition of needing help meant helping her pick out a new shade of eyeshadow. "I can't, Wind." Kite looked around her then made her way through an intersection. "I'm heading to the office to wrap-up a case."

She then steeled herself for the flurry of angry protests Windy would throw her way. When none came, she pulled the phone from her ear to make sure they were still connected. They were.

She pressed the accelerator, blazed through a stop sign, and took a quick right to get to the highway. Windy was used to getting her way. When it didn't happen, she'd make you regret it. But when she went silent, that was bad. Real bad.

"Where are you?"

"Corner of Adams and Lincoln." Windy's voice was shaky. "I need to get out of here before they find me."

"Who?"

"Hurry!"

Kite clicked off the phone, turned onto the highway, and veered the agency's surveillance minivan into the fast lane. Her boss, Jack Eagle, kept at least ten different types of surveillance vehicles in the company parking lot. She'd chosen the beige minivan because it wouldn't stand out at the small church, but apparently this make wasn't known for its speed. She barely stayed ahead of the bright yellow Volkswagen riding her tail.

She switched into the middle lane, and hit the redial

button on her phone. She was still at least fifteen minutes from Windy's location. She didn't know if her sister was on foot or planning to switch cars, but if she was able to meet her at a location closer to the highway, Kite could get to her faster.

No answer.

A second redial went straight to voicemail.

Kite floored the minivan and said a silent prayer that the traffic would remain light, and that she wouldn't attract police. Or maybe the police were exactly who she needed. If it weren't for Windy's history of multiple brushes with the law, she'd call and have them meet her there. But chances were nine out of ten that that'd end in her sister's arrest. Still, she had to take that chance.

She slowed to merge into the right lane and had pressed the first of the three digits for the police when the phone vibrated in her hand. She clicked the talk button. "Windy, what's going on?"

"I started walking south. I'm heading toward Monroe."

"That's even better. I can be at the Federal Credit Union on Monroe in less than five minutes. I'm in a beige minivan. I'll pull up to the steps in front, and you can jump in."

She let out a loud breath. "Thanks, sister. You're by yourself, right? You didn't contact the police, did you?"

Kite turned onto the exit ramp and stopped at the light. "I was about to when you didn't answer. What's going on, Wind?"

"The police are who I'm trying to avoid. They're coming for me. Or soon will be."

Kite tightened her grip on the steering wheel. "Why? What did you do this time?"

"It has to do with Michael."

Figured. Her boyfriend for the last ten years. Michael was a liar, a thief, and a cheat. Kite was also pretty sure he was married. A one-hour investigation by Jack Eagle could've proved that, but Windy wouldn't have it. Every person who tried to talk her into leaving Michael, she broke communication with. To preserve their sisterhood, Kite kept her opinions to herself and prayed that soon enough Michael would be exposed for the rat he was.

"What did he do now?"

"Doesn't matter. He's dead."

Her fingers tightened on the phone. "What do you mean, he's dead?"

"He's dead, Kite. D.E.A.D. I killed him. Stabbed him straight through the heart."

She quickly wiped the phone against her jeans as the sweat on her hand threatened to make it slip. A moment passed before Windy let out a soft chuckle. "Do you know he even had the nerve to look surprised? Like he had no idea of the heartache he'd put me through. Well, he knows now." She took in a quick breath. "Where are you?"

Kite loosened her grip on the phone as the steps to the credit union came into view. "I'm here."

She waited for a gray sedan to pull out of the space directly in front of the building. Her sister, dressed in tight jeans and an oversize dark blue sweatshirt—which she was pretty sure used to belong to Michael—turned in her direction, bounded down the concrete steps, and smiled.

Chapter Two

Priscilla Martin admired her reflection in the window of Rosenberg Jeweler's. She smiled, adjusted her purse strap, and continued her walk, secure in the fact that her four-inch heels accentuated every curve of her shapely legs. She pretended not to notice the stares and double-takes of the men who passed by. At forty-five, she was fully aware that she still had the "it" that made men strain their necks for a longer look. Her deep mocha-skin attracted men from every race and economic background. And she loved every minute of it.

She was glad she was making this trip alone. Most Saturday nights, she'd be accompanied by her friends, Diamond Liz and Lola. It was Lola she was glad not to have in her company tonight. While Priscilla's five-foot-seven frame and long dark locks turned heads, it was Lola's exotic mix of African and French heritage that made them salivate. Add to that Lola's perfect bow lips, her vivacious curves, and her love of sporting the Betty Boop hairstyle and in the presence of Lola, Priscilla was nothing more than background noise.

But not tonight. Tonight, Diamond Liz was to introduce Priscilla to her next victim. Diamond Liz had initially wanted the man for herself, but after four dates had found him to be too needy. And Diamond Liz hated emotionally needy men.

Priscilla wasn't particular. She was willing to stroke a man's ego for as long as it took to get what she wanted. And today, she wanted a rich man.

Her current boyfriend, Jacob, had it all. He was tall, dark, handsome, and rich. But he was also yesterday's news. He didn't know that, but Priscilla did. She had ten years invested in their relationship. If he hadn't started to complain so much about money, she'd have given him ten more. It wasn't just the new Bentley she'd requested. It was his failing and soon to be bankrupt business. A broke man was not a man in Priscilla's world.

She reached the entrance of Jeffrey's, one of the best fine-dining establishments in the Midwest, and stepped inside. Before the hostess greeted her, Diamond Liz appeared. Her blond hair was parted straight down the middle and fell in long golden sheets over her shoulders. And the couture blue dress, one of Liz's favorite colors, was no match for the blue of her eyes. Nothing ever was.

"I'm so glad you're here!" Diamond Liz grabbed Priscilla's arm and pulled her in close. "If I have to hear this man whine one more time about how noisy it is in here, I'm gonna scream."

Priscilla tossed her hair to the side. "He doesn't like the violin playing?"

Liz shook her head. "He's the, 'Can't we go someplace

quiet and snuggle' type." She twisted her nose and mouth, then held out her right hand and stared at it for a moment. A diamond the size of Mt. Everest stared back at her. "Barry definitely has the money to add many more of these to my collection, but I'm done. I already told him. He was about to put up a fuss until I told him I had a friend who'd be more his type."

Priscilla struck a pose and pursed her lips. "How do I look, dahling?"

"Amazing, dahling. Simply amazing." Diamond Liz stepped behind Priscilla, then turned her in the direction of two tables at the back of the restaurant. "Barry is the Bob Dole look alike at table two. He's seventy, six-foot-four, and a real-estate mogul. Self-made billionaire, if you believe his company profile. Not married. Two children, three grandchildren, and he's in great shape. I gladly would've been his next trophy wife. But you know me, Pris. I can't stand clingy."

Priscilla turned to face Liz. "I know it'd take a whole lot more than an old man needing affection to get you to let go of billions. What's the real deal?"

Diamond Liz smiled. "Let's just say I'm a great fill-in, but I'm not exactly his type."

"Oh?" Priscilla tilted her head toward Liz. "And what type is that?"

Liz gave her a push toward Barry's table. "How about I just let him tell you."

Barry stood as they approached and pulled out a chair for Priscilla. He smiled. "My, oh my. Aren't you a lovely little chocolate drop?"

Chapter Three

Lydia Dooley knelt, bowed her head, and embraced the warmth from the hands that gently touched her body. She had been in this position so many times that she easily recognized the women by their scents. Eve smelled of peppermint and was praying softly. Rhoda smelled of fresh lavender, and Lola carried the sweet scent of strawberries and the tropical hint of mango. Lydia breathed in deeper, relishing that scent. Sweet yet exciting. She smiled. That was Lola, all right. She was the only person Lydia knew who could take two distinct scents and make them her own. Lola knelt beside her, massaging Lydia's back while Rhoda stood behind them praying for healing. Lydia's nose told her that several more women had joined their prayer circle. They brought the scents of coconut and roses. Lydia's ears and heart heard every word of every prayer said over her. But her eyes, behind closed lids, envisioned a garden. A beautiful flower garden full of color and splendor. She smiled again.

"Lydia, are you all right?"

She opened her eyes, surprised that she was no longer

kneeling, but in Rhoda's arms. Somehow, she'd toppled over. Using Rhoda's thigh as leverage, she pushed herself into a sitting position. It was times like this she missed her thick, shoulder-length hair. It came in handy when she wanted to hide the rising heat in her cheeks. "I'm sorry. I don't know what happened." She accepted Eve's hand to help her off the floor. "That must've been some prayer you ladies prayed."

Everyone laughed, but Eve nibbled her bottom lip as she clasped Lydia's hand into both of hers. "You appear very weak. When is your next doctor's appointment?"

"I just had one yesterday, so not for a few weeks."

Eve tightened her grip. "What did he say?"

"The same as before. They don't expect me to be around this time next year."

Lola stepped forward. "What does he know? Doctors don't know everything." She placed a hand on her perfectly curved hip then pointed to her chest. "I, on the other hand, will continue to have faith that not only will you be here next year, but for many more after that. How does that sound?"

"Sounds good to me." Lydia stepped away from Eve and pulled Lola into a hug. Even though they looked absolutely nothing alike, Lola was like a daughter to her all the same. Lydia still had a hard time believing that only eighteen months ago, this ray of sunshine had come into her life. Before then, Lola had never stepped inside of a church and knew very little about God, Christ, or the Bible. It was Lola's fiancé, Ram, who had led her to Christ. A few months after they were married, he'd reached out to Lydia and asked if she would be a spiritual mentor to his much younger bride. After he told her about Lola's background, she knew exactly why he'd asked. And there was no way she could've said no.

"Okay, ladies, that's enough of that." Rhoda stepped between the two of them. "My favorite café closes in two hours. It takes us that long just to place our orders." As the ladies gathered their things, Rhoda wrapped her hand around Lydia's elbow. "Have you heard anything from Dinah yet?"

Lydia shook her head. Dinah was the youngest of her four daughters. "I've done everything I can think of. I've called, sent letters, emailed, texted. She's a woman of her word, that's for sure. Seventeen years hasn't changed it. I can't help but admire her for that."

Rhoda pressed in closer. "That was a very broken and hurt young girl who said those things. She's grown now. And she's a beautiful and successful young woman. Attitudes change. Hearts change. She still doesn't know about your diagnosis?"

"No. And I've asked my parents and her sisters not to tell her. I don't want her to feel like she has to reach out to me just because I'm dying."

"But if she knew—"

"I hurt her, Rhoda. I was an awful person. For years I've tried to reach out to her to fix that. And for years she's ignored me. I continue to pray that I'll get to see and hug her at least one more time. To apologize for the horror of a parent I was to her." She blinked against the gathering dampness. "But I won't guilt her into forgiving me. I can't do that to her. I've hurt her enough. I died to her a long time ago. Me taking my last breath in the coming months won't do much to change that."

Rhoda smiled. "Well, if you don't mind, I'm just going to follow Lola's lead and have faith that Dinah will find it in her heart to forgive you. And that you'll be able to have that talk with her. And that hug." Rhoda hiked her chin up, pushed her shoulders back, and placed a hand on her almost non-existent hip in a futile attempt to strike her best Lola pose. "What do you think about that?"

Lydia laughed and retrieved her purse and Bible from the sanctuary steps. "I think you need to pray very hard, my friend." She linked arms with Rhoda as they followed the other ladies toward the exit. "I think you need to pray very, very hard."

Chapter Four

Eve Stockton locked the door to Kay's Café, then waved good-bye to her friends. The café belonged to her mother, but Eve loved how Mom turned over the keys to her on Tuesday afternoons so she could have brunch with her weekly prayer group. The café normally closed at three on weekdays, but the girls tended to arrive late and stay way past closing time. After the last customer left, Eve's mom would hand over the keys and let them have the place to themselves. And despite Eve's protests, the girls never left without helping make sure the café was spotless, ready for the next morning's breakfast rush. They also helped with food prep, slicing and dicing the fruits and vegetables Kay would need for the next day. Eve's mom was so ecstatic the first time they'd done that, she'd asked them to come and visit more than once a week, but like Eve, most of the ladies had husbands and houses and children to tend to. Tuesdays were a day they set aside to spiritually nourish themselves through prayer, Bible study, fellowship, and coffee. And for

Eve, Tuesday afternoons couldn't come fast enough.

As she walked to her car, she glanced at her watch. How was it already after six? She considered going back inside to make a couple of sandwiches for dinner, but decided against it. If Philip didn't have a home-cooked meal when he came home, it could be a very bad night. She placed her purse on the hood of her car, rummaged through it, and pulled out his flight itinerary. His plane was scheduled to land at seven. Add the additional forty-five minutes for him to drive home, and she still had time to shower and prepare a decent meal for her husband. Well, at least by law he was still her husband, though, in his heart, that was another matter.

Eve used the car's remote to unlock the door and start the engine. Thankfully, Mom had placed the café within minutes of each of their homes. If she turned right, she could be at her mom's place in seven minutes and, if she turned left, at hers in five. After she turned left, she checked her phone again to make sure she hadn't missed any texts or email updates from the airline or Philip. Satisfied, she pressed the accelerator and was home in a record three minutes. Inside, she turned on the oven, washed and seasoned two chicken breasts, then placed them inside the giant oven that had cost more than her first car. She pulled a loaf of homemade bread from the freezer, groaned at the lack of fresh veggies in the refrigerator, and grabbed a bag of rice from the pantry. She placed water to boil before heading up the stairs for a shower. Just as her foot hit the top step, keys scraped in the door. She stiffened and retraced her steps as Philip's suitcase rumbled over the threshold.

"Evie!" His shout reverberated through the house louder than the slamming of the door. He took off his suit coat and laid it across his luggage. "Evi—"

"I'm right here." She stopped on the bottom step and glanced at her watch. "I wasn't expecting you home for another hour."

Philip kicked off his shoes and loosened his tie. "Howard and I were able to catch an earlier flight."

"That would've been nice to know."

"Why? Am I interrupting something?" He shook his head and let out a short laugh. Like the thought of her being involved in anything worthwhile was beyond comical.

"No, but it would've been nice for you to keep me informed. I could've started dinner earlier."

"You mean it's not ready?" He walked into the kitchen and looked around. "I don't smell anything. Have you even started?"

Eve gripped the wooden railing next to her. "We're having baked chicken and wild rice with homemade bread. The chicken will be done in less than an hour, and I planned on finishing the rest after a shower."

He turned the knob to turn off the heating water. "We had rice last week. If we're having chicken, I want green beans."

She gripped the railing tighter. "We're out of green beans. I'll stop by the farmer's market first thing in the mor—"

His fist slammed on the counter. "I just spent ten miserable days in less than stellar hotels listening to the most boring speakers on the planet all to stay on top of my game so I can provide you with all this." His arm made a dramatic sweep around the state-of-the-art kitchen. "And I can't even get a decent meal. What is wrong with you?"

Eve stepped off the bottom step and pinched her lips together to stop from calling him out on his lies. He hadn't been gone ten miserable days, he'd been gone fourteen. Several of which she knew had nothing to do with his job. The only thing *less than stellar* about the hotels was they didn't serve caviar. And she was the last person he'd do anything for. She'd had no say in the kitchen when it was being built. He'd done it all for himself. Just like everything else.

She let out a long sigh. "Nothing's wrong with me that a little consideration couldn't fix. You've called me once in two weeks. A quick text would've been nice to let me know you'd be home early. I could've left the café earlier, and your dinner would be ready."

That all-too-familiar vein in his forehead pulsed. He gripped the counter and leaned forward. "You were at the café?"

"Of course, I was. It's Tuesday."

"I told you to stay away from there."

Eve shook her head. "You're not going to stop me from seeing my friends, Philip."

"You know I don't care about those Bible thumpers. I'm talking about your mom. She's a snake."

Eve walked into the kitchen. When she got to the counter, Philip grabbed for her arm. She dodged him then headed straight for the oven. She glanced at the still baking chicken, then punched the timer buttons for thirty minutes. She pulled her keys from her jeans' pocket.

"Where are you going?"

Eve faced him. "I'm going to the store. If I leave now, I should be able to make it there before they close." She brushed past him, but this time he didn't try to stop her. "I'll grab some fresh beans from the produce section, then come back and finish the meal. It'll be a late supper, but that'll give us both time to shower and calm down."

"I bet Howard's wife had his meal ready when he got home."

"I bet she did." Eve twisted the doorknob. "I'll be back shortly."

"Ignore me all you want, Eve. But this little ploy of yours is not going to stop us from discussing your mother. She's a problem and you know it."

Typical Philip. Instead of taking responsibility for his own actions, he shifted the focus to someone else's. "I know you have a problem with her. I don't."

"For thirty years that woman has—"

"I also know that I'm not going to stay away from my mom just because the two of you had an argument."

Philip shoved away from the counter and stomped towards her. "She's poisoned you against me and you know it!"

"And if you plan on continuing to ignore the fact that all of this could've been avoided if you'd let me know your schedule had changed, then you'll be talking to yourself." She opened the front door and stepped onto the porch. "I'm done with it."

"Eve—"

"I said I'm done with it."

A vein in his neck seemed eager to pop. He called her a name, then marched to the door and slammed it inches from her face. While he secured the lock, she wondered if she'd ever have the courage to follow through on what she'd said.

Her heart told her no, but her brain told her the truth.
She needed to be done with it.

Chapter Five

Mary Rabin couldn't believe her eyes. The yard, the same yard she was taken from thirty-nine-years before, was as tidy and colorful as she remembered it. And the house just as tiny. The yellow-framed house with white shutters and blue roof still hosted beautiful arrays of spring flowers. Tall red columbine, blue sage, and sweet Kate surrounded the porch, while bright orange begonias and soft pink impatiens cascaded from baskets along the porch roof. Images of Mary and her mom, kneeling in the dirt with matching gloves and trowels, flooded her memory. So did the names of the plants Mary thought she had long ago forgotten. And she had. Until today.

With a deep breath, she searched the car for a tissue decent enough to wipe her eyes with. She counted the empty tissue boxes. Four. The drive from her home in Delaware to her former home in Missouri had been joyful and full of expectation, but it had also been full of tears. She'd waited almost forty years to be reunited with her family, and now it was happening. She glanced at the car door handle. At least it was supposed to be happening. She put her hand on the handle. Opening that door could be the best thing that ever happened in her life—or the worst.

They had no idea she was coming. She'd had no idea she was coming until a week ago. It'd taken Eagle Eye Investigative Services one day to find her parents. Mary'd asked the investigator to be discrete when verifying information. When Jack verified it, she'd packed her things and planned her road trip. A flight wouldn't have given her the time she'd needed to process everything. Well, the road trip had certainly done that. But just when she thought she couldn't possibly shed one more tear, another one appeared.

She looked into the sun visor's mirror. The makeup she'd carefully applied at the hotel that morning had been cried off. Only a bit of eyeliner and mascara remained beneath her eyes. Ugh. She lifted the top of the car's middle console and pulled out the bottle of water and washcloth she'd stashed earlier. With the dampened cloth, she wiped the tear streaks from her face. She applied a thin layer of her favorite lip gloss. Her shoulder-length brunette hair remained secured at the nape of her neck with a barrette, and her side-swept bangs were holding up well. She flipped the visor shut and said another prayer before opening the car door.

As she walked toward the house, she wondered for the hundredth time that morning if this was a good idea. Her parents would be in their seventies now. Would the shock of seeing her distress them? The best route would've been to do as Jack Eagle had suggested and use him as an intermediary, allowing him to go ahead of her to explain everything to her family. But that was exactly what she wanted to avoid. She wanted—no, she *needed*—to see and experience their reactions first hand. She'd dreamed about it for thirty-nine years, and just when she'd given up hope, she'd received the phone call that had changed her life. Her only regret was that her husband Ethan wasn't here with her. They'd argued for days before she left on the trip. He was adamant that he needed to be with her, and she was just as adamant that she needed to do this alone. She'd fully expected him to plead his case the morning she'd left, but instead he'd helped her pack the car and prayed with her. Fifty miles into her trip, she'd known she'd made a mistake. She needed him. But turning back hadn't been an option. She'd waited too long for this.

As she climbed the first set of steps, the screen door pushed open and an older woman with a silvery bob stepped out holding a watering can. She slid a small stool beneath the hanging plants. When she turned to step on it, she saw Mary and stopped.

Mary sucked in a quick breath, unable to speak. It was the woman's cornflower eyes. They were the same eyes that looked back at her every morning from her seven-year-old daughter. The same eyes Mary remembered from childhood. Eyes full of love, kindness, and laughter. The same eyes that were staring at her now.

The woman stepped back from the stool but continued to stare. Mary put one foot in front of the other and was amazed when she looked down to see that her feet hadn't actually moved at all. This was it. This was the moment that she'd dreamed about for as long as she could remember. But even in her wildest dreams, she'd never imagined that her body would refuse to cooperate.

The woman on the porch set down the water can and

approached. As she descended, she paused on each step. And with every new step, her grip on the wrought-iron railing whitened another shade. When she finally landed on the long concrete walkway that joined the two sets of steps, Mary attempted once again to get her legs to move, but the woman held up her hand, and Mary stopped, not sure what to do next.

The woman's rosy scent reached to Mary. The familiar fragrance brought tears to her eyes.

The woman stepped closer and opened her mouth as if she wanted to speak, but instead she placed her small hand over it. The hand shook.

The woman lowered her hand and stepped closer. "Mary Laura?"

Mary blinked. The name was whispered so softly, Mary wasn't sure she'd heard right. But the tears, like rivers that coursed down her cheeks, assured her she had. "Yes, Mommy." She squeezed her eyes shut in an attempt to stem the flow. She swallowed and whispered back just as softly, "It's me. Mary Laura."

This time it was both hands that covered her mother's mouth. Mary leaned in to hug the woman whose touch she'd been denied for too long. But instead of falling into Mary's embrace, her mother screamed. But the scream wasn't one filled with terror. It was a mixture of anguish and joy. Mary stepped back, but her mother grabbed her arms and pulled her close. Mary was sure that anyone within a ten-mile radius had to have heard that scream.

The screen door opened. Two men and a woman ran down the steps. The woman in front said, "Mom, are you okay? What's going on? Who is this?"

Mary stifled a sob. "Christianna?"

The woman balled her fists and ran toward them. Mary forced herself to pull away from her mother's embrace. The younger woman came closer, fire blazing in eyes that mimicked her own. "What did you do to my mother?"

Her mother placed an arm around Christianna. "Chrissy, it's Mary Laura. Praise God! Can you believe it? She's home." She pulled them together, then lifted her face toward the sky and shouted, "She's home!"

The two men had paused at the bottom of the steps. Mary loved her mother, but from the day she was born until the day she was taken, she'd always been a daddy's girl. The years had been kind to him. As a child, she'd thought he stood as tall and as strong as her mom's favorite oak tree in their backyard. And just as immovable. Today, he seemed the same way. Rooted to the ground. His face, unreadable.

"John, Paul, didn't you hear me?" Her mother wiped at the tears. "Mary Laura's home."

Paul, her older brother by two years, stepped forward. He was as tall and good looking as their dad. A long way from the Pauly she remembered, who had been all legs and arms as he sat at her tiny table, by mom's orders, to play tea party with her. She in return had promised to stay out of his room.

He reached into his back pocket and pulled out a wallet. Mary watched as he used two fingers to pull a photo loose from one of the slots. He looked at the photo, then back at Mary. He did that several times before he stepped close enough for her to grab him into a hug.

"Oh, Pauly." Mary sobbed into his shirt.

After a few seconds, he pulled her tight and cried into her hair. "As soon as I stepped out the door, I knew it was you. I knew it. I just … I just couldn't take it if it wasn't, you know?" His voice cracked. "I just couldn't."

She wept into his shirt until a large hand warmed her shoulder. She turned around and looked into her dad's eyes. His face wet, he reached for her hands. "I punched myself in the leg several times to make sure I was awake this time and not dreaming." He shook his head. "And now…"

Mary clasped his hands tighter and then lifted them to her face. "It's not a dream, Daddy." She pulled her fingers from his as he traced the outline of her face. "I'm home. It's a miracle and a very long story, but I'm here, I'm alive, and I'm home."

His lips trembled.

"It's me, Daddy. Shmumpkin is home."

He pulled her in and hugged her until she had trouble breathing, but she wouldn't dare say a word about it. The mention of the favorite nickname, which she'd never forgotten, had opened the dam. If that meant that she would suffocate in her daddy's arms, then so be it.

"We should move this reunion inside." Mary didn't have to move her head from her dad's chest to know that it was Chrissy who'd spoken. "Mom's scream brought out some of the neighbors."

Mary forced herself away from her dad. The last thing she wanted was attention, which was why she hadn't told anyone about her arrival ahead of time. It was also why she hadn't gone to the police first. *Woman kidnapped forty years ago at age eight, returns, reunites with family.* That headline would bring a media circus for sure. She was not about to put her family through that. Not after everything they'd been through.

"Chrissy's right," Mary said. "It's probably best to go inside. I have so much to tell you."

"It might be too late." Chrissy's focus was now behind Mary. "I bet it's one of those nosy reporters."

Mary turned, ready with the well-rehearsed answers she'd prepared ahead of time for anyone besides family who asked questions. But when she got a glimpse of the guy making his way up the steps, her jaw dropped.

"Ethan!"

She ran toward him and gave him a quick peck on the lips. "What are you doing here?"

He smiled and waved over her shoulder. "You really didn't think I'd let you make this trip alone did you?"

Her mind flashed back to the days right before her trip and the arguments with her husband. And how, on the morning of the trip, his attitude had drastically changed.

"You left right behind me, didn't you?"

He smiled. "I gave you a five-minute head start, but yeah. I was right behind you the entire 936 miles, which included five restroom stops, three fast food breaks, and one overnight hotel stay."

"You were with me last night at the hotel?"

"Right across the hall."

She swatted him on the arm. "Why didn't you say anything?"

"What? And have you fighting with me the entire way?" He leaned in close to whisper in her ear. "I also know how much you wish the kids could be here. I used my cellphone to record a video to show them later."

It had broken her heart to make this trip and reunite with her biological family without her children in tow, especially once they'd learned the entire story. They were eager to meet their biological grandparents, but she'd been afraid that it would be too much, too soon. For her and her family. She gave Ethan another peck then grabbed his hand and turned around. "This is my husband, Ethan. I didn't know he was coming, but he knew I would need his support. I hope it's okay for him to come in."

Mom stepped forward, blinking away tears, and gave a soft chuckle. "I figured he was your husband and that, if he weren't, he oughtta be." She placed a hand on Ethan's shoulder. "You're welcome in our home anytime."

"You have no idea how glad I am to finally meet all of you." Ethan patted her mother's hand." It's been a long hard road for Mary, and I can't begin to imagine how difficult it's been for you."

Mom wiped away another tear. "All I know right now is that every prayer I've ever prayed for the past forty years has been answered."

Mary reached for her mom's hands and kissed them. "And I've felt every one of those prayers. I believe they're the reason we're here today. And I also bet you have a lot of questions."

Mom nodded.

Mary wrapped an arm around her mom's shoulders. "And after almost forty years, I've finally gotten all the answers. But first, let's start with the day I was kidnapped."

Chapter Six

Kite stared at the empty spot on the floor. The same spot where her sister Windy claimed she'd left a lifeless Michael less than an hour ago.

Kite knelt on the gray stone tiles of the kitchen floor and leaned in to get a closer look. Faint streaks of blood smeared the tile. And the grout had a pink tinge to it.

"Looks like somebody tried to clean this area." She looked up at Windy. "Are you sure he was dead when you left here?"

"Of course, I'm sure. Well … at least I think I am."

"Windy!"

"I don't know, okay? Like I told you in the car, I came over to confront him about his latest tryst. We argued. Things got ugly, so I turned to leave out that door." She pointed the key to his house toward the entrance. "Then he grabbed me and threw me against that wall." Kite followed her finger to the wall near the kitchen. "We wrestled, and somehow we ended up on the floor, in the exact spot that you are now. He snatched a knife off the table and threatened me.

I scrambled for the door again, he snatched me back, and the next thing I knew, I was putting the blade through his chest. He tumbled off me and hit the floor. That's when I jumped up, ran out, and called you."

"So you didn't actually check to see if he was dead?"

"There was so much blood …"

Kite pulled Windy down next to her. "Okay. He threatened you, wouldn't let you leave, and you were afraid for your life. Is that what you're telling me?"

She nodded.

"That sounds like self-defense."

Windy lifted an eyebrow and cocked her head.

"You *were* afraid for your life weren't you, Wind?"

Windy ran her hand through her dark brown mane, squinted, and gazed at the ceiling. "It all happened so fast."

Kite took note of how Windy refused to look her in the eyes. With her sister, Kite had learned it's best to keep a mental notepad and pen at the ready. Windy's actions always spoke louder than her words. "It's fine. Once the police hear what you just told me—"

Windy shot off the floor. "The police? What do you want to call them for?"

"This is a crime scene, Windy."

"But we don't know that. For all we know, Michael could've regained consciousness, called 911, or driven himself to the hospital."

"Regained consciousness?"

She bit her lip and shrugged. "You know what I mean. Got up or whatever."

Kite straightened and took another look around the kitchen, living area, hallway, and entryway. Besides the smudges on the kitchen floor, nothing else looked out of place. It didn't even look like there'd been a struggle.

She glared at Windy.

Her sister raised her hands. "I've done a lot of things, Kite, but I've never lied to you. What I told you is exactly how it happened."

Kite crossed her arms and was reminded once again that she and Windy may have looked alike, but that was where their similarities ended. Windy preferred her hair long and flowing while Kite was content with her hair pulled back and secured with 1950's style headbands. Her eyes were the color of root beer and but her sister's resembled milk chocolate. She thrived on the straight and narrow while Windy's personality pursued chaos.

"Do you know where Michael is?"

"No."

"Did you kill him?"

"I don't know."

"Did you cut him up and hide his body?"

She stepped back and mimicked her sister's stance. "Really, Kite?"

When no answer came, Windy tossed hair away from her shoulders and returned her sister's glare. "I thought he was dead when I left him here, but what happened after that I don't know. And I definitely did not hide his body somewhere."

"What aren't you telling me?"

She blinked several times. Silence.

Kite walked toward the door. "Fine. Do it your way, Wind."

She stepped in front of her. "Everything I told you is

true."

"But?"

She took in a quick breath. "There … might be a little bit more."

"Spill it."

"It wasn't just *some* tryst that Michael was having that I was upset about. It was who he was having it with. Her name's Hildy."

"A friend of yours?"

She let out a huff. "Heavens no. This girl wouldn't run in my circles. And that was what made me so angry. I gave Michael anything he wanted, anytime he wanted it. Then suddenly he stopped wanting it. All because of this pure-as-the-driven-snow twenty-something who won't even let him hold her hand unless her daddy said so. And what does Michael do? He chases after her, panting like a dog."

"You've seen them together?"

"Yes. And I've bugged his phone, intercepted emails, and followed their text messages. She and her family recently moved here. Her father was some big-time preacher from upstate somewhere. This girl's completely out of his league, and I told him so. I told him to end it before it went too far. But he was obsessed." She shook her head. "When I found out he bought her an engagement ring, I was furious. I pulled up to his place today, blazed up the steps, and pushed my way through the door. Can you believe that cheatin' mongrel wasn't going to let me in?" She flicked her hand in the air with the same annoyed attitude one had when flicking away a gnat. "Anyway, his neighbor witnessed the entire thing. Well, he was out there when I drove up. An hour later, he was still out there when I ran out of here and sped off.

When I rounded the corner, I saw him pull out his cell. I thought he was calling the police."

Kite nodded. "That could be a good thing. Maybe they came and talked to Michael. Or maybe he saw Michael drive off or leave with someone. Either way, he could've seen Michael alive."

Windy slid her hands into the front pockets of her jeans. "The only person he'd ever call to come get him would be his brother, Frank. He drives one of those loud, obnoxious muscle cars. The whole neighborhood would've heard him."

"Good. Call Frank and see if Michael's with him."

She shook her head. "I don't have his number. Frank's one of those people … let's just say that if you're ever stopped by the cops, he's not one of those people whose number you'd want to have on your phone."

"Do you think he would've taken him to the hospital?"

She let out a small sound that fell somewhere between a gasp and a chuckle. "Definitely not. He would've taken him to Uncle. Their uncle. That's the only name I've ever heard anyone call him by. He's a retired surgeon. And if Michael or Frank ever needed medical attention, that's where they'd go. He has a small house on the outskirts of town. He performs medical procedures out of his basement."

Kite opened her mouth to speak, but all she could do was stare. This whole thing was becoming more bizarre by the minute. And dangerous. Part of her wanted to chastise her sister for associating with people like this—let alone being in love with one. The other part wanted to hold her and keep her safe.

She rubbed the back of her neck. "My hands are tied on what I can do here, Wind. I can't call the cops if you're going to refuse to talk to them. And you'd never agree for me to call Jack and get an Eagle Eye investigator on it." She shrugged. "I don't know what you want me to do."

"You're one of his investigators. Can't you do it?"

Kite shook her head. "Sure could, but I'm not going to. And I'm not going to for the exact same reason you don't want Jack or the other investigators to do it. You're afraid of what they might find. On you, as well as on Michael. And so am I." She took a step forward and pointed her finger at Windy. "You know how I am. If I go down that road, I'm going down it thoroughly. And I'll have an obligation to the law, my conscience, and my God to report anything illegal that I find. And we both know that your hands aren't clean."

Windy pinched her lips and looked at the floor.

Kite let out a sigh. "The best thing for us to do right now is wait a few days and see if Michael pops up. Until then, you'll stay at my place. I don't know what kind of craziness you and Michael have going on, but if he survived that knife wound, your apartment's the first place he's going to look for you. And from what you've told me about the people he surrounds himself with, I don't think he'll be stopping by for a kiss."

"Michael won't come after me."

"His brother or his uncle might."

She scratched at her cheek. "I'm not sure how I want this to end, Ki. Michael deserves to die for the way he's treated me." She looked up without raising her head. "I've waited over a decade for a proposal from him. Then to be kicked aside so he can marry some innocent dove too stupid to know what she's getting into? My intention wasn't to kill him, but if he's found in a dark alley somewhere with his chest sliced open, I won't lose any sleep over it." She tilted her head and used her fingers to comb through her waves, lifting and loosening each one until her hair flowed wild and free. "But at the same time, he's not worth spending the rest of my life in prison for either."

Kite bit her bottom lip to keep from responding. If she'd thought about that earlier, they wouldn't be in this predicament. Vintage Windy. Act first. Think second.

Windy clutched her sister's hands. "But I do want to clarify something. You're right about my hands not being totally clean. But they're not as dirty as you think they are, either."

Kite's eyes darted once again around the small apartment before focusing back on the woman in front of her. The warmth from Windy's hands and the sincerity emanating from her eyes told Kite that she could believe her. Kite's heart cried out for her to believe her. And her soul clung to the hope that she *would* believe her. But there was a problem.

Kite knew that her definition of dirty and her sister's were as different as night and day.

Chapter Seven

It had been three weeks since Diamond Liz introduced Priscilla to Barry. Since then, her life had turned upside down. Priscilla couldn't have planned this any better if she'd tried.

She kicked off her stilettos, stepped onto the silky Persian carpeting, then flopped onto the pillowy king-sized bed, where luxurious Charlotte Thomas sheets surrounded and cooled her skin. Shopping was hard work, especially on a day like today. The calendar told her that spring was still a few weeks away, but the sun and its blazing rays didn't agree.

Barry would be stopping by her room in a few minutes. She chuckled. He was so predictable. He'd also remind her to let Chef Rigalta know what she wanted for dinner. She closed her eyes. A chef. Her own personal chef.

Barry. Barry. Barry.

She'd thought it would be more difficult. But when Jacob found out that she'd been seeing Barry on the side, he'd tossed everything she had—including her Louboutins—

onto the front lawn and lit a match. Shoes that expensive were not meant to burn, but burn they had. Along with everything else he'd ever bought her. As if that weren't enough, he'd sent her personal items, like her journal, to her mom's house. He knew she'd be loathe to go there and pick them up, but at least they'd escaped the fire.

She and Jacob had made a good couple. He'd known from the beginning that she was in it for his money, not love. That arrangement had worked for almost ten years, but somewhere down the line, his emotions and her motives had become entangled in his mind. But not for Priscilla. She'd miss the dark stallion, but her mama hadn't raised a fool. There was no way on earth Priscilla would've ever turned down what Barry was offering.

He was twenty-five years her senior, and she didn't care. Especially after she realized she didn't have to pretend to like him just to keep the arrangement. She'd done that before. Living like that was a nightmare, but she'd endured worse to keep up the lifestyle she desired.

But Barry was different. And smart. After her incident with Jacob, Barry had seized the opportunity to make her his own. Knowing she'd escaped Jacob's wrath with just the clothes on her back, he suggested that if she moved in with him, he'd give her carte blanche to do whatever she liked with his credit card. And when his driver had picked her up—bruised and battered by Jacob's fists—Barry'd brought her into his home, and sent for his own private physician to tend to her wounds. When she was well enough to tour the place, she was left speechless by the opulence that awaited her at every turn. She knew her daddy would call it sinful, bless his soul, but she called it hitting the jackpot. She was all in. And when Barry emphatically said that she wouldn't have to earn her keep by sharing his bed, she almost started believing it was one of those miracles her friend, Lola, was always yapping about.

"Silly, are you in there?"

She smiled at the nickname he'd started using for her. A natural deviation of Priscilla, he'd said. Some women would be offended, but she didn't care. She'd been called a whole lot worse.

She sat up on the bed. "Come in."

It wasn't until he opened the door and stared at her that she realized she hadn't taken the time to check the mirror. She could only imagine how flushed her skin looked from the heat. And she didn't even want to think about what the humidity had done to her hair.

He smiled. "Your beauty knows no bounds. Made up or melting, I've never seen anything so beautiful."

Priscilla smiled. Barry was a talkative one for sure. He sometimes even waxed poetic, which was a refreshing change from Jacob, who gritted and grunted. But it was statements like this that made it tempting for her to break her own cardinal rule—keep the heart out of it.

"You keep talking to me like that, and you're in danger of having more than you agreed upon, mister."

He laughed, then walked to the bed and sat next to her. "I knew from the moment I laid eyes on you that I was in danger of that. And I know you feel it too." He kept his hands in his lap. "Which is why I was adamant about us having separate bedrooms. I don't want to taint whatever relationship we may have in the future. Whether that happens or not, I'll never go back on my word. Everything I have here on this property, you'll always have access to. The home, the cottages, the boats, the pool, the cars, everything." He scooted closer and continued. "This morning, when I met with the house staff, I made sure they were aware of that too. There won't be any problems because, apparently, they've fallen in love with you too. They couldn't say enough good things about you."

The heat of a blush attempted to color her cheeks. Thankful for what the staff had shared with Barry, she closed her eyes and smiled. Not because she was trying to win them over, but because she hated it when people treated others like they were beneath them. She'd been there. Too many times to count. No one would ever feel like that around her. She was glad that his staff hadn't.

He laughed. "You're blushing."

She raised her hand to her cheek. "Nice try. My skin's a tad too dark for that."

He shook his head. "I didn't see it in your cheeks. I saw it in your smile."

"Barry—"

"I know what you're going to say. You've said it a hundred times before. 'This is just how you make a living. Your heart is never involved.' And like I said earlier, I accept that." He thrust his chest out. "But I haven't become this successful without knowing exactly what I want. I've kept company with many a young woman, but everyone knew they were just arm candy for a lonely old man. I never ever invited any of them into my home, and that includes your friend Diamond Liz. And I definitely didn't introduce them to my staff.

"I don't know if you've noticed, but the majority of my

staff are in their late sixties or early seventies like me. A couple of them, a few years older. Some are children of the staff my parents hired eons ago. I've grown up with them. They're family to me." He held up a finger. "I'm highly protective of them. I only invited you to be a part of their lives because of my feelings for you. I *know* we're going to have a future together. I can feel it. You don't, not yet, I know that, but I'm usually right about these things." He lifted an eyebrow and smiled. "I may not be a young man, but I'm a patient man. And I'm prepared to do whatever it takes to woo you." The smile turned into a confident grin.

"You just met me," she said. "You know I have a past, and you know it's not that pretty." Suspicion clawed its way up her spine. "So, why in the world would someone like you want to have a relationship with someone like me?"

He shrugged. "I just explained that. And everyone has a past. Who cares?"

The suspicion slid away as she looked into his eyes. There was nothing there that suggested he had a hidden agenda. For some strange reason, that made her feel sorry for him. "You should care, Barry. I haven't met a lot of good men in my life. But the ones I did meet, I eventually hurt."

He nodded. "I understand."

She shook her head. "No, I don't think you do. My only priority in life is looking out for me. I don't have that same passion for anyone else."

He bowed his head. "I'm willing to take that chance."

She leaned closer and placed her hand on his thigh. "Even when you're not getting anything out of it?"

He stared at her hand. "I'm getting more out of it than you think." He chuckled, then looked her in the eyes. She watched as the humor faded from his. "You have no idea how sweet my desire is for you. And being this close, knowing you're only a touch away, drives me mad." He pushed off the bed and headed for the door. "But I'm asking you for more than that."

She tossed a handful of hair over her shoulder. "You do realize that there's a strong possibility you'll wake up one morning and I'll be long gone. Off chasing another offer, from another guy, whose dollar signs were also too good to refuse." She hoped her face didn't betray her lie. She wasn't an idiot. He was offering her a life of leisure and luxury with no strings attached. But he needed to be reminded of what this was and what it wasn't. If he didn't quit all this romantic nonsense, she was in danger of losing it all before it even began. Despite his assurances that she'd still be able to enjoy her lifestyle on his dime, Priscilla knew better.

He paused near the doorframe, his back still toward her. "I know. But I wouldn't regret one minute of it."

She closed her eyes as the bedroom door clicked shut and the soles of his shoes tapped along the marbled hallway. The fainter the sound of his steps became, the more she realized something.

She wanted him to come back.

Chapter Eight

Lydia smiled at the framed photograph Ada handed her. "Oh, my heavens!" Dinah's daughter smiled up from the glossy print. "She looks just like her mother did at this age. Big blue eyes and bouncy brown ponytails."

Ada took the picture and placed it on the mantle. "And she's just as feisty and spirited as Dinah was before she was …" Ada paused and shook her head. "I'm sorry, Mom. I didn't mean to bring up the past."

Lydia poured her firstborn another cup of coffee. "No need to apologize. What happened back then is part of your memories, so of course it's gonna come through when you're talking. Please don't feel like you have to filter things like that for me."

Ada took the steaming mug and sat on one of the stools in front of the breakfast bar. "But I feel like I do, Mom. I worry about you being in this big old house by yourself all day. I worry about your health. I worry about Dinah not replying to any of your letters. I know all of that weighs on you. The last thing I want is to add more stress."

Lydia leaned against the breakfast bar and smiled. "I'd feel a whole lot better if you stopped worrying so much about me."

Ada wrapped her hands around the mug then stared into it. "Have you heard anything new from the doctors?"

"No. But I do have another scan scheduled in a few weeks. One of my doctors called it a PET scan. I'm looking forward to this one. I've been feeling better for quite some time now, and I'm excited to see if there's been any change."

Ada pointed to the cluttered counter next to the stove. "I'm not sure I can even name all the different types of fruits and vegetables you have over there. And I definitely don't know what those funny-looking appliances you bought are supposed to do. But if all of that's responsible for the extra energy you've had lately, I'm all for it."

Lydia patted Ada's hand. "Enough about me. How's Daniel's job with his new promotion coming along?"

"He loves it. Though he is having to spend more time in the office on Sundays. It's not the same going to church without him. He's spoken to his boss about it, so I hope things'll settle down soon. Keep the prayers coming."

Lydia loved going into her prayer closet to pray for her daughters and their families. She was blessed beyond measure that her parents had instilled their common sense in her girls. If only she hadn't had such a rebellious heart growing up and had listened to her parents like they did. If only. But her girls now had their own struggles, and she planned to be there spiritually for them for as long as the Lord saw fit to let her. "I will."

"And while you're at it, add your two middle daughters to your prayer list.

B & C are fighting again."

Lydia moaned. "Seriously? What are they fighting about now?"

"Something about how one doesn't appreciate everything that the other does for them, yada, yada, yada. You know how they are, Mom, best friends one day, enemies the next."

Lydia silently counted to ten. Her doctors had warned her that stress would only make her condition worse. She let the breath seep out with a small sigh. She'd had Ada when she was seventeen, and both Bethany and Claudia—affectionately nicknamed B & C—were born before she turned twenty-one and were less than a year apart. She'd hoped that would increase their sisterly bond. Instead, it only increased their bickering. And she knew why. Bethany sought to control everything Claudia did, and that never ended well. "I'll call Bethany this afternoon. She never stays angry for long. I'll wait until the weekend to call Claudia."

Ada laughed. "Good idea."

Lydia glanced at the framed picture on the mantle and waited for Ada to share news about the youngest girl in the family. After about a minute, Ada took a sip of her coffee, and gazed out the kitchen window.

"And, well … Dinah is being Dinah. Busy, busy, busy. All. The. Time. Luckily, I get to see Jenny when I pick my kids up from school." She pointed to the mantle in the dining area. "That's how I'm able to snap photos of her. Dinah'll never give me one herself because she knows I'll give it to you. She's a bad daughter but a good mom. She'll squeeze us sisters into a group phone call, but she always makes time for Jenny."

"I'm glad to hear that." Ada didn't always share updates about Dinah, but she'd shared enough recently for Lydia to know that the past couple of months hadn't been easy for Dinah. She was going through a tough divorce, and there seemed to be no end to the child custody battle. "But I fear with her ex-husband moving thousands of miles away, she won't take it well if the courts decide on shared custody."

Ada shook her head. "She won't take it well at all. Having Jenny that far away, for weeks or even months at a time, will devastate her."

Lydia closed her eyes. The last thing she wanted was to see her daughter hurt, but she also knew the importance of having a father in a child's life. Life had taught her that lesson. All four of her girls had different fathers, two of whom she didn't know the names of. One of her biggest regrets was not being strong enough to provide her girls with a sound family life. "Hopefully, they'll work something out. If not, perhaps she'll move closer to her ex."

Ada choked on her coffee. Lydia handed her a napkin. After a few seconds, Ada continued. "Mom, she won't move that far away. I know my little sister, and a move like that would be the proverbial straw that breaks the camel's back. She's worked so long and hard on Bliss, and if she moved, she'd have to sell it. She'd chain her ex to the radiator before she let that happen."

A few years back, Dinah had purchased a farmhouse that came with acres of prime real estate. She'd had it refurbished into a quaint bed-and-breakfast, wedding chapel, event center, bookstore, and café, which she'd named Bliss.

Ada continued. "Now, with the addition of another chapel on the lake, the reservations are pouring in. She's always said that her priority list was short because it only included Jenny and Bliss. Which may explain why Ralph filed for the divorce. There was no room for him."

"But he is a good father, right?"

"Yes. Jenny's definitely a daddy's girl, and he absolutely adores her. But Mom, you're missing my point. I'm telling you all this because I'm hoping you'll reconsider letting us tell Dinah about your diagnosis. She'll never admit it, but if something happened to you, it would haunt her forever. She'd never forgive herself for refusing to make peace with you. She needs her mom. And if this custody battle goes south, she'll need you more than ever. More than that, you need to see your daughter's face again. And you need to meet your grand-daughter before it's too late."

Lydia blinked away tears. There was no way Ada could know that she'd been praying for those exact same things for the past decade. And her diagnosis had increased those prayers from day-by-day to minute-by-minute.

"I'm going to continue to reach out to Dinah in all the ways I know how. But I can't have you girls telling her about the diagnosis. Not yet. For one, it has to come from me, and I'll only do that face-to-face. Two, I haven't felt a peace in my spirit yet to do so. I can't say I understand why God hasn't given me the green light, but if I had to gander a reason, I'd say that right now, her knowing about my diagnosis would do her more harm than good."

Ada bowed her head.

"That's the only reason I can think of right now, sweetheart. I wish I could give you more, but I can't. I'm sorry."

Ada let out a shaky breath. "I sure hope you're hearing

right from God on this, Mom. I really do."

Lydia opened her mouth to respond, but she had no more words. She believed with everything in her that she was hearing from God correctly. But the words flitting around her brain and the thumps in her heart kept asking her the same question.

What if she wasn't?

Chapter Nine

Eve walked into Roarke's Music Studio an hour early. She hung her purse and spring jacket on the ornate oak coat rack and clutched her music notebooks to her chest, glancing down the hall. The recording area was empty. She turned the opposite direction, walked to Roger's open office door, and knocked.

"Evie, hey!" Roger Roarke shot up and pulled her into a quick hug. When he released her, he pointed to the black leather chair in front of his desk and gestured for her to sit. "How's it goin', love?"

Roger's easy-going, laid-back, no-worries-in-the-world personality always brightened her day. But she was sure the puffiness under her eyes showed her weariness. She placed the notebooks on his desk and settled into the chair. "It was a rough night."

"So I heard." He sat in the matching chair behind his desk. "Philip called after you went to bed."

She'd figured he had. Which was why she'd showed up early to talk to Roger about it before the band arrived.

Philip had been intent on continuing the argument about her mother. After dinner, she'd locked herself in the bedroom, and Philip had slept on the couch.

She took a deep breath and thought a moment about what she was going to say. Roger was her friend, but he was Philip's *best* friend. She must keep in mind that anything she said could get back to him.

Roger was looking at her hands. She looked down and saw that she was mindlessly twisting her wedding ring. She could only imagine what Roger must think. "I'm sorry." She folded her hands and forced them to stay put in her lap. "Philip and I are going through a tough time right now. But please don't think that'll affect my playing in any way, because it won't."

He placed his forearm on the desk and leaned forward. The black ponytail at the nape of his neck shifted and landed on his shoulder. "Evie, I've been working with you for over a year now. If I'd had any concerns, I wouldn't have invited you back to play on Three-Sixteen's second album. I'm convinced that it was your masterful touches on *Come to The Altar* and *Cry Unto Thee* that made the first album such a surprise success."

Heat flushed her cheeks. Three-Sixteen was a popular local Christian band that had used Roger's recording studio to make their first CD. She'd only played the piano and keyboards on the songs that he'd mentioned, and even though they were the first two breakaway hits, Roger saying that her small part had anything to do with their success made her blush.

"Oh, Evie." Roger's perpetual smile faded. "You don't get many compliments, do you?"

Tears brimmed her eyes. He had no idea. Her mousy brown hair, dull gray eyes, and almost non-existent lips certainly didn't lend to many compliments. She knew beyond a doubt that she was a talented pianist. The award-winning music tutor her parents had hired when she was four years old had made sure of that. But until Roger had asked her to record with Three-Sixteen, her music had always been a private affair, and the only compliments she'd gotten had come from her mom. Heaven knew Philip never gave her any.

She swallowed. Time to steer the conversation in another direction. She nodded toward his office door. "It's awfully quiet out there. Is Three-Sixteen the only group you have recording today?"

His eyebrow rose and his lips parted as if he were about to say something else, but to her relief, he backed off the desk and leaned back in his chair. "Yeah. We want to get as much done in the next few months as possible. Strike while the iron is hot, so-to-speak. The industry is fickle. If we don't get something new out there soon, they'll easily become yesterday's news."

"What's on the schedule for them today?"

"We'll be putting the finishing touches on *But He Did* this morning, so we'll only need you for two hours. After that, they'll be working on *Warfare*." He smiled and let out a chuckle. "You're welcome to stay for that if you like."

Roger knew full well she wouldn't be sticking around for that one. As much as she'd come to love the band members, especially Gabby, the female lead vocalist, the majority of their songs had too much of a rock feel for her taste. But the lyrics ministered, so if adding loud drums and shrieking guitars got the salvation message out to the next generation, she was all for it. That didn't mean *she* had to listen to it.

"I think I'll slip out before they begin that one."

Roger's chair creaked. "You know, Gabby's been campaigning hard for the band to record *Kingdom Child*. Her constant phone calls, emails, and text messages have sold me on it, but the band is resistant. They think it's way too mild for their brand."

Eve shot back in her chair. "What?" *Kingdom Child* was her baby. She'd written it years before when she'd been inspired to write a song about the benefits of being a child of God. She'd had no idea Gabby was trying to get the band to record it. They were right to dismiss it. It called only for a vocalist and a piano accompanist. Not Three-Sixteen's style at all.

"I don't want *Kingdom Child* recorded. The only reason Gabby knows about it is because she heard me singing and tweaking the lyrics one night. Come on, Roger. You know my music and especially my songwriting, is personal. I thought I was alone here in the studio, then suddenly, there she was standing over my shoulder. That was over a month ago. We haven't talked about it since. And I definitely didn't know she was trying to get the band to record it."

"She must've heard more than you thought because she sent me an audio recording of it."

Eve gripped the arms of her chair. "She did what?"

"A recording of her playing the piano and singing the vocals. It's a really great song, Evie."

Eve loosened her grip, lowered her shoulders, and sat still. Her tutor had trained her to always remain poised and professional. She had a few choice words for Gabby, and she was close to grabbing the phone off Roger's desk and punching in her number. But she had to think clearly, and giving a name to the emotion she was feeling always seemed to help. The first word that came to mind was *violated*. And by Gabby, of all people.

"She had no right to do that."

Roger raised his hand. "Calm down. She's let everyone know that you wrote it, so she's not trying to take credit for it. I know how private you are with your music. When she first came to me, I asked her how she came across it. She gave me the same explanation you did. Then she added that the song spoke to her so much that she was able to remember it without even trying. She did a rough recording of it and sent it to me. It's not a great fit for their band. At least, that's what I thought at first."

"What do you mean?"

He scratched at one of the silver sideburns that stood out against his tanned skin, dark green eyes, and dyed black hair. A color combination that shouldn't have worked. "The more I listened to it, the more I realized it is exactly what their band needs. They're at their best when they do Christian rock, but that first album had a little bit of everything. Rock, gospel, contemporary, and even a hint of bluegrass. *Kingdom Child* is soft, melodic and gives a nod to the folk songs of old. It could work."

Eve shook her head.

"Would you at least listen to the audio she sent? Gabby's powerful voice and passion for the song gives it a soulful feel. That's sure to take it over the top."

"The answer is no."

He threw up his hands. "She wants to do this for you,

Evie. Her plan was to surprise you with it at one of the recording sessions."

Eve stood. "I don't care what her plan was. What she did was wrong, and I'm going to confront her about it when she gets here."

Roger pushed a button on the lower right side of his chair, and it jerked him forward. "The saddest thing in all of this is that it's Three-Sixteen recording in my studio and not you. I've heard you sing a thousand times. Your voice has a depth and uniqueness that can't be matched by a million Gabbys. You're a great pianist, and the songs you've written, *especially* the ones about you and Philip, can only come from someone who's lived a lot of life and learned even more from it. Songs like that speak to people." He tilted his head back and let out a chuckle. "Heck, they speak to me, and I'm not even a Christian."

Eve resumed her seat. "That can be fixed in a matter of minutes."

He smiled. "Evie. Forever the evangelist."

"Shall I get my Bible?"

"Nah. Not unless it's going to help *you* understand the importance of the gifts you've been given." He glanced at his watch. "Look Evie, I know you love helping people. What I don't know is why you won't use your music to do it. I know how Philip can be. I've been divorced five times, so no marital advice, but you haven't been happy in a long time. I wonder if you focused less on Philip and more on your music, if you'll smile again."

Eve took in a quick breath. She had no idea how to respond to that.

He reached across the desk, palms up. She placed her

hands in his. "Let's just give this a try, okay? If you totally hate Gabby's rendition of *Kingdom Child*, then it's over. It won't be recorded. I'm your friend first, producer second."

"I'll consider it. But if you're hoping for a quick yes or no, then the answer is no."

"I didn't expect a quick answer. I just wanted you to hear it from me and not Gabby. I've blown her surprise, but I had to tell you."

She withdrew her hands from his. "Thank you."

He relaxed into his chair. "You're still upset. If you'd like to step out for a bit, or call off today's session, that's okay. I can switch the schedule around."

Eve thought about that for a minute. Last night it was Philip and this morning, Gabby. She only had enough emotional energy left to go home, curl up under the blankets, and scream until she had no voice left. Or tears. But …

"No, you've hired me to do a job, and I'm here to do it."

He ran his thumb across his chin. "Does Philip know you're here?"

"Not unless you told him. I haven't spoken to him since last night."

"Mind if I give him a call? He should be here supporting you in this."

She chuckled. "Go for it."

Roger would get Philip to show up, even if he had to drag him in by his collar. But it wouldn't change anything. His body would be here, but his heart wouldn't.

And no matter how much she wanted to remain professional, she knew hers wouldn't be in it either.

Chapter Ten

Mary accepted the cool glass of water from her mother. She and Ethan sat on the sofa across the coffee table from her father, and Pauly had settled in a leather recliner. Christianna chose a pastel multicolored wing chair. The furniture and decorations looked much newer than the forty years she'd been absent. Her mother wiped her hands across the pant legs of her crisp white capris, then took the seat next to Daddy.

Mary glanced around the tiny living area looking for anything that'd help her remember the times spent in this room from her childhood. Nothing looked familiar. But she also didn't remember spending much time in here as a child. It was where her parents came to relax when Dad returned from work. After school, she and her siblings usually played outside until dinner, and then it was bath time.

She sipped her water, placed it on the table next to the sofa, and tried to tighten her grip on Ethan's hand. Every moment she sat there, her palm became sweatier.

After a deep breath, she tilted her head toward Ethan.

"My husband and I live in Delaware." On a corner shelf were several photos of three children. Two girls and one boy. They looked like they could be brothers and sisters, but more than likely were cousins, belonging both to Pauly and Christianna. How would her parents take the news that they had two more grandchildren? It hurt to think of how much her kids had missed out on by not knowing her biological parents. She used her forefinger to wipe her damp lashes. "We have two children." Mary paused when her mom's eyes widened, but when the beginning of a smile started, she continued. "Our oldest is Levi. He's fifteen and on our state's champion swim team. Our daughter Israela is seven and the cutest little ballet dancer you'll ever meet." Mary tamped down the urge to reach into her wallet to prove it. "They've known all their lives that they had additional family somewhere, but it wasn't until last week that we knew where."

Their faces reflected a myriad of questions.

Ethan released her hand and slid his arm around her shoulder.

"I'm sorry." She secured a lock of hair behind her ear. "On the drive here, I kept wondering where in the world I would begin to tell a story that's been thirty-nine years in the making." She shook her head. "I never came up with an answer, but the short version is that I remember very little about the day I was taken. I know it was summer, and I know it was early morning because Mom and I always got up early to water the flowers." She closed her eyes. "I remember a man coming up to me with a flower I'd never seen before. He asked if I knew the name of it. Before I could answer, someone from behind put a handkerchief over my nose." She opened her eyes. Her mom's hand was over her mouth. It trembled badly. Should she go on? She looked to her father, who leaned forward, his forearms on his knees, his hands balled into fists.

Daddy nodded. "Go on."

"I remember waking up, I guess the next morning—but I can't say for sure—in a room with eight other girls. We were all about the same age and were dressed in matching white blouses and tan skirts with white tights. When I asked the girls where we were and how I'd gotten there, they said someone named Miss Autry had brought me in. I ran toward the door, screaming."

She swallowed hard, hoping it would dislodge the memory and the lump in her throat. Daddy's posture and expression were frozen in place, but Mom looked to be struggling to keep upright on the sofa. Mary pulled away from Ethan and stood. "I'm sorry. Maybe this is too much too soon. Me showing up here, the abduction .... Everything." She turned to Ethan. "We should come back aft—"

"No!"

Pauly jumped from his chair and faced their parents. "Sorry." He dropped back into his seat. "Everything you're telling us we're just now hearing for the first time. All we've known is that you vanished while Mom was in the side yard. She's beaten herself up every day since. It's hard to hear, but we want to hear it. Mom too."

Daddy had pulled her mom close. Her head rested on his chest. She wrapped an arm around his middle and nodded to Mary. "Pauly's right. We need to hear the rest."

Christianna launched from her chair and headed down

the narrow hallway. When she returned with a box of tissues, Mary remembered that it led to the powder room. Christianna handed Mom several tissues, then placed the box in the middle of the coffee table.

Christianna's eyes were tight, her nostril's flared, and her mouth pinched. It was obvious she had something to say, but she'd have to wait. Mary had to get the rest of her story out before she second-guessed herself and ran out of the house and back to Delaware.

She leaned forward, pulled a tissue from the box, and clutched it in her hands. "I'm not sure if it was two days or two weeks later that I awoke in the middle of the night and again ran towards the door. I banged and pulled and did everything I could to get that door open. It was then that Miss Autry came, sat in one of the chairs, and pulled me into her lap. She tried to soothe me by telling me that she knew how much I wanted my parents and that she wished that they could be there too. But then she said—Mary met her mother's eyes—she said that it was you who sent me there."

"That's a lie!" Mom jerked away from Daddy's chest. "Straight from the pit of hell! We did no—"

"I never believed it." Mary held up a hand. "But she told me and the other girls that all the time. That our parents loved us, and that you gave us to her so she could find good homes to take care of us because you couldn't anymore." Mom was about to interrupt again but Mary shook her head. "I didn't believe that either." She fingered the crumpled tissue in her hands. "Shortly after that, she told me there were some people she wanted me to meet. Mr. and Mrs. Isaacs. They'd visit with me every couple of days or so. We'd play board games. Go out for lunch, take walks—"

"Hold on a minute." Pauly held up a hand. "These people took you for walks, like outside someplace?"

Mary nodded. "Yes. And I was grateful for it. Miss Autry never let us outside. She'd put up quite a fuss with the Isaacs when they'd first suggested it, but they insisted. They took me to the park and even to a local fair once."

"How long after you were taken did these walks take place? A week? A month?"

"I'd say a couple of months." Mary shrugged. "But to be honest, I have no idea. It could've easily been much longer than that."

He looked at Daddy, then back to Mary. "We had people and organizations working with us in every state. Dad and I visited some of those places with the media, and we posted missing person flyers of you everywhere. I'm ticked that nobody recognized you."

"The Isaacs never tried to hide me."

Her brother's face now mimicked their sister's.

"The Isaacs eventually adopted me, though at the time I didn't know what that meant. They explained that Miss Autry worked for an agency and that eventually all of the girls there would be adopted into loving homes. I told them I had a home, and I wanted to go back there. But they said that the agency's lawyers had told them that I was not allowed to go back home. The next thing I knew, I was saying good-bye to Miss Autry and the girls. I left with the Isaacs early the next morning. Hours later, we pulled up to their home in Delaware."

Mary wiped her nose with the tissue. "It wasn't until a week ago that I found out about the extensive search to find me. It all makes sense now why Miss Autry was so against any of the girls going outside. But I want you to know that…" Mary looked at her mom, who'd now taken refuge again in her husband's chest. "I was never abused in any way. Miss Autry was strict, and I hated the place we were kept because there were no windows, but she never harmed me or any of the other girls. And the same with the Isaacs. Their names are Ezra and Aviva. They still live in the same home in Delaware. And I know that if they'd had *any* suspicions that I was kidnapped or that Miss Autry wasn't who she'd said she was, they would've called the authorities immediately. When you meet them, you'll see the kind of people they are. They're one of the many reasons I'm able to be here today."

She took a deep breath and continued. "When I first arrived at their home, I begged them to bring me back here. Told them I wanted to see my family again. Mrs. Isaacs told me again what Miss Autry's lawyers had told them, but she added that when I was eighteen, they'd help me find my family again." She let out a small chuckle. "I didn't know back then that it would take ten years for me to reach that point, but I held on to the fact that I'd see you guys again. And sure enough, on my eighteenth birthday, Mrs. Isaacs woke me before dawn. We'd been planning a huge celebration, so I thought it had something to do with my party. But it didn't. She kissed me, wished me a happy birthday, then gave me a cardboard box. In it was all the paperwork they'd received from Miss Autry's agency regarding my adoption. But also inside …." Mary tilted her head back to dam up the tears starting to flow.

Ethan handed over her purse and she pulled out two small articles of clothing. Mary held them out. "Were these."

Mom reached for the clothing. "Oh, my …"

Mary handed her the colorful little girl's short set. A white T-shirt with pink and green flowers strung across the front and a pair of pink denim shorts that had a green embroidered flower on the upper corner of the right pocket. Mary no longer fought the tears. "I remember sitting with you when you sewed those flowers on for me, Mom." She took what was left of the crumpled tissue and dabbed at her cheeks. "And knowing what I know now, I can't believe Miss Autry kept them, let alone gave them to the Isaacs. But as you know, that's the outfit I was wearing when I was taken."

Chapter Eleven

Kite sat at her desk and focused on the paperwork for the DeMint case. Jack had suspected there wouldn't be much to the wife's claim of adultery, but now they had proof. The hard part was going to be telling Mrs. DeMint what they'd actually found out about Mr. DeMint.

The door to the office clicked open. Kite expected to see J.S., whom she'd asked earlier to retrieve staples from the supply closet for her, but instead it was Jack. "J.S. told me you'd returned. I expected you back hours ago. I was just about to come look for you."

Kite scribbled the last of her thoughts regarding the DeMint file onto a sticky note and stuck it on the folder. "I'm sorry, Jack. Windy needed my help with something."

"Uh-oh."

She nodded. "Uh-oh's right."

He stepped into the office, leaving the door open. "Anything I can help with?"

There was a whole lot Jack could help with. But Jack Eagle was the last person she wanted to drag into Windy's madness. She pulled open the center desk drawer and tossed the DeMint file inside. "No. We put our heads together and got a pretty solid plan going."

"Solid plan with Windy?" He chuckled then plopped a box of staples on the desk before sliding into the seat across from it. "Is that possible?"

"Give me a few days. I'll let you know."

His brown eyes locked onto hers before he clasped his hands together and leaned forward. "Hungry?"

"We've talked about this."

"We've talked about you not being ready to date. I'm thinking greasy bacon burgers and chili cheese fries. That's not a date. That's dinner." He lifted his brows and gave her a lopsided grin. "I promise to have you home at a decent hour."

She glanced at her watch and immediately regretted it. The watch was a beautiful, diamond-accented gold watch that looked more like a bracelet. Which was exactly what she'd thought it was when Nethaniah first walked toward her with it at their twentieth wedding anniversary dinner. She'd grabbed it from him, pulled him close, and let a flurry of kisses exclaim her joy. She fought back tears as she remembered how every time he saw her put it on after that, he'd demanded more kisses. Then suddenly one day, there was no one there to kiss.

Jack leaned forward. "Kite, I'm sorry. I wasn't thinking. I should've known—"

She shook her head and blinked to keep the tears at bay. "It's okay." She gave him a quick smile and tilted her wrist. "Anyway, it wasn't the invitation that brought on the memories, it was my watch."

He lifted her hand to get a closer look. "I've never seen you wear this before."

She let her hand fall from his grasp. He'd never seen her wear it before because she'd never worn it to the office. Or outside of the house for that matter. Because every time she wore it and every time she looked at the time, it was a constant reminder. And right now, it reminded her that it had been three years, ten months, three hours, nine minutes, and— she glanced at the time again—twenty-two seconds since Nethaniah died.

"I normally don't wear it. This morning I was feeling emotionally brave. I thought I could handle it."

Jack stared at her wrist for a moment, then stood and nodded toward the door. "Come on. I'll give you a ride home."

She reached for her purse and keys aware of the fact that any other time she would've turned Jack down, fearing she'd be encouraging his romantic intentions. But she also knew that if she didn't accept his offer, it was going to be a long, sad, and teary drive home.

"You're clearly in no condition to drive." He stepped closer and smiled. "If I let you drive out of here like this and something happens to you, Windy'll kill me."

She chuckled, though her body stiffened at the truth in that statement. "Thanks."

"Was that the DeMint file you were working on?"

"Yes. Mrs. DeMint was right about one thing. Her husband's definitely not telling her the truth about where he's spending his Tuesday evenings. But it's not with some other woman. It's with a group of kids at a church thirty miles outside of town."

"What's he doing there?"

"He's a volunteer. I was able to get a phone number from the ministry's website. I called and talked with the couple who runs the program. They said Mr. DeMint has been working with the kids for the past year."

Jack rubbed at his neck and groaned. "His wife's going to have a harder time with that than if you'd caught him cheating."

"My thoughts exactly."

He switched off the lights and locked up. "I'll get the file from you tomorrow morning. Lauren DeMint is a difficult client. I'll take it from here."

"You don't think I can handle her?"

"It's not that." He scrunched his brows together. "I know Lauren. She's gonna swear Eagle Eye botched the job. Then she'll threaten legal action."

She swallowed. "You're right. Better if you handle this one."

"I've worked with her type before."

She handed him her purse and retrieved her jacket from the wall hook in the building's foyer. "Better you than me."

"That's not the only reason I want to take her off your hands. We have a local case that's going to cause a media frenzy. I'd like for you to act as our public relations person." He cleared his throat. "I know you've done it before with the photography studio you and Neth operated. I've seen the videos. You're a natural. I don't mind handling the DeMint case if it means I can back out of this one. I don't like talking with reporters. They ask stupid questions."

Kite laughed. "Risen Son Photography got its fair share of media attention, but it was nowhere near a frenzy. But, I'll do it. The media can be a nuisance, but they're not so bad when you get to know them." She pulled the other arm through the jacket. "You said this has to do with one of our clients?"

He held out her purse. "Remember the woman who wanted to find her biological parents? She lived out of state but had recently learned that her parents' last known address was here in Habakkuk."

She slung the purse over her shoulder. "I remember. I take it you were able to find them?"

"In one day. They never moved. Apparently, it was a pretty big case before I moved here."

"What's her name? If it was on the news, I'm sure I'd remember."

"Mary Rabin."

Kite shook her head and walked toward the door. Jack held it open. "The name doesn't ring a bell. Habakkuk's a small town. I grew up here. Everybody knows everybody. If it were a huge story, I don't know how I could've missed it."

"Rabin's her married name. Her maiden name was Melson."

Kite stopped mid-step. "Her name was what?"

"Melson. Mary Melson."

Her breath hitched. "As in, Mary Laura Melson?"

"Yeah." He let go of the door and reached for her elbow. "Are you okay?"

She gripped his forearm and turned to face him. "You're sure she said her name was Mary. Laura. Melson." She deliberately enunciated each word. She couldn't take it if he was wrong. But of course, he was wrong. It couldn't be. She had to know.

He nodded, then slowly guided her back into the small waiting area. "Did you know her?"

She sat on one of the cushioned seats as memories from forty years ago stormed her vision. As her breaths came quicker with each inhale, Jack ran out of the room, and returned seconds later with an opened bottle of water and crouched in front of her. "Drink this."

She tried to reach for the bottle, but her vision blurred, and her fingers went numb. Jack placed his hand near her mouth and gently squeezed. With his other hand, he grabbed the bottle and let the water drip into her mouth. She took small sips at first. Then more as her breathing calmed.

She wiped the moisture from her lips with the back of her hand. "Have you seen her? Talked to her? Oh, my word … are you …?" She paused and let out a shaky breath. "Are you telling me that Mary Laura is alive?"

"I met with her and her family today." He placed the bottle of water on the floor. "You knew her?"

She bobbed her head, tried to make it stop, but couldn't. "She was my best friend."

Jack squeezed her hand.

"And mine was the last face she saw before she disappeared."

Chapter Twelve

Priscilla smiled at Liz and Lola then inserted her fork into the mushroom risotto. Earlier, she'd asked Chef Rigalta to fix lunch for her and two friends. A few hours later, he'd ushered them to the rose garden, which was outside the formal kitchen area. In the center of the garden was a small table covered with a beautiful white cloth, and a vase of fresh-cut roses in the center. Chef had set the table in the European dining style, which meant their salads would follow the main course. Priscilla took a quick glance around the table. There was no way they were going to make it that far.

After a scrumptious appetizer of grilled spring onions and goat cheese spread on the best homemade sourdough flatbread she'd ever tasted, she was just now finishing off her main course. Diamond Liz sliced through the last pieces of her sautéed salmon, and Lola had just taken the last bite of her braised endive. Chef Rigalta had catered to their every request, which only encouraged their over-indulgence.

Lola closed her eyes and laid her head back against the

white wrought iron chair. "I simply cannot take another bite."

"Well, change into your bathing suit and swim a couple of laps to regain your appetite." Priscilla tapped a fingernail against Lola's plate. "Because we *are* going to enjoy dessert."

"What are you trying to do, kill her?" Diamond Liz let out a small laugh. "Best not to swim after you eat. And especially not after everything *she* just ate."

Lola tossed a crumpled napkin in Diamond Liz's direction.

Priscilla shook her head. "That's a myth."

Lola scooted her chair back and stood. "Myth or not, a swim sounds like a great idea. The weather's perfect. Which way to the pool house?"

Priscilla pointed to her right. "Take the path just right of the gazebo. We'll join you in a few."

As she disappeared out of sight, Liz said, "Just so you know, before this day's over, she's going to wrangle you into joining her at church this Sunday."

Priscilla ran her fingers through her hair. "What do you mean, wrangle?"

"That's what she did to me the entire ride over here. She wouldn't take no for an answer. And she's not going to take one from you either. She says some people you grew up with attend there. Some lady named Kite, and another one na—"

"She's mentioned them to me before." Priscilla reached for her napkin. "Kite and I didn't get along, but her sister, Windy, and I had a blast together in high school. The rest of them? No comment." She wiped her mouth with the napkin. "I'll just remind her of the lightning bolt that'd strike the church if I ever dared to step inside."

"Nope. Won't work. I tried that. The next thing I knew, I'd agreed to meet her there on Sunday morning. Still not exactly sure how that happened."

Priscilla smiled. "She always has been the persuasive type."

"That's the truth." Liz leaned closer to Priscilla. "Speaking of persuasive, you and Barry are obviously doing okay. Personal chef. Free reign of his estate. Choice of cars *and* drivers. Do I know how to pick 'em or what?"

"I can't thank you enough for introducing us. He's … different. Not in a weird, creepy way. In a good way. Too good of a way. He's the first man I've met who I don't think *I'm* good enough for. What a strange feeling."

Liz jerked back. "Are you okay, Pris? You don't sound like yourself at all."

"I know, and it's all Barry's fault. He's always saying things that keep me awake at night."

"Like what?"

"Actually, it's what he's *not* saying that keeps me awake at night. He finally got the message that I don't like him verbally professing his love for me, so he stopped. But now, it's in the way he looks at me. Through me. Not in a lustful way, just … I don't know. I can't explain it. And that's what keeps me up at night."

"And you two still haven't—"

"Nope. The only thing we do in our bedrooms is talk."

"Still have the separate rooms, I see."

"I'm not complaining. I'm just not used to getting something for nothing is all. Not sure what to make of it."

"Hey!" Lola bounced around the corner in a bright

yellow swim set. "I thought you guys were going to join me."

Priscilla took one look at Lola and regretted suggesting the swim. Lola's suit was modest but stunning. The high-waisted bottoms and tankini top did nothing to tone down the natural hourglass shape of her body. If anything, it highlighted it.

"Uh, no." Liz shook her head. "No way I'm putting on my suit with you looking like that. Not gonna happen."

Priscilla chewed her lip. She and Liz had nothing to be ashamed of because they both looked good in their bikinis. Even the tiny ones. But they didn't look *that* good. "Lola, don't you have a fat-lady jogging suit or something you can wear over that? Because that's the only way I'm going anywhere near a pool with you beside me."

Lola folded her arms across her chest. "Really, girls?"

Chef Rigalta opened the glass door and stepped into the garden with a tray of chocolate strawberries. When he saw Lola, the tray hit the ground.

"My apologies." He bent to pick it up. Priscilla watched as his gaze snaked upward, taking in every inch of Lola's golden-brown legs. He stood and pointed at the berries. "I'll send someone to clean that up. The cake will be served in a few minutes."

His heart looked like it was about to thump through his chef's jacket.

Priscilla joined Lola and stood in front of her to block the chef's view. She loved Chef Rigalta, and the last thing she needed was for Lola to give the old man a heart attack. Priscilla turned to him and smiled. "No hurry on the dessert, Chef. As a matter of fact, would you mind if we wait an hour?" She jerked her head toward the pool house. "We were hoping to get in a quick swim."

He nodded, walking backward to the kitchen until he stepped inside, leaving the glass door open.

"So, you ladies are going to join me? Great, come on!" Lola waved them forward, then turned and jogged down the stone path to the pool. "I'll be in the deep end."

"Well … it's a good thing your chef went back inside." Liz sidled up next to her. "I'm pretty sure *that* view would've landed him in the hospital."

Priscilla laughed. "Oh, my. Yes."

Liz's face turned serious. "Barry'll be home soon, right? Are you sure you want him to see Lola in her bathing suit like that? I mean, men can't help themselves. They like to *look,* and we both know what that can lead to."

"I already told you, Barry's not that type."

Diamond Liz took in a deep breath and shrugged. "If you say so."

"But, it wouldn't do any harm to ask him to pick up some snacks on the way home. That'll give us enough time to enjoy our swim and throw a shower curtain around Lola before he gets here."

Liz grabbed her friend in a hug. "Now *that's* the Priscilla I know. The one who remembers how dangerous it can be when you get too comfortable." She walked in a semi-circle, pointing at the house, pool, cars, boats, and other amenities while sunlight danced off the diamond on her middle finger. "Complacency will cost you all of this."

Priscilla nodded. Her friend was right. But it wasn't the material things she was afraid of losing.

No. What she feared was a whole lot worse.

Chapter Thirteen

It wasn't like Kite to send cryptic text messages. Lydia scrolled through the message again. *"Urgent. Meet me in room 157 at the church. Noon sharp."* The same text had been sent to Eve.

She glanced at her watch—five minutes to eleven—then hit the down button for the elevator. Her doctor's appointment had just ended, and she was thirty minutes from the church. She had a medical update to share with her friends, but she hadn't expected to do it this soon. It was easy enough to meet up with Eve and the other ladies at the church, but Kite had been hit or miss in Bible study and prayer meetings ever since she'd decided to work full-time for Rhoda's brother, Jack Eagle.

The elevator dinged, and Lydia dialed Eve's number as the doors slid open.

"Hi, Lyd! I was just about to call you."

"Have you seen Kite's text?"

"Yes. I texted her back asking for more information, but she hasn't responded."

The elevator jolted to a stop. Lydia headed toward the parking lot. "That's not like her. She always responds to texts and emails quickly."

"I know. And why meet at the church instead of her home?"

Lydia used her car remote to unlock the door. "I guess we'll find out in a few minutes." She slid into her seat. "I'm leaving the doctor's office. Would you like me to swing by and pick you up? We can grab lunch on the way."

Eve sighed on the other end. "I'd love to, but I'm at the music studio. I won't be done here for another half hour. I'll barely make it to the church on time."

"I'll bring lunch to the church. What do you want?"

"Whatever you're having."

"Veggie burger and garden salad?"

Laughter filled her friend's voice. "Um … no. However, considering the comments Philip has been making about my weight lately, I should say yes. Chicken salad on rye will be fine. Thanks."

"I'll grab some water, too." Lydia bit her lip to stop there. She had a lot to say about Philip *and* his comments but now wasn't the time. "See you in a bit."

Lydia ended the call. Despite the irksome comment by Philip, she couldn't help the smile that spread across her face. Eve was back in the studio. Talk about talent. And that's where her friend was the happiest. Eve had been so down on herself lately. If only her no-good husband …

Lydia slowed as she spotted a sandwich shop. She parked, and leaned forward, resting her forehead on the steering wheel. *Lord, I'm sorry. I shouldn't think those things about Philip. I just know what Eve's going through.*

Philip was a jerk decades ago when I dated him, and he's only gotten worse with age. She fought to keep the painful memories of that relationship from reaching her heart. *Bring Philip closer to You, Lord. As much as I dislike him, Eve loves him, and she wants their marriage to work. If that be Your will, may it be so. Amen.*

She got out of the car, locked it, and walked toward the restaurant. She wasn't going to let memories of her past ruin the day. The doctors had been shocked that the new scans showed no progression of her tumor. And their eyebrows had lifted when "Thank you, Jesus!" spilled from her lips. It was an answer to the many prayers she and her friends had lifted to heaven. Her physician, however, said it was a glitch and re-ordered the scans. No matter. The cancer was still in her brain, but it hadn't spread. She *knew* she had been feeling better the last few weeks, and the scans proved it. Well, to her at least. And when the new scans showed the same thing next month, she prayed the doctors would see it too.

Her phone buzzed with a text from Eve saying she was leaving the studio early and on her way to the church. Lydia glanced at her watch and decided to skip the veggie burger. She ordered one chicken salad sandwich, one BLT, two garden salads, and three bottles of water in case Kite hadn't had lunch either.

Lydia parked in the lot at Resurrection Church, grabbed the lunch sacks, and headed inside. Eve waited for her by the entrance and she handed her the sack with the chicken salad in it. "Have you spoken to Kite yet?"

"I haven't been inside. I think she's in a meeting." She motioned toward the parking lot. "Lots of staff here."

Lydia opened the church door. "I'm too curious to wait.

Room 157 is the one with all the windows, right?"

Eve nodded.

They headed down the first hallway. "Good. If they needed privacy, they would've taken the one next to it." She gave Eve's elbow a nudge. "Let's find out what we can see through the glass."

Eve giggled but slowed her pace. "No way. Listening to you is what got me in trouble in high school. My parents still won't let me live the squirrel incident down." She stopped. "You go on ahead and tell me what you see."

Lydia tried to frown at her best friend. "Scaredy cat."

Eve smiled but stayed put. "This cat has learned her lesson."

A door clicked further down the hall, followed by footsteps.

"Evie, Lyd!" Kite hurried toward them and embraced them both. "Sorry about the crazy text. I'll explain in a minute. I was just meeting with Pastor Greene and the administrative staff. Here they come now."

Pastor Greene and his wife approached. Lydia hugged his wife, Ruth, while the pastor placed a gentle hand on Lydia's shoulder. "Every time I see you, you look better and better. How are things?"

Pastor Lloyd Greene and his wife had held her hands through some very dark times. If anybody deserved to hear about her latest medical update it was them. She was about to share when she overheard Kite and Eve wrapping up their conversations with the other members of the staff.

"I was at the doctor's office this morning. I have some exciting news." She glanced over her shoulder. Kite and Eve were walking down the hallway toward the meeting rooms.

"But Kite said she needed to meet with me. Urgently. I should probably catch up to them."

"That's right." Pastor Greene removed his hand from her shoulder and placed it on his wife's. "You haven't heard."

"Haven't heard what?"

He waved off his comment. "Go see Kite. Afterward, stop by our office to let us know what the doctor said."

Kite and Eve were already walking into one of the rooms. She waved good-bye to the Greenes, then made her way to the room.

Kite closed the door behind her. "I hate all this cloak-and-dagger stuff, but good news travels fast, and I wanted the two of you to hear it from me first."

Lydia handed Kite one of the salads and a water, then pulled a chair out from one of the smaller meeting tables. "Are you and Jack Eagle getting married?"

Kite's neck, cheeks, and ears turned crimson. "What? *No!* Who said—"

"I'm kidding!" Lydia laughed. "Just ignore me. I'm on cloud nine right now and feel like I glided into this church today." She hitched her thumb at Eve, who'd sat in the chair next to her. "Just ask her. If you hadn't shown up when you did, there's no telling what kind of shenanigans I would've talked her into out there in the lobby."

Kite sat across from them and opened her water. "Good news from the doctor?"

"The scans showed that the tumor is not progressing like they thought it would. It hasn't grown at all since my last scan two months ago."

Kite and Eve's voices melded together. Lots of questions with several, *Praise the Lord's* mixed in. Lydia held up a hand. "I have to add that the doctors aren't that excited. They want to run a new scan to rule out any machine errors, but I'm not worried. Only God knows for sure what this means, but it's given me hope, and I'm holding on to it."

Eve pulled her into a side hug. "And we're holding on with you."

"Have they set a date for the next scan?" Kite asked.

Lydia pulled her salad out of the bag. "Sometime next month."

"Let me know when you have a date." Kite said. "If one of your girls can't make it, I'll go with you."

"Thanks. I don't want the girls to worry, so I usually don't tell them about my appointments until afterward. I also don't want to get their hopes up just yet either, so I'm not going to say anything to them about today's results. I'll wait until the next scan is completed. I may just take you up on that offer."

"One of the best things about working with Jack is that I get to set my own hours, so definitely let me know." Kite took another sip of her water and motioned toward Eve. "And how're things with you and Philip?"

Eve straightened. "Not good. He's frustrating me and I'm annoying him. It's obvious we're long overdue for a heart-to-heart." She shrugged. "I've avoided having one because I'm afraid. Afraid he'll say he wants out. Afraid he'll say he doesn't love me anymore. Afraid. ..."

Lydia gripped her friend's hand. Kite reached across the table and did the same.

Eve continued. "But something has to be done. I can't keep living like this. If he had just a *smidgeon* of love left in his heart for me, I could work with that." Her eyes brimmed with tears. "But I'm afraid that ship has long since sailed."

Lydia fought to keep her thoughts from spilling out of her mouth. She wanted to encourage Eve, but she also knew that Philip had never loved anyone but himself. She'd never understood how their marriage had lasted for three decades.

Eve pulled her hands away. "That's enough about me." She wiped her tears and smiled at Kite. "If the good news isn't about you and Jack, then what is it?"

Kite's eyes narrowed but she let out a small chuckle. "Uh-huh. I see what you two are up to. And I wouldn't be surprised if Jack was the one who put you up to it. But for the record, Jack and I aren't even dating, let alone getting married. I'm afraid you'll have to put your matchmaking skills to rest."

Eve winked at Lydia. "It was worth a try."

"Busted. So, what's the good news?"

Kite pressed her lips together and screwed the top back on her water bottle. She focused on Eve. "This news also involves Philip. The plan was to try to meet with everyone around the same time. To share the news with friends and loved ones before they heard about it through the media." She glanced at her watch. "But we're running a bit behind. And since it involves Philip's best friend, you'll probably be getting a call from him soon."

Eve leaned forward. "His best friend? This has something to do with Roger?"

Kite shook her head. "Paul."

Lydia watched Eve for a clue as to what in the world Kite was talking about. Paul Melson would never do anything that would put him or his family in the news. Nothing bad anyway. But Eve's face looked just as bewildered as Lydia imagined hers looked.

Eve squinted. "I don't get it. Paul's okay, isn't he?"

Kite leaned forward, her arms resting on the table. "It's about his sister, Mary."

Lydia pressed a hand to her chest. "Mary Laura?"

Kite blinked several times before she answered. "She's alive."

Lydia's hand fell away. Did Kite just say Mary Laura was alive?

"Mary and her family wanted to take their time and meet with everyone personally and share her story. But the media found out. So now we're in scramble mode. I agreed to meet with the two of you, and Paul said he'd meet with Philip, Roger, and their other friend Howard. Mary's parents are meeting with their family and friends. But, as hard as it is to believe, it's true. Mary Melson, now Mary Rabin, is alive and well. She's been reunited with her family."

Lydia's heart raced. How could that be? It had been years. Decades. She hadn't been close friends with Mary growing up like Kite and Eve had, mainly because she was a few years older, but she remembered the friendly, freckled-face little girl who'd lived across the road. Kite's family had lived next door to the Melsons back then, and Eve's family a few miles south, closer to town, but that hadn't stopped her and Mary Laura from becoming best friends.

Eve's eyes were wide. Lydia grabbed her hand. "You okay?"

Eve blinked. "I ... I don't understand what you're saying."

Kite rubbed the back of her neck. "To be honest with you, I don't even know what I'm saying. I haven't had the chance to process any of this. The past twenty-four hours have been a whirlwind." She straightened in the chair. "And if I hadn't seen Mary yesterday morning with my own eyes, I wouldn't believe any of this."

Eve didn't respond.

Lydia scooted her chair closer to Eve's and wrapped an arm around her shoulders. "Kite, I think it'd be easier if you start at the beginning."

"A few weeks ago, Eagle Eye received a call from a woman who wanted to hire a private investigator to help find her biological parents. The last known address she had for them was in this area so she called someone local. Jack took the case, and he located the family quickly because, as we all know, the Melsons never moved. It wasn't until after she arrived that she told him the whole story. That's when he mentioned it to me." She fell back into the chair. "He told me the family was planning a press conference and asked that I be the spokesperson for Eagle Eye when the media started asking questions."

Lydia looked to Eve again to see if *she* had any questions.

Silence.

Lydia cleared her throat. "Then what?"

"I had to see Mary. It was late, so Jack suggested I call the Melsons instead. The family assured me that it was true, and then they put Mary on the phone." Tears streamed down her face. "All I could think about was how *I* was the last person to see her on the day she went missing." She got up from the table and walked back and forth behind her chair. "I peeked out the kitchen window that morning and saw Mary working in the yard with her mom. I ran out, still in my pj's, and told her to come over when she was done to jump rope with me and Windy. She agreed, and I hurried back inside before my mom yelled at me for being outside in my jammies. Minutes later, I heard her mom calling her name." Kite slid her fingers underneath one of the sleeves of her blouse and withdrew a small bundle of clean tissues. "Sorry. I left my purse in the car."

The retro blue-and-white striped jumper Kite wore was adorable, even if it did put her in the mind of something her mother would've worn decades earlier. She'd never seen Kite wear anything that even slightly resembled today's current fashion trends. Wicker bowknot wedges and one of her famous headbands completed the style.

Kite blew her nose. "I prayed so hard that I'd see Mary again. But the years went by, and I gave up praying that she'd be found. Instead I prayed that they'd find her remains in hopes that would give her family peace." She dabbed at her eyes. "But when she came on the line and asked if she could still come jump rope with me and Windy, I melted. Poor Jack. Thank goodness he was there to catch me. I was a weeping mess after that phone call. I thought for sure Jack was going to call one of you ladies to come take me home, but he stayed with me until Windy called wondering where I was. She's temporarily staying at my place." She stopped pacing and pinched her lips together. "That's a whole different story that I have yet to tell you ladies. But because she was there, Jack drove me home. He wanted to stay longer in case I needed him for anything, but Windy kicked him out. I told her about Mary and we stayed up talking about it the rest of the night. The next morning, I went to see Mary."

Lydia let out a breath. Some of what Kite was saying

sank in, but it was still so hard to believe.

Eve remained silent.

Lydia held out her hand for Kite to hand her some of the tissues. "You've seen her. You've actually *seen* her? Did you get a chance to talk with her?"

"Some. A bit. I got up early the next morning and arrived at her parent's home right after sunrise. I couldn't get my mind off Mary. I was ready to apologize to her family for the early hour, but when I pulled up, there were already several cars there and more arriving. I had to park down the block. She told me later that her parents had contacted family members all over the country because they didn't want them to hear it through the media. So yes, I did get to see her. Sadly, we only had about twenty minutes together. But after that, the house became more of a staging area to figure out how to get the information out and to whom."

Lydia nodded towards Eve. "When will we get a chance to see her?"

"Unfortunately, not until after tomorrow. The family scheduled a press conference for nine a.m. Eagle Eye has received inquiries and requests for interviews from journalists all over the world. Jack hasn't agreed to any of them, but it will be a frenzy. And the rest of today, Mary's bogged down with interviews of her own. She's scheduled to meet with the FBI and Interpol.

Lydia straightened. "Interpol?"

"The man who kidnapped her was part of an international kidnapping ring."

Eve shot forward. "Stop. I don't want to hear the rest if you're going to tell me she was trafficked."

"No, nothing like that." Kite blew out a breath.

"Apparently, the guy who took her was part of an illegal adoption ring. They kidnapped kids from all over the world then placed them in so-called agencies to be adopted. Some of those families still have no idea that the children they adopted years ago were kidnapped."

Lydia trembled. She remembered the day Mary was taken as if it were yesterday. It'd started with Donna Melson calling her daughter's name. After about the third time, she sounded annoyed, but then her calls were more panicked. Lydia had gone to the window and watched as Mary's mom walked around the house and searched behind every bush and tree along the way calling for Mary. Then she'd stood in their driveway, cupped her hands around her mouth, and called for her again. When she didn't receive a response, she took off like lightning. She went to each neighbor's house, banged on doors, and asked if they'd seen Mary. Lydia's mom had run outside to see what all the ruckus was about. When she found out what happened, she helped Donna search the neighborhood.

Fourteen at the time, Lydia still remembered the sinking feeling of something being terribly wrong. Then the police had come. And more neighbors. She'd never forget how Mr. Melson roared into the driveway, screeched to a halt, and jumped out of his truck the instant it stopped. Or how ten-year-old Paul held a three-year-old Christianna as she cried on his shoulder.

And the whole time, little Mary had probably been beaten, tied up, and thrown into a car trunk. Scared. Alone.

Now she was back.

Thirty-nine years later.

Lydia knew firsthand what could happen to a person

during that vast amount of time.

She hoped for John and Donna's sake that the Mary they remembered was the same Mary who'd returned.

But experience told her otherwise.

Chapter Fourteen

Eve sat in her favorite chair and stared out the garden window. Hummingbirds perched, took off, and came back to suck sweet nectar from the colorful feeder outside her window. Her thoughts resembled the hummingbird's wings. Its wings flitted so fast it was hard to see them. To capture the movement of them. The only thing visible was the blur. And ever since she'd left the meeting with Kite and Lydia, her thoughts had been just like that—a blur. They flitted around her head faster than the bird's wings.

What a dolt she must've looked like, sitting there, frozen, as she heard her best friend was alive. She'd wanted to say something, to ask questions, but her tongue couldn't keep up with her heart and her brain. Which was the main reason why her piano tutor, all those years ago, suggested she take deep breaths when she felt anxious and overwhelmed. But Eve had learned giving a name to what made her feel that way was what truly helped.

Joy. Disbelief. Fear. Shock. So much so that Kite and Lydia refused to let her drive herself home. Kite had to return to her office to prepare for the press, so it was Lydia who'd brought her home. She stayed and made them both cups of hot tea. Lydia must have made conversation, but Eve struggled to remember any of it.

Mary. Her childhood best friend. Alive.

According to Kite, Mary was doing quite well. How could that be? After all this time? After so much heartache? Eve had struggled with the disappearance of her friend until her parents were advised to take her to a child psychologist. A lot of good that did. It only confused her more. How could her friend—whom she'd had more sleepovers with than she could count—disappear without a trace? The friend she'd played paper dolls with had vanished into thin air and no one could tell her why.

She closed her eyes against the memories. The tea Lydia made had calmed her some when it was hot. Now lukewarm, it agitated more than relaxed her. She needed to get a grip on her emotions.

She rose and walked into the backyard, past the vegetable garden, to the shed she'd managed to piece together when they first bought the house. There was only enough space for a sofa, two small chairs, and a table big enough to hold a couple of books and a cup of coffee, but it worked. When she couldn't stand being in the house with Philip, she retreated here to read, pray, and write music.

But those things had to wait. She walked to the east corner of the shed and stepped on one of the floorboards. It popped loose. Beneath it, a small, brown leather purse stared at her. A gift from her mother shortly after Mary disappeared when she realized Eve was wrapping their treasures in plastic wrap.

Eve picked up the purse. Dirt and mud still clung to it from its original burial site—the backyard of her childhood home. She'd only lived two places since then, and she'd carried this with her both times, securing it in safe places. She didn't want people asking questions and bringing up memories. She'd also never expected to open it again.

Five years after Mary's disappearance, during a memorial prayer service, she'd overheard some of the adults talking. They commented about how too much time had passed. How there were no new tips, and how Mary was surely dead by then. They remarked that her parents should give up hope, stop praying, and start the grieving process so that their family could move forward.

Eve had been holding a cup of lemonade. She'd dropped it and run out of the church crying. In all those years, she'd never thought about Mary being dead. Her parents never told her that and neither did the doctor during her therapy sessions.

That night, she'd asked her parents directly. When they admitted the possibility, she ran to her room, and pulled out the small leather purse from under her bed. It held her and Mary's favorite things.

Paper Dolls.

She'd cried rivers in her parents' arms that night. Mary was no more.

Her parents had let her have a small, make-shift memorial in the backyard. Her father prayed, her mother cried, and Eve placed the last remnants of her friendship with Mary in the ground. The hope of returning the dolls to Mary—gone.

She'd dug up the purse and taken it with her when she

left for college. When she'd married Philip, she'd brought it with her and reburied it. Always keeping her friend close. She'd never again opened the purse.

Eve let the memories fade. She dusted off the purse and placed it on the tiny table. When she saw Mary again, they'd open it together.

"Hey."

Eve jumped and spun. Philip stood in the doorway and nodded at the purse. "I see you've heard about Mary."

Eve let out a breath and nodded. "Yes."

He stepped over the narrow threshold. "Didn't mean to scare you."

"It's fine."

He sat on the couch. He wore blue jeans, tennis shoes, and a navy polo. Not his usual work attire.

He rubbed a hand along his jeans. "I didn't make it into work today. Paul called and asked me, Roger, and Howard, to meet him for lunch. When he told us about Mary's return, all I could think about was you. I didn't know if you knew already or if you were okay. I came by the house, and you weren't home. Then I called your cell, but it went to voicemail. I figured that must've meant you were at the studio. I drove over and you weren't there either."

Eve narrowed her eyes and chewed her bottom lip. Philip put in all that effort to look for *her*? She couldn't figure out if he was telling the truth or if this was another one of his lies. If it was, it was a cruel one.

He shook his head. "I know what you're thinking, but I'm telling you the truth. I know we have to work things out between us, but I wouldn't lie to you about this. I care about you Eve. And I know how much Mary meant to you. I wanted to be there for you."

Philip was being kind, and that was progress. But she couldn't deny that her heart took a deep dive when he said he *cared* about her. No mention of love.

"When I couldn't find you, I decided to come home and wait. I saw your keys on the counter so I knew you'd be out here." He motioned toward the small brown purse, then leaned forward, elbows on his knees. "Are you okay?"

She sat in the chair across from him. "I don't know."

He patted the seat on the sofa next to him. "Come sit by me." He reached for her hand. "Please."

Eve hesitated. She couldn't remember the last time she'd sat that close to her husband. Let alone at his invite.

"Philip—"

"Please."

She sucked in a breath and joined him on the sofa. She leaned against the armrest, but he put his arm around her shoulders and pulled her close. Tears filled her eyes.

"I'm here for you, Eve. I really am. Please know that."

She sniffed and rubbed the back of her hand under her nose. The warmth of his body against hers reminded her of how much she'd missed his touch. His embrace.

He wiped her cheeks, then lifted her fingers to his lips. He kissed each one softly, then held her hand.

"When you feel overwhelmed, I know how hard that can be for you. The shock of Mary's return I'm sure has your mind spinning." He kissed her hand one more time and rubbed her shoulder. "Wanna talk about it?"

Her mind spun all right. Mary's return, Philip's tenderness, his closeness. The familiar leather-and-spice scent of his cologne.

"Talk to me, Eve."

She took in a deep breath. She had to wrangle her thoughts. At least one of them. She exhaled, then said, "I don't think I'll be able to accept Mary's return as real until I see her with my own eyes."

He rubbed her shoulder again. "That may take a couple of days. Paul said law enforcement had her tied up with questions and interviews, including meeting with the original investigator on the case. You might not get a chance to meet with her until next week. Will you be okay with that?"

"I guess. I'd love to see her right now, but if waiting a week means that I'll be able to visit her without any distractions, it'd be worth the wait."

"The press conference is tomorrow morning at nine. I took off work." He gently squeezed her hand. "I think it'd help if we go together."

Eve couldn't hide her shock. Philip rarely called off work. And if he did, it was never for her.

He kissed her forehead. "Or we can sleep in and watch it on TV. All the morning news shows will be broadcasting it. You decide. Whichever way will make it easier for you."

She tried to take in everything he'd just said. And who was saying it. "Um, the TV will work best. I don't want my first glimpse of her to be amongst a huge crowd. But I also don't want to watch the broadcast live. Could you record it for me? I'd like to watch it after I meet with Mary, not before."

"I'll set up the recorder tonight. We'll watch it together whenever you're ready."

She debated whether or not she should jump up and ask

this man who he was and what he had done with her husband. She decided instead to wrap her arms around his waist and lean into his chest. "Thank you."

He slid his hand from around her shoulder, up the nape of her neck, and into her mousy, untamed hair. He turned her head toward him and kissed her. She relished in the deepness and intensity of it.

She pulled away when he shifted in his seat to stand. He stood over her a moment before he reached for her hand. She placed it in his. He led her outside. She gripped his hand tighter and followed.

"Where are we going?"

He glanced behind him and smiled. "It's been a long day for both of us. I think it'd be nice if we relaxed a little."

Eve bit her lip. His mouth said the word *relax*, but his eyes promised more.

"Philip, I don't think—"

He placed a finger to her lips and shook his head.

Eve's heart raced as he led her into the house and up the stairs. Each intimate experience with her husband was a trip to a wondrous land. Complete with kaleidoscope colors, harmonic angelic voices, and reverberating harps. And it had been a long time since she'd been to wonderland.

But this wasn't right. There were too many things broken between them. She pushed away to remind him of that before it went too far.

"Phil—"

He covered her open mouth with his.

She was done. Her body responded to his without her permission. She blinked away the tears. She knew what would come of this. Today, he desired her. Next week, he'd be back to calling her a fat cow without an ounce of common sense.

But none of that mattered. Because tonight, her body wanted to go on an adventure.

Chapter Fifteen

Of all the things Mary'd had to do the past couple of days, this was going to be the hardest.

Her adoptive parents, Ezra and Aviva Isaac, sat across from her. They'd flown in as soon as she'd called and told them that she'd reunited with her biological family. That part she'd told them over the phone. The next part had to be done face-to-face.

She'd planned on having more time to tell them, to help them prepare for what was to come. She'd hoped to fly back to Delaware and tell them in their own home, but the press conference had been pushed up to tomorrow, and time was a luxury she no longer had.

The joy and excitement that had accompanied her parents ever since their arrival, faded as her mom reached for Mary's hand. "What is it, sweetie? You know you've always been able to tell us anything. We're here for you no matter what, you know that."

Her dad threw his arm across the sofa. "Go ahead. Spit it out."

That was Dad all right. Always straight to the point. But after he heard what she had to say, he might've wished she'd beat around the bush a little.

She took a deep breath. "I need to tell you how I came across the information that led me to my biological parents." Mary bit her lip and closed her eyes. This next part was going to shock them. "I got the information from Seema."

Dad leaned forward. Mom pulled her hands away and squished her eyebrows together. "How would Seema have any information on your biological family?"

Before they adopted Mary, Seema had been the Isaacs' housekeeper and cook. When Mary joined the family, Seema worked as the nanny, too. When Mary went to college, she continued her employment with the family until an illness left her blind. After that, she'd moved back to her native India.

Mary swallowed. "Do you remember her younger brother, Amit?"

"Of course." Dad let out a low groan before continuing. "Trouble from the day we hired him. Only lasted about a year and a half. Gave him the boot for stealing. Surprised you remember him. He was only there for a few months after you arrived."

Oh, she remembered him. Amit had been hired as a handyman. She didn't see him often, but when they did cross paths, she'd run the other way. Something about him had frightened her. Now she knew what it was.

"Amit knew you were looking to adopt?"

Dad shrugged. "Probably. Most of the people we knew back then did."

"How'd you come across Miss Autry's agency?"

"I don't know." He turned to his wife. "Do you remember?"

"At our annual dinner party, several people handed us business cards of adoption lawyers, agencies, ministries, and orphanages. I put the cards in my purse. We visited the ones that weren't too far away. Miss Autry's was one of them. Why?"

"The person who handed you Miss Autry's card. Do you remember who it was?"

"There were over five hundred people at that party. Half of those who handed us cards we didn't know. But I do know that Amit wasn't there."

Mary knew that too. Amit had worked with an older white gentleman, a man investigators had identified as Dr. Thomas Roth. That name had led to a dead end. Literally. He'd passed away twenty years before.

What she had to say next wasn't going to get any easier, and she knew her dad well enough to know that his patience was fading fast. She decided to follow his advice to get on with it. "The man who handed you the card was Dr. Roth. He worked with Amit and several other people, including Miss Autry. They ran an illegal adoption ring."

Mom's head jerked back. "*Illegal*?"

Dad pushed his shoulders back and lifted his chin. Just as he'd done when he'd chastised her growing up. Like the time he'd caught her skipping class in high school. "Daughter, I want to hear all of it. Now."

These people, whom she loved dearly, were about to have their worlds turned upside down.

She sucked in a quick breath, then let it seep out before answering. "All of the adoption papers from Miss Autry's agency and their supposed legal team were false. My parents never put me up for adoption. I was kidnapped out of my own front yard. And Amit was the one who did it."

Mom's mouth was slightly open as if she wanted to speak.

Dad crossed his arms and lowered his brows. But it was his mouth that told her everything she needed to know. He. Was. Ticked. Good thing Amit was no longer alive either. Her dad's temper rarely flared, and when it did, it was because someone had harmed a loved one. He wasn't a violent man, but his reach was far and wide. Amit would've felt the length of it. He would've had to go a lot further than Asia to dodge the wrath of her dad.

Mom broke the silence. "Are you telling me that Seema …" She put her hand over her mouth and blinked back tears as she talked through her fingers. "Who was more like a daughter to me than an employee … was using her job with us to kidnap children?" Her voice squeaked out the last six words.

"No." Mom's chin quivered. Mary hoped the words she spoke next would ease her Mom's fears. "It was only a few months ago that Seema found out what Amit had done. When she returned home, her brother had to go too. But his criminal activities didn't start here in the States. He'd left quite a few enemies in India. And apparently, they had long memories. They eventually caught up with him, and when they did, it wasn't pretty.

"Seema had nothing to do with this. I've looked at it from every way possible, and so have the police, the FBI, and other international authorities. Amit left a full confession on videotape. He'd made arrangements for it to be delivered to

Seema if he went missing or if his body was found." Mary left out the fact that the only part of Amit's body that *was* found was his head. "Seema couldn't see the video, of course, but she heard every word. It broke her heart. She couldn't bring herself to tell us because she couldn't stand the thought of us thinking she'd had anything to do with it."

Mary swiped at a tear that trickled onto her chin. "But she also knew that we needed to know. I received a call from her a little over a month ago. She said it was urgent and to come to India right away. It was about my biological family. That was all she said. Ethan and I boarded a plane. We watched Amit's confession. A four-hour video that detailed several kidnappings. Mine was one of them."

The muscles in Dad's face tightened.

"He also gave the names of those he worked directly with. The kidnapping ring itself expanded across several countries. He claimed that he participated in ten kidnappings in the United States, but he only gave details on three. Mine and two others. A young girl named Grace, and a little boy named, Li Wei. The FBI located Grace, but so far they haven't found Li Wei."

Mary left her chair and sandwiched herself between her parents. "I know this is a lot to take in. And the last thing I wanted was for you to find out like this." Mary waved her arm around the modest hotel room. "But my biological mom, Donna, called every one of our relatives in the Midwest and told them that I'd returned. They all came to see for themselves and to welcome me home. They'd all sworn to keep the information private until my parents and siblings, the law agencies, and the two of you were ready to make it public. But one of those relatives, or someone they knew, contacted the media. It's been chaos ever since. Journalists want more details. Right now they only know that I was kidnapped and then adopted by a wealthy family. But it won't be long until it's front page news. I couldn't let you find out that way."

Dad placed an arm around her shoulder. "We knew something was wrong yesterday when you called. Didn't sound like yourself at all. We would've been on the next plane even if you hadn't asked." He lowered his voice, his thick Jewish accent becoming more prominent. "But now that your mom and I know what's going on, we're here to help."

"I appreciate that, Dad. But there's more." Mary's stomach churned. She'd rather drink cat vomit than share what she had to say next. "There are whispers circling that you and mom must've known—"

"I figured as much." He rubbed her shoulder. "It's all right. We can handle it."

Mary cried into her hands. "I'm so sorry, Daddy. You and Mom don't deserve this. The media is looking for someone to blame, and they haven't even heard my story. I'm not going through with this. I'm not going to let them—"

He grabbed her shoulders and turned her to face him. "Look me in the eyes, daughter."

She blinked away tears to look at him.

"Do you think I or your mother knew about your kidnapping?"

She stopped her head from doing a double take. "*What?* No!"

His eyes glistened. "Then do what you've come here to

do. Tell your story. Enjoy your family."

She glanced at the floor. "But—"

He pulled at her shoulders until she faced him again. "Who am I?"

"Daddy."

He chuckled and said it again. "Who am I?"

Wisdom-filled brown eyes of the only father she'd known for thirty-nine years stared back at her. "You're Ezra C. Isaac. Child of God. Devoted husband. Wonderful father. Superhero grandfather, and agricultural specialist extraordinaire."

"And I'm married to … "

"The only woman in the world full of grace and mercy, but who still knows how to give a mean uppercut when needed." Mary finished one of her father's favorite sayings. Mom gripped her elbow.

Dad continued. "Have you ever seen us get upset at what people say about us? Or let them back us into a corner?"

"Never."

His eyes flashed. "And you never will."

Mary wrapped her arms around her parents. It would be a cold day in the underground inferno before either of her parents let a difficult situation get the best of them. Even one as shocking and surprising as this.

Kite had shown her some of the questions the media wanted to ask at the press conference. Not only were they gunning for her adoptive parents, they were going after her biological family as well. Any reporter trying to make a name for himself would consider them fair game, especially since those involved in the actual kidnapping were dead. But it was the theme of the media's questions that unnerved her.

They screamed conspiracy. That the families had somehow been working together. And come tomorrow morning, the whole world would be asking the same question.

Had they?

Chapter Sixteen

Kite fell into her kitchen chair and rested her forehead on the table. Oh how she wished her arms weren't too tired to provide cushion, and that her neck had enough strength for her to bang her head against the wood.

The phone rang.

Again.

The press conference had been set up for Mary to thank everyone who'd supported her family through the years with prayers and words of encouragement. She ended with an inspiring message to those still waiting for loved ones to return. She'd left the details of her kidnapping and how she had been reunited with her family to the FBI.

After the FBI shared their updates, the media went haywire. The questions fired in.

What proof did the FBI have that it was an actual kidnapping?

Who was Amit Patel and were the feds able to locate the rest of his body?

Did the nanny have anything to do with it?

Wasn't it true that the kidnapping was a ruse and that the financially struggling Melsons actually sold their young daughter to the wealthy Isaacs?

Her phone rang.

Windy answered it. She told the caller to go kick rocks and to not bother her sister again. Except the words she used were a lot more colorful.

Windy staying with her had its benefits.

Kite winced as the chair across from her creaked. "Kite, how in the world did they get your mobile number?"

"I have no idea. The only phone number we gave out was to the office. When Jack didn't answer, I guess they got creative to find my mobile number. No way would they have been able to find his. With the cybersecurity steps he has in place, it'd been easier for them to get into Ft. Knox."

"I can set up your phone like that, too."

Kite lifted her head. "Go for it."

Windy grabbed her phone from the middle of the table, then plugged it in.

"How long is that going to take?"

"With your internet speed, not long at all. You need to call someone?"

"Several someones actually." Kite massaged the back of her neck. "Jack to get an update on the DeMint case. Mary to see how her folks are doing. Eve wasn't at the conference. Lydia said she'd stop by her place on the way home to make sure she was okay. I'd like to check in with both of them."

Windy grabbed her computer from the sofa, added a small device, then connected it to Kite's phone. "Your first call should be to Mary to make sure Christianna's not in jail. If she is, I have bail money. That reporter deserved it. I wish

Paul hadn't stopped her before she got a fistful of that woman's Raggedy Ann locks. I would've recorded it and made sure it went viral. A warning to idiot reporters everywhere."

Kite squished her eyes to shut out the memory. It didn't work. "Unfortunately, I think it's going to go viral anyway."

The reporter had pointed her finger at Mrs. Melson and accused her of selling her

daughter. Christianna had practically leaped off the small platform toward the throng of reporters. Her brother grabbed her before she seriously injured the woman, but she left a long scratch along the woman's jawline.

"I still can't believe that happened."

"Wasn't your fault." Windy tapped away on her computer and the phone. "You didn't know what that reporter was going to say or how Chrissy would react."

"Still, I hope Jack didn't see it. He'll never put me in charge of anything again. What a nightmare."

Windy shrugged. "Wasn't so bad. Well, maybe for the reporter it was. I'm sure having four flat tires wasn't a great end to her day either."

Kite leaned forward. "What are you talking about?"

Windy lifted an eyebrow and grinned.

"Windy!"

"Hey, you know how I love the Melson family, and Chrissy's like the little sister we never had. There's no way I was gonna let that reporter get away with what she said."

"Christianna's not little! She's a grown woman with two daughters. Sarah's just starting high school. How do you think she's going to feel knowing everyone at school saw her mom acting like that on TV?"

"Proud?"

Kite grunted. She wasn't going to win this argument nor be able to convince Windy that what both she and Christianna did was wrong, and she was too tired to try. "Are you done with my phone?"

Windy restarted it and slid the phone across the table. "Your number has been cyber-secured and your phone is now hacker-proof. No one will have access to anything on there unless you want them too."

"What about my contacts?"

"Still there."

"Thanks. I couldn't take that constant ringing."

Windy narrowed her eyes. "When was the last time you slept?"

That was a good question. "I remember going to bed the past couple of nights and trying to sleep, but somehow I never quite got there."

"I bet you haven't eaten either." Windy made her way to the refrigerator. She pulled a bowl from the shelf, removed the lid, and retrieved a plate from the cabinet. "I made tuna salad earlier." She spooned some on the plate then added crackers from the pantry. "Eat and go to bed."

She glanced at the kitchen clock. Four p.m. Pastor Greene had arranged for the church to host a reunion dinner for Mary's friends and family at seven. A two-hour nap sounded divine. She took the plate from Windy and scarfed down the snack. "It's getting harder and harder to keep my eyes open. Wake me at six so we won't be late."

She handed me a glass of water. "Will do. Would you mind if I asked Michael to come?"

Kite coughed up some of the water and wiped her mouth

with her sleeve. "Michael? The same Michael that you thought you killed?"

She slid back into the kitchen chair across the table. "Yeah."

"He's alive?"

She shrugged. "He says he's okay. He called last night to say there'd be no hard feelings as long as I let him and that girl live in peace. Said he stopped loving me a long time ago. That he's happy now and looking forward to getting married and starting a family."

"By *that girl* you mean the twenty-something he was cheating on you with? Hildy, I think her name was, right?"

"Mm-hmm."

"Then, why in the world would you want to invite him to dinner?"

"Because I think it'd be good for our relationship."

"You don't have a relationship."

"Michael says one thing and does another. He's always been that way."

Kite tried to ignore the ache pulsating in her temples and thought for sure she heard her bed calling her name. But she knew that if she didn't straighten this out with Windy now, as soon as she was asleep, Windy would go visit Michael, and possibly Hildy, and who knew how that would turn out.

"Windy, he's offering you a clean break here. He'll retaliate against you for stabbing him if you don't let this thing go."

She scratched at her cheek. "What do you think I should do?"

"You should take him up on his offer. Let him be happy with Hildy. Maybe she'll be good for him."

Windy's head jerked backward. "You mean, just let him walk away from me?"

"Yes."

She folded her arms. "Um … no. That man made me promises, and I intend to make sure he keeps them."

"Now you sound like a stalker."

She gripped the table and leaned forward. "What I sound like is a woman who refuses to be used."

If Windy had been used by Michael, it was her fault, not his. But telling her that now was not going to get me out of this conversation quickly.

"I thank God that Michael's alive. If you'd killed him, we'd be having an entirely different conversation right now. But it doesn't change the fact that he's disloyal and dangerous. His offer is actually a blessing. The sooner you wash your hands of him and his violent family, the better off you'll be."

Tears filled her eyes. "He was supposed to marry *me*. He said he wanted to raise a family with *me*."

Heavens. She'd actually thought about having kids with this man? "I know. But he's made it pretty clear. He's now going to do that with Hildy."

Her eyes tightened, and the tears were replaced by a flash. Kite had said the wrong thing. A storm now brewed behind those caramel browns.

She leaned away from the table and turned her head to the side. "I thought you said you were going to take a nap."

Kite didn't say anything more. She knew better. A week before they were born, their mom had a dream. When she awoke, she told their dad she'd dreamed that their twins were in the air. One dived and looped through the sky with ease and soared when the winds of adversity blew. The other was a gentle breeze that refreshed and relaxed everyone around them. But when challenges came, that same breeze turned cold and calamitous.

Dad, being an avid kite enthusiast, decided that day that if the twins were girls, he'd name the firstborn Kite, and the second, Windy.

Our parents had a strong faith, but neither of them put much stock in the dream being prophetic. As our personalities developed, however, they referred to it more and more.

She was Mommy's darling, but Windy was Dad's favorite. She was always wild and impetuous, but Dad had a way of talking with her that veered her away from many disastrous decisions.

He passed away shortly after their eighteenth birthday. It changed Windy. She blew through life without care or caution. And when Kite sensed a change in the wind was coming, she ended the conversation and prayed.

Because she knew her sister. And from the look in Windy's eyes, one thing was certain.

Catastrophe loomed.

Chapter Seventeen

Priscilla swayed to the slow tempo of the soft music filtering into Barry's multimedia room with no idea where the sound came from.

Barry walked up beside her. "I didn't like the look of the large speakers, so my sound guy made them invisible." He smiled. "Which, according to him, means they're hidden inside the walls."

When he'd first given her a tour of his home, this room had been reserved by one of his employees. It wasn't until their after-dinner walk and they came upon the massive extension to the main house that Priscilla realized she'd never had the chance to see inside.

The room was circular. In front of her was a movie screen that had six plush leather chairs and two sofas facing it. To her left was a large kitchen area with a convection oven, two stainless steel refrigerators, and a soda fountain. The entire area was surrounded by gleaming black granite countertops and bar stools that matched the dark gray sofas and chairs. To her right was a round stage. Three guitars, a drum set, several keyboards, and a couple of microphones finished off the space. Next to the stage was an entryway covered by a long black curtain.

She pointed to the curtain. "What's back there?"

"The restrooms and a couple of dressing rooms. Every now and then we like to have live entertainment. But usually, this room is where I host Super Bowl and holiday parties or watch movies with the grandkids. My staff uses it for birthday parties and other celebrations."

He pulled his cell phone from his pocket. "Watch this." He pushed a button and, behind her, a fireplace kicked on and the shades on the floor-to-ceiling windows slid closed.

"Wow."

He stepped closer, wrapped his arm around her waist, and looked up. She followed his gaze and saw a glass domed ceiling. Moonlight filtered through the panes. "This is my favorite feature." With his free hand, he pushed another button on his phone, and the ceiling went from clear to black, then slowly faded into a soft gray. He pressed the button again, and the starlit moonlighted sky reappeared.

She leaned into his chest. "That's going to be my favorite feature as well."

He pulled away and slid his phone back into his pocket. As soon as he did, the music changed from the soft instrumentals to a lively tune she remembered from the seventies. He smiled. "I can control the music from my phone too."

She laughed. "Al Green's 'Let's Stay Together?' Really, Barry. Could you be any more transparent?"

He pulled her in close and sang along.

The soulful lyrics and Barry's deep baritone voice

warmed her. "You're a great singer."

He extended their arms, gave her a twirl, then pulled her back in. "And a great dancer as well?"

"Fred Astaire has nothing on you."

He laughed. "I feel like a kid on Christmas morning." He gave her another twirl, drew her in tight, and rocked their bodies from side-to-side. "The same way I used to feel when I realized that everything I'd ever wanted was right there under the Christmas tree."

She tilted her head to the side. "You're going to tell me how much you love me again, aren't you?"

"That bothers you, so I'm not going to." He lowered his head and nuzzled his nose in her hair. "Instead, I'm going to tell you how the smell of your hair reminds me of a trip I took to the Caribbean. And how your eyes are filled with so much passion that it makes it hard for me to sleep at night. And how your lips—"

The smooth voice of Al Green faded, and the sultry one of Dorothy Moore filled the room. He slowed their lively dance to a sway as "Misty Blue" made its way through the invisible speakers.

Diamond Liz had been right when she'd said Barry reminded her of former U.S. Senator, Bob Dole. The facial features were similar, but Priscilla didn't remember the senator being as tan or as muscular. The white button-down short-sleeve shirt Barry wore gave her a glimpse of his strength.

"Look at me, Silly."

She forced her gaze from his arms to his eyes.

"I know how Dorothy feels. Not being able to get someone off of your mind." He slid his hand from her waist, along her spine, and into her thick waves. "I wake up thinking about you. I go to work thinking about you. I go to sleep thinking about you."

Her survival instincts had the words, *but I don't think about you* on the tip of her tongue. She didn't say that though. That would've been a lie. Funny. She'd never had problems lying to men before.

He tightened his hold on her waist and stared at her lips. How fast her heart had betrayed her. The same heart that repeatedly told her to flee from love was now eagerly anticipating an act of it.

Dorothy's song of heartbreak continued as Barry held her and swayed, but he never let his lips touch hers.

She was falling for this man.

Whether it was love or something else, she wasn't sure, but somehow he'd been able to change her when none of the others could. She released her arms from his waist and wrapped them around his neck, bending it slightly. If he wasn't going to make the first move ...

He pulled away. "No, Pris. Not until you're mine." He took a step back, quirked an eyebrow, and spread his arms wide. "To enjoy all of this, you'll have to be my wife."

She placed her hands on her hips and laughed. "All of that, hmm? Perhaps this would be a good time for me to remind you of how old you are."

He grinned. "And I guess I'll have to show you that age is just a state of mind." He yanked her in close, their lips almost touching again. "When you become Mrs. King, I'll show you what the term age-defying really means."

Dorothy's song ended. Barry stepped back and walked toward the kitchen. "But right now, I need something cold.

Would you like a glass of water?"

No man had ever walked away from her. Not when they were that close, the mood that intense. But she didn't feel rejected. It was that other "R" word her mother loved to toss her way.

She felt respected.

She closed her eyes to shut off thoughts of her mother. When she opened them, Barry was staring at her. "Don't mind me. Just trying to block out the past." She pointed toward the kitchen counter. "Is that a working soda fountain?"

"It is."

"Then I'll have a root beer float."

Barry pulled a carton of vanilla ice cream and two frozen mugs from one of the refrigerators. "Do you like yours spoon thick or straw creamy?"

"Creamy, please."

She sat on the sofa. A minute later, he handed her a float with whipped cream and a cherry on top. She placed the red-and-white straw in the center and took a sip. It was the perfect blend of roots, herbs and vanilla bean sweetness. "Mmm. This is good. Thank you."

"Nothing but the best for you, my sweet."

She shifted on the sofa and faced him. "You intrigue me, Barry King. Did you know that?"

He sat next to her. "How do you mean?"

"I know you ... well, I know how you feel about me. And I know a few other things that you've told me here and there, but I don't know a whole lot more. For instance, you've mentioned that your wife passed away years ago, but I never hear you talk about her. And I know you have a son and a daughter, but you don't talk about them either."

"I don't talk about my wife because it still hurts. She was the bride of my youth. We married at seventeen and stayed that way until her death parted us." He took a sip of his float then laid his head against the sofa. "And I don't talk about my kids because they hate you."

Her eyes widened. "They *what*?"

"They're against me having a relationship with you."

"But why do they hate me? They haven't even met me."

He turned his head toward her. "That's why it doesn't bother me. They haven't met you. When my daughter realized you were living here, she and my son joined forces to find out more about you. They found out that you're twenty-five years my junior and that you're beautiful. To them, those two things equal gold-digger."

She let out a sigh. If *finding out more about her* meant they'd contacted some of the men from her past, no wonder they hated her. "They're not exactly wrong, Barry."

He bolted upright. "Silly, they are wrong." He took another sip of his float then placed it on the coffee table in front of them. "They're judging you by the mistakes you've made in the past. You're not that person anymore."

She blinked. She wasn't?

He scooted closer. "We both know how this relationship started, and that doesn't bother me. And it bothers them that it doesn't bother me. But if you took every dime I'd ever earned and disappeared into the night, I still would not regret one moment of it. I fell in love the moment I saw you. It wasn't your beauty that I fell in love with. It was the essence of you that poured out of every pore. I saw what you still refuse to see."

"And what's that?"

"That you're worthy."

Worthy? She placed her mug next to his on the table as a tear made its way down her cheek. She didn't know why it was there or how it had made its way so far before she'd noticed. She swiped at it. Worthy. She wanted to unpack what he meant by that, but it had been a long time since a man had said something that made her emotional enough to cry. She needed to divert the conversation.

"You're always talking about us getting married. How do you think that will work? Your children hate me. Can't you see what would happen if I became the next Mrs. King? It'd be chaos. And in the end, blood is thicker than water. I can be replaced. Your kids can't."

He placed a hand on her knee. "I'll do anything in the world for my children— within reason. But they're not little anymore. They're married and have families of their own. I hope they'll allow themselves the chance to get to know you. If they don't, I'll understand. But how they feel and what they decide will have no bearing on us. I love you, and they can't change that."

She stared at the floor. "We'll see."

"Yes, we will." He gently rubbed her knee. "Enough about my family. What about yours?"

She smiled as a memory from childhood filled her vision. Her father at the pulpit. His salt-and-pepper beard and the way it stood out against his dark skin. One hand raised in the air praising the Lord. The other holding a Bible. "Daddy was a preacher. Pastored a small congregation a few miles outside of Habakkuk. Did that for as long as I can remember." She frowned as another memory made itself known. "Then, after church services one morning, he went to sleep and never woke up."

"Oh, Silly. I'm so sorry. How old were you?

"Twelve."

"And your mom? Is she still alive?"

"Oh, yeah. She's alive, all right."

"Tell me about her."

She folded her arms across her chest. How in the world did one describe Mabel? "She's a good Christian woman. How 'bout we just leave it at that?"

"I take it you two don't get along?"

"She thinks I'm ruining my life, that I'm on my way to hell in a handbasket."

He guffawed, then covered his mouth. "Sorry."

"It's fine." She pulled the sofa pillow from behind her and placed it on her lap. "It's not completely her fault. She had high hopes for me. After college, I started my own style magazine. The first couple of years were a huge success. I was on my way to becoming the black version of Martha Stewart. Then the economy tanked. People were more interested in paying for their homes than decorating them. The magazine never recovered. I tried working for a few companies after that, but I've always had a hard time with people telling me what to do." She laughed. "I blame it on being a PK. Too many do's and don'ts. Anyway, I got fired more than once and soon found myself deep in debt and penniless. Then one day, a former colleague made me an offer I didn't want to refuse. It was at one of his parties— and that's putting it nicely—that I met Diamond Liz and Lola. To me, it was making a living. To my mom? Her worst nightmare."

He nodded slowly. "Does your mom know about me?"

"I didn't tell her, but I wouldn't be surprised. Somehow she always finds out where I'm at and what I'm up to."

"Are you her only child?"

"I have an older sister, Penelope. A doctor. She moved to Guyana a few years back. Works at a mission hospital over there. She's the golden child."

He wrapped his arm around her shoulder. "So, your mom and your sister are the only family you have?"

"A few extended family members here and there. But growing up, it was just the three of us."

He squeezed her shoulder. "See, Silly, that's why you need me. Your dad's no longer with us. You and your mom are at odds, and your sister lives thousands of miles away. You need someone you can count on. To have your back. To be there for you."

"*I've* been there for me."

"And that's sad." He glanced away, then back at her. "You don't have to live that way. Everyone needs someone."

She blinked away tears. Once again, Barry had penetrated her defenses. If she didn't act now, it would be too late. When the heart was involved, mistakes were made and possessions lost. He needed to be reminded once again what this relationship was about. But before she opened her mouth, she realized something.

She didn't care.

She didn't care what his kids thought about her.

She didn't care what her mom was going to say.

She didn't care if Barry never gave her another nickel.

She only cared about this man, who for some reason thought she was worthy.

But one question remained.
Was she?

Chapter Eighteen

Lydia stared at the flowery sticky note stuck to her front door.

It couldn't be.

She read the note again. *Call after ten p.m.* Attached to the bottom of the note was a business card that had *Bliss Wedding and Event Center* in bold letters at the top, and in the lower right-hand corner, in a much smaller font, the name *Dinah Dooley O'Keefe*.

Lydia took a deep breath and removed the note from the door. Dinah. Her baby. The one who'd ignored all of her phone calls, letters, and gifts for seventeen years, had stood on this very porch.

The note shook in Lydia's hand as she fumbled to unlock the door. She tossed her purse and keys on the foyer table, shut the door with her foot, and ran toward the phone hanging on the wall near the kitchen.

She pressed the number one button and held it down until her firstborn's name popped up on the screen. Thank goodness for speed dial.

After the fourth ring, she chewed her lip. *Please, Ada. Answer the phone.*

Finally, her daughter's voice. "Hi, Mom."

"Have you talked to Dinah today?"

"No." Her daughter stretched out the word, then added, "Why? Is everything okay?"

"Yes, I'm fine. It's just—"

"You sound out of breath. I'm coming over."

"No." Lydia walked to the kitchen table and sat. "I'm fine. I'm out of breath because I ran to the phone. And because I'm excited. Dinah stopped by today."

"She did *what?*"

"I know. I couldn't believe it either."

"What did she say?"

Lydia closed her eyes. For years she'd been waiting for this day. The day that her estranged daughter would show up at her door. She'd prayed years for this. And Lydia hadn't been here when it happened. She grabbed a napkin off the table and wiped her eyes. "I don't know. I wasn't here. I was at the salon."

"Oh, Mom. I'm sorry."

"So am I." Lydia sniffed. "She left a note on the door."

"What did it say?"

"To call her after ten. She left the office number for Bliss."

"Dinah doesn't leave there until midnight most nights, so that makes sense."

Lydia sniffed again.

"Mom, please don't cry. You didn't know she was going to stop by today. None of us did."

"And you girls didn't tell her about my diagnosis, right?"

"No. And the four of us were together last weekend for Jenny's recital. If she knew then that she was planning on stopping by, she didn't tell us."

"I just wanted to see her so badly." Lydia's voice hitched. "To touch her. To look at her face."

"She left a note, right? Asking you to call her? That means she's not shutting the door again. She wants to talk. That's a good sign."

Lydia rubbed her thumb over the card. "You're right." She looked at the clock on the stove and wiped at another tear. "How will I survive another four hours before I can call her?"

"I made fettuccine for dinner. I'll bring some over, and you and I can have dinner together. That'll help pass the time."

"Thanks, sweetie, but I'm too nervous to eat. I think I'll just go into my closet and pray."

"For four hours?"

If her daughter only knew that most of her closet prayer times easily exceeded that. "Yeah. It'll help calm me, and I need to pray for wisdom. It's been a long time since I've spoken with her. I want the conversation to go well. The last one we had ended with her vowing to never speak to me again. I don't think I could take another seventeen years."

Ada was quiet on the other end. Then she said, "Mom, just remember that Dinah is still Dinah. I truly believe this is a huge step on her part, but ..." Ada let out a loud sigh. "I guess I just don't want you to expect too much from her. Not at first."

In other words, Dinah was still angry.

"I don't want you to be too disappointed if the first

conversation doesn't go well."

"That's why I'm going to pray for wisdom, honey."

"Call me after you two hang up. I don't care how late it is."

"Ada—"

"Promise you'll call, and I'll shut up and hang up."

Lydia placed her elbow on the table and rested her head in her hands. "I promise. Now go enjoy dinner with your family."

After Ada hung up, Lydia got a bottle of water from the refrigerator, kicked off her shoes, and walked up the stairs to her bedroom. She exchanged her black slacks and navy blouse for a pair of gray sweats and a white T-shirt, then stepped into her closet. In her favorite corner, her Bible, notebook, several pens, and two twin-sized pillows waited for her on the floor. As she settled in next to them, the phone rang. She groaned. This was why she preferred her prayer times to be in the early mornings. Fewer distractions and no interruptions. Nobody called. Nobody rang the doorbell. She climbed out of her spot, walked into the bedroom, and picked up the extension.

"Hello?"

"It's Dinah."

Lydia tightened her grip on the phone. The voice on the other end was more mature and had more of a depth to it than the voice she remembered, but the familiar soft tone with an edge confirmed that this was indeed her daughter.

Over the years she'd imagined what she would say if given the opportunity. She'd rehearsed conversations in her head a thousand times. She closed her eyes to recapture some of those words, but the sudden rapid beat of her heart caused her to feel lightheaded. She sat on the edge of her bed. Dinah was on the phone. She needed to say something.

"Hi." She scrunched up her face. After all this time and all that rehearsing, that was the only thing she could think of?

"Hi."

Lydia waited for her to say more. Nothing came, so she cleared her throat and decided to start the conversation. "I saw your note when I got home. I'm sorry I wasn't here. I wanted to call right away, but the note said to call after ten. I was going—"

"It's all right. One of my assistants is looking for a promotion. I handed her the reins tonight to see how she does. So far, I'm not impressed. Just wanted to give you a heads-up in case you hear me screaming at someone."

Lydia decided not to respond to that. "Lately, it seems like no matter where I go, someone is talking about how great your venue is. Just today, there was a lady in the salon talking about her friend's wedding and how beautiful and well-managed Bliss was and that she was even thinking about doing her upcoming nuptials there. I'm so proud of you, honey. I know how hard you've worked. I'm not surprised it's been such a huge success."

"The salon. Is that where you were when I stopped by?"

"Yes. The gray strands were quickly turning into white patches."

"I'm glad you weren't home. I was hot under the collar when I stopped by earlier. I've calmed down a bit since then."

Lydia's hand trembled. Oh, how she wished she'd gotten off the phone with Ada earlier so she could've prayed. She needed words. She needed wisdom. She'd hoped Dinah reaching out meant they'd somehow be able to start rebuilding their relationship. Right now, it seemed she'd reached out for the opposite. Lydia couldn't let this conversation go downhill.

Give me words, Father.

Lydia's stomach tightened. "You came to see me because you were upset about something?"

After a slight pause, Dinah answered. "I ran into Mr. Melson today and he mentioned that he'd dropped Mary and her mom off at your church. I swung by to apologize for missing the reunion dinner. As I was leaving, Pastor Greene stopped me in the hallway and told me he and his wife wanted to speak to me about something."

Lydia rubbed the back of her neck. She knew where this conversation was headed. The Greenes had known Dinah since she was little. Her parents had made sure that all of Lydia's girls not only attended church but were active in it. They grew up there. Three of her daughters and their families still attended. And so had Dinah, until Lydia started attending a few years back. Her message was clear. She didn't want to attend the same church with the woman she'd vowed to never speak to again.

"Dinah—"

"Do you know what they wanted to talk to me about? Forgiveness. They sat me down like the new kid in Sunday school and preached a mini-sermon to me on forgiveness." She let out a loud sigh. "How could you do that to me? Wasn't ruining my entire childhood enough?"

"Dinah, I didn't—"

"And don't tell me you didn't put them up to it. It was

obvious from the conversation that they'd been talking with you."

"That's not what I was going to say."

"Have you been talking to them about me? I asked them that question too. They didn't confirm it, but they didn't deny it either."

Lydia sucked in a breath and let it out slowly. "He's my pastor. Of course, I seek their counsel when I'm struggling with something."

"So that's a yes?"

"Yes."

Dinah breathed heavily into the phone. "How much did you tell them?"

"They know everything, Dinah."

"How could you! If I'd wanted people to know the details of what happened to me, *I* would've told them. You had no right."

Lydia thought about that for a moment. Did she have a right? She wasn't the one who'd hurt Dinah. Not physically anyway. But in her drug-induced state, she'd allowed it. She'd allowed those men to hurt her daughter. And for the promise of more drugs, she'd allowed it to happen again.

She knew her daughter didn't want to hear what she was about to say. In the past, it only made her angrier. But she had to try. "I am sorry. I hate what I did. That's why I was seeking counsel. If I could—"

"I have to go."

"No!" Lydia jumped off the bed. "Let's not end it this way, please." She paced the floor and desperately searched for something else to say. Anything to keep Dinah on the phone, to change the course of the conversation. Finally, it hit her. "You said you were glad that I wasn't here earlier because you were pretty angry but have now calmed a bit. Can I ask why?"

She thought she'd heard a slight chuckle. "Because in the end, I knew that the Greene's were right. But what they didn't know is that I've tried forgiving you. Many times over the years. Every time you sent a birthday card, a Christmas gift, or a letter, I tried. Then I'd have another nightmare. And I'd end up in the shower scrubbing my skin until it was red and raw and bleeding. Then I'd do it all over again because I couldn't stand the stench. All these years later, I can still smell the stench of those men."

Lydia wiped at the tears streaming down her face. *Father, help me. I know You've forgiven me. I know I'm not that person anymore. But I'll take any punishment You deem necessary for my child to be free of those nightmares.*

Dinah sniffed and continued. "I don't even know how I ended up at your house. I was so angry when I left the church that I just got in the car and drove. When I saw where I was, I ran up the steps and banged on the door loud enough to bring out the neighbors." She blew out a breath. "When I got back to the office, I couldn't think straight and I couldn't work, so I locked my door and prayed. The more I prayed, the more I realized that Pastor Greene was right. This needed to end. That I was never going to have peace until I forgave you and extended an olive branch to mend our relationship. That's when I gave my assistant her to-do-list and called. I knew if I didn't do it now, it would be another seventeen years."

Lydia stopped pacing. Did she just hear what she'd thought she'd heard?

Dinah clicked her tongue. "I don't know what's next because I don't know how to forgive something that I can't forget. But I figured a phone call would be a good place to start."

Lydia nodded before she realized Dinah couldn't see her. "Thank you."

"I want to say I'll call you tomorrow or next week. But I don't think I will. I need time to figure this all out. I can promise that I'll call again in the next couple of weeks. That's all I can offer right now. I hope you'll be okay with that."

Lydia nodded again before she pinched herself and spoke. "Yes."

"Bye … Mom."

Lydia continued to grip the phone until she heard a soft click and a dial tone. She walked to her nightstand, placed the phone back on its base, walked into her prayer closet, and lay prone on the floor.

She thanked God and cried. Thanked Him for His mercy and for answering her prayers for her and Dinah to be reunited. She cried because of her guilt and shame. She'd been so addicted and so strung-out when those things had happened to Dinah that she didn't know the extent of it until child services stormed through her door and removed her girls. She would've spent time in prison if her parents hadn't intervened and begged the court to give her the chance to complete an intensive rehabilitation program. The court agreed but with the caveat that, if she missed even one session, she would be removed from the program and spend the rest of her time in prison.

It had been the longest eighteen months of her life, but

she finished. The thought of prison hadn't scared her, but the thought of never seeing her girls again had. She eventually lost custody of all four of them to her parents, but she finished the court's requirements and even volunteered to do two additional years at a sober living home, which included weekly counseling.

But when she was allowed to visit her girls, they weren't the same. Ada hated her, Bethany and Claudia were afraid of her, and Dinah hadn't spoken a word in three years.

Ada was thirteen when she'd found out what was happening to Dinah, and she'd immediately called her grandparents, who'd called the authorities. It had taken years for Lydia to mend that relationship, and more years to do the same with Bethany and Claudia.

Dinah hadn't spoken to her again until she was fifteen, ten years after the incidents took place. And she'd had a lot to say to the mother who'd fed her to the wolves.

Lydia reached across the floor of her closet to where she kept the tissues. She snatched one before another sob escaped and blew her nose. She knew Dinah had suffered, but she also knew her grandparents had made sure she'd had counseling.

But like Dinah said. There were some things you just couldn't forget.

Chapter Nineteen

Eve smiled across the small café table.

Her mother, Kay, took a sip of coffee then waved as a young couple with a small child entered. "Welcome to Kay's Café. A server will be with you shortly." Mom stopped one of the waitresses walking by and pointed to the couple who'd taken a booth by the window. "I think that couple with the little girl is new. Please let them know their order will be on the house." Mom turned back to Eve. "You look happy. How are things between you and Philip?"

Eve shrugged, then took a bite of the warm, cream cheese-filled bear claw. As she chomped into one of the plump raisins, she closed her eyes. Her favorite pastry. The one Mom always baked fresh whenever she knew Eve would be stopping by.

She sipped her orange juice. "Philip's about seventy-thirty. Seventy percent his old narcissistic self, thirty percent new and improved." She set the glass down and reached for the mug of almond flavored coffee that Mom had poured from a pot in the center of the table. "This morning was great. We slept in, and he attempted to make breakfast for me. The oatmeal was soupy, the bacon was rubbery, and the eggs were burnt, but I appreciated the gesture, and we laughed about it. He went to work after that. Depending on how his day goes, he could be leaning toward that seventy percent again." She pulled a napkin from the holder and wiped her mouth. "Or he could surprise me and remain in the thirty. I hope that's the case. But I'll be okay either way. I've learned to adjust."

Mom's lips tightened. "You've been adjusting to his moods for thirty years."

"I know, but something is different. I see him making an effort this time."

Her mother's lingering look of doubt told Eve it would be best to change the subject. The war between Mom and Philip had started the day of her wedding, when Mom swore she saw Philip and one of his female "friends" in a very compromising position in a back room of the church. Mom had been livid and had done everything in her power to stop the wedding, including telling everyone within earshot what she saw, leaving nothing to the imagination. Both families were horrified, but Eve stood her ground and decided to believe in her future husband's plea of innocence. He'd somehow managed to convince her that Mom was off her meds and hallucinating. Thing was, Mom hadn't been on any medications.

Eve cleared her throat. "Anyway, Philip's attempts at trying to rebuild our marriage aren't what have me smiling this morning. Last night, Mary and I came here after the reunion dinner and talked into the wee hours of the morning, just the two of us."

Mom smiled and her eyes softened. "I know how much you were looking forward to that."

Eve nodded. "We cried, laughed, and caught each other up on our lives. She introduced me to her husband, Ethan. He's a gem for sure. I also got to meet her adoptive parents. What a nice couple. It was fun to hear about Mary's antics growing up, but odd as well. It blesses me to know that she was well taken care of and had a safe and loving family, but at the same time, I also recall the torture and grief the Melsons endured, not knowing where their daughter was."

Mom stared at the table. "I remember the fear that gripped this town when Mary disappeared." She let out a small laugh. "Your dad slept on the floor by your bed for months after that. Do you remember?"

Eve smiled. "I do. And I remember him nailing my bedroom window shut so it couldn't be opened from the outside."

Mom leaned back in her chair. "But the Melsons never gave up. Donna told me time and time again that her daughter was alive. I'm ashamed to say I didn't believe her."

"A lot of people didn't believe her."

Mom stared out the café window. "I know. But to have that type of faith. For four decades, she never stopped praying and she never gave up hope." Her gaze darted to Eve, then back out the window. "I'd like to think I'd have that same type of faith if that had happened to you, Evie. But I honestly don't think I would have."

Eve moved their plates and mugs to the side and leaned on the table. "Until we're in that situation, none of us knows what we would do. Some would stand strong like the Melsons, and others would crumble, blame each other or blame God. Mary told me her family went through all of those emotions. But when they saw that wasn't getting them anywhere, they decided as a couple that even though they didn't know where Mary was or who she was with, they knew the God who created her. And that together, no matter the outcome, they would trust Him. That was what gave them the strength to continue."

Mom blinked away tears. "I would've curled up in a ball and never recovered."

Eve shook her head. "You might've curled up in a ball, but you wouldn't have stayed that way. The Melsons had tons of people praying for them. And you were one of them. You didn't think Mary would be found alive, but you still prayed for their family, just like everyone else. And those same people from across the country who were praying for Mary and her family would've been praying for you." Eve straightened in her chair. "Besides, remember when I was six years old and little Billy Bluett chased me home, throwing rocks at me and calling me ugly? I saw the fire in your eyes when you snatched him by the arm. I was so glad when Dad stepped out and intervened. You were about to fling Little Billy down concrete steps."

Mom frowned. "I was going to make him eat those rocks too. The little brat. I couldn't stand him or his skinny-minny mother."

Eve laughed. "See what I mean? You're not the type to stay in a fetal position. With God's help, you wouldn't have given up until you'd found answers. Or the man who took me. And he would've been in a world of trouble if you got to him before the authorities did."

Mom let out a small chuckle. "Thanks for making me

feel better."

A waitress hurried to their table. "Kay, there's a phone call for you."

Mom glanced at her watch and stood. "Be right back."

When she was sure her mom was out of earshot, Eve pulled out her cell. All afternoon she'd been wanting to call Philip. Their morning had gone so well, she was hoping his lightheartedness would continue into the evening. He picked up on the first ring.

"What?"

Eve closed her eyes. There went her nice evening. "I just called to see how your day was going."

"I work with a bunch of idiots. How do you think my day is going?"

"I won't keep you then. See you when you get home." She aimed her finger at the button to end the call.

"Wait. I'm sorry, Eve. You didn't deserve that. It just looks like it's going to be one of those days, you know?"

She lifted the phone to her ear again. "What can I do to help?"

"Just have dinner ready when I get home."

"Fine. Anything else?"

"Where are you?"

"I'm enjoying a cup of coffee." She left out the part that she was at her mom's café. With the mood he was in, he'd probably storm in and make a scene. "I'm headed to the studio, then to the mall with Lydia and Lola. I'll be home by six, and dinner will be ready."

"I'll be home at four. Have it ready by then."

Eve let out a sigh. Calling the girls to let them know she wouldn't be joining them wasn't a problem, and she'd do it in a heartbeat if Philip had a legitimate reason. He didn't. He was doing this to agitate her. "I'll be there at four, Philip. But there'll be no cooking or eating until we talk."

"About what?"

"You. Me. Us. Our marriage. Your being angry one minute, tender the next."

"Angry? You want to see angry? Let me come home to an empty house or no dinner and I'll show you angry." The call ended before she even had a chance to pull the phone away from her ear. She grabbed her purse and was about to stand when she felt a hand on her shoulder.

"I take it that was Philip?"

Eve dropped her purse to the floor and looked up at her Mom. "I can't believe I'm getting ready to say this, but you were right. I never should've married that man."

Kay kissed Eve on top of her head. "I want to talk to you about something, but there's not enough privacy in here. Come with me."

Eve snatched up her purse and followed.

The employee break area at the café was right outside the rear exit. The café was too small to have an indoor area, so her mother had added an awning for the employees, to protect them when it rained, and tables with umbrellas for when the weather was sunny. She also had a fire pit for them to enjoy in the winter. Despite all of that, their favorite place to gather was right outside the door, where they'd sit on wooden crates to chat or make phone calls.

Eve threw her purse over her shoulder, walked to one of the crates, and plopped down with a sigh. She tried her best to make it sound more irritated than sad, but her voice trembled and tears followed.

Mom handed her a tissue. "Let me guess. He was more seventy than thirty on that phone call."

Eve nodded and wiped away the tears.

Mom pushed one of the crates in front of Eve and sat. "You know how I feel about Philip, so anything I say will be jaded, but I have to ask. Why are you still married to that man?"

Eve blew her nose. "I used to say it was because I loved him. Which I do. And I can't imagine my life without him. Which I can't. But now it's to the point where I can't imagine my life *with* him either. He constantly has me on a roller coaster of emotions. And he does it on purpose. What I don't know is why." She shrugged. "Maybe he enjoys seeing me an emotional wreck all the time." She sucked in a deep breath and held it. She didn't want the next words to come out as a whine. "But *why*?"

So much for that.

Mom scooted her crate closer. "*Why* is the right question, Evangeline Annette Stockton. Not why is he doing this to you, but why are you letting him?"

Eve sniffed and wiped a tear off her chin.

"Philip has always been scum. He thought his dad being the mayor of small-town Habakkuk was the same as his dad being the President of the United States. Rumors of his—and his dad's—indiscretions are legendary. Except he knows that I was an eyewitness to one of those so-called rumors. He knows what I saw the day of your wedding. And he's been trying to make me out to be a raving lunatic ever since."

Eve nodded despite wanting to defend her husband. Philip had gone to great lengths to make her mother look bad. He'd never forgiven her for making public what she saw that day.

Mom leaned forward. "Do you know that for at least a year after you two were married, he sent me threatening letters?"

Eve's eyes widened. "He did *what*?"

"He sent me letters, at least once a week, accusing me of ruining his—and his father's, and his grandfather's—careers. He told me that if I didn't retract what I was saying, he would make my life miserable."

Eve gasped. She knew Philip had been obsessed with ruining her mother's reputation. And she'd witnessed him having a total nervous breakdown after his father lost his re-election, and his grandfather, who at the time was a member of the state legislature, was asked to resign. But she had no idea he'd threatened her mother.

Mom folded her arms. "I spit on every last one of those letters and sent them back to him."

Eve stared at her mom. Philip never, ever let her get the mail. If her mother, or anyone else for that matter, had sent her something through the mail, she'd never known. She had no idea what their bills were or what assets they owned. Or didn't own. And not once did he mention that he'd sent letters to her mom, or that she'd returned them. Eve balled her hands into fists to stop them from shaking.

Kay put her hands on top of Eve's fists. "When you went ahead with the wedding that day, I cried because I felt like I had failed as a mom. But despite the disagreements that Philip and I had, I never stopped praying that he would become the man of your dreams. That's the main reason I kept quiet all these years. I didn't want the way he felt about me to poison any true connection that might've developed between the two of you." She shook her head. "But he hasn't changed, honey. And as much as I'd like to place the blame solely on him, I can't. You've let him get away with treating you like this. You've always been drawn to people who abuse you. Even after Little Billy pelted you with rocks, you ran after him, begging to be his friend. And what did he do? Pelted you with more rocks. Philip and Little Billy are the same. One was a boy, the other is a man. The only difference is that the man has had more time to fine-tune his terror."

Eve yanked her hands away. Did her mom just call her husband a terrorist? She threw the balls of tissues in her hand on the ground. "You've never understood."

Mom tilted her head. "Understood what?"

Eve used her hand to make a circular motion around her face. "What it's like to be ugly."

Mom took in a deep breath and Eve rolled her eyes. She knew what was going to come next. A lecture on inner beauty. They'd had this conversation a million times. They both had dull brown hair, narrow eyes, and pointed noses. Although no one would call her mother a great beauty, those features had a way of making her attractive. Eve didn't have to look in the mirror to know that those same features made her look like a rodent.

Kay shifted on her crate. "Help me understand how what you look like has to do with any of this. You let Philip abuse you because …?"

"Because I like having someone around who needs me. Because I like coming home to a house with someone in it. Because I like going to bed and waking up next to someone, sharing life with someone." Eve sucked in a breath and continued. "Philip's not perfect, but he is that someone. And he has been since high school. No other guy ever showed me the attention Philip did. Heck, none of them showed me any attention whatsoever. Do you know what it's like to be in a group of girls and all the guys you come across gaze right past you to the pretty ones? To the girls with thick, silky hair, long lashes, and beautiful smiles? It was like I wasn't even there. Like I was invisible. I tried once to get one of those guys to notice me. I smiled at him and waved. You know what he did? He frowned and looked like he was about to vomit." She shook her head to stop her mind from revisiting that nightmare. "But not Philip. He not only acknowledged me, he sought me out. Whenever he'd see me with that same group of girls, he'd walk up to *me* and hold *my* hand. He was tall, good-looking, athletic, the grandson of a member of the Missouri General Assembly, and the son of the mayor. The other girls couldn't believe it. All of a sudden, *I* was the one being envied. *I* was the one attending high-profile parties, and *I* was the one he married." She sniffed and blinked away tears. "I knew he wasn't faithful, and my gut told me that he cheated on me the day of our wedding. But I let him convince me otherwise because I needed him to go home with *me*. And I'm pretty sure he's cheated again since then. But from the moment we said *I do,* I've held on to the Scripture that says what God has put together, let no man—or in my case, woman—tear apart."

Mom leaned in closer. "Are you sure it was God who put the two of you together? Because it sounds more like you latched on to Philip out of desperation, and still clinging to him out of fear. That sounds more like your doing than God's."

Eve swallowed. Was it her doing? She'd needed love and

desperately wanted affection, and Philip had heaped both upon her. But she'd never prayed about their relationship. She'd been afraid of the answer. She'd never listened to her parents' warnings or paid attention to the red flags that were now on fire because she was afraid he'd leave. And now the ashes were collecting at her feet. All for a man she didn't know. A man who kept secrets. A man who'd threatened her mother. A man who'd demanded her attention, affection, and undying loyalty while he played loose and free with his.

A man who was about to get a wake-up call.

Eve stood, gathered her purse, kissed her mother on the cheek, walked back through the café, out the entrance, and into her car.

What her mother didn't know was that Little Billy had not only thrown more rocks at her, he'd thrown her up against a tree, pushed her to the ground, and kicked her until she begged him to stop.

It had taken a physical beating for her to realize that Billy didn't want anything to do with her.

She wasn't going to wait for that to happen with Philip.

Chapter Twenty

Mary blew a kiss to the two adorable faces saying goodbye to her on the screen. She handed Ethan the electronic tablet and plopped down on the hotel bed. "I miss them so much."

"I do too." He sat next to her. "And before you ask, I still don't think the time is right for them to join us."

As much as she wanted to hug her handsome fifteen-year-old and snuggle with her tutu-wearing seven-year-old, her husband was right. Things had calmed since the press conference and reunion dinner, but there were still a few reporters looking for a story where there wasn't one. Until they realized that, she didn't want the kids getting dragged into something that could potentially have their faces splashed across the television screen. Or have some immoral reporter trying to question them. Right now her beautiful children were anonymous. And she and Ethan planned to keep it that way.

She kicked off her shoes and folded her legs under her. "I'm glad your sister took them back with her to Tel Aviv.

That way they won't hear the lies being spread. But I'm also sad. They've been waiting their whole lives to meet their real grandparents. And now this delay."

Ethan leaned against the headboard. "Even hungry reporters get tired of eating dirt. In another week or two, they'll move on to the next story. That is, as long as Ezra follows his lawyer's advice and doesn't give any interviews."

"I know. He's pretty heated about the lies that are out there and the effect they could have on his career."

"Your dad has worked in his field and built business relationships in the States and Israel for over sixty years. And he did it with character and integrity. Nobody who knows him believes any of that stuff."

Mary sighed. "I know. But I think he's hurt by it all. Not only the lies that are out there but also that he trusted Miss Autry's lawyers instead of having his own legal team handle the adoption. And he fired Amit for stealing, but he didn't have him arrested because of the family's relationship with Seema. He mentioned to my biological dad how badly he feels about that. If he'd had him arrested, perhaps that would've stopped him from kidnapping the other nine."

"Ezra *would've* had him arrested in a heartbeat if he'd had any idea what Amit was up to. He'd have had him drawn and quartered when the authorities looked the other way. But he didn't know. No one can be held responsible for what they don't know." He tapped her knee. "Speaking of don't know. Do you have any idea what Christianna is so ticked off about?"

She sighed again. "I have no idea. I'll find out in about an hour."

"She finally agreed to talk with you?"

"She replied to my text saying she couldn't talk for long and that it couldn't be at Mom and Dad's house or in public. She agreed to come here when her girls get home from school."

"There's a rec room downstairs next to the pool. I can work out for a couple of hours while the two of you talk. But you still have no idea what she's so upset about?"

"I don't. But you know, she's hasn't really been mean to me. That first day she was obviously agitated, but after that, it's been more avoidance. I walk into a room, she walks out. That sort of thing." Mary stretched her legs out on the bed then laid on her stomach. "The past couple of weeks I've had the opportunity to talk and catch-up with tons of relatives. Some I remember, some I don't. Mom and Dad and I have talked at length about everything. What happened the day I disappeared, the efforts to find me, the struggles they've been through. They've updated me on those who've died, like my grandma and grandpa, and the new additions to the family. Pauly and I have pretty much been inseparable, and I absolutely adore his wife and children. I've even had the chance to catch-up with Eve and the girls and their lives. But I know very little about my baby sister. I know from others that she's married and has two daughters. She didn't even show up for the reunion dinner."

Ethan chuckled. "I think that had more to do with the fact that she was almost thrown in jail earlier that day for attacking that reporter. The video was all over the news networks and social media. Her family was probably trying to avoid any further media attention."

"I know, but it breaks my heart not being able to reconnect with my sister. She's the only one I have—"

"Shhh. We're not going to have any of that." Ethan pulled a tissue from its box on the nightstand. "You don't want to start the waterworks before she gets here, do you?"

Mary smiled at her husband's lighthearted attempt to distract her, then snatched the tissue from his hand. "I know what you're trying to do, but you're right." She dabbed at the moisture under her eyes. "No sense getting upset before I even talk to her."

"That's all I was saying."

"You were calling me a crybaby."

He kissed her forehead. "Okay, that too." He leaned in again and kissed her on the lips. "But you're the prettiest crier I've ever seen. Your makeup doesn't even smear."

She gave him a playful punch in the arm. "I just want things to go back to the way they used to be with me and Christianna. Pauly and I know that there are huge gaps to be filled in, but we instantly fell back into that brother-sister dynamic. I was hoping for the same with Christianna."

"But she was only three when you were taken."

"I know. But the three of us were close. Pauly tried to be tough in front of his friends and act like he didn't want his little sisters around, but he did. He didn't like doing girly stuff, but I can't tell you how many trees he and I used to climb. And we'd drag Christianna along with us. She'd have mud pies waiting for us when we came down. We'd emerge from the woods with dirt in our mouths and on our faces. Pauly and I would get in trouble because Mom said we'd made her baby eat dirt. In reality, Christianna was the one shoving it in *our* mouths. She'd threatened us. Told us she'd tell on us for playing in the big sticks—that's what she called trees—and tell Mom that we made her climb the trees too. It was get spanked or let her feed us mud. We chose the mud.

"She was a little stinker but we loved having her around. I remember the times when we'd play tag and Pauly would run with Christianna under his arm like a football. That drove Mom crazy but Christianna loved it. She and I would eventually get thrown in the tub and bathed. We shared a room with twin beds. In the mornings, I'd wake up with her snuggled next to me." Mary frowned. It had been way too long since she'd allowed herself to indulge in memories from her childhood. Growing up she'd kept the memories at bay because the pain of not having her siblings with her was too great. By the time she was in her twenties, the memories had blurred and by her thirties they'd completely faded. At least she'd thought they had.

A knock sounded on the door.

Ethan pushed off the bed and reached for her hand. When she stood, he pulled her into a hug. "I'll grab my gym bag out of the closet and head out." He leaned in and, when his lips parted hers, Mary's heartbeat quickened. What had she been thinking telling Christianna they'd have time alone to talk? Ethan couldn't leave. Mary needed his calming presence. What if she said something stupid and Christianna never spoke to her again?

Ethan's warm hands kneaded her tense shoulder and back muscles before he pulled away. He placed his forehead against hers. "I can be back here in a few minutes if you need me."

"Please don't go."

"I'll be right downstairs."

She swallowed and nodded.

He gave her another peck then grabbed the canvas

athletic bag from the closet. He turned and looked at Mary, waiting for her nod. She offered it, and he opened the hotel room door. He greeted Christianna as she walked in, then he turned back to Mary. "Can I get you ladies anything before I go?"

"I don't think so," Mary said, "but I'll call if we need anything."

He nodded, then closed the door.

Christianna stood inside the small foyer and folded her arms. "I can't stay long."

"I know." Mary sat on the sofa and patted the space beside her. "But I'd like to at least sit while we talk."

Christianna wore a pair of black jeans with a white button-up blouse and a light tan leather jacket. Mary motioned toward the closet. "You can hang your jacket in there if you like."

"Not staying that long." The only thing she carried was her keys. She slid them into her back pocket and sat at the opposite end of Mary. "What did you want to see me about?"

So much for small talk. "I'd like to talk about why you're upset with me."

Christianna let out a loud sigh. "I don't know. This is why I've avoided you. I'm annoyed, and I can't even tell you why."

Mary waited for her to say more, but Christianna just stared at her.

"The past couple of weeks have been a whirlwind." Mary tried to keep her emotions in check, but sitting here with her baby sister, trying to explain how she felt … She hardly knew where to start. "My emotions have been all over the place, and I wouldn't be surprised if yours have too. You're going about your normal day, and then, out of nowhere, the sister you haven't seen in forty years shows up. I can't begin to imagine what that would be like. Feel like. I've been looking for you guys forever, and I'm still having a hard time absorbing it all. I'm willing to bet that what I'm dealing with is nothing compared to the emotional upheavals you, Pauly, Mom, and Dad are going through. But I hope that we can talk about it."

Christianna raised an eyebrow. "Just like you and Pauly, right?"

"Pauly and I have a long way to go. We've missed decades of each other's lives. The same with you and the rest of the family. But they're not avoiding me. They're helping me try to reconnect. To—"

"You want to know what made me angry?" Christianna's lips drew tighter and so did her eyes.

Mary nodded.

"It was the way you looked when you showed up. Your rental car was a Mercedes. The pantsuit you wore looked like it came straight off the runway, and I'm pretty sure your purse and shoes cost more than my Honda." She shot a fiery gaze at Mary's left hand. "And don't even get me started on that mountain sitting on your finger."

Mary glanced at her wedding ring. "I'm not sure—"

"We grieved for you, and you show up looking like a million bucks without a care in the world."

Mary shook her head. "That's not what I—"

"Mom cried herself to sleep for years. I know because she held me while she did it. Dad and Pauly were never home because they were too busy traveling the country putting up posters of you. And every night I did everything I could to stay awake, because if I fell asleep, I'd dream that I was back in the bathtub with my sissy Mary, splashing water and blowing bubbles."

Mary reached for her sister's hand, but Christianna pulled it away. "In elementary school, I was known as the sister of the girl who disappeared. They called you *eerie Mary*. Pauly constantly got into fights. We were never allowed to sleep over at friends' houses, and Dad never let me go anywhere alone. He chaperoned everywhere I went until I was twenty-one and moved out. Even then he slept outside my place in his car a couple times a week. It was ridiculous, but that was our normal. And that's just a *small* fraction of how our lives changed. Not knowing what happened to you not only broke our hearts, it messed with our minds." She blinked away tears then pointed at Mary. "But you … you didn't look like you'd been through what we'd been through."

Mary shook her head in disbelief. "Are you saying you don't think I've suffered?"

Christianna pulled a tissue from her jacket pocket and blew her nose. "Then I met your adoptive parents. Mr. Ezra and Miss Aviva." She rolled her eyes. "The idiots had the nerve to ask me if I remembered your infectious laugh. How it made everyone around you want to join in. The dunces. Of course, I remembered your laugh. We laughed together as a family. But what I couldn't understand was why you were laughing with *them*. The laughter in our house stopped the day you disappeared. And there you were, laughing it up with another family."

"Christianna—"

"And when they started to share about your school years,

I couldn't believe it. While I was being teased and Pauly was beating people up, you were singing in musicals and dancing in ballets."

Mary pointed to her chest. "You think my life was all giggles and tutu's?"

Christianna wiped her nose with the tissue and shrugged.

Mary sucked in a deep breath and held it. Tears filled her eyes. She leaned back and stared at the ceiling until they dried. She had to remain calm. She slowly released the breath and hoped that would keep her voice from rising again. "From the moment I opened my eyes at Miss Autry's, my family was all I thought about. One minute I was helping Mom in the garden, the next I was in a room full of strangers with a woman I'd never met, telling me my parents didn't want me anymore." She blinked to keep the tears at bay. "I knew that was a lie. I couldn't wait for Dad to show them that by kicking down the door and taking me home. But that never happened. And the whole time I had Miss Autry whispering in my ear that this is what my parents wanted. Then I'd think about you and Pauly. I cried every time I thought about you, tiny and alone, in a place like I was. I can't begin to tell you how many times I had to stop and listen and look around because I could've sworn I heard Pauly calling my name. And it didn't end at the agency. For years after I went to live with the Isaacs I'd wake up screaming. I didn't know I'd been kidnapped, but I knew something awful had happened. Then I started to think that all of you had been murdered. I couldn't eat, I couldn't drink. I ended up in the hospital. The doctors told the Isaacs that my issues were mental, not medical, and advised they seek psychiatric care because they feared that I'd take my own life. They weren't wrong. Many times I'd thought about ending the voices and the pain by slicing my wrists. But the Isaacs decided to make me a promise instead. They said when I was old enough, they'd do everything in their power to help me find my family. They didn't know if we'd find everyone dead or alive, but I held on to that promise with everything I had in me. If I laughed and sang and danced it wasn't because I'd forgotten, it was because it was the only way I knew how to survive."

Christianna's lips trembled, and she looked down at her lap before she scooted closer to Mary. "I didn't know." She pulled Mary into a hug. "I am so, so sorry."

"It's not your fault, Chrissy." Mary hugged her baby sister tighter as her own tears made their way into Christianna's auburn hair. "Neither one of us knew what the other was thinking or how we were feeling. As the oldest sister, I apologize. I never should've waited this long to talk with you. I'm the one who should be sorry."

Christianna's head moved from side to side on Mary's shoulder. "From the day you arrived, you've been going non-stop. The police had you tied up for weeks, and then there was the media. And besides, it's not like you didn't try. I was the one who wasn't ready."

Mary relished the warmth of her sister in her arms. Her mind went back to the times when Christianna scrambled up next to her in bed. "The kidnapping taught me that lives can be changed in an instant. I knew something was wrong the moment you realized who I was. I should've insisted that we talk then. I could've lost that opportunity if anything had happened to either one of us over the past couple of weeks."

Christianna laughed. "Yeah. I could've been locked up."

Mary chuckled and pulled away to look into her sister's eyes. "That reporter wanted her fifteen minutes of fame. But I am glad we're not having this conversation in jail."

"Me, too."

Mary let out a shaky breath. She had to clear up one more misunderstanding. "Please don't think ill of Ezra and Aviva. They were an answer to the many prayers that were said on my behalf. Yes, they're rich. My dad had made his fortune decades before I joined the family. But they provided much more than money. They rejoiced with me when I was happy and cried with me when I wasn't. They were by my side when I was sick and, when I misbehaved, they were there with discipline. My teenage years were an emotional time for them. One day I would be in hysterics and the next day I'd have no memory of what happened. The doctors told them there was a medication for that. But they refused. Instead, they'd come to my room, and the three of us would sit on the floor, eat pizza, drink cola, and talk. We talked about anything and everything, but mostly my dad told stories of people he knew who had overcome great adversities. Including some of his family members who'd survived the Holocaust. Then he'd open the Bible and read more great stories. It took a long time for me to understand what he was trying to teach me. I'd still throw tantrums for no reason at all and sometimes refuse to get out of bed, but they still kept coming to my room, talking, reading, and praying. As I got older my symptoms subsided, but my point is that my parents never let me face any battle alone. They weren't perfect parents, but they were great parents. And they were always there when I needed them."

Red crept across Christianna's cheeks. "I never

should've said those things about them. I'd mentioned to Dad what they'd shared about your childhood, and he told me that they'd shared that for my benefit, hoping I'd feel better if I'd known that you'd had a nice home. It didn't make sense to me at the time, but now I understand what he meant. I feel like a jerk. They were only trying to help and I was so cold toward them."

"They understood."

Her eyes widened. "They told you?"

"They weren't upset. They just feared they'd done more harm than good."

Christianna looked around the room. "Are they staying here? I'd like to apologize."

"Their suite is a couple of floors above us. I'm not sure if they're back yet. They had a meeting with their lawyer earlier. As far as the investigation goes, they've been officially cleared of any wrongdoing. In the next day or two, they'll probably be heading home."

"To Delaware?"

Mary shook her head. "Tel Aviv first. They have a home there, and Ethan's sister lives there as well. That's where our kids are. Mom and Dad will spend some time there then bring the kids back with them to the States."

"Tel Aviv. That's where you met Ethan, right?"

"Not exactly. My dad was working in both countries back then, so we had a home in Mevaseret Zion. That's where Ethan was born and raised. We ran across each other a couple of times, but it wasn't until we both ended up at the university in Tel Aviv that we started dating."

Christianna looked down at her hands. "Does that mean that you and Ethan will be leaving soon as well?"

Mary placed a hand on Christianna's shoulder. "I'm not ready to leave you guys yet. There's still so much more I want to say, do, and see before we leave. We agreed to stay a couple more weeks. After that, we're hoping that everyone will agree to come and stay with us for a while. By then, my parents will be back with the kids, and we'd love for everyone to meet them."

"When you say everyone, you mean…?"

"Mom, Dad, your family, Pauly's family."

Christianna jerked her head back, eyes wide. "How big is your place?"

"Ethan's a consultant for several high-tech companies in the States, Japan, and Israel. We have enough room."

Christianna raised an eyebrow. "Well, Brad isn't a consultant for any major corporations. He works in construction, but he does make a decent living. He and our girls—Sarah is fourteen and Rose is twelve—have given me endless grief about the fact that they have yet to meet the sister-in-law and aunt they've heard so much about. And if I don't extend an invitation for you to join us for dinner tonight, then I might as well not go home."

Mary let out a small laugh. "Of course. We'd love to."

"I'm afraid it won't be anything fancy. I'm not a gourmet cook, but I do make my own pasta, sauce, and bread. The veggies will be fresh from the garden. Our kitchen is small, so I can guarantee it won't be the ritziest place you and Ethan have ever dined, but I can also guarantee that you'll never come across a better spaghetti."

"You had me at homemade pasta. What time?"

Christianna glanced at her watch. "Brad doesn't usually get home till around six, so our family is used to having late dinners. If you guys are okay with that, I can leave now and have dinner on the table at seven."

"That's perfect. Ethan and I had a large lunch, so by seven we'll be ready to refuel."

Christianna stood. "I can't wait to call Brad and the girls."

Mary pulled Christianna into a hug. "Thanks for inviting us. I'm looking forward to meeting your family, especially your girls. Mom and Dad's eyes light up every time they talk about them."

Christianna's front pocket dinged. She pulled her cell phone from it, typed a quick message, then returned it to her pocket and smiled. "They must've heard us talking about them."

"I have an idea. Kite and I are getting together this weekend to have some fun. You know girly stuff. I'd love it if you and the girls could join us."

"They have track-and-field practice. I'm free, however," Christianna looked at her feet then back up at Mary. "I have the feeling what you and Kite consider fun might not be up my alley, so I think I'll pass."

"We're getting hot stone massages and avocado facials. Not to mention lavender mani's and pedi's. You don't consider that fun?"

Christianna tightened her lips and shook her head. She seemed to be fighting the urge to laugh.

Mary crossed her arms and pretended to be offended. "Did I mention that Windy will be joining us?"

Christianna's face morphed into skepticism. "Windy's not getting a hot stone massage."

"No, but she's joining us. She mentioned that while

we're getting spa treatments, she'll be zip lining or cable jumping or something like that."

"I'm in." Christianna walked to the door, opened it, then paused. She turned on her heel and frowned. "I'm sorry. This was something you wanted us to do together as sisters, right? Forget what I said. It wouldn't hurt for me to have some kiwi—"

"Avocado."

"Some of that on my face. Windy and I can do our thing some other time."

Mary walked toward her. "The whole reason I mentioned Windy was to entice you to come. We'll have breakfast together, enjoy some retail therapy, then Kite and I will go get pampered while you and Windy hang from steel ropes in the sky."

Christianna's smile lit up the room. "You sure you don't mind?"

"You promise to join us for the after-dinner pajama party later that night?"

Christianna let out a quick laugh. "Yes."

"Then I don't mind."

Christianna stepped into the hall. "I'd better dash if I'm going to have dinner ready on time. But be sure to call Kite and tell her I'm in." She waved good-bye and sprinted toward the elevator.

Mary rubbed her thumb across her bottom lip. She was glad Christianna had decided to join them, but the more she thought about it, the more she regretted extending the invitation. Individually, Christianna and Windy were magnets for trouble, and she didn't have to dig too deep to imagine what they'd be like together. And that didn't include them planning an adventure that involved flying high over jagged rocks.

Especially when one of them already had one foot over the edge.

154

Chapter Twenty-One

Kite didn't want Priscilla Martin mistaking her for her twin sister.

Kite's hair was shorter than Windy's, but they shared the same brunette shade, so she gathered it at the nape and secured it with a clip. She tossed the blonde wig she'd considered wearing onto the back seat of the surveillance car and opted instead for the nondescript faded gray baseball cap that Jack had left in the trunk.

After a quick glance around, she plopped into the driver's seat and slid on a pair of dark shades. A limousine came into view. Investigating someone you didn't know had its risks, which was why Jack had insisted she get her concealed weapons license. But investigating someone you did know also had risks.

Especially if you liked them.

Priscilla stepped out of the limo and walked along the trendy boulevard in downtown Habakkuk. The slick black Lincoln shadowed her. She paused at some of the massive window displays and chatted with someone inside the limo.

She glanced Kite's way and waved. Kite slapped the steering wheel. How could she slip-up and get caught so easily? As she began to return the wave, a young attractive black woman ran up to Priscilla sporting a short sexy bob, a tan off-the-shoulder blouse, skinny jeans, and the cutest ankle boots she'd ever seen. The two embraced, and Priscilla gave her a quick kiss on the cheek before they disappeared inside a boutique.

Kite let out a loud sigh and scooched down as the limo parallel-parked in front of the boutique entrance. She grabbed her camera from the passenger seat. Having a photo of the make, model, and plates of the limousine would be helpful, but the heavily tinted windows gave her pause. Someone inside could also have a camera—or something worse—aimed at her.

A noise sounded to her right.

She clutched her arms to her chest.

Priscilla peered through the passenger window, and tilted her head. Her teeth were straight and pearly white and the perfect addition to the white long-sleeve bodycon dress that fit her like a glove.

Kite reached over to unlock the door as her heavy heartbeat lightened.

Priscilla climbed in and turned the smile up a notch. "Hi, Kite."

Her ebony hair was parted on the right side, and Shirley Temple curls cascaded over her shoulders. She grabbed a handful of those curls and tossed them back.

"I must not be doing my job right if I was that easy to spot."

Priscilla laughed. "I'd like to tell you I have a sixth sense about these things or that I spotted you a mile away. But the truth is I had a bit of help."

Kite flinched. "Help? From whom?"

"Windy told me to be on the lookout for Eagle Eye investigators. That Barry's family'd hired them to find evidence I was scamming their dad."

Kite sucked in a breath. She hated being caught off-guard. And she hated showing that she'd been caught off-guard. But thanks to her twin, she'd been caught doing both.

When Priscilla's file had come across her desk, she'd casually mentioned it to Windy. She knew she was friends with Priscilla, but it hadn't crossed her mind that Windy would betray that confidence. She clenched her teeth as the heat that flushed through her body demanded she head home and confront Windy. She pressed the button to open the driver's side window and closed her eyes. A breeze wafted in, cooling the air and her temper. She unclenched her teeth. "What else did she say?"

"That's it." Priscilla stared at Kite a few seconds then wrinkled her brow. "Don't be mad at her. She wasn't positive you'd be assigned to the case. She just wanted to give me a heads up. She's always said us girls had to stick together."

"*Us* girls?"

Priscilla's gaze dropped to her lap then back at Kite. "Girls like me and her. Girls like Liz, Lola and a few others. Girls who our town looks down on because of how we live our lives."

There were people in Habakkuk who were well-known for looking down upon others, but their focus was on those who broke the law. The Habakkuk police knew my sister well. Diamond Liz was also no stranger to the department. It wasn't unusual for people to turn their noses up at them, but Priscilla was no criminal. There were rumors about how she'd made her money, but rumors were a favorite past time for people who lived in small towns. It was because of those rumors that the Eagle Eye agency had been hired. Kite rubbed the back of her neck. "Why are you here, Priscilla?"

"I thought it'd be easier this way. Windy's been my best friend since high-school, and I didn't want this situation to get in the way of that. I've always respected you, Kite." She let out a slight chuckle. "I never wanted to hang out with you back then, but that's because we ran in different circles."

Habakkuk was small, but it was also diverse. Their high school had just as many black, Hispanic, Asian, and other students as it did white. The reason they hadn't run in the same circles was because of the type of girls Priscilla hung out with. She was friends with the ones who drank, smoked, and met up with boys during school hours. Girls who were one step away from being expelled or landing in prison. Girls like Kite's sister and her friend Lydia.

She'd enjoyed Priscilla the few times she'd had the chance to be around her. Their moms were friends, so it wasn't unusual for them to be at each other's houses. But Kite had always gotten the impression that Priscilla thought she was one of those who looked down on her. Not because of her race but because Kite was a nerd. She loved school. She arrived early, stayed late, and took part in every academic challenge offered—and she usually won. When she didn't win, it was Priscilla's older sister, Penelope who'd beat her. When their mom visited, Penelope would sit at the kitchen table with Kite, their noses stuck in a book. Priscilla, on the other hand, always made a beeline toward Windy's room.

Priscilla narrowed her eyes. "It felt weird knowing someone I knew would be following me around town, documenting my every move. You have to do what you've been hired to do, but because of Windy, I wanted to make things easier. I'm here for you to ask me questions. Interview me. No matter what I say, Victoria is going to accuse me of lying, but I'd rather talk face-to-face instead of pretending that I don't know you're here. Take notes or use a recorder if you like. I've got nothing to hide."

At this point Kite couldn't figure out if Jack was going to fire her for opening her big mouth to her sister and ruining their chances of catching Priscilla unawares or if he would promote her for getting an inside scoop, saving the agency tons of money in man hours and fuel. If Barry's daughter, had anything to say about it, she was pretty sure it was going to be the former. Perhaps she could save her job if she at least had something to offer them.

She pulled her mini voice recorder from the cup holder. Priscilla settled against the passenger door and crossed her legs. Her silver strapless high-heeled pumps glistened in the sun beaming through the windshield. It reminded Kite of the boutique and the limousine driver waiting for her outside of it. "I saw a young lady walk into the boutique with you, and I'm guessing the limo driver is waiting for you to return. Are you sure you want to do this now?"

She nodded. "The girl is my niece, Alexandria. You remember my sister, Penelope, right?"

"Of course. Last I heard, she was working in the mission field."

"Alexandria is her daughter. Alex's husband just graduated from law school. She's in the boutique having a gown designed for an event being held in his honor. She'll text me if she needs me. And the driver is Munro. He's worked for Barry and his family for decades. I'm pretty sure he's taking a nap right about now."

Kite smiled. "Munro was a good friend of my dad's. They used to build kites together." She glanced at the limo. "Is it normal for him to follow you around while you're shopping?"

Priscilla shook her head. "We were in a talkative mood, so we chatted as I window shopped and waited for Alexandria to arrive."

Kite rubbed her thumb across the recorder. "Before we start, you need to know that just because you're doing a sit-down with me doesn't mean Eagle Eye won't continue to investigate you. Victoria was adamant that she wanted more than one person on this team. She hired us to do a deep dive into your present and your past."

Priscilla shrugged. "It wasn't an investigation I wanted to avoid, just bad blood among you, me, and Windy."

Kite switched on the recorder and dictated her name, time, date, and location. Priscilla acknowledged that she was with her and gave her verbal consent. Kite didn't know when her niece might summon her, so she wanted to get to the heart of the client's concerns quickly. Problem was, there was no easy way to do that. She cleared her throat. "Victoria King-Wycroft, Barry King's daughter, hired our agency because she believes that you're out to scam her father. Can you confirm that you know Mr. King?"

"I do."

Kite swallowed. The next question regarded Priscilla's personal life, and she hadn't given her fair warning before they started. But Priscilla nodded and mouthed that it was okay. Kite hated doing this and found no comfort when her conscience assured her that she was just doing her job. She let out a breath. "Mrs. Wycroft is under the impression that you're a prostitute. Is that true?"

Priscilla narrowed her eyes and gazed out the windshield. "Not anymore."

It wasn't something Kite hadn't heard before, but she'd never believed it. Priscilla had never struck her as the type to go down that road. "Is that how you met Mr. King?"

She turned her gaze toward Kite. "I never worked the streets, but at one time I was a personal escort. However, Mrs. Wycroft knows that I haven't done anything like that in over fifteen years. I met Barry through a friend."

"When did you meet him?"

"Several months ago."

"She's also under the impression that you're staying with her dad at the King Estate. Is that true?"

"She's not under the impression of anything. She *knows* I live there. Barry introduced her to me and told her. What she really wants to know is how I managed to get through the front door. She refuses to believe that I was invited, even though she heard it from his own lips. I did not lie, manipulate, deceive, or seduce him into anything. His invitation was an act of mercy. I needed medical attention and a place to stay, and he provided both." She crossed her legs and hiked an eyebrow. "And I didn't have to pay for them. Not with money or anything else."

Kite pressed the power button to close the driver's side

window, and turned on the cars air conditioning. She hoped the quick blast of cool air would hide the flush that had made its way into her cheeks. She did not agree with Priscilla's lifestyle, and the last thing she wanted to hear about was what she did or didn't do with the men in her life. But the more Priscilla spoke, the more Kite believed her. It wasn't what she was saying, so much as how she was saying it. Still, she knew she had to dig deeper. "Have you participated in illegal drug use with Mr. King?"

She jerked forward. "You've got to be kidding me. She thinks I'm drugging him?"

Kite nodded.

Her lips tightened before she let out a long breath. "I've never used illegal drugs in my life. Or even legal ones. And I've definitely never done anything like that with Barry. The man's a health fanatic and wouldn't take them anyway. It's a shame that I know that and his own daughter doesn't."

"Are you blackmailing him?"

Her eyes widened. "Am I what?"

"Have you threatened to use photos, videos, texts, emails, or anything of that nature to get Mr. King to do your bidding?"

This time it was her mouth that widened. She closed it then shook her head. "I don't know what upsets me more. That she thinks I'd be stupid enough to try to blackmail one of the most well-known and respected businessmen in the state of Missouri, or that she thinks her father would be gullible enough to fall for it." She folded her arms. "I am *not* blackmailing Barry."

Kite pulled a manila folder from her purse. "As I mentioned before, Victoria asked for three investigators on this case. Two were assigned to look into your background. According to them, some men from your past have stated—"

"That I threatened or blackmailed them, and they're correct. But in every single instance, it was to show those imbeciles that two could play at that game. I'm sure your investigators also told you that happened a long time ago. The relationship I was in before Barry lasted ten years. His name was Jacob, and I wouldn't be surprised if he said a lot of bad things about me, but I know for a fact that drug use and blackmail would not have been among them."

Kite flipped through the pages in the folder. Priscilla was right. Her ex had called her a few names, and he'd lamented how she'd broken off the relationship without warning. But the investigator also jotted in his notes that Jacob said he'd take her back in a heartbeat if she gave him the chance. She shoved the folder back into her purse, eager to wrap-up this surprise interview. "You said that you're staying at the King estate as Barry's guest and that there's nothing salacious about it. Why did you feel the need to emphasize that?"

Priscilla leaned her head backward before letting out a sigh. "I'm not an idiot. The things I've done in my past *should* concern Barry's family. I'm not upset they're looking into it, I expected it. Rumors about me have spread far and wide in this town. That's not new and it's never bothered me. But now, my previous lifestyle has cast shadows on Barry. People look at him differently, and he doesn't deserve that. I want the truth to be known. I love him and—"

She stiffened and sucked in a quick breath.

Kite waited for her to continue. When she didn't, she placed her hand over the mic and leaned toward her. "Are you okay?"

Hand to her chest, Priscilla paused. Her fingers then made their way to the diamond-accented pendant necklace that lay perfectly below her collar bone, fingering the emerald in the center. She turned her gaze back to the windshield.

She blinked slowly as the tiniest curve of a smile began to form on her lips. "I'd always wondered what that would feel like. To say, *I love him* and mean it. For the words to roll from my heart to my tongue without any conscious effort." She looked down at the emerald. "A lot of men have given me a lot of expensive jewelry over the years. Last night, I tossed every single one of them in the trash." She tapped the verdure gem. "This is the only one I didn't have to work for. Barry gave it to me yesterday morning. When I asked him why, he said it was because he knew I'd like it."

She bowed her head. "I didn't go to medical school like my sister, and my past proves I'm not the smartest person in the world, but I do know that hearts don't speak, they beat. As sure as I'm sitting here, I'm telling you Barry's heart spoke to mine the moment he gave me this necklace. And at that moment something changed in our relationship, and we both knew it." She tossed another handful of curls away from her shoulders. "I'm familiar enough with jewels to know that this one is worth a fortune. What I wasn't familiar with was someone thinking I had more value than this tiny piece of stone. For decades, I'd accumulated diamonds, gold, silver, and other material things to show my worth. And I only knew one way to pay for them." She pressed the pendant against her chest. "Little did I know how far that road would take me. Or how okay I would be traveling it. It wasn't until

I met Barry that I realized just how much each one of those transactions cost me."

She closed her eyes, but not before a tear escaped. Kite grabbed tissues from her purse, only then realizing that the recorder was still on. She switched it off.

Kite handed her a couple of tissues and kept one for herself. Whether or not Barry and Priscilla's love story was one for the ages, she had no idea. But it did remind her of when she'd first met and fallen in love with Nethaniah. Theirs was a love story that ended way too soon. She winced as the all-too-familiar throes of grief beckoned. She dabbed at her cheeks with the tissue. Experience had taught her that the only way to avoid thinking about Neth was to focus on something else. And right now she needed to focus on finishing up this interview.

"Have you received the Lord Jesus Christ as your Savior, Priscilla?"

Whoa. What in the world? Where did *that* come from?

Kite was sure the puzzled look on Priscilla's face mirrored her own. Her heart raced. This day was going from bad to worse. Not only did she find out her sister had betrayed her and handicapped her investigation, but now she was about to be chewed out by the very person she was supposed to be investigating. Priscilla's father had been a preacher, for cryin' out loud. And anyone who knew her mother knew that Mabel wasn't shy about her faith. Kite had personally seen her lead some of the most atheistic people she knew to Christ. And here she was questioning her daughter?

Priscilla cleared her throat. "Barry asked me that same question." She uncrossed her legs and straightened in her seat. "And I'm going to tell you the same thing I told him. I have no idea."

Oh.

She let out a small laugh. "The look on your face tells me you're wondering how that could be—especially since my father was the beloved Reverend Martin and my mother's a fire-and-brimstone evangelist. According to her, my father led me to Christ when I was ten years old. I remember the moment. I remember the day. I even remember the prayer." She shrugged. "But that's all it was to me. A prayer."

Kite's heart slowed from its rapid beat. She'd had every intention of asking the final questions to wrap-up this interview, but maybe this was what this afternoon was really supposed to be about. Not the investigation but Priscilla's salvation. The question she'd asked hadn't come from out of nowhere. Priscilla had talked about her past, her lack of self-worth, and how she'd felt when Barry looked past all of that and loved her regardless. As Christ had done for both of them. She hadn't mentioned it because she'd figured Priscilla already knew all of that. She now realized that she was wrong. God knew exactly what she'd needed to say.

Kite leaned closer to Priscilla. With just the two of them in the car, this was the perfect opportunity to discuss it further. "Prisci—"

Chimes filled the air. Priscilla grabbed her cell as the chimes increased in volume.

Kite nodded toward the phone. "Your niece?"

She furrowed her brow and stared at the phone. "It's Christianna."

Christianna, Mary's younger sister, was also a good

friend of Priscilla's and Windy's. "Do you need to take it?"

"I better. It's not like her to call this time of day. She's normally at work." She tapped her phone. "Hey, Chrissy. I have you on speaker. What's going on?"

"Pris, I've tried everyone I could think of. I called Eagle Eye, the church, her landline, and her cell a zillion times, but I haven't been able to find her. Then I remembered Windy mentioning something about her investigating you. Have you seen her?"

Priscilla glanced toward the driver's seat before answering. "Are you talking about Kite?"

"Windy's in bad shape. I'm in the E.R. with her right now. Have you seen Kite?"

Windy was in the hospital? Kite fumbled with the keys. This had something to do with Michael, she was sure of it. *Please, God. Please don't let anything happen to my sister.*

Priscilla opened the passenger door. "She's here with me now. What hospital?"

"St. Matthews."

"We're on our way." She ended the call and stepped out of the car. "Get in the passenger seat. I'll drive."

Kite started the ignition. "I have to go now."

"Your whole body is trembling." She was on the driver's side, tugging on the door before Kite could focus on what to do next. "Unlock it and move over."

"What about your niece and Munro?"

"I'll text them when we get there."

Chapter Twenty-Two

Priscilla pressed her hands against the cold steel that separated the waiting area from the burn unit. Through the small glass window, men and women in lab coats and two teenage boys in hospital gowns dotted the hallway. No sign of Kite or Windy.

She pushed off the door, made her way back to Christianna, and plopped into the chair next to her. When she and Kite arrived, Christianna had rushed to tell them what had happened, but Kite was only interested in finding someone to take her to her sister. Priscilla turned toward Christianna. "Tell me again. Slower this time."

Christianna scrubbed a hand over her face. "I took off work because Windy and I had planned to go shopping for the upcoming girls' weekend. On our way to the mall, we dropped off a box of her ex-boyfriend's stuff at his house. He and his new girlfriend, were standing in front of his car, looking at something on a phone." She shrugged. "Windy didn't even get upset. All she did was tell him to grab the box in the backseat so we could take off. But Michael was ticked. He called her a stalker and a whole bunch of other names. He yanked her out of the car. His girlfriend stood there frozen, so I jumped out of the car to help Windy. Uh … I mean to ask Michael to stop. That's when his girlfriend went nuts and started screaming for *us* to stop. By then, Michael had Windy by the throat. I kicked him. When he doubled over, Windy grabbed his hair and slammed his head against her knee. Then something splashed against my arm, and Windy cried out in pain. That crazy girlfriend of his had thrown scalding hot coffee on us. The left side of Windy's face and arm were bright red. I got her in the car and rushed her here as fast as I could."

Christianna's jacket sleeve had been rolled up, part of her arm bandaged.

"Are you okay?"

She looked at the gauzy wrapping. "My jacket protected me from most of it. They treated me in the emergency room but wheeled Windy up here. They wouldn't let me go back there with her. That's when I tried to call Kite."

Priscilla adjusted her dress and sat further back in the hard plastic chair. "Kite had her phone off. She said she typically does that when she's working a case."

When there was no response, Priscilla glanced around the waiting area before turning her gaze back to Christianna. "Where's your family? Do Brad and the girls know you're here?"

"I didn't want them to know until I knew how Windy was doing."

"Brad's going to be livid when he finds out you were hurt and he didn't know about it."

She clasped her hands together then rested her elbows on

her knees. "I can barely think straight. Brad's going to ask tons of questions. I want to let him know what happened, but then he'll show up and demand I go home so he and the girls can take care of me. I can't leave until I know that Windy's okay. She was in so much pain." She closed her eyes. "By the time we arrived at the hospital, her skin had already started to blister. And it looked like some of it was beginning to peel."

Priscilla tapped a fingernail against her chair. She wanted to be at her friend's bedside. The nurse at the desk had made it clear that the only person allowed to see Windy was Kite. She could send Kite a text to get an update but decided against it. She didn't want to distract Kite from her sister. Besides, surely they'd know something soon. Priscilla adjusted in the chair again. She wanted to do more than just wait. She couldn't remember the last time she'd felt so helpless.

"You do know that when you get up from that chair, your dress will no longer be white."

Priscilla wiped at several smudges. Neither the silver heels nor the dress had been made for a hospital waiting room. "I know." She wiped at a few more spots then gave up. "When we hear something from Kite, I'll text Barry and ask him to bring me some clothes."

"He knows you're here?"

"I called him when we first arrived. He knows Kite from church, though he hasn't met Windy yet. He wanted me to let her know that he's praying for her sister and that he contacted the church's prayer team."

"Crap." Christianna rubbed her forehead. "That means my parents and Mary are going to know as well. That's the last thing I need.”

“You didn’t call them either?”

She slapped her hands against her thighs. “I didn’t call anyone, Pris. No one needs to know anything until—”

The metal door swung open and Kite appeared. Priscilla and Chrissy stood. “Wind has been seriously injured.” She glanced between them. “She has second-degree burns on her face, neck, and upper left arm. The doctors assured me she’s going to be okay but she’ll need to stay in the burn unit for a few days. After that, they think she’ll be able to go home as long as someone’s there to help her. She’s been staying with me anyway, so that won’t be a problem. They don’t want infection to set in, and they said it’ll be easier for her if she had help applying the different ointments.”

Christianna asked, “Can I see her?”

“She’s pretty out of it, Chrissy. They gave her something for the pain, and she was on her way to sleep when I left. But the doctor said the two of you could visit briefly, one at a time.”

Priscilla motioned for Christianna to go first. As the door shut behind her, the double-doors that led to the main area of the unit burst open. Jack Eagle looked around. When he spotted Kite, he rushed toward her and swept her into a hug. “I came as soon as I heard.” She wrapped her arms around his neck, and he pulled her in tighter. When he noticed Priscilla, he placed Kite back on the floor and wiped at the tears on her face. “Everyone wanted to know if I knew where you were, but it wasn’t until Lydia called that I heard about Windy and Christianna.” He slipped Kite’s hand in his. “Please tell me they’re both okay.”

Kite seemed to rein in her emotions before she spoke.

"Windy has significant burns and some bruising around her neck. Michael tried to choke her, but the doctors told me she's going to be fine. Christianna has been treated and released. She's with Windy."

He pulled Kite into another hug. "Lydia and Eve will be here any second. Pastor Greene and his wife are also on their way, and so is Christianna's family." He nodded at Priscilla. "Barry's on his way."

"Thank you." She moved to the other side of the room. It was obvious Jack wanted some time alone with Kite. Priscilla'd had no idea they were an item. Jack was one of the most sought-after bachelors in Habakkuk. And Kite was a widow. Priscilla knew from Windy that a piece of Kite had died with her husband. To see her now with Jack warmed her.

The double doors opened again. Eve, Lydia, and Barry dashed in, followed by two female police officers.

Eve and Lydia ran over to Kite. Barry came to Priscilla and wrapped his arm around her waist. "The officers are here for Christianna."

Priscilla grabbed his arm. "What?"

He rubbed her back. "That's what I overheard downstairs."

"What do they want with her?"

"Something to do with an assault charge."

Priscilla yanked away from him. "Assault charge? The girl threw hot coffee on them. Windy could be scarred for life. They're the ones who should be filing assault charges."

"The girl is claiming self-defense." He kissed her forehead. "I wish I had more details honey, but I wanted you to know in case she was led out of here in handcuffs."

Priscilla's mind reeled. Christianna had never lied to her, and she wouldn't start now. There was no reason to. They knew each other's darkest secrets. If Christianna said that girl attacked them, then that's what happened. The only one who could file assault charges would be Michael. He wouldn't. Not because he cared about Windy or Christianna, but because he wouldn't want law enforcement looking into his own illegal activities. Which was something Windy had extensive knowledge of and would use to throw him under the bus —in a heartbeat—if he dared try to have her arrested.

But Barry said the officers had only mentioned Christianna. Is that what Michael was up to? Accusing Christianna would be a back door way for him to hurt Windy without saying that she was directly involved. But it wasn't him making the charges, it was his girlfriend, Hildy. Was he using her to get back at the two of them?

Priscilla eyed the officers, who'd stepped away from the nurse's station and toward the heavy metal door which squeaked open. Christianna appeared.

Priscilla grabbed Barry's hand.

Things were about to get ugly.

Chapter Twenty-Three

Lydia listened as Christianna's verbal tirade increased in volume. She needed to intervene before Christianna made matters worse. She hurried over to her. "Chrissy, I've been in situations like this before. Trust me. Things will go a lot smoother if you calm down."

Christianna took a step back. "That girl is lying! *She* attacked *us*."

One of the officers reached for her arm. "You need to come with—"

"Not on your life." Christianna took another step back. "I didn't do anything wrong. And if you're planning on hauling me out of here, then plan on doing it with me kicking and screaming."

"That can be arranged." The officer reached for her cuffs.

When the other reached for her Taser, Lydia lifted her hands and took a step forward. "Please. Give me a few seconds to talk with her?"

When the one with the cuffs nodded, Lydia turned

toward Christianna. "Have you lost your mind? This is a hospital. You know that there are patients on the other side of that door. Patients who are wounded and hurting, and that includes Windy. Is this really where you want to make a scene?"

Christianna clenched her teeth. "I. Didn't. Do. Any. Thing."

Lydia mimicked the action. "It. Doesn't. Matter. There's someone out there who said you did. Right now, the police just want to talk to you. That'll change to resisting arrest if you don't go quietly. Do you really want your family to see you hauled out of here like a wild animal?"

Christianna's eyes widened. "What are you talking about?"

"Brad is downstairs. And so are your parents and Mary. Paul said he was on his way, but that was thirty minutes ago. He could be down there as well."

"Are you serious?"

"Yes." She placed a hand on Christianna's shoulder. "Listen, Mary said that Ethan's already hired a lawyer who'll be waiting for you at the police station. If you cooperate and leave with the officers now, you'll likely be home before the girls get out of school."

Christianna inhaled a deep breath and held it. Her face turned a deeper shade of red by the second. Finally, she scrubbed a hand over her face and glanced at the officers. "Fine. I'll go. But there's no way I'll be able to talk Brad and Mary out of following me to the station. My parents will try as well. I don't want them to have to go through that. Ask them to pick the girls up early from school."

"You got it," Lydia said.

Christianna pressed her lips together and marched to the officers. As they led her toward the double doors, Lydia said a silent prayer that the misunderstanding would be wrapped up quickly. The poor Melson family had been through enough.

Someone touched her shoulder. Eve and Priscilla had joined her, and she hadn't even noticed. Eve leaned in close. "I'm glad you were able to convince her to go along with them."

"I'm not sure I did. She'd dug her feet in until I mentioned her family being downstairs. She didn't want to upset her parents."

Eve folded her arms. "Whatever convinced her, I'm glad she's gone." She motioned toward Jack and Kite, who'd settled into a pair of chairs on the far side of the room. Kite's head rested on Jack's shoulder. "She's having a hard time. The last thing she needed was an incident between Christianna and the cops."

Priscilla glanced that direction. "I had no idea they were a couple."

Lydia let out a small laugh. "They're not." When Priscilla scrunched her brows together, Lydia added, "They'd make the perfect couple, and nothing would make Jack happier, but Kite's not ready for a new relationship."

Priscilla glanced their way again. "Are you sure? They look pretty comfortable to me."

"According to Kite, they're just friends."

"Oh." Priscilla lowered her head.

Lydia quirked her brow. "Everything okay?"

Priscilla nodded without lifting her head. "I was just kind of hoping that they were. Windy told me how difficult it's been for Kite since Neth passed away. I hoped she'd found happiness again." She lifted her head. "But honestly, I don't know why it bothers me so much that she hasn't."

Eve swung an arm around Priscilla's shoulders. "Don't give up hope yet. Kite never imagined spending the rest of her life with anyone except Nethaniah. She didn't want to go on living after he passed away. Windy was right when she said that it's been a long and rough road for her." Eve gave a quick nod toward Jack. "Lately, she's taken some baby steps. We're praying that soon she'll be able to embrace the blessing God has placed before her."

"So there's still hope?"

"There's still hope."

Priscilla smiled just as Barry and a nurse from the burn unit joined them. He placed a hand on the small of Priscilla's back. "Windy asked to see you."

After they said their good-byes, Lydia went to Kite and crouched in front of her. "Where are you staying tonight, sweetie?"

"In Windy's room, if they let me."

Kite hadn't moved her head or hand away from Jack's chest as she spoke.

The odd look in Kite's eyes had Lydia asking, "Is there something else? Windy's going to be okay, right?"

She nodded against Jack's chest. "It's just that … I had a chance to see her face before they bandaged her up. Lyd, she didn't even look like my sister." The last word came out with a sob. Jack rubbed her shoulders, but not before another sob escaped. "And it could've been so much worse. Michael's a dangerous man. I could've lost my sister today. To lose her and Neth? I wouldn't be able to take it. I just wouldn't."

Lydia tapped Kite on the knee. "You didn't lose her. She's alive. Let's focus on that."

Kite shook her head. "You should've heard the list of things they said could still go wrong. What if something happens and she doesn't recover?" She wiped at her eyes. "All Neth had was food poisoning. Five days later he was dead. If he could die of something like that, what are Windy's chances of recovering from something like this?"

Lydia now realized what that odd look in Kite's eyes was about. She'd never seen it on her before, so she hadn't recognized it. But there it was. Fear. Fear of the past. Fear of the unknown. Fear of the what-ifs. It had gripped Kite's soul and had no intention of letting go.

Jack whispered reassuring words in Kite's ear, but Lydia knew this was war. A spiritual war that could only be won on their knees.

Lydia grabbed Kite's hand. "There's a chapel off the main floor. Why don't you come and pray with me?"

Kite was silent for several moments before shaking her head. "If Windy needs me, I'd like to be here."

Just like she was there when Neth died.

"That's okay. Eve and I will go. Then we'll go to your place and pack a bag. Text us if there's anything in particular you'll need."

"Thank you."

Lydia rose to her feet.

It was time to go to war.

Chapter Twenty-Four

Eve was no slouch when it came to prayer, but it had been a long time since she'd been in an atmosphere this thick with the presence of God.

Lydia had called down every stronghold, principality, and vain imagination they could think of.

Eve had raised her hands and sung with abandon as hymns and worship songs—new and old—made their way from her lips toward the heavens. As Lydia waged war in the spiritual realm, Eve continued to sing and listened in amazement as her songs melded perfectly with Lydia's prayers. As they knelt and cried out before the Lord, the atmosphere shifted. A beautiful, fragrant stillness had filled the sanctuary. She whispered, *"Thank You,"* to the God of Angel Armies that they'd had the wisdom to drive to their own church to pray instead of staying at the hospital's small chapel. The Glory that surrounded them was massive, and she wouldn't be surprised if it permeated the sanctuary walls, broke through the church's concrete borders, and filled the streets.

Eve closed her eyes and hummed a tune she'd never heard before. When it increased in volume and intensity, she leaned closer to the altar and moved her lips, trusting the God of heaven and earth to fill her spirit with the words. When they came, her feet itched to dance, and her arms ached to wave with joy, but her soul longed to be still underneath the wings of the Almighty.

"I didn't want to wake you," Lydia said. "But we still need to go by Kite's place."

Eve blinked and looked around. "What happened?"

Lydia's face and posture had been so intense moments ago when she was praying next to Eve. Now, it didn't look like she'd been to battle at all.

Eve shifted into a sitting position. "Oh, no. Don't tell me I fell asleep. But I must have because I haven't felt this rested in ages."

"And you did it while still kneeling." Lydia laughed. "I'd never seen anything like it. You looked so … peaceful. Like a sweet sleep ordained by Jehovah Shalom Himself had made its way into your spirit."

Wouldn't it be just like God to bestow indescribable peace and rest upon her on a night when she'd need it the most?

Lydia helped Eve off the floor. "Are you okay? Your face went from peaceful to distressed in a nanosecond."

Eve pulled her phone from her purse. She sat and rubbed her forehead as she scrolled through the missed call log and text messages. Philip had called twenty-seven times and had sent twice as many texts. She glanced at her watch. It was a little after nine. The last time she'd talked with him was around four. She'd told him that one of her friends was in the hospital and that she didn't know when she'd be home. She didn't expect sympathies, promises of prayer, or offers to come and support her, but she did expect understanding. What she'd received instead was an earful of curse words.

Lydia sat next to her. "Is Philip upset that you haven't made it home?"

"He's way past upset."

"Don't let Satan steal your joy or your peace, Eve." Lydia scooted closer. "Tonight we experienced something miraculous. I don't know why and I don't know if it has something to do with us, the people we prayed over, or the situations we prayed about. But we did what the Scriptures told us to do—called upon the Lord in our day of trouble. And heaven knows we have trouble. Windy's recovery. Me and the issues with my health and Dinah. You and your marriage. Kite and her grief over Neth and her worries for Windy. Mary and the entire Melson family have their hands full with Christianna's situation. Priscilla needs salvation. We came here with aching hearts and weary souls and experienced a Presence so real it was palpable. Something happened here tonight. Will we get to know what it was this side of heaven? I don't know. But I do know that I'm not going to let anything take away my joy." She took Eve's hand. "I know that's easy for me to say because I'm going home to an empty house and not a raging husband. But I believe that God has already gone before you and that He's given you the courage and the strength you'll need to face the fiery darts coming your way. No matter what happens, don't let the enemy steal the peace God has given you."

Eve nodded. This wasn't the first time Philip had gone on a rampage, and she was sure it wouldn't be his last. The difference now was that her hands didn't shake like they usually did, and she wasn't searching her brain for ways to calm him down and make things right. Like Lydia, she wasn't exactly sure what had happened here tonight, but she definitely felt peaceful.

She grabbed her purse and stood. "We'd better get going. I'm pretty sure Kite thinks we've forgotten about her."

"You sure you still want to go with me? I'm okay going to Kite's place by myself if you'd like to go home and deal with Philip."

Eve waved off the comment as they made their way toward the exit. "I want to go. Philip will be just as mad no matter what time I get home. Besides, Kite didn't look so well earlier. I'd like to check on her and offer to stay if Jack can't. And I want to get an update on Windy."

In Lydia's car, Eve called Kite. She explained that they were just now heading to her place, then she grabbed a pen and notebook from her purse to scribble some additional items Windy needed.

Eve called Philip next and told him she'd be home before midnight. He told her it didn't matter because he'd packed his stuff and left the house hours ago. And that he'd called a lawyer.

Eve tapped the phone off. His last four words still rung in her ears.

He wanted a divorce.

Chapter Twenty-Five

Mary grabbed Ethan's hands to keep hers from shaking. Christianna was no saint, and heaven knew she was as hot-tempered and strong-willed as they came, but there was no way her younger sister could've done the things that she was being accused of. Which meant the young lady sitting across from the detective in the other room was lying.

To make matters worse, the person telling it was none other than Hildy Carson, the twenty-five-year-old daughter of the famous televangelist, Reed Carson.

It made no sense.

According to Mary's mom, everyone loved the Carsons. When Reed's wife was diagnosed with multiple sclerosis a year ago, he'd retired and returned to his hometown of Habakkuk, where he frequently shared the pulpit with Lloyd Greene, Pastor of Resurrection Church. The same church Mary's family and friends had attended for years.

Ethan stepped closer to the glass partition. "Something's not right. Her hands are shaking worse than yours."

Mary leaned in to get a closer look. Hildy sat on one side

of the table, her arms extended across the top of it. Ethan was right. Her hands shook terribly. To her right sat Windy's ex-boyfriend Michael, who sported a black eye, which, according to Christianna, was given to him by Windy's knee.

"What do you know about this Michael guy?" Ethan asked.

"Just that I attended elementary school with him and his brother, Frank. And that my dad disliked the entire family. He often mentioned that if a crime was committed in Habakkuk, the Kildares were behind it. I'm pretty sure their house was the first place my dad went when I disappeared."

"Do you know if anything came of that?"

"Not that I know of. Everything else I know about Michael came from Christianna and Kite. That's how I knew that he was Windy's ex-boyfriend and Hildy's current one. What I don't know is why she's lying for him."

Ethan pointed at the window. "He's smirking at us."

Ethan and she were watching and listening to what Hildy and Michael were saying because Ethan's lawyer had pulled some strings. Christianna was being questioned down the hall in another interrogation room. If the detectives interviewing her believed even half of the tale that these two were spinning, her sister was in big trouble. And all because of the guy smirking at them through the window. She wanted to yank open the door, jump across the table, and throttle him. But the officers were doing them a favor by letting them be here, and she didn't want to get on their bad side.

Ethan scratched at his neck. "A lot of interesting things happen in this small town."

"It's definitely not the storybookish little town I remember." She shook her head. "Maybe it never was.

Maybe it was just the idyllic memories of a scared eight-year-old girl."

Ethan pulled her into a hug and kissed the top of her head. "You've seen enough of this nonsense." He nodded to the officer by the door that led to the rest of the police station. When he opened it, Pauly leaned against the opposite wall. He motioned for them to follow him down the hall toward the exit.

Mary turned to her brother. "How did Christianna's interrogation go?"

He smiled. "She's been released."

"*What?* How did that happen?"

"Jack Eagle sent a team to scour Michael's neighborhood. One of his neighbors had a security camera aimed at the street. The police reviewed it, and the video showed that Michael attacked Windy first, then Hildy threw a cup of hot coffee on them."

"Which is exactly what Chrissy said happened."

"Right. Windy and Chrissy never laid a hand on her. But Michael sure did."

"What do you mean?"

"After Chrissy left to drive Windy to the hospital, the film showed Michael slapping Hildy across the face and shoving her into his car."

Mary gasped.

"Yeah. And a few hours later, they showed up here saying that it was Chrissy who'd slapped her."

Ethan wrapped an arm around Mary's shoulder. "It's okay, honey. Chrissy's been released. She's going to be fine."

She looked at Pauly. "Where is she now?"

"Brad took her home."

"I'm glad Chrissy's okay, but now I'm worried about Hildy. She's still in there with that monster."

Pauly pointed his thumb toward the entrance. "Her parents are here. Hopefully, she'll go home with them, and leave that scumbag to rot."

Mary asked, "Your wife teaches Sunday school with her, right?"

"Yeah. Fawn teaches middle-school and Hildy the younger ones."

Mary made a mental note to arrive early on Sunday morning. What little she knew about Hildy Carson was that she tended to be naive and impressionable. The last thing someone like that needed was a Michael Kildare in their life. Especially if he was using her for a punching bag.

She glanced at her watch. "I'd like to go back by the hospital before it gets too late and thank Jack in person for getting his team involved. I'm pretty sure he hasn't left Kite's side. And I'd also like to see if Windy's up for another visit. There's a reason she broke up with Michael. If she tells me what it is, maybe I can use that to help Hildy."

Ethan reached into his jeans pocket for his keys. "We'd better hurry."

She kissed her brother on the cheek before following Ethan to their car. He opened the door for her. "You don't want to see Christianna first?"

"No. Brad was pretty upset earlier, especially about Chrissy being injured. We'll stop by tomorrow morning after they've had a chance to calm down and get a good night's sleep."

She reached for her seatbelt and stopped. Michael

Kildare's gaze cut through the windshield. On each side of him was a Missouri State Trooper. When they got to a waiting patrol car, one of the officers opened the door, and Michael got into the backseat. But not before she noticed that the smirk that she'd wanted to wipe off his face earlier had morphed into a sneer.

After the patrol car made its way out of the parking lot and onto the main road, she shuddered.

Ethan turned to her. "What's wrong?"

"I don't know." Mary opened her door. "But we need to go back inside and talk to the police."

Ethan snatched the keys out of the ignition. "Okay. But why?"

"Because my sister and her family are going to need protection. And they're going to need it now."

Chapter Twenty-Six

Kite placed her cell on Windy's hospital table and put it on speaker. Mary sobbed on the other end. Kite leaned closer to the phone. "Can you say that again?"

Mary's sniffles came through the line louder than her words did.

"Kite." Windy grimaced and inched closer to the table. "Turn up the volume."

She increased it to the max.

Mary cleared her throat. "Michael sent a gunman to my sister's house." There was a long pause. "She's fine, and so are Brad and the girls. But if the police hadn't taken us seriously, they could've been killed."

Kite glanced at Windy. The right side of her face and her arm had been treated and bandaged. The look she gave but tried to hide screamed that she was in pain. But after what they'd just heard, Kite didn't know if her pain was physical or emotional. The love of her life had tried to kill her best friend.

Kite slid the table out of the way and scooted her chair

closer. She lifted the phone. "Tell us exactly what happened."

Mary sucked in a breath and released it. "I'm … not exactly sure what happened. As Ethan and I were leaving the police station, I saw Michael being escorted out by state troopers. The look he gave me sent chills up my spine. It wasn't just the look, his whole demeanor was frightening. Then I knew—I don't know how—but I knew that he was going to try and hurt Christianna. Ethan and I asked the police to provide protection for her, but they couldn't because we weren't able to give them anything to go on. And also because Michael was on his way to some type of holding center or whatnot. However, one officer was familiar with the Kildare family. Since Christianna lives in his patrol area, he said he and his partner would drive by. I thank God he did. Minutes before they arrived, Brad had heard a noise outside. He went to check on it and ended up surprising the gunman. They fought, and the gun discharged. When the gun went off, the girls went to check on their dad. The gunman broke away from Brad and grabbed Rose. When the police arrived, he pushed Rose toward Brad, shot at them twice, and ran into the woods."

Kite gasped. "Are they okay?"

"Brad grabbed Rose and threw them both to the ground. Officers found one of the bullets in the grass. Inches from where Brad fell."

She swallowed and closed her eyes. "And Rose?"

"Bruised, but okay. Well, about as okay as one can be after someone tries to kill you."

Windy groaned. Kite grabbed her hand and held it. "Mary, we're so sorry. Were they able to catch the guy?"

"A K9 unit found him."

Windy leaned back against the pillows and closed her eyes, her lips pinched. Whatever her pain was, it didn't allow her to talk.

"What makes you think Michael had anything to do with this?" Kite asked.

Mary's voice took on a slight edge. "Because the gunman said he did. And like Michael, this guy had felony warrants all across the state. He sang like a canary."

As much as she wanted to, she couldn't connect the dots. "You saw Michael being escorted away by troopers. How could he have gotten word to someone?"

"Michael's brother Frank hired him. He was told to kill Christianna— and if he couldn't get to her, to take out one of her daughters. Who else could've told him my sister was involved if it wasn't Michael?"

Kite wiped at a tear. She cried for what Christianna's family had been through and because she knew what Michael did would sear her sister's heart worse than any amount of scalding liquid. "Mary … I don't know what to say. I'm so … I—"

"You don't need to apologize, but I do for my tone. It's been a stressful day for all of us. I think what I need, what we *all* need, is a good night's sleep."

"Christianna—"

"She's fine. She'd already taken the pain meds the doctor had prescribed and was asleep until she heard Rose scream."

"You're at her place?"

"We're all staying the night. Mom, Dad, Pauly and Ethan are here as well. Chrissy's fine now, but she was a wreck when she'd found out how close Brad and Rose came to being hurt. Or worse. Took forever to calm her down. What helped was the police nabbing Frank and letting us know. How's Windy?"

Tears streamed down Windy's face. Kite wiped them away. "Still in a lot of pain and not able to speak much, but she heard everything you said. I know she's glad everyone's all right. She hasn't been able to sleep because she's been so worried. Even the sedatives the nurses gave her haven't helped." Kite left out the part about how guilty she felt. Before the pain had settled back in, she'd gone on and on about how all of this was her fault. That conversation was barely an hour before Mary called with this latest bombshell. "Hopefully after her next dosage she'll be able to rest."

"Windy, if you can hear me," Mary's voice came through softer and calmer. "Please know that we're all praying for a quick recovery. The shouting in the background is Christianna saying none of this is your fault. She loves you and she'll be by to see you first thing in the morning." Mary sniffed and continued. "Kite, please let Jack know how thankful we are that he got his team involved. We'd planned to stop by tonight to thank him in person, but—"

"I'll let him know."

"Thanks. We'll see you ladies in the morning, okay?"

"See you then." Kite clicked off the phone and leaned against the bed rail. "You okay?"

She nodded slowly. After a moment, she squinted then tilted her head toward the door. "Go tell Jack what Mary said."

"I'm not leaving you. I'll send a—"

"I'm okay."

"I'm not leaving."

"Please, Kite." She adjusted herself in the bed slightly. "I need a few minutes alone. Go grab something from the cafeteria. I'll be fine."

The way she grimaced every couple of seconds told her otherwise, but arguing with her would only make the situation worse. She stood. "Fine. I'll go. But promise me you'll try to rest."

Windy closed her eyes and nodded.

Kite reached the door and glanced back from the doorway. The tears that had streamed down her sister's face earlier had returned. Kite still didn't know if they were tears of pain or regret, but there was one thing she knew.

Michael Kildare was going to pay.

Chapter Twenty-Seven

Priscilla set her juice glass on the table and yawned. Her lids were heavy, her eyes watered, and the yawns repeated themselves. She glanced at her watch. Eight a.m.

Barry reached across the wrought-iron breakfast table. The morning sun reflected off of his white shirt and had already begun darkening his already tanned skin. He laid his fingers on top of hers. "Silly, you didn't get a wink of sleep last night, did you?"

"I woke up shortly after you left." She stifled another yawn. "After everything that happened at the hospital, I was glad you were there to hold me until I fell asleep. I still don't know why I was so restless." She also didn't know the last time she'd slept in the same bed with a man and all they did was sleep. He'd stayed until around nearly two. "After you left, I checked my phone. There was no going back to sleep after that."

"Why?"

Priscilla rubbed her free hand across her forehead. "There were several text messages from Christianna. A gunman tried to kill her husband and her daughter last night."

Barry jerked his hand away. "What?"

"I don't know the whole story. Apparently Windy's ex-boyfriend was behind it. Or someone in his family. Or his entire family." She let out another yawn. "I'm not sure at this point."

Barry narrowed his eyes. "Those—"

"They're okay. The police have the shooter and Frank Kildare in custody. I also had texts from Kite updating me on Windy's condition. Physically, she's going to be okay, but emotionally—"

"She's blaming herself."

Priscilla nodded. "It's not her fault. It's Michael's. I hope he rots in prison."

"Well, if my friend Lauren has anything to say about it, he will."

Priscilla blinked. "Lauren. As in District Attorney Lauren DeMint?"

"She's the A.D.A. not the D.A., but yeah."

"I didn't know she was a friend of yours. Or anyone's friend. She's ... mean."

Barry chuckled. "Yeah, I'd like to say a lot of that is just for the cameras. But it's not. She really is mean."

"How do you know her?"

"Her dad and I were partners at one time. She and my daughter are still really good friends. When she became the A.D.A., we consulted each other on different cases. Fraud, property issues, criminal bids, etc. She's definitely tough on crime. And she's been after the Kildare family for years."

"Why?"

"One of them killed her sister."

Priscilla's hand flew to her mouth. "No."

"Happened about fifteen years ago. Her younger sister was in a relationship with one of the Kildare brothers—there are so many of them, I honestly can't remember which one. According to Lauren, the day Rebecca broke-up with him is the day she disappeared. Her remains were found a year later by the river. Lauren's always believed the brother did it. It went to trial, but he was found not guilty. Not enough evidence."

"Was she dating Michael?"

"I'm pretty sure it was one of the older ones."

Priscilla swallowed. "If Michael's family went after Christianna, do you think they'll go after Windy, too?"

The warmth of Barry's hand as it clasped hers eased some of her fears. "Windy's been entangled with the Kildare clan for a long time. If she thought she was in danger, I'm sure she'd go to the authorities."

Priscilla looked at the toast and eggs untouched on her plate. Barry didn't know Windy. The last thing she'd do was go to the authorities. But would the Kildares go directly after Windy? Or her family? The only family Windy had within a thousand-mile radius was Kite. And heaven help them if they tried to harm Kite. Windy would wipe them clean off the planet.

Barry squeezed her hand. "You okay?"

"Yes. I'm just—" A loud yawn burst from her lips. "Still tired, I guess." She shook her head to free it of the cobwebs. "But it doesn't matter. I have to get to the hospital and see Windy."

"Of course you do." Barry scooted his chair back and

helped her stand. "But right now, I'm taking you back upstairs. I don't even think you're fully awake yet. Sleep for a couple more hours then join me back down here for lunch. After that I'll take you to see Windy myself."

She smiled. It had been a long time since someone cared about her needs.

"Barry?"

"Yes?"

"I love you."

He took a step backward, then stared at her.

She stepped in to close the gap. "Did you hear me?"

He nodded.

"You don't have anything to say?" She traced the muscles in his upper arm.

"I have a lot to say. But none of it involves words."

She smiled.

He cleared his throat and grabbed her hand. "But right now, I want this. This moment. The pleasure of enjoying that look in your eyes."

"What look?"

"The look that says you've found something. And you're happy with it."

She let out a small laugh. "Don't get too cocky. Remember, I am still a little sleep deprived."

"Which means your defenses are down." He lifted her chin. "That makes this moment even sweeter." He wrapped an arm around her waist and leaned in until their lips touched, then pulled away slowly.

She smacked his arm. "Barry, you can't keep teasing me like that."

He squeezed her waist. "I don't want to start that fire

until—"

"I know. Not until we're married."

He pulled her close, his breath ragged in her ear. "Please, don't keep me waiting long, darling." He placed a tender kiss near her ear. "Please."

He stepped out of the embrace and through the glass door that led into the kitchen.

She'd broken the cardinal rule. Her rule. The one she'd made when the repercussions and consequences of succumbing to love had haunted her.

And yet here she was.

Diamond Liz would call her a fool.

Lola would call her loved.

But the only name she cared about being called right now was Mrs. Barry King.

Priscilla wrapped herself in a hug and stared at the ground. Before that could happen, she needed to pay her mother a visit. If Mabel found out that Priscilla was even *thinking* about getting married, and that she wasn't the first to know, all—

Priscilla shuddered. She didn't want to think about her mother's reaction or the reception she'd get when she showed up at her mother's door. It'd been months since Jacob had sent her mother all of Priscilla's journals, several of which contained intimate details of the men she'd been with and why she'd been with them.

Priscilla made her way to the spiral staircase that led to her bedroom. She'd sleep for a few hours, have lunch with Barry, visit Windy, then mentally prepare herself for the long overdue visit to her mother. Because the words "fool" or "loved" wouldn't come close to the words Mabel would

have for her.
Not even close.

Chapter Twenty-Eight

Lydia pulled into the VIP parking space and turned off the ignition. She'd visited Bliss many times in the past. The women's ministry at her church often chose it for seminars, conferences, and retreats. Most of the women knew her daughter owned the place, but they didn't know of their estranged relationship. She doubted Dinah had known Lydia'd been on the premises.

But today she would.

Dinah had extended the invitation. It'd be the first time in over a decade Lydia'd see her daughter's face again.

She sucked in a deep breath and tried to wrap her mind around the invitation. It had come out of the blue. Sure, she and Dinah'd had several phone conversations over the past few weeks, and a couple of text messages, but the conversations were short and the texts were just about random things going on at Bliss.

Lydia didn't care. Her daughter had opened the lines of communication, and she was taking everything she could get. Dinah had mentioned several times how she still needed to process a lot of the things that had happened, and Lydia was prepared to give her the time she needed.

Then this morning, Dinah'd called and asked to meet at nine o'clock. Lydia hadn't even had her first cup of tea, but she knew that it was a now-or-never moment. She'd scurried to make it on time.

Thankfully she'd remembered to pick up her black skirt from the cleaners the day before. It went perfectly with the black kitten heels and the cream blouse. She'd tucked her not-quite-dry hair into a bun and decided she'd rather be over-dressed than under-dressed when reuniting with her daughter.

She'd managed adding eyeliner, mascara, and a touch of lipstick on the drive over and slid on a pair of pearl earrings with a matching bracelet. But what she hadn't done was calm her pounding heart. She should've been prepared for this. After all her prayers over the years, this invitation shouldn't have taken her by surprise.

But it had.

Through the windshield, the bold red-lettering on the VIP sign stared at her. The fancy, cursive script looked like it belonged on a wedding invitation. It was beautiful and welcoming. Normally, she'd have parked further back on the lot, but this was where Dinah had told her to park.

Lydia bit at her bottom lip. Surely, the VIP gesture was a good sign. If Dinah'd called her here to chew her out, she wouldn't have asked her to park so close to the entrance. Or maybe it was so Lydia would be able to enter and exit unnoticed, especially if Dinah had her escorted out by security.

Lydia slapped the steering wheel. Time to stop the

madness. She'd already driven herself crazy worrying about the *why now and what-ifs*. Time to go inside.

Lord, give me the strength and the grace to handle whatever is before me. She exited the car and smoothed her skirt and her blouse, then paused to take in the view. It was spectacular. The well-manicured grass was the deepest shade of green she'd ever seen. The landscape was dotted with several small ponds that featured geese gliding on the water. Hundreds of flowering dogwoods graced the property. A brook babbled to her right. To her left was a dazzling waterfall that had several fountains in front of it that sprayed rose-colored water into the air. The setting was surrounded by the rolling and breathtaking hills of the Ozark Mountains. She'd never tire of admiring all that her daughter had accomplished.

"Excuse me. Are you Mrs. Dooley?"

The dark brown eyes of a young man, maybe mid-twenties, greeted her. The eyes were kind and so was his smile.

"I am, yes." His demeanor was so welcoming, Lydia didn't have the heart to tell him the *misses* designation had never been a part of her name.

He extended his hand. "My name is Blackwell. I'll be your concierge during your stay."

"I'm sorry. I'm afraid there's been a misunderstanding. I'm just visiting."

"There's no misunderstanding, ma'am. I have direct orders from Mrs. O'Keefe to escort you to her office, then to your room."

"My room?" Lydia blinked. "But I didn't pack anything. I didn't know that I'd need—"

"Mrs. O'Keefe has arranged everything. A personal stylist will chat with you about your fashion preferences and take your measurements. Then she'll have a selection delivered to your room. Couture is an option as well."

"There's no way I'll be able to pay for any of that."

"Everything will be taken care of by Bliss."

Lydia opened her mouth to protest but thought the better of it. She'd had no idea that Dinah had planned all of this and wasn't sure how she felt about it. But the last thing she wanted to do was appear ungrateful.

"Um … Blackwell?

"Yes, ma'am?"

"Would you happen to know how long Mrs. O'Keefe has arranged for me to stay?"

"As long as you'd like."

"As long I'd like?"

"Yes."

Lydia then realized that Blackwell's hand was still extended. "Mercy me. I am so sorry."

After they shook, he clasped his hands behind his back and tilted his head toward the huge oak doors that marked the entrance. "Shall we?"

She held up her hand. "I forgot my purse." She retrieved it from the car, then lifted the remote to lock it.

"There's no need. We have the best security in the state and you have VIP parking. Trust me, no one will approach your vehicle without the proper credentials."

Lydia pushed the button on her remote. "I think I'll lock it anyway. I'll sleep better knowing that I did."

He gave a slight bow, then extended his arm toward the front of the building. "After you, ma'am."

She followed the circular cobblestone walkway that led to the entrance. Blackwell stepped around her and opened the door. Inside, she instinctively turned to the right toward the conference rooms, but Blackwell continued on to the reception desk. He went behind the semi-circle counter. Lydia caught up with him before he opened a narrow door that led down a long hallway. They passed several more employees who wore the same impeccable black blazers, pants, and white shirts so crisp they might break if you tried to fold them. They all wore silver name tags, but only a few had the Missouri state tree engraved into them like the one Blackwell sported.

After they passed several glass-enclosed offices, Blackwell stopped at one at the end of a hallway. Unlike the others, the glass surrounding this particular office was designed with glass blocks that resembled crystal and were not see-through.

Blackwell paused at the door. "Mrs. Dooley, are you ready to greet your daughter?"

Absolutely not. She was nowhere near ready. She swallowed, then whisked a mirrored compact from her purse, checked her hair, and snapped it shut. She smoothed her skirt one more time and nodded.

Blackwell twisted the crystal knob.

Across the room on the far side of a large mahogany desk, a woman looked out the window. Her back was toward Lydia, but Lydia would recognize that beautiful mane of dark brown hair anywhere. It fell down the woman's back in waves. It was the same color and texture as those long-ago ponytails. Lydia smiled at the memory.

Blackwell whispered something and left, the door

closing behind him with a soft click.

The woman at the window rubbed her thumb over a crumpled tissue, but she didn't turn around.

Lydia placed her hand over her mouth. She longed to shout Dinah's name and run across the room and embrace her. But Dinah had always frowned at open displays of affection. Lydia lowered her trembling hand then took a few steps forward. She strove to sound calm and cordial. "Dinah, you have no idea how glad—"

Dinah spun. Water-filled royal blue eyes stared at her. Lydia placed a hand over heart. God had answered her prayers. She was looking at her daughter's face again. It had been a long time since she'd seen it, but it hadn't changed. The eyes, the nose, the mouth … they were just as she remembered them. "Oh, Dinah."

"Mom."

Lydia steadied herself as Dinah made her way around the desk and raced toward her. She'd barely opened her arms before Dinah flew into them.

"I'm so sorry, Mom." She hugged Lydia tighter. "I've missed you so much."

Tears flowed down Lydia's face. The last word Dinah uttered carried such heartache. Her daughter trembled in her arms. Lydia rubbed her back. "I've missed you too, sweetie. You have no idea how much. But there's nothing to apologize for. You did what you needed to do. I've always understood that."

Dinah sniffed. "You forgive me?"

Lydia gently lifted Dinah's head from her shoulder and looked into her eyes. "There was never anything to forgive."

Dinah dabbed at her eyes with the tissue. "I've said so

many hurtful things to you in the past. I've kept your grand-daughter away from you. I've—"

"But look at what God has done. Today, we're here in each other's arms. None of that other stuff matters."

Dinah took a step back. "I haven't overcome the past, Mom, but I have decided to not let it control me. However, it may take me a while to get there."

"Now that I've seen you again, I have all the patience in the world. We'll get there."

Dinah grabbed her mother's hands, stepped back, and smiled. "You haven't changed a bit. A wrinkle or two here and there, and a few crow's feet, but you look just how I remember you."

Lydia chuckled. "If those are the only things you noticed, then I'm afraid you need a pair of eyeglasses, dear. But you … you're as beautiful as always."

"I've put on a few pounds, but at this point in my life, I don't care. I stay active and exercise regularly, but if the pounds don't want to come off, I'm okay with that, too."

Lydia studied her daughter from head to toe. She might have gained fifteen pounds or so, but the extra weight enhanced her figure. She'd been the thinnest of her four girls, and she still was. She wore a satin blouse, navy wide-leg pants, and beige heels. She looked professional and casual at the same time.

"Oh!" Dinah snatched her cell phone from the top of her desk. "I'm sorry, Mom. I just have to do this." She wrapped an arm around Lydia and snapped a selfie. "I'm about to be hated." She grinned and tapped her phone. "I just shared that photo of us with Ada, Bethany, and Claudia. They had no idea about this. I wanted to keep it quiet in case it didn't work out. They're going to be so mad at me for not telling them."

Lydia bit her lip. After the initial shock and being a little miffed that she was left out of the loop, Ada would be ecstatic that her mother and her sister had finally mended fences. Bethany and Claudia would both get worked up, but after a few days, Bethany would calm down and be excited for them like Ada. Claudia, on the other hand, was a different story.

She'd have to convince all of them that she'd been kept in the dark.

Dinah led her to a sofa that was tucked into a nook along one of the glass walls. As she sat, their phones dinged multiple times. Lydia fished hers out of her purse. When she tapped open one of the messages, it rang it her hand.

Dinah used her index finger to scroll through her phone. "Yeah. They're mad. Well, Ada's just kind of glad-mad. But B & C? Whew."

Lydia answered her phone. "Good morning, Ada. Yes, it's true. I would've told you but I didn't know myself. I understand, but I'm with Dinah right now. Can I call you back when I get to my room?" Lydia squeezed her eyes when Ada's next question burst through the earpiece with a screech. "Yes, I have a room. No, I don't know which one."

Dinah leaned in. "She'll be staying in the Bluebird."

Lydia paused. The first time she'd visited Bliss with her church group they'd been given a tour. The Bluebird, also known as the Bluebird Loft, was like staying in the penthouse of a luxury hotel. Bliss only had three floors, and the Bluebird took up almost the entire third one. She'd speak to Dinah about her staying there, but right now, she needed to get Ada off the phone. Her other line was already beeping, and she didn't have to look at the caller ID to know that it was either Bethany or Claudia. "Dinah says I'll be staying in the Bluebird. Yes, I know. All right, I'll see you in a bit, but please call your sisters and let them know that I'm not ignoring them, and that I'll call them later after I spend more time with Dinah. Okay, thanks." Lydia turned off her phone then slid it back in her purse.

"I'm sorry about this, Mom." Dinah continued to tap away on her phone. "I've been thinking about this reunion for a while. I didn't tell them what I was planning because I didn't want them to pressure me into it before I was ready or try to talk me out of it. That's also why I sprung this on you at the last minute. You talk with them all the time, and I didn't want them to feel like you were hiding something."

Lydia nodded. "That was a smart move. I don't know if I could've held in my excitement. Ada for sure would've gotten it out of me."

"I know." Dinah chuckled then placed her phone in her pocket. "Whenever she's put her interrogator's hat on with me, I've cracked." She sat next to Lydia. "I didn't want to put you through that type of torture." She glanced down at her pocket. "Things should get quieter now. I've sent them all messages letting them know I'll explain everything later."

Lydia tried to hold back a new set of tears. "I don't have the words to explain how I'm feeling right now. But I want to say thank you for giving us a second chance."

"I know." Dinah wiped at her eyes. "I don't have the words either. But it was time. Past time." She let out a long breath. "We don't have to share and solve everything right now. I have questions. Lots of them, and I'm pretty sure you do, too. But there's no rush. I hope you enjoyed meeting

Blackwell."

"Oh, I did. Such a nice young man. Very gentleman-like."

"He is. You may know his grandmother, Deborah Lowell?"

She knew Deborah from church. "I had no idea her grandson worked here."

"He's been with me about seven years now. Started off doing dishes here as a teen. He's impressed me so much over the years, that I've heaped tons of additional responsibilities on him with each new promotion. He's never let me down." She let out a small laugh." And I'm tough on my employees, so that's saying a lot. He's also the only employee I completely trust. That's why I assigned him to you. Did he get the chance to explain everything I have planned?"

"He did." Lydia leaned forward. "But none of that is necessary. Just being able to spend time with you is enough."

"I know. But I really wanted to do something special for you. Enjoy some of it, all of it, or none of it, your choice. I promise not to get mad either way. But it'd bless me so much to be allowed to spoil you a little bit."

"A little bit? A personal concierge, unlimited shopping, and a custom tailor are more than a little bit. And the Bluebird? Dinah, it's too much."

Dinah clasped Lydia's hand in hers. "Please let me do this."

Lydia didn't want to take advantage of her daughter, and that's what she felt like she'd be doing. She wasn't even sure that being in the same building with her daughter at this point in their relationship was a good idea. It was too soon. Dinah also said she had questions. Lydia wasn't sure if she could provide the answers. How would Dinah respond? Would she think her mom was deliberately withholding information, or worse—lying? And the answers Lydia had, would Dinah really want to hear them? She knew from her other daughters that Dinah's temper could still be explosive. She didn't want this reunion to go south. But one look in her daughter's eyes made the decision for her.

"You're sure you want to do this?"

Dinah nodded.

"And it won't cause you any type of hardship? Financial or otherwise?"

Dinah smiled. "Not even close."

Lydia pulled her daughter into a hug. "Fine. I'll stay. But promise that if things become too stressful or—"

"I'll keep the lines of communication open I promise. You'll do the same?"

Lydia nodded against her daughter's shoulder and kissed her cheek. This is what she'd needed. What she'd waited for. To see, kiss, and embrace her daughter. The rest would be nice, but she honestly didn't need anything more.

But she knew her daughter would. And Lydia wasn't sure she'd be able to provide what she needed. Because one question sent chills up her spine. Like the rest of her daughters, Dinah would want to know who her father was. Lydia had thought a lot about that since they'd started talking again. And she didn't like the answer. It wasn't good.

Not good at all.

Chapter Twenty-Nine

Eve listened for the sound that had awakened her—footsteps on the stairs. Her pulse slowed with each moment of silence. Nothing. A figment of her half-asleep state of mind and a dark room. She fluffed her pillow and closed her eyes.

A breath on the back of her neck and an arm around her waist popped them back open. Heat from the arm radiated through her thin chiffon night gown to her cool skin. She fumbled for the pen she kept on top of her nightstand. She grasped it, turned, and aimed it at the intruder's temple.

When lips pressed against hers and the grip tightened, her pulse quickened. She knew those lips. And the kiss that followed. And the slight arch of her back confirmed it.

Philip.

She dropped the pen but fought the urge to surrender to his intentions. What was he doing here? More importantly, how had he gotten in? He'd stormed out weeks ago and swore to never return. But he had. Every time she left the house, he'd come in and help himself to items that were precious to her. The locksmith had put an end to that. Or so she'd thought.

She pulled away from the kiss. He gripped her waist and smothered her lips again. Her body protested, but she knew that she couldn't wave the white flag on this one. If she didn't stop this now, he'd go on treating her any way he wished. Full of disdain one moment. Searing with passion the next.

She untangled her legs from his and shoved him off. When he rolled to the other side of the bed, she flipped on the lamp.

"Why are you here, Philip?"

He blinked several times. "Dim the light. It's blinding me."

She dimmed it a few notches. "What are you doing here?"

He wiped his eyes and propped himself on his elbow to face her. "It's my house. I can come and go as I want."

Eve folded her arms. "I've never had a problem with that until you started taking things that weren't yours, like my father's watch. You know how much that watch means to me. Why would you do that?"

He grunted and dragged a hand over his face. "There you go complaining again. And you wonder why I don't want anything to do with you anymore."

The muscles in her stomach clenched. How could she have not seen this disgusting side of him before? Had it always been there? Could she really have turned a blind eye to it for all those years? Was it even a blind eye?

No. She couldn't blame this on blindness. She'd jumped into this relationship with her eyes wide open. What she needed to know now was why had she put up with it for so long, but that wasn't a question that Philip could answer. However, he could answer this one. "Why did you want anything to do with me in the first place? You were tall, good-looking, and wealthy when we met. Girls— who I know you enjoyed being around— threw themselves at you. There were plenty to choose from, but I'm the one that you asked to marry. Why?"

He placed a hand on her thigh. "It's been weeks since I've seen you, Eve. Longer than that since I've been this close to you. I know you've missed me. The way you responded to my kiss let me know that." He inched closer and cupped the side of her face. "Why don't you just relax and let me do this for you."

She slapped his hand away and scooted off the bed. "You're a monster, you know that? I don't know what I ever saw in you. Ever."

He laughed and stood. "You're kidding, right? You know *exactly* what you saw in me. Someone who'd take your ugly behind."

She felt the color drain from her face. "What?"

"I asked you to marry me and not one of those other women because you were desperate enough to say yes and they weren't."

Her head jerked back. "Desperate?"

"Yes. And desperate women make good wives." He pushed up the sleeves of the black pajama shirt he wore. "Well, a good wife for me anyway. I had no intention of settling down, but my grandfather said I needed a wife for my political career. None of those other women were desperate enough to put up with my shenanigans. But you were. When grandfather found that out, he told me to marry you. He said you'd be so grateful that someone like me wanted someone like you that you'd be as loyal as a rescued hound."

Eve wished she still had the ink pen in her hand. Or something, anything to throw at him. She eyed the lamp on the nightstand.

Their whole relationship was a façade. A charade. A sick joke dreamed up by his late grandfather, who she now hoped burned in hell.

Philip had never loved her.

That's what hurt the most. She'd hoped that somehow, somewhere, or maybe even once upon a time, he'd loved her. How could he not? She'd been good to this man. She was a great girlfriend, a doting fiancée, and a faithful wife. He was the only man she'd ever shared her body with. When things were good in their marriage, she was his biggest fan. When things were bad, she'd jumped in the trenches and worked by his side. When he was sick, she was his caretaker. When it became clear that a political future was no longer an option for him, she'd supported every career change and crazy endeavor he'd come up with, all without complaint. All of it for nothing. He'd never loved her. He'd just used her. While she'd remained as loyal as a rescued hound.

Just like his grandfather had predicted.

Eve cut her eyes from the lamp to Philip. "So I'm just a joke to you, is that it?"

Philip placed a knee on the bed. "This is not why I came here tonight, Eve. You started this. You're the one who brought up the past."

"Answer me."

He narrowed his eyes. "Are you okay?"

"For thirty years, you and your family have been laughing at me behind my back."

"Well, kind of, yeah."

She opened the top drawer of the nightstand. "It was clear twenty years ago that you'd never have a career in politics." She quietly slid loose papers and other items around the drawer until she found what she was looking for. The stainless-steel barrel of her dad's Smith and Wesson glinted under the dimmed light. "So why did you stay? You could've divorced me then, since I was no longer of any use to you."

He tightened the string to his pajama bottoms. "I'm not doing this." He walked toward the bedroom door. "When you come to your senses, let me know. Then I'll give you what you need." He opened the door. "I'll be in the guest room."

Eve wrapped her hand around the grip of the loaded revolver. Images bombarded her vision. Images of her screaming and pulling the trigger. Images of Philip sprawled across the floor, blood pouring from the back of his head. Sirens. Police. Philip's body being zipped into a black bag. Voices. Questions. Her wrists. Handcuffs. The click from them loud enough to clear the images. She gasped and jerked her hand away from the revolver. "Thank you, Lord, for not letting me succumb to temptation." She slid the drawer shut.

Philip turned to face her. "Who are you talking to?"

"Your Savior."

He paused in the doorway. "I should've had you committed a long time ago."

Maybe he should have. Nobody in her right mind

would've put up with what he'd put her through. She glanced at the drawer and shivered. Maybe she should commit herself.

"Goodnight, Philip."

He stalked out of the bedroom. She shuddered when he slammed the door behind him.

She slunk to the floor beside her bed. "Lord, I almost killed that man tonight." She pulled her knees to her chest. "Truth be told, I still might." She squeezed her eyes shut and waited for the tears of regret and repentance to come. When her eyes remained dry, she dropped her forehead on her knees. "Help me, Lord Jesus. I feel like I could kill Philip tonight and not lose an ounce of sleep over it. When did this spirit of hatred overtake me?"

She tightened her arms around her knees. "I don't know what to do, Lord. I feel like I'm losing my mind."

Philip's grandfather had called her a dog.

"I need You, Lord."

Philip had called her desperate.

She rocked back and forth.

He'd used her.

She squeezed her knees tighter.

He'd never loved her.

Tears made their way through her closed lids.

He'd never love her.

She sniffed then shuddered as a sob started in her toes, parked in her chest, crawled up her throat, and made itself known. She tightened her lips to control the volume, but it was of no use. The last thing she wanted was for Philip to hear her crying. He'd no doubt think it was over him.

But it wasn't. It was over how she'd wasted three

decades of her life. Years she'd never get back. Time she could've spent building a life for herself. Perhaps she would've gone into business with her mom, something she'd often thought about doing. Who knew how many cafés they'd have by now? And what about her music career? If she'd taken Roger's advice all those years ago and hired a manager, who knew where she'd be now? Maybe she could've found a God-fearing man. A man who knew what true love was. A man who would've appreciated her faithfulness and loyalty. A man who would never have let her be mocked, joked about, or laughed at.

A man who was probably still out there.

What was she thinking? When she was young, she couldn't turn heads. What were the chances of doing so now, all these years later? None. It didn't matter. She didn't care anymore. She couldn't stay married to Philip a moment longer than she had to. She'd tried. She'd given everything she had and then some. And he still wanted more. Still wanted to use her for reasons only he knew about. But her chasing and pining after him ended tonight.

She was done.

She lifted her head and wiped her eyes. "Lord, I don't know what to do next. I know what I want to do. I want to call my lawyer and tell her to speed up the divorce. That Philip can have everything. As long as I'm left with my dignity, I'll be happy." She sniffed and shook her head. "But I don't want to do anything without hearing from You first, Lord. If I'd done that in the first place, I wouldn't be sitting here contemplating killing someone I once loved. Who You still love. You gave him life, not me. I have no right to take it. Help me with this dark feeling I have toward him. A feeling with such force, Lord, that I'm still shaken by it. Please replace that feeling with brotherly love."

She rested her head on her knees again and let the tears flow through the sheer layers of her gown onto her skin. All she'd ever wanted was for Philip to love her. In pursuit of that, she'd unwittingly given him control over her emotions. So much so that she'd almost let him turn her into a murderer.

She rubbed at the tears that had made their way down her legs.

With the Lord's help, she wouldn't let that feeling take root. Too much time had been wasted on Philip. She wasn't going to spend more of it in prison—physical or spiritual.

She made her way to the bathroom and filled the sink with cold water. In the mirror, the reflected image looked like her, but something was different. Eve smiled when she realized what it was. She no longer had what she could only describe as that "please love me" look.

She dipped a washcloth in the cold water and washed her face. It bothered her to no end that she couldn't name the new look on her face, but things were going to be different now, she could feel it. She'd go back to sleep, wake up whenever, and if Philip was still around, fine. If he wasn't … She shrugged at the image in the mirror. Whatever happened, she'd remain at peace until the Lord showed her the next move.

She blotted her face dry. When she returned to the bedroom, the clock read 3:45 a.m.

As she pulled back the bedding, she was stirred by a feeling she recognized. A feeling she knew better than to ignore.

Sleep would have to wait.

She picked up her cell and dialed. A groggy but kind voice greeted her on the other end.

She took in a quick breath, then let it out slowly. "Roger?"

"Hey, Evie."

"I'm on my way over."

A slight pause and then, "See you soon."

She clicked the phone off. Things were going to be different all right.

Very, very different.

Chapter Thirty

The short, overweight, and deeply wrinkled woman in front of Mary wore a fuzzy blond wig with long strips of bright pink and baby-boy blue along the front. The wig was topped with a large straw hat that touched the rim of large sunglasses.

The woman tugged at the hat with a gloved hand, then glanced in both directions before speaking. "I saw on the news how you had been reunited with your family." She lifted the sunglasses, looked Mary in the eyes, and smiled before slamming them across her nose again. The gesture took only seconds, but the soft green eyes sent chills up her spine. The woman's face was older, but those were the same eyes that had looked Mary in the face night after night and lied to her. The eyes back then were as kind as they were soft now. And more than likely, just as deceptive.

The woman looked over her shoulder before continuing. "I tracked down your parent's address, spotted you leaving, and followed you in my rental. When you stopped here, I knew I wouldn't be able to find a better place to talk with you."

The farmer's market was crowded with people talking with vendors, walking their dogs, shopping, and eating. It was surrounded by a large circular parking lot with easy access from multiple angles. The perfect place for someone to make a quick exit. And Mary was sure the woman was already planning her escape.

The woman tilted her head to the side. "I came to tell you how sorry I am for my part in what happened. I could give you a thousand reasons why I did what I did, but they'd all come down to the same thing. Greed. I needed money, and Dr. Roth paid me lots of it to take care of the girls he brought to me. I knew it was likely that you girls had been kidnapped or worse, but I didn't care. Years later, my conscience got the best of me, and I called in a tip to the authorities. I called in anonymously, but Roth found out, and that's when I witnessed firsthand just how dangerous he was. He made sure I paid a steep price for what I did, but I haven't let that stop me. I can't undo the harm I've done, but when I'm able to track down the girls who were in my care, I won't rest until I look them in the eyes and apologize. A part of your childhood was stolen from you, and I played a role in that. I'm—"

Mary held up her hand. She still couldn't believe that she was standing in front of the same woman who'd held her captive all those years ago. Not to mention all of the other girls. Mary at least had gone to a good home. But what about the others?

"What matters is that you're here now. There are still families out there looking for their children. You can help them."

"I just wanted you to know how sorry I am about what happened." She straightened the oversize jean jacket she wore. "You have no idea how happy I am to know that things turned out well for you and your family." She turned to leave.

Mary grabbed the woman's jacket. "Miss Autry, wait."

The woman frowned. "Ann Autry was the name on the fake ID that Dr. Roth gave me."

The FBI had said the same thing. Apparently, the cheap wig, overalls, extra-large hat, and jacket were extra measures she'd taken to keep her identity a secret. "What should I call you, then?"

She shrugged. "You always referred to me as Miss Autry. No need to change that now."

Mary loosened her grip on the woman's jacket. She'd continue to use the name, but she'd drop the Miss. She wasn't a respective little kid anymore. She was a grown woman who wanted answers. But Autry was jittery. Mary knew she had to handle her with kid gloves or she'd scare her off. And this time it could be forever.

"I'm sorry." Mary let her hands drop to the side. "It's just that you might have information that could help reunite other families. I just thought that—"

"If I go to the police, I'll spend what's left of my life in prison. That can't happen. I have seven grandchildren I'm responsible for."

Mary stepped forward and lowered her voice. "What if it was one of your grandchildren who had been kidnapped? If there was someone out there who could help find them, wouldn't you want them to help?"

The woman stuck her gloved hands in her pockets. "It

was nice seeing you again, Mary."

"Don't leave."

Autry turned and moved quickly through the crowd. Mary followed and pulled her cell phone from her purse. She dialed the agent who'd handled her case. When Autry stopped at a homegrown tomato vendor, Mary lost track of her. The crowd at the tomato stand almost wrapped around the entire booth. Autry, with her pink and blue dyed wig and large straw hat had somehow managed to disappear in that crowd.

She left a voicemail for the agent, and dialed Ethan.

"Hey, love."

"You'll never guess who just approached me."

"Where are you?" The panic in his voice stopped her in her tracks. What was she thinking? With everything that had happened over the past couple of weeks with Christianna and Windy, he probably thought she was in some type of danger.

"Honey, I'm fine. Everything's okay."

He let out a breath. "Sorry, it's just that—"

"I know. I know."

After a brief pause, he continued. "This person who approached you. It had to be someone from your past."

Mary adjusted her purse and strolled to a nearby vendor selling natural soaps. "How'd you know?"

"Your voice. It takes on a certain tone when you talk about people from your past."

She picked up a bar of soap made out of goat's milk and honey. "Yeah, well, this one's a doozie." She told him about her conversation with Autry.

"She must be really sorry for what she did to take a risk like that."

"I know." Mary sniffed the soap, then grabbed a small carrying basket from the ledge of the booth. She dropped the soap inside, then tossed in two more. "She could've easily used an untraceable phone line and told me all of that over the phone. But she said she'd wanted to do it in person. Which made me think, that maybe there was some real regret for what she'd done. And I thought I saw that in her eyes, but when I mentioned that she could help some of the other families, she bolted."

"Sounds like she was scared."

Mary placed a jar of pomegranate and brown sugar scrub in her basket. "She was. She said she couldn't spend the rest of her life in prison, but surely they can't arrest her for something done that far back."

"Depends on what she did. There is no statute of limitation on murder."

"Oh." Mary tossed a bottle of beard oil for Ethan in her basket. "Do you … think she could've murdered someone?"

Ethan grunted. "Babe, with all the craziness that has happened since we arrived, I'm not ruling anything out."

Mary jumped when she felt a soft touch on her shoulder. She turned and a saw a girl, about fifteen, with bangs, a short red ponytail, and a face full of freckles. Mary spoke into her phone. "Ethan, hold on a second." She nodded toward the girl. "Can I help you?"

The girl smiled and extended her right hand. In it was a piece of white paper folded in half. "An old woman in a straw hat came up to me and my friends over there at the fruit stand," She glanced behind her then focused again on Mary. "She asked if one of us would like to make a hundred bucks. I told her yeah, and she gave me this, and a hundred dollar bill. She then asked that I deliver this piece of paper to you."

Mary looked over at the fruit stand. Several girls stood there, staring. Mary could tell that they were taking in every inch of her, perhaps in case they had to give a description of her to the police if anything happened to their young red-headed friend.

Mary took the note, surprised by the weight of it. "The woman who gave this to you, do you know if she's still here?"

The girl shook her head. "I doubt it. She asked me to wait ten minutes after she left to give it to you."

"Thank you."

The girl smiled then jogged over to her friends. They grabbed her hand and made their way through the crowds. Mary waited until they were out of sight before lifting the phone back to her ear again. "Ethan, did you hear any of that?"

"I heard all of it. What does the note say?"

Mary placed her basket on the counter and unfolded the note. "It's a handwritten address and a local post office box number. There's also a small key taped to the paper."

"You called Agent Rudd after you ran into her, right?"

"I got his voicemail."

"I'll try and see if I can reach him. That paper and key may have fingerprints on it. Maybe they'll be able to track her down using that, and hopefully she'll be more agreeable to helping solve the other cases if the FBI knocked on her door."

Mary clicked her tongue. That's why Autry had been wearing gloves on this beautiful, warm, and sun-filled morning. She didn't want to leave any prints, but it was still worth a try. "Okay."

"Can you wrap things up? Until they find out what this woman is up to, I'll feel a lot better if I were by your side."

"I'm checking out now. See you in twenty minutes."

"She completed her purchase and walked toward her car. She loved strolling around the Farmer's Market. She'd also planned on doing a lot more shopping, especially since she had two lists full of items from Christianna and her mom. But Ethan was right. Until they found out what was going on with Autry, it was probably best that she had someone else with her. She didn't mention it to Ethan, but she was disappointed in herself for not being aware of her surroundings. How could she not know that she had been followed? And from her parent's house of all places. Try as she might, she couldn't remember anything odd or out of place on the quiet street her parents lived on. She also didn't remember seeing a vehicle that didn't belong to any of the neighbors. But Autry wouldn't have been stupid enough to park on a street that had so little traffic. If Mary hadn't noticed the car, one of her parents' neighbors surely would have. More than likely, Autry parked on another street close by, and when she saw Mary emerge from her parent's house, ran to her car and followed from there. Mary blew out a breath. She knew there was no way she could've known that, but it still bothered her. Autry had not only followed her to the market, she'd also followed her as she'd walked around as well. Mary had visited several booths and vendors before Autry approached her. She would've had to have been followed for at least a good thirty minutes. How could she have not known?

Mary used the remote to unlock her doors when her car

came into view. When she reached the driver's side, she reached for the handle, then stopped. She wasn't going to make the same stupid mistake. The last thing she needed was to get in her car and have someone pop-up and surprise her from the back seat. She leaned in to look through the windows, but the tint stopped her from seeing inside. She took a deep breath, then yanked open the back door of the sedan. She looked for anything out of the ordinary. Satisfied that everything looked exactly the way she left it, she tossed in her purse and her packages, then popped the trunk and searched it as well. Nothing out of place there either, so she walked to the side of the car and looked under it. No tracking device. She stood, wiped her hands on her jeans and walked back to the driver's side and got in. After locking the doors and starting the ignition, she let out a deep breath. She was over-reacting. But under-reacting was apparently just as bad. Fortunately, it was Autry who'd followed her this morning, who, as far as she knew, didn't mean any harm. But what if it had been someone else who did? What if it had been one of Frank's or Michael's minions? She could've been dead already. The police had assured her that they were all locked away and no longer a threat, but she'd also thought that everything that had to do with her kidnapping was done and over with as well.

This was the one place she'd always felt she'd be safe. Habakkuk. Her hometown. The town she'd dreamt of returning to when she was a kid.

Now she wanted to leave. She wanted to be on the next flight to Israel with Ethan. She wanted to reunite with their kids and smother them with kisses.

She retrieved the white folded paper from her purse and

stared at the key. As much as she wanted to, she knew seeing the faces of her children would have to wait. Because if her hunch was right, the key attached to this paper was going to keep her here a lot longer than she'd anticipated.

A whole lot longer.

Chapter Thirty-One

Kite plugged in the blow dryer and set the temperature setting to low. Blow drying Windy's hair would go a lot a faster if she used a higher setting, but Windy hated using heat on her hair. The only reason they were doing it now was because they were meeting up with the girls in ninety minutes. Kite knew there was no way Windy's hair would be able to air dry in that time, but at the current setting, blow drying wasn't going to get the job done any faster either.

Kite grabbed a hairbrush from the vanity their dad had made for her. He'd given it to her after she'd moved into her very first apartment. The color had deepened over the years, but the grain of the cherry wood was just as smooth as the day he'd made it.

She aimed the dryer at a section of Windy's hair. "You know, if you'd kept your phone on, we would've gotten Christianna's message earlier, and we wouldn't be rushing now trying to get ready."

She tried to turn her head to look at Kite, but she used

the brush and dryer to keep her facing forward. Wendy frowned at her in the vanity mirror. "That hurt."

"This'll go a lot faster if you keep your head straight."

She rolled her eyes. "I didn't keep my phone on because I'm not up to talking to everyone just yet."

"Then why'd you agree to meet up with them?"

She looked down at her lap. "I owe it to them."

Kite nodded and gently rolled and pulled the brush through Windy's hair while she aimed heat at it. It had been several weeks since Windy's release from the hospital. Until today, she'd refused to see anyone and only checked her messages at night. The scars on the right side of her face were healing nicely. One of the wounds on her arm had become infected, so her right hand and lower arm were still bandaged.

Kite grabbed a clip from the top of the vanity and used it to separate the dried hair from the wet and wavy mass waiting its turn. "You owe it to them?"

She started to nod, but Kite tightened her grip on the brush. "I've put Christianna's family through hell, yet they still love and support me. I haven't returned Priscilla's calls in forever, but she still sends inspiring and encouraging texts every day, which I've never responded to. Every morning, I get a new devotional in my email from Lydia. And Eve has mailed handwritten notes."

Kite smiled at Eve's thoughtfulness. Her letters always lifted Windy's spirits. The envelopes were always exquisitely hand-decorated, with an array of musical symbols adorning each one. "Funny how I've not been getting the same inspiring and beautifully handwritten messages that you have. When I see them tonight, I'm gonna ask 'em what's up with that."

Windy chuckled and Kite paused the dryer for a moment. It had been weeks since she'd last heard her sister laugh. She'd forgotten how much it reminded her of their dad's.

It was good the girls had given Windy the space she'd needed. But they were still there for her—whether she'd wanted them to be or not.

"Well, I, for one, am glad that you've agreed to go out tonight. Some fresh air would do us both good."

Her smile faded.

Kite clicked the dryer back on and began drying another section

of her hair. "What's wrong?"

"I don't know. I just … I thought it'd be a good idea to get out, but now I'm not sure."

Kite switched the dryer off and laid it on the vanity. "What's really going on, Wind? If you're worried about running into one of Michael's cronies—"

"I don't want anyone else getting hurt because of me, okay?" She held her gaze through the mirror. "It's bad enough that I put Christianna in harm's way. I should've known better. I *did* know better. I knew Michael would be ticked if I showed up at his place, especially with that girl there, but I didn't care. If it had been just me, that would've been fine. But putting someone else in danger was reckless."

"You didn't know things were going to turn out the way they did."

She scooted the stool back and stood. "I did know, Kite. That's what I'm telling you."

"You knew that Hildy was going to throw—"

"I knew confronting Michael would end in violence. And

I still drove there. With Christianna in tow."

Kite laid the brush down next to the dryer and folded her arms. "You're afraid Michael's not done trying to get back at you."

She rubbed the back of her neck. "I don't know. The reports I'm getting from Michael's inner circle are saying that he and his family have bigger fish to fry—especially with all the new charges the district attorney has thrown at them. But I don't want to take that risk. Not again. I am ready to venture out, but if you or one of my friends get hurt again because of me, I'd never be able to live with myself."

Michael Kildare was in prison, and it didn't look like he'd be getting out any time soon. And if our local news was correct, the ADA was on a mission to dismantle the entire Kildare family criminal enterprise. Dozens of arrests had been made, and one of Michael's brothers had been indicted on a murder charge. Windy was probably the last person on any of their minds.

But she had to be careful. She didn't want her sister to be afraid of going out and spending time with her friends. That would be torture for Windy. She was the definition of an extrovert. This caring, less self-centered side of her was new. It blessed Kite to know that she'd matured, but she needed to learn how to balance the two. They'd be perfectly safe dining out with the ladies tonight, and part of her wanted to push Windy to do that, but the look on her face told her that she wasn't ready.

"How about we have the ladies come here instead? They've been bursting at the seams to see you, so I don't want to cancel. But instead of getting dressed up to go out, we'll ask everyone to come here and make it pizza casual."

She raised an eyebrow.

Kite pulled her phone from her skirt pocket. "I'll send a group text and ask if everyone will be okay with the change in plans. Clothing is casual, shoes are optional. I'll ask them to stop by the pizzeria and bring their favorites here. It'll be fun."

Windy glanced at her watch. "I don't know. We're supposed to meet them in a little over an hour. I'm pretty sure Pris is already glammed up and waiting for her limo."

"Which would make you feel more comfortable? Meeting them at the restaurant or having them come here?"

"Having them come here."

Kite sent the text. "Done."

"But they're going to want to know why."

"I told them we'll explain when they get here."

She laughed her beautiful laugh and shook her head. "You know you're the best sister in the world, right?"

"That's what you've always told me."

She gave Kite a quick hug then sat on the stool. She faced the mirror and gave her head a vigorous shake. "Now we don't have to worry about trying to make a miracle out of this mane. How about just a ponytail?"

Kite picked the brush up again. "What type of ponytail? High-pony? Slicked-backed pony? Side—"

"Messy."

"I can do that." She loosened some of the tangles Windy'd just made. "This is definitely going to be a messy one."

"That's okay. Michael always said that I looked gorgeous when my hair was a mess."

Kite stopped the brush in mid-stroke.

Windy glanced up at her, then lowered her head. "I can't believe I just said that."

"That's okay." Kite squeezed her shoulders. "Old habits are hard to break."

When she didn't lift her head, she continued. "You still love him, don't you?"

She shook her head, but the tears that fell onto Kite's hand told her otherwise.

She gathered Windy's hair and wrapped an elastic band around it. She'd never understood Windy's attraction to Michael. She'd always leaned toward bad boys, but Michael was beyond that. His dark curls and eyes and rugged good looks she was sure had played a part in her attraction, but anyone who'd spent any time in Habakkuk knew that he was bad news.

Windy had fallen for him, regardless of the fact that every time Kite had been in the same room with him, she'd gotten a bad feeling. Numerous times she'd mentioned that to Windy. She'd assured Kite the feeling would go away once she'd taken the time to get to know him.

The feeling hadn't gone away and neither had he. The longer they were together, the stronger the hold he seemed to have on her. Even now, after everything he'd done, she was here in front of the mirror, sadly remembering some lame compliment he'd given her.

Kite had waited for this day. The day where Windy's eyes were opened, and she saw Michael for who he really was. Unfortunately, it'd taken him trying to hurt someone she loved. That was a line you didn't cross with her. But apparently she didn't mind when he'd crossed it with others. As long as it didn't come nigh her dwelling she either dismissed it or ignored it.

But now that the enemy had found its way into her camp, she had to face it head-on. Kite was proud that Windy had found the strength to stand strong even though her heart was breaking. If she'd only realized earlier that this was the type of heartache and pain she'd been trying to save her from all along.

She kissed the top of her head. "We'll get through this, Wind, I promise. And we'll pray that someday you'll meet the man of your dreams."

"I thought Michael was the man of my dreams. I thought for sure we would've been married by now with a couple of kids." She paused then looked at her sister again through the mirror. "He was never going to marry me, was he, Kite?"

She shook her head.

Windy nodded, and wiped at a tear that had trickled down her cheek. "That's ten years of my life I'll never get back." She rubbed her hands on her jeans and stood. "So, am I going to call the pizzeria to order our favorites, or are you?"

Their phones dinged at the same time. Kite grabbed hers and looked at it. "Um, well … looks like we're too late. The girls are just around the corner. They'll be here in a few minutes."

Windy grabbed her phone. "I have the pizzeria's app on my phone. One of the owners there has a crush on me. I'll ask him to rush the order."

Kite raised an eyebrow. "This owner, have I met him? Is he cute?"

Windy swiped through her phone, then held it up and showed her a man's photo.

"Oh, yeah. I know Anthony. He's always real nice to me

when I go in. He's definitely a looker. Do you think, maybe in time, that you might go out with him?"

"Nah." She tapped away on her phone. "He's too much of a goody two-shoes. Goes to church every Sunday, takes his Mom to brunch afterwards, volunteers at food pantries. You know the type."

Kite took a step back. "Well, we certainly couldn't have you going out with someone like that, now could we?"

She tossed her phone on the vanity. "Sorry, Kite. He's just not the kind of guy I'd be interested in."

Excited voices filtered in from the front porch. Kite started toward the living room. When Windy didn't follow her, she turned back toward her. "Aren't you coming? They're here to see you."

She blinked several times. "Tell them I'll be out in a few minutes." She made her way over to Kite's bed and lay down.

The doorbell rang. "I'll tell them. But if you're not the first person Christianna sees, you know she's going to come looking for you."

"I said I'll be out in a few minutes."

The bell rang again, longer this time, as if someone was leaning on it. Kite jogged to the door and opened it to the zesty aroma of Italian cuisine. Her mouth watered.

Mary nodded to one of the many bags she was holding as she entered the room. "Don't worry. We ordered for you guys too. We got Windy the Cajun chicken fettucine and mozzarella cheese sticks with a jalapeno dip. For you, we picked up the cheese tortellini and their house salad."

"Oooh." Kite grabbed two of the bags from Mary and followed Eve and Priscilla to the kitchen. They had already transferred several of the entrees onto large plates from her cabinets. She placed the bags on the table. "I love the tortellini from Vinny's."

Mary smiled. "So I've been told. We also brought two jugs of iced tea, pizza, and enough bread sticks and hot wings to feed a small army."

"I have no idea what we're going to do with all this food." She poked her thumb toward the bedroom. "Windy just placed an order for us."

Mary shrugged. "Whatever is left over, we can take home to our families." She patted her on the elbow. "You can save your order for tomorrow night and share it with Jack."

How did she know Jack had been stopping by to have dinner with her? Before she could ask, Christianna walked in carrying a clear container holding the most decadent triple-layer chocolate cake she'd ever seen. Christianna placed it on the breakfast bar. "Where's Windy?"

Kite pointed to her bedroom. "She said she'll be out in a few minutes."

Chrissy turned, but Mary grabbed her arm. "You can't just waltz into someone's bedroom without asking."

She gave Mary a mock frown then faced Kite. "May I please enter your bedroom?"

She chuckled. "Go ahead. She's expecting you."

Lydia poured the iced tea. "Kite, is Windy okay?"

"No. Which is why we changed plans at the last minute. The support you ladies have shown over the last several weeks has meant a lot to both of us. She'll share the details, but she's still a bit nervous about seeing everyone again."

Priscilla stepped forward. "If this is about her scars—"

"It's not." Windy and Christianna walked in. Christianna pulled out a chair for Windy to sit.

She sat and bowed her head before looking up. "It's about shame, humiliation, and embarrassment. You've stood by my side even though my actions could've cost Chrissy and her family their lives. And possibly even yours. I don't deserve the love and support you've shown. That's why I didn't return calls and texts. I didn't know how to respond to messages that should've been filled with anger and cursing, but weren't." She shrugged and gestured toward me. "I'm not like Kite. She puts everyone else's needs before hers. I'm not like that. Everyone here knows I have a dark side. Kite loves me regardless, but she's my sister. You ladies don't have that obligation." She wiped at a tear. "But you love me in the same way she does, and I don't know how to deal with that."

Eve swiped a napkin off the table and knelt next to Windy. "You deal with it the same way we deal with it—you accept it. The only reason we're able to extend mercy and grace is because it's been extended to us." She handed Windy the napkin. "We're loved by the Great I Am, and so are you. When you finally say yes to Him, you'll understand."

Windy wiped her tears with the napkin.

Eve reached for her hand. "Would you like to say yes now?"

"I'd like to talk with you some more after everyone leaves. Would that be okay?"

Eve smiled. "Absolutely." She squeezed Windy's hand and stood.

Kite grabbed a glass of tea, sipped it, then closed her

mouth around a cube of ice and sucked. Seriously? After all the years she'd prayed and witnessed to her sister, Eve was going to be the one to lead her to the Lord? She bit into the cube. Apparently, she wasn't as selfless as her sister thought. Windy's life was about to be changed for eternity, and here she was stewing that she wasn't the one leading her there.

Christianna thumped Windy on her shoulder. "Are you done feeling sorry for yourself?"

Windy nodded.

"Good." Christianna dipped a mozzarella stick in the jalapeno sauce and handed it to Windy. "These are your favorite. You'll feel better after several of these and the fettucine. Let's eat and be merry."

"Christianna's right." Kite gestured toward the living room. "I'll clean off the coffee table, and we can move everything in there."

Priscilla grabbed a couple of the plates. "A few of these need to be warmed up. Are these plates microwaveable, Kite?"

She nodded and moved toward the living room. After Kite cleared the coffee table and threw several large pillows on the floor for the girls, Lydia and Mary placed a steaming hot platter of sausage pizza squares in the center of it and placed a bowl of salad next to it. Windy and Priscilla followed filling the rest of the table with bread sticks, wings, pastas, hot pretzels, and various sauces. Kite was just about to clear a side table for the cake when the doorbell rang.

"Oh!" Windy placed a hand over her mouth. "I forgot we had more food coming." She opened the door, and there stood all six feet and four inches of Anthony De Santis. He held out a slated wooden crate. The crate and bags of food in it had the name Vinny's emblazoned across the front, but his clothes didn't. Instead of the usual red-and-white T-shirt's and khaki's with the Vinny's logo on them that everyone in the restaurant wore, Anthony had on a crisp white button down shirt, black slacks, and dark brown Italian loafers.

Windy took the crate and invited him to step in. "Ladies, this is Anthony. He owns Vinny's restaurant with his brother." She motioned toward the table and everyone sitting on the floor around it. "Anthony, these are our friends. We were all about to indulge in the food your staff prepared for them earlier."

Anthony made his way to each of the women, shaking their hands and asking their names. Since everyone except Priscilla was now sitting on the floor, he had to bend to do it. And Kite noticed that he'd managed to do it all without stepping on a single pillow.

"So nice to meet all of you. I hope you're enjoying everything."

After several nods and thank-you's, he turned to Windy. She placed the crate next to Kite on the floor, who noticed a bottle of red wine and two glasses tucked inside.

Windy turned toward her sister. "Kite, be sure to put the food in the refrigerator for tomorrow." She leaned over and grabbed the bottle of wine and the two glasses. "I'm going to say good-bye to Anthony and thank him properly for what he's done for us this evening. We'll be in my room. We'll only be a minute." She grabbed his elbow and led him down the hallway and around the corner to Kite's guest bedroom. The same bedroom that Windy had been recuperating in since she'd left the hospital. The same bedroom that she was now calling her own.

A disturbing thought crossed Kite's mind, and she sucked in a breath. Surely she wasn't going to—

Mary placed a warm bowl of tortellini in her hand. "Don't let your mind go there." She handed her a fork and sat on the floor next to her. "She said she'll be back in a minute. What could possibly happen in one minute?"

"With my sister?" Kite sighed and brought a forkful of pasta to her mouth. "And did you see the way he looked at her when she touched his arm?"

Mary nodded. "It was smoldering."

"Exactly." Kite bit into the pasta and closed her eyes as an explosion of spices and various cheeses burst into her mouth. She tried to savor it, but her mind kept wandering toward thoughts of what her sister might be up to in the other room.

She reached for a bread stick and remembered the conversation Windy had at the kitchen table with Eve. Anthony or no Anthony, there was no way Eve was going to leave without having that conversation with Windy.

She chomped on the breadstick and pointed it down the hall. "She needs prayer."

Lydia chuckled. "Don't we all? But the evenings not over yet." She winked at Eve. "If He accepted me as His child, then Windy'll be a breeze."

Kite nodded even though she didn't agree. The difference between Windy and Lydia was that Lydia's heart was ready to change. She'd genuinely desired a relationship with their Heavenly Father. Windy's heart was fickle. Kite had given up trying to figure out what she desired years before.

Priscilla slid a plate of hot wings in front of her. She took one, bit into it, and said a silent prayer that her sister's heart would finally be ready to make the right decision tonight.

She also prayed for Anthony. Because if Windy's heart wasn't right and she was back to her old ways, she would either leave him heartbroken or lead him down the garden path.

Or worse.

Chapter Thirty-Two

Priscilla sprinkled parmesan on top of her manicotti and turned away from Kite. The look of concern and disappointment on Kite's face had nearly brought Priscilla to tears.

She wanted to tell Kite not to be concerned with what Windy was doing in the other room. Anthony had a serious crush on Windy, but a shared glass of wine and a peck on the cheek would be it. Windy could flirt and tease with the best of them. She and Priscilla had taken turns in the past to see who'd be able to string along some poor sap the longest. If they'd benefitted from it somehow, of course. Whether or not Windy planned on doing the same thing to Anthony didn't matter. There was no way Windy would ever do what Kite was imagining. She respected Kite too much and she'd never take advantage of her sister's home like that.

Priscilla shoved a forkful of manicotti in her mouth. How could Kite not know that? Or at least give her sister the benefit of the doubt? So many times, Priscilla had been accused of doing something horrid that she hadn't done. She was no saint, but her sins weren't ever as bad as people had made them out to be. And no one close to her—especially those who should've known better, like her family—defended her. Seeing Kite's reaction to what she only speculated her sister might be doing … Had her own family had those same looks of concern? Had they shaken their heads in disappointment?

She swallowed the manicotti before she choked on it. Hopefully they hadn't, but the thought of her loved ones seeing her as someone who'd do those things shook her.

Could she blame them if they did? Yes, she could. There were just some things you should know about the people you grew up with, cared about, shared life with. They should've put a stop to those rumors. They should've had her back.

"Well, look who decided to return to the party." Lydia pointed a fork toward the hallway, where Windy was escorting Anthony to the door.

Anthony said his good-byes. Windy locked the door behind him then made her way to the coffee table. Priscilla nudged Windy's leg. "It's a good thing you returned when you did. Your sister thought the two of you were doing something naughty back there."

Windy's head jerked toward Kite. "You thought what?"

Kite cut her eyes at Priscilla then looked at Windy. "I did. And I apologize."

Windy glared. "How could you think that? I know how you feel about sex outside of marriage. And this is your home. What made you think I'd do something like that?"

Kite opened her mouth, but Windy plunged on. "Anthony and I talked and shared a glass of wine. That's it. Shall I bring in the sheets to prove it?"

Christianna laughed and leaned forward. "Yeah. I think you should."

Mary smacked Christianna's arm. "Stop stirring the pot."

Kite grabbed Windy's leg when she tried to storm off. "You don't have to do that, and you know it."

"Do I?" Windy yanked her leg free. "Because I thought you knew I'd never do anything to hurt you."

"You'd never intentionally hurt me, no."

"What is that supposed to mean?"

Kite placed her plate on the floor and stood. "It means that you act first and think second. You do what you feel in the moment without a second thought about those who love you and how they'd feel."

"If you thought I was doing something wrong, why didn't you come back there and say something?"

"I was going to," Kite rolled her eyes at Priscilla, then turned back toward Windy. "In private. Not in front of everybody."

Priscilla prepared to stand, but Lydia placed a hand on her shoulder. "Enough. This is not what tonight is about." She walked up to Windy. "We came here tonight to see you, to talk, catch-up, and have fun. Not to watch you and your sister fight."

Windy bowed her head.

Priscilla cleared her throat. "It's my fault. I started it, and I'm sorry."

Kite plopped down and retrieved her plate. "Then why did you do it?"

Priscilla narrowed her eyes. "Because I know what it's like to walk into a room with an elephant the size of Africa in it. It's a horrible feeling. Especially when everyone acts like you weren't the topic of the conversation." She let out a breath. "I didn't know that you'd planned on speaking with Windy. I projected my own feelings into the situation and spoke without thinking. It was all based on my emotions." Her eyes softened. "But I didn't want you and Windy to argue. I'm sorry. I really am. Forgive me?"

Kite smiled. "Of course. You were looking out for my sister. I understand."

Windy placed several slices of pizza on her plate and bounced down next to Kite. "I'm sorry I yelled at you." Kite pulled her into a hug.

Lydia made her way over to Priscilla and sat next to her on the couch. "And I'm sorry you've had to endure those things. I know what that feels like."

Priscilla broke off a piece of a mozzarella stick and popped it into her mouth. "My insecurities have a way of showing themselves at the worst possible times."

"Unfortunately, I know what that feels like too."

Christianna guzzled the last of her tea and stood. "The mood in here is too melancholic for me. Anybody want cake?"

Hands shot into the air. Priscilla tapped the coffee table with her fork. "Since I'm the one who darkened the mood, how about I lighten it with some good news?" When she had everyone's attention, she stretched out her left arm and splayed her fingers. "Barry and I got married."

The room exploded with voices. Christianna fought through the crowd of women, who were now on their feet. She grabbed Priscilla's hand. "For you to have caught the biggest fish in Habakkuk, he sure did buy you an awfully small ring."

"Christianna!" Mary leaned toward the table. "How could you say something like that?"

Windy folded her arms across her chest. "Forget the ring. I want to know why I wasn't invited to the wedding."

Priscilla raised a brow. "You weren't answering my phone calls, remember?"

"Oh." Windy lowered her eyes, then lifted them defiantly. "Still, that's no—"

Priscilla laughed. "There was no wedding. Not really. Only a handful of people even know that we're married. Diamond Liz was there since she introduced me to Barry, and so was Lola. Her husband and Barry are close friends."

Eve tilted her head. "But why all the secrecy? I would think that the future bride of Barry King would've planned the wedding of the century."

"I would've loved to, but there was more at stake than my dream wedding. No one in his family would've agreed to attend, not even his children. For those who don't know, they hired private investigators to dig into my past for proof that I'm a gold digger."

Windy rubbed the back of her neck and sat back on the floor. Kite did the same.

Priscilla twisted the ring on her finger. "Anyway, you ladies know how I feel about money, and so does Barry. He knows that was the only reason I'd initially agreed to our relationship. But Barry is a heck of a good man. He really is. Over time and after multiple marriage proposals from him, I said yes."

Christianna groaned. "That still doesn't explain this tiny ring."

"Or the secrecy," Eve said.

"His family threatened to stop the wedding, so we kept it a secret until after we were married. But now, I'm keeping it as hush-hush as possible until I can break the news to my mom."

Windy gasped. "You haven't spoken to your mom yet? You made plans to visit her weeks ago."

"I did, but I chickened out every time. If you remember, Jacob sent her my personal journals, where I'd written in graphic detail about the different men and trysts I'd had over the years. I took excellent notes in case anyone ever tried to blackmail me. But when I left Jacob for Barry, he gave those journals to my mom to hurt me. And he succeeded. Before, she'd only heard rumors about the way I used to make a living, now she has proof of it in my own handwriting." An image of her mother reading through her journal flashed through her mind. Her stomach roiled. She pressed her hand against it and waited for it to calm. "So far I haven't summoned up enough courage to face her."

Lydia placed a hand on her shoulder. "When did you and Barry get married?"

"March fifth."

"That was weeks ago. If she hasn't heard by now, she will soon. You need to be the one to tell her. Don't let her hear it through gossip."

Priscilla swallowed. "It's bad enough that I have to look in her eyes and talk to her about the diary. When I tell her I married Barry, she'll think what his kids think—that I married him for his money. And now that she's read the diary, there's nothing I'll be able to say to change her mind." Priscilla swiped at a tear. "As a daughter, you hope that if anyone in the world truly knows you, it's your mother. The one person on this earth who can say that they nurtured you for nine months. That you shared a body with until you took your first breath. You'd think they'd know your heart, know the essence of you." She shook her head and continued. "But Mabel has always judged me by my actions. And now she has several hundred pages from my journals to back it up. I can't take one more look of disappointment from her. I can't."

Lydia squeezed Priscilla's hand. "Honey, don't you see? What Jacob meant to hurt you can actually help you. Those journals are the perfect springboard for you and your mom to open up about feelings that have been buried way too long. It'll be hard at first—I know because Dinah and I are still working on our relationship—but we've been able to understand each other better since we started communicating. As a mom, I'll be the first one to say I dropped the ball. I wanted to be the best mom my girls could've had, but it didn't work out that way. To say I failed would be an understatement. Even though Dinah wasn't speaking with me at the time, it broke my heart when she got married without me. She had good reasons and so do you. But hearing about it from someone else? I can't begin to describe that type of hurt."

"It all happened so fast. Barry and I returned home from the amusement park and over dinner he asked me again to marry him. I surprised him by saying yes. A few hours later, I was the one who was surprised when his pastor showed up along with Liz and Lola. They ushered me into the small chapel on his estate, and we said short, heartfelt vows to one another. Next thing I knew, Pastor Greene announced that we were married." Priscilla's cheeks warmed. She reached for her glass of tea and took a sip.

Windy tapped the table. "Don't stop there. Tell us what happened next."

She placed the glass back on the table. "After that we kissed. It was our first. He'd teased me with it for so long that I practically melted from the anticipation of it." She picked up her glass and took another sip.

Windy snatched it from her hands. "And?"

"And it was just as tender and as passionate as I'd dreamed it would be." Priscilla stopped there. As life-changing as that kiss was, it paled in comparison to the first night she shared her body with her husband. She sucked in a breath as the memories bombarded her and left her gasping for air. Every promise Barry had made regarding the experiences she'd enjoy as Mrs. Barry King, he'd delivered on. Time and time again.

Eve giggled. "Windy, I think you need to return her glass. And add a lot more ice to it."

Priscilla blinked away the memories. "My point is, there wasn't the usual type of wedding planning. I didn't even have a gown. Lola brought a spectacular floor-length silver-and-white dress for me from a nearby thrift shop. I got married in that—barefoot by the way, because I didn't have shoes to match. There were no flowers or caterers, not even a violin in the background. Seven people in total were there, and five of them watched two of them make a vow before God."

Lydia nodded. "I understand. It was a surprise and rushed probably because Barry wanted to make sure you didn't change your mind. There was no time to get your mom involved. But she needs to know."

"You're right. I'll do it first thing in the morning."

Christianna placed her hands on her hips. "I'm going to stand right here until you tell me what's up with that pea-sized diamond."

"Barry gave me what I asked for. I've had tons of large and extravagant gems with no meaning behind them. I'm so done with that." She glanced at the tiny solitaire on her left hand. "This one may be small, but it has a lot of meaning. And for some strange reason, I'm crazily okay with that."

Eve smiled. "You're okay with that because you're in love. It's written all over your face."

"I guess … I guess you're right. Who would've thought that Priscilla Martin would find true love?"

"Priscilla King," Eve corrected her.

Priscilla lifted her brows. Eve was right. Priscilla Martin didn't exist anymore. And neither did the thoughts, desires, and behaviors that were associated with that name—the only name her mother had ever known her by. It was time to introduce Mabel Martin to the new Priscilla.

Tomorrow morning couldn't come fast enough.

Priscilla King was ready for it.

Chapter Thirty-Three

Lydia was glad she'd been able to persuade Priscilla to talk with her mother sooner rather than later. The conversations would be difficult, but once that was over, the better off their relationship would be. She didn't want Priscilla to end up estranged from her mother. After Dinah had stopped talking to her, there were times that Lydia wished she'd been more active in forcing a conversation with her daughter. As the silence between them had grown, so had Dinah's bitterness and resentment. In Dinah's mind, it was her mother who was to blame for what happened to her, so it was her mother who should've stepped up to resolve the situation. Lydia had wanted to, but her counselors had warned her against it. They'd said Dinah needed time to process what happened to her and when she was ready to talk, she would, and if Lydia forced her to relive the trauma before she was ready, that would only cause her more harm.

But recent conversations with Dinah revealed just the opposite. Yes, she was mad at Lydia for not protecting her, but at the same time, she'd needed her mom. She'd wanted Lydia to hold on tight, even though she was actively pushing her away.

Something hit her hand. A piece of pizza crust landed on her empty plate. Eve was preparing to toss another piece her way. "What in the world are you doing?"

Eve rolled the crust in her hand. "You're a million miles away. I'm just trying to bring you back to the present."

"Sorry." Lydia placed her plate on the table. "I was thinking about Dinah."

Kite folded her legs. "Eve said you've been staying at Bliss the past couple of weeks. How's that going?"

Lydia leaned back into the couch. "A lot better than I expected. Not only am I staying in the Bluebird—without paying a dime—her staff has been taking very good care of me. But what I look forward to the most, or at least I used to, is that Dinah comes to my room every morning to have breakfast. We eat there instead of the dining areas so we can talk privately."

Mary raised a brow. "Used to?"

"Yeah." Lydia looked down at her hands then cleared her throat. "The conversations we've had have been therapeutic for both of us. Lots of tears, but there've been some laughs too, especially when we got through the difficult stuff. But just like her sisters when they welcomed me back into their lives, she wants to know who her father is. With Ada and Bethany, I was able to tell them what little I remembered about their dads. They eventually connected with them, so those situations ended well. With Claudia it was more difficult. I shared what I knew. But with Dinah … "

Priscilla leaned in closer. "It's okay. You were a

completely different person back then. Dinah will be upset at first that she may never know who her father is, but in time—"

"I know who her father is."

Priscilla's eyes widened. "You do?"

"It took me a while to clear the cobwebs from my brain and do the math, but I'm a hundred percent sure I know who her father is."

Mary scooted forward. "You don't have to tell us who he is, but have you told her?"

"No."

"Do you plan to?"

"No."

After a long stretch of silence, Lydia added, "To clarify, I will tell her that I *know* who her father is, I'm just not going to tell her *who* he is. I have a good reason for it, and I ask that you ladies pray she'll understand. Dinah and I have come so far. This is the last thing I'd want to come between us, but—"

"It's Philip, isn't it?"

Lydia glanced at Eve and was tempted to prepare her lips to deny it. To reassure her friend that it wasn't true, but Lydia couldn't do it. She couldn't lie to Eve. She'd never done it, and she wasn't going to let a deceiving spirit lead her into doing it now.

Lydia ran her fingers through her hair. How had she allowed the conversation to get to this point? As soon as they'd asked about Dinah, she should've changed the subject. Since Dinah has asked about her father's identity, it was all Lydia could think about or pray about. And now it had spilled into her conversation with the girls. But she'd kept everything as vague as she could. How did Eve—?

"It's okay, Lyd." Eve rose and came to the couch. Priscilla scooted over, and Eve sat next to Lydia. "Everybody here, with the exception of Mary, knows that you and Philip were an item before I married him. When Dinah was a toddler, I often thought I saw glimpses of Philip in her. They have the same sable brown hair, blue eyes, and dimpled chin. Even some of her mannerisms remind me of Philip. I asked him about it. He denied it, of course, and made a comment about how any hot-blooded male in the town of Habakkuk could be her father. I quit pressing him on it because he'd get so angry. Also, I knew your history with men back then, so I just chalked it up to me having an overactive imagination."

"I'm so sorry." Lydia scratched the back of her neck. "It wasn't until Dinah started asking questions that I allowed myself to think about that time in my life again. I paid a visit to my parents' ranch after she and I had talked because I knew my mom had kept a box full of junk from my teen years. I went through it and found stacks of letters written between me and Philip. The dates, the events ... everything added up."

"So my suspicions were right. And once again, Philip made me think that I was crazy for thinking it."

"I put all of this together a few weeks ago and wanted to talk to you, but it happened after you and Philip separated. I didn't want to bring it up when you were already going through so much. And I needed to handle the situation with Dinah first. She can't stand Philip. His company conferences are at Bliss. There have been issues regarding his behavior there. She had him escorted out by security the last time.

They exchanged words, and it got pretty heated. I can't imagine how she's going to react when she learns he's her father. And her daughter's grandfather."

Eve frowned. "He's stormed home multiple times in a rage after being escorted out. He has no idea that your Dinah and the Dinah at Bliss are one and the same. I didn't tell him because I thought that would make the situation worse. Now I'm thinking that I should have. Maybe their encounters wouldn't have gotten so far out of hand."

"Eve." Kite stood and collected empty plates and pasta dishes from the coffee table. "Do you think you're going to tell Philip, now?"

"Not until Dinah knows. Given what Lydia said, she may not want to acknowledge him. Her name and her resort have a stellar reputation, and she rubs shoulders with some of the most influential people in town. If Philip knew that she was his daughter, he'd exploit it to his advantage. Her having any type of relationship with him could ruin her business and her life. I'm living proof of that."

Kite balanced the dishes in her arms and made her way to the kitchen. Windy, Christianna, and Mary gathered additional items off the table and followed.

Priscilla rose from the couch. "Obviously, everyone thinks the two of you need some time alone to talk." She grabbed her glass off the table then joined the others in the kitchen.

Lydia adjusted herself on the couch until she was knee-to-knee with Eve and able to look her in the eyes. "I didn't want you to find out like this. If I'd known that you'd had any suspicions at all, I would've avoided speaking about it until I'd worked everything out with Dinah."

"Don't worry. I'm not upset. When you said she'd asked about her father, all of those old suspicions flooded back. You didn't say it was Philip, I did. Besides, we're among friends who already knew about you and Philip. I could tell they were shocked about him being Dinah's father, but things like that happen. The two of you were an item back then."

Stuff like that did happen, but Lydia and Philip were never an item. She'd been an addicted soul willing to do anything to fill a need—heroin—and Philip had been eager to help her do it. He was mean and he was cruel, but he'd had an unending supply of drugs, so she endured his treatment. And she'd endured it for way too long.

But not as long as the woman sitting in front of her. Eve married Philip about a year after Dinah was born. Lydia knew what she was getting into with Philip—she'd used him and he'd used her. Neither one of them were innocent, but Dinah and Eve were. Two innocents damaged by the same man. Dinah had no say in who her father was, and Eve's heart had fooled her into thinking that Philip was somebody he wasn't.

Eve had to be devastated. Philip had promised her they'd start a family once they were married. She'd dreamed of being a mother for as long as Lydia could remember. But after the wedding, Philip changed his mind. Eve held onto the hope that once they were pregnant, he'd come around. Six months later, Eve was pregnant and she couldn't wait to tell Philip, but her joy was short-lived. Philip accused her of betraying his trust and stormed out of the house. When he didn't return, Eve went looking for him. She lost control of her car in a storm and slid into a ravine.

Lydia had been by her side when the doctors told her she'd lost the baby. Due to her injuries, the chances of her carrying a baby to full-term were almost non-existent. Lydia had held on to Eve and cried as they waited for Philip to arrive.

He never did.

And now, here she was, all these years later, telling that same friend, who'd never been able to have a child with the man she loved, that not only did her husband have a child, but he also had a seven-year-old grand-daughter.

All thanks to her best friend.

Lydia blinked back tears. This was no time to start crying. Her past mistakes made a regular habit of rearing their ugly heads, and she always seemed to lose someone dear to her in the process.

But she couldn't lose her relationship with Eve. It was too precious to her.

If the enemy wanted to fight her on this one … fine.

She grabbed Eve's hand and uttered a short prayer over their lives, their friendship, for Godly wisdom on how to move forward, and for the courage to do so.

Afterward, they clasped their hands and smiled.

Victory was already theirs.

Chapter Thirty-Four

Eve pressed her lips together. Philip was Dinah's father. She'd been right all along. What would Philip have to say about this development? Eve looked at Lydia and smiled. It didn't matter. Weeks ago, news like that would've sent her spiraling. She would've been in a daze, stuttering and muttering and looking like a simpleton. But she'd spent the last couple of weeks reacquainting herself with her first love.

She was at peace.

Mary entered carrying a tray with three bowls of ice cream. She handed a bowl of vanilla to Eve and a bowl of strawberry to Lydia.

"The kitchen rumor mill states that these are your favorites. The rest of us are enjoying some too. Is it okay if we rejoin you ladies?"

Lydia swallowed a spoonful of strawberry before answering. "Of course. Who doesn't love an ice cream party?"

"She's right." Eve dipped her spoon into the creamy

concoction. "And so was the rumor mill. I love vanilla, but be warned. If anyone comes out here with a bowl of butter pecan, they'd better run, because I'm stealing a scoop."

Mary yelled over her shoulder, "Christianna, if I were you, I wouldn't come out here unless you're ready to share. Or better yet, grab the pint of butter pecan and bring it. Along with the black walnut." She faced Eve and Lydia and pointed at her bowl. "I love this stuff."

Kite carried in two quarts of ice cream. Christianna was right behind her with a third.

Kite dropped to her knees at the coffee table. "Sorry we disappeared like that, but we knew the two of you could use a minute or two to talk alone."

Mary lifted her spoon. "We also said a prayer. I didn't know much about what was going on, but it still broke my heart. I couldn't imagine being in either one of your positions. It has to be hard."

Eve tilted her head. "Not as hard as you might think."

Christianna elbowed her sister. "See, I told you. Even his wife knows that Philip is a first-class—"

"Really, Christianna?" Mary gave Christianna a stern look. "You know, you don't always have to say exactly what you're thinking."

Christianna shrugged. "I call 'em as I see 'em."

"She's right." Eve added a scoop of butter pecan to her bowl. "Philip's a piece of work."

"I would've chosen a different word than work." Christianna mumbled around a mouthful of ice cream.

Eve laughed. If they were giving out awards, Christianna would win for funniest comment of the evening. Mary was annoyed by her sister's candor, but she found it refreshing.

Chrissy didn't mince words and Eve loved that about her. You never had to guess what Chrissy was thinking or where she stood.

"Eve." Kite licked her spoon. "What did you mean when you said it might not be as hard as we think?"

"A few months ago, information like that would've rocked me to my core. Not because Dinah's his daughter, but because I would've been scared spitless about his reaction to the news." She shrugged. "Now, I don't care."

Kite nodded. "Well, that's good news, right? I mean, that sounds like you and Philip are in a better place in your marriage?"

"Hardly. As soon as he signs the documents my lawyers sent him, we'll be officially divorced."

Lydia gasped. "I had no idea!"

She shrugged again. "There's no point in me trying to fix things anymore. I fought the good fight. I was patient, forgiving, and I extended copious amounts of grace and mercy. I've put up with decades of verbal and emotional abuse, and I stood strong even when he refused to go to counseling. And I'd still be standing if he hadn't told me that the only reason he married me was because he knew that I was desperate enough to put up with anything. When he said that, something inside of me broke." Eve paused and waited for old and familiar tears to brim her eyes, but they never came. "Of course, my heart was broken, but it was more than that. I realized I'd never have a successful and rewarding marriage. I was a joke to him back then, and he's made it abundantly clear that I'm still a joke to him now. I hated to move forward with the divorce, but it needed to be done."

Lydia placed a hand on Eve's knee. "I'm so sorry."

Eve rubbed her hand. "I was a wreck after I signed those papers. And I second-guessed myself for days. But the next thing I knew, I was back in the studio. Not just to finish recording with Three-Sixteen, but also to write and record some of my own music. I wrote more songs about Philip, and I wrote songs about how God is seeing me through it all. It's amazing how much I've been at peace lately. Writing and singing those songs not only brought me into a deeper relationship with my Savior, but it also showed me how much time I'd spent on a daily basis obsessing over Philip. Where was he? Who was he with? When was he coming home? Was he coming home? Did I do his laundry the way he liked it? Or was I going to get yelled at again for being stupid? Since I've been back in the studio and focusing more on God and less on Philip, I've been in a better place. I haven't felt this free in ages. When I say I no longer care what Philip thinks or how he'll respond, I truly don't."

Lydia frowned. "I know how you feel about divorce. And for you to have signed those papers, you must've really felt like he'd left you with no other choice."

"You've been telling me for years that I had a biblical basis to divorce him. I knew you were right, but I also knew it didn't mean that I had to. I wanted to make sure I gave us every opportunity possible for a successful marriage. But it takes two."

She paused as Windy and Priscilla carried in a bowl of strawberries and a couple of jars of toppings. Windy handed a jar of caramel topping to Kite. "Are we interrupting something?"

Kite took the jar. "Eve was just letting us know that she and Philip are getting divorced."

"Oh." Priscilla sat on the couch next to Lydia. "I'm sorry to hear that Eve."

"It's not what I wanted, but the good news is that he's not being a complete jerk about the divorce. He comes from a wealthy family, so of course he made me sign a prenuptial agreement before we were married. So far, he's insisting I keep the house. It's paid for, so that's a blessing. He's also insisting on giving me a substantial amount of money monthly. However, I won't believe anything he says until everything's final. He's had the divorce papers for a week and still hasn't signed them."

Lydia's jaw clenched. "Has he said why he hasn't signed them?"

"He sent a text two days ago saying he'd been too hasty in agreeing to the divorce. He asked if we could get together and talk."

"You've got to be kidding me. What did you say?"

"I said no. I know what he's up to. He knows it's harder for me to stand up to him when we're alone. He asked what he could do to change my mind. I said I have an appointment Monday morning at church for counseling. If he really wanted to see me, he'd join me there."

"Do you think he will?"

"I have no idea. I haven't heard from him since."

"And if he does show up?"

"Then I'll …" Eve ran her fingers through her hair. "Then I have no idea what I'll do." She pulled out her cell phone. "That's all I'd like to say about Philip. What I'd really like is for you ladies to listen to this song and tell me what you think."

She pressed the play button and took in each of the girls'

faces as they listened. She couldn't believe she was being this bold. Rarely did she share her music with anyone. It was too personal. Each lyric was an expression of her heart, an extension of her soul. But working with Roger in the studio over the past month had boosted her confidence. His kind words and encouragement not only helped her songwriting, it also helped her voice soar. He'd helped her pull out aspects of her voice that she'd never explored before. And this latest song, "Faithful," was just a sample of the beautiful music they'd compiled together over the past couple of weeks.

She relaxed when Kite raised a brow as she listened, and Windy hummed along with the melody. Priscilla nodded and swayed with the rhythm, while Lydia listened with her eyes closed. Mary and Christianna looked at each other and smiled. After the song ended, Eve pressed the stop button.

"Wow." Priscilla's eyes were wide. "Lady, I knew you could sing, but I had no idea you could sing like *that*."

Windy nodded. "Yeah. I've heard you sing several times on those Sundays Kite dragged me to church. I loved hearing your solos. But this was different, more … powerful. I don't know how to explain it, but I felt something as I listened."

If the song touched someone like Windy, then it was worth all of the prayer, hard work, and late nights.

"That was just you and the piano, right?" Christianna reached for the phone.

"Yes. However, Roger and I are having a tough time deciding what to do next with the song. The initial plan was to add in band instruments and have Gabby from Three-Sixteen sing backup vocals. But after we heard the song in this form … " She lifted her shoulders and let them drop. How could she explain this so that her friends would understand? "Roger and I talked about it earlier today. He ultimately left the choice up to me, so I said I'd have you ladies take a listen, see what you think, and make a decision afterward."

Lydia's mouth formed an O. "You were at the studio earlier today?"

Eve nodded.

"But weren't you there last night as well? I mean, when I talked with you on the phone last night it was pretty late."

"Roger has a lot of established artists that he works with during the day. We work on my stuff at night, and sometimes it carries over to the next day." She shrugged her right shoulder. "Neither one of us has anybody waiting at home, so late nights work for us."

Lydia gave a slow nod.

"What?"

"Just … be careful, Eve." Lydia paused for a moment, then continued. "Divorces can be hard, and you're emotionally vulnerable right now. Roger's been eyeing you since college. Not only that, he's Philip's best friend. If you're not careful, things could get real messy real fast."

Eve's head jerked back. "Roger's never had eyes for me."

Every face in the room had the same look as Lydia's. A look that said they knew something she didn't. "You ladies are wrong."

"No, we're not." Lydia softened her eyes. "Perhaps you've never noticed it because you've only had eyes for Philip, but Roger's had a crush on you for a very long time."

Her mind raced back through the interactions she'd had with Roger over the years. "He's never acted inappropriately with me. Not once.”

“Of course not. Roger Roarke may be a godless man, but he’s a good one. And Philip’s friend. He’s also been married a time or two … or three.”

“Five. He’s been married five times. Which proves my point. You’ve seen the women he’s married. Every one of them looked like a supermodel or was one. What on earth would he be looking at me for? And besides, I’m sure he’s heard a lot of horrible things from Philip about me over the years—lies, of course—but nonetheless, he’s heard them.”

“He also knows Philip well enough *not* to believe them.” Lydia templed her fingers. “All I’m saying is, be careful. Guard your heart. Please.”

As the ladies resumed talking, Eve slouched against the couch pillows and folded her arms. Why would Lydia say something like that about Roger? She wasn’t the type to make stuff up, so if she said she saw something, she saw it. But Roger? Having feelings for her? Eve chuckled. Not in the slightest. Roger liked his women young and he liked them beautiful. Eve was older and not. But he was also kind, gentle, respectful, always willing to listen, and he’d never ever called her stupid. Unlike Philip who’d done it so many times that she’d often wondered if he’d forgotten what her real name was.

Roger also encouraged her in her music. Always had. If he’d had any longing looks toward her back then it was because for decades he’d longed to get her into the studio to record. She’d resisted because she was focused on creating a family with Philip. But when that didn’t happen, she just focused on her marriage. Since that was about to end, she’d delved back into her music and agreed to start singing again.

That was Roger's doing. He'd always loved her voice. Said so many, many times over the years. Unlike Philip, who'd never liked her voice, and hated to hear her sing. Hated to see her happy. But Roger loved to hear her sing. And he knew how to nurture her voice, knew how to—

She bolted upright and almost knocked a spoon full of ice cream from Lydia's hand. She apologized and rushed to the bathroom. She splashed cold water on her face. What in the world was she doing? Thinking? Was she really comparing Philip and Roger? She was. Unintentionally, but she'd been doing it. How long had that been going on? Had she been unintentionally sending Roger the wrong signals? No, that couldn't be. She loved Philip and only Philip.

Were the girls right about Roger? And what about her? Did she deep down, way beneath the surface somewhere, suspect that Roger liked her? Was it possible? What was the likelihood of them exploring a relationship after her divorce was final? Could they really become a couple?

She splashed more cold water onto her face. Again, what was she thinking? How did her mind go there? No. She and Roger would never become a couple, because Roger was no Philip.

She stared in the mirror. The dripping face staring back at her said what her heart wasn't ready to hear.

Roger was no Philip.

He was better.

Chapter Thirty-Five

"Be right back." Mary rose. "I'm going to check on Eve."

Lydia lifted a hand. "No. Let's give her a few more minutes. If she's not out soon, I'll go check."

Mary looked at her watch and sat back on the floor. "Ladies, it's almost midnight, so I should probably take off soon. Ethan texted earlier. The FBI wants to meet with me again at seven tomorrow morning."

Kite shifted toward her. "I thought the investigation officially wrapped up weeks ago."

"It did. At least that part of the investigation." Mary scratched at her forehead. "There was a new development. One of the women who was involved in my kidnapping found out where my parents live. She waited in a car one morning, then followed me to the Farmer's Market." Mary put a hand up to halt the concerns and questions coming her way. "No, it wasn't like that. She didn't come to harm me, she'd had a change of heart over the years and wanted to apologize. But she did hand me a note with a key taped to it.

Ethan and I gave the note to the FBI. They found partial prints on the note and the key, and were able to determine that they belonged to Ann Autry. The name is an alias that she used, but it was the same woman who approached me at the market and who was pretty much my babysitter at the agency before I was adopted. The key led to a lockbox with papers in it that looked like they'd been pulled from a fire. The majority of them were still legible. They helped the FBI locate more of the girls who'd been kidnapped and taken to that bogus agency. They are in the process of helping them reunite with their families."

"Oh, my word!" Kite pulled her into a hug. "Mary, that's something you've been hoping for ever since you've been back. To somehow find a way to reunite the girls you were with at the agency with their families. I can't believe that woman would take a risk like that, but I'm so glad that she did."

Mary nodded. "She was scared and in a disguise when she came up to me. And I don't think it was in her plan to help me at first. When I'd asked her to, she said no and scurried off. The next thing I know I'm given a key to a post office box. It was a goldmine of information, but a lot of it was incomplete. The best files had pictures and names attached to them, along with the families they were adopted by. Others had names but no photos, and there are tons of photos without names. The meeting is to see if I can help place a name to some of those girls."

Christianna rubbed her sister's shoulder. "Would you like me to come with you? I know that's going to be hard."

"I'd like that. Ethan's going to be there, but he's worried about me seeing all of those faces again and where that might lead. He remembers the nightmares. I used to call out the girls' names in my sleep. I'd reach out to hug them, but they'd disappear, and I'd start bawling. He doesn't want to see me go down that road again. Things were pretty dark for a while, and that's when I stopped looking for my biological family. I had to, to keep sane.

"Having *you* there will be a reminder that God is in control, and I need to leave everything in His hands. Almost a year to the day after I stopped looking, Seema contacted me, which led me back here. But I've wondered about the friends I left behind at the agency. Did they end up in a good home? Were they trafficked or abused? Neglected? Agent Rudd let it slip a few of them died young. He didn't say how, but my imagination has a way of getting the best of me." She smiled at Chrissy. "You'll be a great distraction. Think you'll be able to make it?"

Christianna returned the smile. "I'm already there."

"Already where?" Eve reclaimed her seat on the couch next to Priscilla and Lydia. Priscilla gave her a quick update.

"I'll be praying that everything goes well."

Mary nodded. "Thank you."

Lydia yawned. "Kite, I'm about to fall asleep on your couch." She picked up several bowls and utensils from the table in front of them. "I'll wash dishes and clean the kitchen, but if I stay much longer, I'm afraid you ladies will kick me out for snoring. If my daughter can be believed, I sound like a bulldozer stuck in the wrong gear."

Kite laughed. "Don't worry about the dishes, you go ahead and take off. I'll get them later."

Lydia snorted. "You haven't seen your kitchen. The last time I was in there, the sink was full, and dishes were scattered all around the kitchen. Besides, I'm the only one here who actually enjoys doing dishes. I'll have the entire space spotless in no time."

"It'd be a lot easier if my sister had invested in a dishwasher." Windy turned toward Kite. "Who in the world doesn't have a dishwasher?"

"Someone who lives alone and works most of the day. Who needs a dishwasher for a handful of dishes?"

"But you don't live alone anymore. I'm here, and so is Jack most nights."

Kite placed a hand on her hip. "Jack only stops by periodically for a home-cooked meal. Unlike you, he helps with the dishes, so again, no need for a dishwasher."

Christianna giggled. "Especially when your dishwasher is a former Marine, has rugged good looks, his own business, and drives a Ferrari."

Kite balled up a napkin and tossed it at Christianna. "Don't start. Half the women in this room already think Jack and I are two steps away from the altar."

"Not two," Windy corrected. "Just one. Jack's already standing there. He's just waiting on you."

Kite rolled her eyes and was about to speak when there was a knock at the door.

"That'll be Ethan here to pick up me and Chrissy," Mary said. She went to the half-wall that separated the living room from the back of the house. "I'll grab our stuff."

"Okay. I'll get it while you gather your things." Kite went to the door.

Mary reached for the straps of her and Chrissy's purses, but hers fell behind the wall. She knelt to pick up the spilled items. Ethan and Jack greeted Kite. After Kite's response,

Jack asked Ethan to excuse them for a moment. Footsteps shuffled closer to where Mary crouched.

Jack was probably about to whisper something sweet to Kite. Mary knew she should let them know that she was there. That would be the right thing to do. But she couldn't make herself do it. She wanted to be a part of this romantic moment. She placed her wallet back in her purse and leaned against the wall for balance as she listened.

Kite giggled. "Jack, we were just talking about you."

"We were at my place watching the game, so I thought I'd tag along." He cleared his throat and lowered his voice. "I also wanted to let you know there's an issue with the DeMint case."

"Issue? I closed that case weeks ago. Mr. DeMint is not cheating on his wife."

Uh-oh. This wasn't Jack and Kite whispering sweet nothings. They were

discussing a case. She grabbed the purses and was about to stand when Jack continued.

"Your investigation showed that Mr. DeMint was a volunteer for Gideon's Club, the one hosted by that tiny church on Main Street. She thinks that her husband has been brainwashed by them. She wants you to find out if they're a cult."

Of all the nonsense … Mary stood and plopped her fist on one hip. "A cult?"

Kite jumped. "Mary, what are you—"

"I'm sorry. My purse fell."

She looked around the room. Ethan waited patiently by the door. Christianna and Windy were still in the living area, but they were having a quiet conversation of their own. The rest of the ladies were in the kitchen.

Mary lowered her voice. "I heard what you said about Gideon's Club." She placed both purses on her shoulder and lowered her voice even further. "Our dad's been friends with the pastor of that church since I was a baby. I know I've been gone a long time, but I also know that they're still friends. There's no way that church is a cult. Who would say such a thing?"

"Mary," Jack glanced around the room before facing her. "You can't tell anyone what you just heard. Not even your dad."

"What? I'm going to let my dad know, Jack. He has to warn his friend."

Jack tightened his jaw. "Mary, you can't."

Of course she couldn't. If Mrs. DeMint found out about this breach of confidentiality, the legal fallout would be tremendous. She nodded her agreement, but once again, the small town she'd longed to return to had disappointed her. Why would someone set out to try to destroy a church that had been a blessing to the community for almost a hundred years?

Mary said her good-byes, then followed Jack, Kite, Ethan, and Chrissy to the front porch. Ever since she'd been back home, it had been one chaotic moment after another. Granted, she'd been a huge part of all of that by rocking the town with the news of her return, but there was also the situation with Michael Kildare and his family trying to harm Chrissy, Barry King's adult children and their hatred toward Priscilla, the decades-long entangled web involving Lydia, Eve, Dinah, and Philip. And now someone was trying to dig up dirt on her dad's best friend.

She waved good-bye to Jack and Kite as she and Chrissy walked toward Ethan's car. As he drove along the streets, Mary looked out the passenger window. The outside of the town looked exactly how she remembered it. She couldn't say the same about the people in it.

She wiped at a tear. This was not the reunion she'd dreamed about over the years. She was beyond grateful that she'd been reunited with her family and friends, and she'd never take that for granted. Her meeting with the FBI tomorrow morning was a staunch reminder that not everybody was given that chance.

But still … something was missing. She'd always dreamed that when she returned to the place from where she was taken, that something would … click. Like pieces of a puzzle coming together. That she'd feel safe … at home.

But she didn't feel safe.

And she didn't feel at home.

She wiped at another tear.

Her dream had been fulfilled, but she'd been reminded daily that real life wasn't like her dreams. Dreams ended with happy endings.

And she wasn't sure that this one would.

Chapter Thirty-Six

Kite's weapon was inside her purse. She didn't need it, but knew it would probably be best to secure it. She opened the desk drawer, removed her office keys from the purse inside, then nudged the drawer shut with her foot and locked it.

She glanced at her watch and stifled a sharp word. It was almost ten. Lauren DeMint would be there any minute. She was the last person Kite wanted to deal with this morning. Jack's birthday was coming up and she and J.S.—short for Jack's shadow, the teenaged intern who admired Jack and followed him everywhere when he was at the office—had been secretly planning a backyard BBQ blast for him. She'd rather be doing that than meeting with Lauren. Her personal vendetta against Gideon's Club and their host church already had Mary stirred up and upset.

She closed her eyes and prayed for patience.

A knock at the door interrupted her prayer. "Come in."

Lauren entered and sat in the chair across from Kite's desk. Her blond hair was pulled tightly into a bun that rested on top of her head like a sentry. Her gray eyes matched her blazer, and they looked directly across the desktop. "Is your first name really Kite?"

She nodded.

Lauren chuckled. "Your parents were fans of cannabis, I bet. Or perhaps LSD?"

Kite narrowed her eyes. "How may I help you, Mrs. DeMint?"

She lifted her chin. "Straight to the point. I like that." She crossed one leg over the other. "The last time we met, you said that there wasn't any evidence of my husband cheating on me. But he still disappears every Tuesday night."

"I showed you everything when we went over the case file, and that included where he was going."

"Gideon's Club. Faith Church. Six p.m. to nine p.m."

"Then why are we here?"

"We're here to solve a problem." She twisted her lips and paused. The red lipstick she wore was bold and contrasted beautifully against her fair skin. What a shame. Beautiful on the outside. Ugly as sin on the inside.

"Normally, my David is so … obedient. We've been married for seven years and, when I tell him to stop doing something, he stops. But when I told him to stop volunteering at that church, he refused." She shrugged. "Something has to be done."

Kite folded her arms across her middle. "Something like what?"

"I've visited that church several times over the past couple of weeks. I wanted to make sure it wasn't some cult trying to keep my David away from me. I talked with the pastor, his family, the staff, and the volunteers. I even went through several of their background checks. Nothing. The church and the people who run it are on the up and up."

"Again." Kite let out an annoyed breath. "Why are we here, Mrs. DeMint?"

"We're here because no one is that squeaky clean. Unfortunately, my job is too time consuming for me to look into this further. *I'm* here because I need to find something on the pastor of that church. My David respects him. Looks up to him. I need a reason for him not to. *You're* here because you're going to help me create that reason."

This time, it was Kite who let out a chuckle. "Excuse me?"

"You're going to create a file on this pastor. Then you'll toss in some phony photographs of him walking into a motel with a hooker or something. I'll tell David that your team found something on him while investigating another client. We'll then set up an appointment, and you'll show him the bogus file. Case closed."

Kite leaned back against her office chair and counted to ten. She wasn't going to ask Mrs. DeMint if she was serious. Her demeanor already told her that she was.

Who in the blazes did she think she was talking to? Kite continued to count. Not only because she was angry, but also because she was offended. Did this woman honestly think that she'd jeopardize her job, and Jack's livelihood—not to mention his reputation, over a lie? A lie that she wanted *her* to create? The audacity. And as if lying weren't bad enough, she wanted her to concoct a lie about a beloved pastor in their community. A pastor who'd sacrificed much to help other people. Obviously, this woman didn't know who she was dealing with.

Kite pushed her chair back and stood. "Have a nice day, Mrs. DeMint."

"Oh." She uncrossed her legs. "Is there a problem?"

"There is if you think I'm going to commit a crime for you."

"I don't think it, I know it, Kite." She bit off her name like you'd bite off a piece of licorice. "Because if you don't, your twin will pay the price."

Did she just threaten her sister?

Lauren leaned forward. "While taking down the Kildare family, Windy's name came up a *lot*. I have enough witnesses and corroborating evidence to send her away for a long time." She pointed to Kite's desk. "An hour or two of you playing around on Photoshop and thirty minutes of meeting with me and my David can make all of her troubles go away. We'll meet Wednesday morning, and your dealings with me will be over by noon. After that I'll hand you a legal document stating that my office will not be pursuing charges against Windy Jordan." She stood and straightened her skirt. "I'll need an answer by nine tomorrow night. If you decline, instead of you being rid of me by Wednesday afternoon, your sister's face will be splashed all over the news, and her arrest will be one that'll go down in Habakkuk history. I know Windy well enough to know how she'd react to my office linking her to the Kildare crime family. She won't go down without a fight—a literal one, and I plan to have the local news teams there to cover every bit of it."

She tilted her head and smiled. "Windy could end up in prison for a very long time. But I'm not after her. I have all of the Kildare brothers, and that's enough for me. Everyone in town knows that Windy and Michael were joined at the hip, so persuading a jury that she was also his partner in crime will be easy. Too easy. But you want to know what would be easier? A few hours of your time for your sister's freedom. By Wednesday night, this entire conversation could be just a bad memory. I'll expect to hear from you soon." She walked to the door and placed her hand on the knob.

"I'll give you my decision now." Kite met her at the door and removed her hand. "I said I'm not going to do it, and I meant it. Blackmailing me won't make a difference. If you're going to bring charges against Windy, then do it." She twisted the knob and opened the door. "I'm sure you'll be able to see yourself the rest of the way out."

Lauren glared at her. "I hope Windy likes the color orange."

"We'll get her the best lawyer in town."

"I'm the best lawyer in town."

"We'll go over your head."

She snickered. "To the D.A.? Good luck with that."

"I was talking about God."

"I don't believe in God."

"Your point?"

"Obviously, Windy doesn't believe in God either, unless parading around with known criminals is in the Bible." She raised an eyebrow. "Or perhaps I have that wrong. Maybe it's God who doesn't believe in Windy."

Kite threw the door open wider. "Good day, Mrs. DeMint."

She lifted her chin and walked out. Kite slammed the door behind her and took a deep breath to slow her racing heart. She hoped that she'd called Lauren's bluff. She hoped she'd come across as brave and immovable. How she was able to keep her hands from shaking while the assistant D.A. talked so casually about sending Windy to prison, she had no idea.

She sank to her desk chair and concentrated on not hyperventilating. This was a nightmare. A total nightmare. What in the world had Windy gotten them into?

She had to think.

There was no way she was going to throw an innocent man under the bus, but there had to be some other way to stop that … woman … from pressing charges. She couldn't let Windy go to prison. Kite would never survive it.

With everything Windy knew about Michael, neither would she.

Kite snatched her cell phone off the desk, speed-dialed Windy, then clicked it off. The last person she needed to talk to right now was her sister. She'd pick up on the panic in Kite's voice and get upset. And if she told her about Lauren's threat, Windy would set off on a path that they'd never come back from.

Windy could be dangerous when she lost her temper, but it was always a targeted anger. She took it out on those who'd directly hurt her in some way. Never on random people. The Kildares had been linked to murder. That wasn't Windy's style. She'd beat and maim someone, but she'd never kill them.

Kite bristled as she wondered about what type of charges Lauren had up her sleeve.

Or even if she really had any. More than likely she was using Windy's known relationship with the Kildares to entice Kite to do her bidding. She had no doubt that Lauren would take it as far as she had to, just to get her to lie so that 'her David' could spend Tuesday nights at home with her.

Ruthless.

And just last night, after speaking with Eve for hours, Windy had given her life to Christ. Twenty-four hours haven't even passed and she was already being tested.

Kite only had the chance to speak to Windy briefly over breakfast. They were both still tired from all the fun and drama of the night before, so it was hard to tell, but she'd thought Windy had seemed different. She'd talked about how it was time for her to do some soul-searching and make some changes in her life. What happened after that, Kite had no idea. She could've studied the chapters in the Bible that Eve had highlighted or she could've left the house and met up with Anthony, like they'd planned to do the night before.

Either way, she still needed time and prayer for her faith to grow. Not a prison sentence.

The office phone rang. Kite hoped it was Jack. Maybe he'd be able to help her figure out what to do.

"Eagle Eye Investigative Services. This is Kite. How may I help you?"

"Hi, Mrs. Tanner. This is Jack Shadow."

Kite yanked the headband from her head and ran her fingers through her hair. Not the Jack she'd hoped for. "Hi, J.S. What can I do for you?"

"You asked me to call during my class break, remember? Said you wanted me to take down some notes on ideas you had for Jack's party?"

She smacked her forehead and grimaced. Her fingers were wet. Her scalp must've been damp. Goodness. She was more nervous than she'd thought. She had to figure out what to do about the Lauren and Windy situation quick. "Thanks for calling, J.S. I lost track of time and forgot. My apologies, but something's come up, and I need to take care of it right away. Do you know where Jack went after he dropped you off at school? He wasn't in his office when I got here."

"He went to pick up his mom and his sister Rhoda. Said he was going to take them to breakfast before going to the office."

She nodded. He had mentioned that the night before. "Thanks, J.S. I'll wait another hour or so, then try his cell."

"Mrs. Tanner?"

The respectful way he referred to her made her long for her late husband. What she wouldn't give to be able to pick up the phone and call Neth right now. "Yes?"

"Is everything okay? You sound ... upset."

Well, it was a good thing she hadn't called Windy. If a sixteen-year-old boy whom she'd only known for a few months, could pick up on that, Windy would've been all over it. "Everything's fine. Or, it will be. I don't know. I'm sorry, J.S., I have to take care of something right now."

"You should call Jack."

"I will, I'm just going to—"

"Call him now. He loves you. If you're in trouble, he'd want you to call him right away."

She opened her mouth to respond, then closed it.

"Call him. Whatever the problem is, he'll be able to fix it."

She smiled at the young man's reassuring words. "Okay. I will."

"Good. He won't let you down."

"Thank you." She tapped the plastic headband against

the desk. "And I promise I'll get back to you about the party, okay?"

"Okay."

When he clicked off his phone, she placed hers back on the receiver. Love? Did he just say that Jack loved her? Jack had never made it a secret that he had feelings for her, but … love?

She leaned her head back against the chair and closed her eyes to hold back the tears. This was why she'd resisted getting close to Jack. Pretty soon, he'd be asking for more than she could give him.

She could never love another.

Neth would always have her heart.

If Neth were here, he'd take control of the situation.

She squeezed her eyes tighter. But no matter how much she wished it, she'd never be able to see his face, hear his voice, or seek his counsel again.

And right now, she needed help. Jack *was* here. He was also well connected politically. In a matter of minutes, he'd be able to connect her to the people she'd need to talk to about Windy's situation. She retrieved her cell phone, dialed the first two numbers and stopped. Before she called him, she needed to speak with Someone else.

She pushed the chair back, got on her knees, and folded her hands on top of her desk.

Chapter Thirty-Seven

Priscilla stepped onto the porch of her mother's small craftsman-style home and lifted her hand to knock.

"Well, well, well. Guess who finally decided to show up."

Priscilla took a step back. Was this really happening? Had she finally been able to gather enough courage to knock on her mother's door? The furrowed brows and pinched lips on the beautifully rounded brown face that glared at her assured her that she had. What a mistake. Priscilla bowed her head and mentally prepared herself to be beaten with the emotional stick her mother had the ability to swing at any given moment.

"Mama, I—"

"Don't 'Mama,' me." Her mother pushed the door open wider, then moved her slight frame to the side. "I haven't seen or heard from you in months. Not a phone call, a letter, or a postcard to let me know that you were even still alive. Someone who keeps that kind of distance doesn't have the right to call me Mama. It's Miss Mabel to you."

Priscilla hadn't even stepped over the threshold, and the beating had already started. But her mother was right. She hadn't returned one of her mother's phone calls or seen her in almost a year. Mama had every right to be angry. Priscilla lifted her head and locked eyes with her mom. "You're right. And I'm here to apologize, to explain, and to share some news with you. Good news. But I'd rather do that inside and not on the porch. May I please come inside, Miss Mabel?"

Her mother narrowed her eyes. "Ditch the sarcasm. I'm not in the mood." She hitched her thumb toward the foyer. "I'm having breakfast. You want to talk to me, I'll be at the kitchen table."

Priscilla stepped in and closed the door behind her. The scents of pine and orange greeted her as she made her way to the kitchen. The wooden floors, banisters, and doors gleamed. She let out a quiet chuckle. Some things never changed.

Mama made her way to the stove. "I have extra, if you need breakfast."

Priscilla sat at the table and glanced at her mother's plate. Half a waffle and a boiled egg were on one side of it and a strip of bacon on the other. Next to the plate was a small bowl of blueberries, a mug half-filled with black coffee, and a mason jar containing maple syrup.

Priscilla licked her lips. No one made waffles like her mother. Or had a better tasting homemade syrup—made with maple, vanilla, and a host of other ingredients Mama had vowed to never share. Priscilla had traveled to a lot of hole-in-the-wall joints and high-end restaurants in the Midwest and on both coasts. Not once did she come across waffles or a syrup that rivaled her mom's.

"Just one waffle, please."

Her mother picked up a glass mixing bowl. "There's enough batter left for two. Might as well use it all." She picked up a small measuring cup that was a quarter full of what looked to be liquid gold. She poured it into the mixture and then picked up a whisk before plugging in her waffle iron.

Two Belgian-sized waffles would be all Priscilla would eat today. She and Barry still hadn't decided on whether they'd have an actual wedding, but she didn't want to take any chances. She planned on looking stunning in her wedding dress.

"The days of worrying about your figure should be long gone."

Priscilla's head jerked back. She'd forgotten how well her mother could sense what she was thinking. She smiled. Once again, some things never changed.

"I've missed you, Mama. I really have."

Her mother turned and faced her. "Have you now? Because I haven't noticed."

Priscilla's cheeks burned. How could she make her mother understand? "I've … wanted to pick up the phone or stop by many times. I just couldn't. I was too—"

"Ashamed?"

Here it comes. Priscilla dipped her head. "Yes."

"You oughtta be. After reading what I read in those journals, you should be downright disgusted. That was not the behavior of the daughter *I* knew, the daughter *I* raised. How do you even look at yourself in the mirror? How did you sleep at night knowing you were involved in some of the seediest acts known to man?"

The words stung. "I wish I had an answer for you, Mama—"

"Miss Mabel."

"I wish I had an answer for you, Miss Mabel, but I don't. I'm trying to figure a lot of that out now."

Her mother tossed the whisk on the counter, then placed both hands on her hips. "What does that mean? You're seeing some type of mental doctor or something?"

"No. Not yet. That may eventually be a part of the process, I don't know."

"Then what are you talking about?"

"I have someone very close to me who's been pointing me in the right direction."

Her mother's face tightened. "If they're not pointing you in the direction of Christ—"

"He is."

Mabel's face softened, then she turned back towards the counter. "Who is this person?"

Priscilla placed her hand over her left shirt pocket. She'd dropped her wedding ring in there earlier. She didn't want her mom to see it without an explanation first. "I came here to say I'm sorry, Mama. I'm sorry for everything that I've done. I'm sorry for hurting you, and for everything you've had to endure because of me. I can only imagine how difficult it was for you to read those journals. And as bad as my imaginings were, I know they didn't come close to how you actually felt reading them. For years, you've had to listen to rumors about me. I've caused a lot of stress and worry, and I can't believe I did that to you. You worked multiple jobs after Daddy died just to make sure that me and

Penelope had everything we needed to succeed in life. You worked six days a week and still made sure we went to church on Sundays and did our homework. You were Mama, doctor, teacher, counselor, spiritual advisor, and more.

"When you said that you didn't raise me that way—you were right. You didn't. But somewhere along the line, I began to see things a little hazier than you did, than the way I was raised. Suddenly, everything wasn't so clear cut, and before I knew it, I had no boundaries. I did what I wanted, when I wanted, regardless of who I hurt. I've disappointed you as a daughter, and for that I am so sorry." Priscilla sucked in a breath, then continued. "But I also want you to know that I'm not that person anymore. Jacob sent you those journals because he was mad that I broke things off with him and pursued a relationship with someone else. That relationship was the start of a new life for me in ways that I never could've imagined. It didn't start off that way, but it ended up being a blessing. And ..." Priscilla reached into her pocket and placed the ring on her finger. "I ended up marrying that man. Before you say anything, there was no wedding, just him and me and a couple of close friends witnessing our commitment to one another. I wanted you there more than anything, but it all happened so fast. I had no idea that I'd be married by the end of that day, but I knew if I didn't go through with it then, I never would, and I'd lose out on one of the most amazing gifts that God had placed before me. I hope you understand."

Mabel mumbled something under her breath before she turned around. She glanced at the ring on Priscilla's finger, then looked up at her. "What's his name?"

Priscilla swallowed and straightened her shoulders.

"Barry King."

"Priscilla!"

"I know. I know. Trust me, I've heard all about why I shouldn't have married him. His daughter and his son made sure of that. But Mama, this isn't about me taking advantage of a widower and trying to take all of his money. It started out that way, yes, but not anymore. I truly love Barry, Mama. I really do."

The waffle iron sizzled. The same waffle iron that Priscilla knew had helped make breakfast for the entire family for as long as she could remember. And according to her mother, it was the same iron her own mother had used to make waffles for her. Since Alexandria, Penelope's daughter, was a frequent visitor to her grandmother's table, that same iron had now fed three generations, and created a million memories. How her mom kept it working after all these years, she didn't know.

Mabel reached for the mixing bowl, whisked it, poured batter into the iron, and closed the lid. She placed her right hand on her hip as she watched the iron. "Priscilla, I knew Mr. King's late wife, Edith, pretty well. We were close. When you say he's a good man, that's not hard to believe, because I know that to be true." She flipped the iron before turning around. "But what is hard for me to believe is that your intentions are pure. I've read your journals. Words written by your own hands. If you're using Mr. King just to get access to his money, get up and leave my house now."

Priscilla shook her head. "Mama, haven't you listened to anything I've said? I'm not that person anymore. I honestly and truthfully love Barry. Please believe me."

Mabel grabbed a plate from the cabinet, placed the

waffle on it then poured more mixture into the iron. "I heard you. Just finding it hard to believe you."

"Then don't believe me. After breakfast, pack a bag and come stay with us for a few weeks. I miss you, Mama, and there's so much more I want to share with you, things I've been dying to talk with you about. Come judge our relationship for yourself. Witness with your own eyes if we're the real thing or not."

Mabel flipped another waffle on the plate and reached for the butter dish. "How are Elizabeth and Lolalana?"

Priscilla winced at the abrupt change in conversation, but wasn't surprised by the question. Despite being aware of their backgrounds, her mother always had a soft spot for Elizabeth Decker and Lolalana Bojali—known by everyone else as Diamond Liz and Lola.

"Liz is doing great. We needed witnesses for the ceremony, so she and Lola and Lola's new husband were there. They're both doing well. Lola and Ram still act like newlyweds, and Liz still loves the single life."

Mabel nodded, her back still toward Priscilla. "When you became friends with those two, I figured there was some truth to how you made your living, but I still hoped that my little girl hadn't gotten herself involved in anything like that. Those girls came from difficult situations and saw what they did as a way to get out of them. But you experienced none of that, yet those journals confirmed my fears. Why did you get involved in that lifestyle, Priscilla? I don't understand it."

"I'm not that person anymore, Mama."

Mabel turned around and pinched her lips together.

"Fine. I'm not that person anymore, Miss Mabel."

Her mother slid the plate of waffles and melted butter in

front of her. Priscilla reached for the syrup and drowned her waffles with it. Her mother handed her a knife and fork, and after savoring the first bite of buttery goodness, Priscilla continued. "Lola no longer engages in that lifestyle either. She's been out of the game for almost two years now. I've seen first-hand the changes that being married to a godly man can bring. She's still Lola, full of life and endless energy, but she's more confident now in who she is. She's made peace with her past. Honestly, she's been my inspiration. I'll never tell her that 'cuz she'll never let me live it down or stop trying to drag me to church. But she's been ministering to me without her even knowing it, by her actions. She also has this … light from the inside. I want that, too."

Her mother sat across from her. "Ram Boaz is a good man. But the Light inside of Lola didn't come from her being married to him."

Priscilla cut off another square and placed it in her mouth.

"And it won't come from you being married to Barry either."

Priscilla swallowed. "I know. But I think he's leading me in the right direction."

Mabel opened her mouth, closed it, then walked to the counter and poured a cup of coffee. She handed the mug to Priscilla.

After taking a sip of the super strong brew, Priscilla continued. "Liz, on the other hand, is perfectly content with the way she's living her life. I don't see her changing that anytime soon. If ever."

Her mother shook her head. "There's still a lot that she's

dealing with."

"I know." Nine-year-old Liz had been found chained and shackled in her parent's attic. Priscilla hadn't known Liz then, but she'd never forgotten the images the reporters had showed of her rail-thin arms and legs and how they'd been covered in rat bites. "But she never talks about it."

"That's what I was sayin'." Mabel plucked a blueberry from the bowl in front of her and plopped it in her mouth. "Sweet little thing doesn't realize that by living the lifestyle she's living, she's still chained."

Priscilla placed her fork down. She'd never thought of it that way. Immediately after that news report, Liz disappeared for several years. Everyone had been told that she'd been sent to live with relatives in another state. She didn't return to Habakkuk until she was in her early twenties. But there was no trace of the undernourished, rodent-bitten little girl who'd had chain marks on her wrist. The Liz who returned had skin that was as smooth as silk, and she had an abundance of charm and personality to match. She never said where she'd been, only that it *wasn't* to live with relatives.

"Fine, I'll go."

Priscilla looked across the table at her mom. "Go where?"

"With you. To your home. You're right. The only way I'll ever truly know if your relationship with Barry is real is for me to see it for myself."

Priscilla hoped her face didn't show the pain from the dagger in her heart. Her own words were now no longer good enough. Part of her wanted to rage against her mother. Let her know how hurtful it was that she'd put stock in what other people had said about her, but doubted the words that came from her daughter's lips. She wanted to rage about the fact that she now had to prove herself to her mother.

Her own mother.

After a deep breath, she realized that as much as she wanted to rail, the truth was that it wasn't her mother who'd eroded that mother-daughter bond of trust. It was her, and her own foolish actions. Besides, her mother had said that she'd never fully believed the rumors. Which was news to Priscilla, because she'd always acted like she had. "It'll be an honor to have you in our home, Mama … I'm sorry, Miss Mabel. It really would." And none of that other stuff mattered now. She needed to rebuild that bond. Even if it meant eating a whole lot of crow.

Mabel snatched a piece of bacon from the plate next to her and broke it in two. "If we're gonna be spending as much time together as you say, I guess you can call me Mama."

Priscilla smiled.

"But if you leave me in a corner somewhere while you and Barry gallivant all across town, I'm revoking that privilege."

"I'm not going to do that."

"'Cause if you are, just let me know now, and I'll keep my black behind at home."

"I understand, Mama."

"I'm not kidding, Priscilla Ann."

"Neither am I."

Mabel bit into the bacon and took a sip of her coffee and frowned.

Priscilla stood. "Give me your cup, Mama. I'll refresh it for you."

"Do you want me to go with you or not?"

Priscilla blinked. "Of course, I do."

"Then stop worrying about my coffee and get my travel bag. It's in the hallway closet."

Priscilla turned toward the hallway.

"And don't get that old raggedy one your daddy gave me when we got married. Get that nice new animal print one that Penelope brought me. If I'm going to stay at Barry's King estate, I at least want to look chic."

"It's my estate as well." Priscilla mumbled the statement under her breath, hoping that her mother's antennae ears didn't pick up on it. Saying that out loud would send the wrong message, but it still pained her that her mother couldn't just be happy for her.

Priscilla opened the closet door and rolled out the travel bag her mom had referred to. Wow. Penelope had spared no expense. The last time Priscilla bought her mom something nice, she'd returned it saying that she didn't want gifts purchased with bedroom money. But Penny's gifts she accepted. No questions asked.

She hoped the next two weeks would change that. Whether her mother ever believed that she truly loved Barry didn't matter. Barry knew it, and she was okay with that.

She needed this time with Mama. She wanted it. They'd missed out on so much of each other's lives this past year. She'd missed her Mama being there. They rarely agreed on anything, but Mama had always been there when she needed her the most.

She grabbed the handle, but before rolling it along the hallway to the bedroom, she stopped and listened. Mama was praying. The prayer that she was praying left both faith and fear in Priscilla's heart.

The next two weeks were going to be very interesting. Very.

Chapter Thirty-Eight

Lydia had no idea how she was supposed to return to her humble dwellings after living in a luxury suite for the past couple of weeks. She tied the belt on her thick, white bathrobe. The Bluebird had everything. A full kitchen, two spacious bedrooms, a corner office, and an en suite that was big enough to hold the entire main floor of her home.

She sat on the bed and gazed at the amazing view of the Ozark Mountains. Beautiful as the view was, it couldn't bring about the peace of mind that she'd hoped for.

Today was the day she and Dinah had agreed to talk about her father and anything else they needed to share that they hadn't already. Dinah was scheduled to leave for a business trip that was only supposed to last a couple of days but had been extended to a couple of weeks.

Though they'd spent every day dealing with past hurts and going over their lives, Dinah said that she still sensed that her mother was holding back on some things. Lydia had hoped that when she'd agreed to share what she knew about Dinah's father, that Dinah would let it go. But she didn't.

She said she'd still sensed there was something more.

There was.

Telling Dinah that Philip was her father would upset her, but Lydia was ready to share that information, and she'd prepared herself mentally to do that.

The other secret she'd hoped to carry to her grave.

She'd never planned on telling Dinah about her terminal diagnosis. Though with every doctor visit, it was looking less and less terminal, still, that was the official diagnosis. Things were going great between her and Dinah, and the last thing she wanted was pity from her youngest daughter. It was bad enough that her other girls knew, but she needed her connection with Dinah to be true and not based on sympathy.

She pulled out her Bible and tried to read the next chapter in her study plan. She shut the book minutes later and returned it to the drawer next to the bed. She loved the Word but couldn't focus.

She slid to her knees and clasped her hands together. A knock at the door interrupted the beginning of her prayer. She sighed. "Who is it?"

"It's Blackwell, ma'am."

She stood, tightened her robe, and the bath towel that she'd wrapped around her wet hair. She walked to the door and opened it slightly. "Good morning, Blackwell."

"Good morning, Ms. Dooley. Will you be having breakfast in the dining area this morning?"

She hadn't been to the café, bistro, or other dining areas in a couple of days. No doubt the kitchen staff mentioned that to Dinah, and she'd sent Blackwell up. "No, but I would like to take lunch in my room around noon, if that's okay."

Blackwell pulled a notebook and pen from his pocket.

"If you know what you'd like, I can take the order down to the kitchen."

She nodded. "I absolutely loved the grilled chicken in the sprouted grain tortilla that I had last week, and I'd love to have that again. Oh, and if they could add an extra dollop of that delicious spread they put inside of it, then that would be great."

"Would you like for me to ask them what's in the spread?"

"No. Probably best I don't know how the sauce is made."

Blackwell chuckled. "I understand. Anything else, ma'am?"

"A bowl of carrot soup would be nice."

He nodded. "Around noon, you said?"

"Yes, and some chocolate chia pudding for dessert. I haven't eaten in three days, so I'll be starving around that time."

He blinked. "Is everything okay? Do I need to call a doctor?"

"No, I'm fine. Just been on a spiritual fast."

"Oh." He smiled. "My grandmother used to do that."

"So did mine."

"I can bring up some fruit if you'd like. That was something my grandmother always requested after she'd fasted for a while."

"Yeah, mine did too, but no. I'll be fine. Thank you."

He tucked the pen and pad back into his jacket's pocket. "I'll make sure that your lunch'll be here at noon."

"Thank you."

He bowed, then made his way to the glass elevators.

Lydia closed the door and glanced at the massive wall

clock in the next room. She tossed the hair towel onto the bed, then stepped into the large, circular closet to get dressed.

In the bathroom, she brushed her hair and took another look at the clothes she'd chosen. The long, denim skirt and brightly colored tee fit her mood perfectly. Usually, after she and Dinah had their morning talks, she'd run a few errands, but today, she'd stay in and read a book. If everything went well with Dinah, that was.

If things didn't go well, for companionship, she'd take Lola up on her invitation to go bowling. Lydia grinned. Bowling with Lola. That would be a sight to see for sure.

The door to the suite clicked open. "Mom?"

"I'm in the bathroom, sweetie. Be right out."

After another quick brush through her hair, she tucked the sides behind her ears, then glanced at the make-up on the counter. No. If she went somewhere later, then she'd apply some.

"I brought up a cup of hot tea for you."

"Thanks." Lydia made her way to the tiny but ridiculously high kitchen table that had been placed in front of a large picture window. She climbed onto the chair across from Dinah and looked out. Several people had already taken to the lake. Many were on jet-ski's. Others were in paddle boats or taking in the morning sun along the shore.

"I ran into Blackwell on the way up. He mentioned that you'd been on a fast. I hope tea is okay. I didn't add anything to it. It's peach flavored herbal tea."

Lydia lifted the lid off the warm to-go cup and inhaled. "This smells wonderful. Yes, tea is okay. Thank you."

Dinah smiled and sipped her coffee. "Well, do you think

we're ready to do this?"

"Without arguing or getting mad at each other? I hope so."

"Don't worry about that. No matter what you have to tell me, I promised myself that I wouldn't throw a tantrum, and that I'd respond like a grown-up."

"Then you're a stronger woman than I am, because that is not how I initially responded."

Lydia flashed back to when she'd confirmed that Dinah was Philip's daughter. She'd screamed and tossed the box of memento's against the wall at her parent's house. She then snatched a picture of her younger self from the floor and yelled at her for being so blazingly stupid.

She cleared her throat. "Before we discuss your father, there's something else I need to tell you."

Dinah raised a brow.

Lydia lifted the cup of tea to her lips. It was still too hot to drink. She removed the lid and placed it on the table. "Almost a year ago, the doctors discovered I had a brain tumor."

Dinah's hands flew to her mouth.

"It's okay, and I'm fine. Or at least I will be. The diagnosis was terminal, but recent scans have shown miraculous improvements. I believe God is healing me. But if entering into my eternal rest is a part of that healing, then I'm okay with that, too."

"No, Mom, don't say that. Don't you dare say that. Not now. Not after how I've treated you. Not after all the years I've let go by. Please, please don't tell me this is ending before we can even get started."

Lydia grabbed Dinah's hands. "Do I look like I'm dying

to you?"

"No, but—"

"Do I look sick?"

"No."

"Then that's what I want you to focus on. When I say I feel great, I mean it. I feel better now than I have in years. I'm following the advice of my medical team, and I'm also under the care of a group of holistic doctors. Together, we've come up with a plan that everyone approved of ... well, mostly approved of, and I've been feeling fantastic as a result. But as much as I trust and respect them all, I follow what God asks me to do first. The medical team thinks I'm going bonkers and the holistic group winces every time I don't follow their plan to the T, but none of them can dispute the evidence."

Dinah tightened their grip. "But don't you think—?"

"I think that's all that I want to say about it right now. Your sisters have known from the beginning, and none of them agree on how I'm approaching this. They've scoured the internet and consulted with some of the best specialists and alternative medicine doctors from coast to coast. They've pointed out all the pros and cons of what I'm doing. Eventually, I told them the only thing I wanted from them was to pray and to have faith in my decisions. It took a while, but they've settled down."

Dinah's eyes blinked rapidly. "They knew? My sisters *knew* you were seriously ill and didn't tell me?" Her voice rose on the last word.

"They wanted to, Dinah. All of them, but I begged them not to."

"But why?" She wiped at a tear on her cheek. "Why

didn't you want me to know? To punish me for not wanting a relationship with you? So I'd have seventeen years of regret if you died? So my daughter would know that *I* was the reason she didn't get to meet her grandmother?"

"No! That's not why at all."

"Then why!"

"Because I didn't want to put any additional pressure on you. I knew about the divorce and the custody battle and how hard you were working to open up the new additions here at Bliss. But mostly, it was because you had every right to your anger toward me. I didn't want you to feel like you had to repair our relationship before I ran out of time."

Dinah rested against her chair and stared out at the lake. After a few minutes, she grabbed her coffee and took a sip. "If you'd died, and I'd found out that you'd kept it from me that you were sick, I would've hated you forever."

Lydia nodded. "That was a risk I was willing to take."

Dinah turned back toward the window.

"It was a risk I was willing to take because I'd already hurt you so much, Dinah. I didn't … I couldn't hurt you anymore. My heart just wouldn't let me. I know that sounds ridiculous because you would've been hurt either way, but I really did think it was the best thing to do at the time."

"Would you have ever told me?"

Lydia lowered her head. "No."

Dinah gasped. Lydia raised her head and continued. "I didn't want it to ruin what was going on between us. We've traveled some rough roads the past couple of weeks, but we've muddled through and made it to the other side. We were both so proud of that." Lydia shrugged. "I didn't want to create any new wounds. We loved, we smiled, we laughed, we forgave. We were happy. I wanted our renewed relationship to be based on those things. Not fear and not regret."

Dinah ran her fingers through her hair. "I knew you were hiding something from me, but I had no idea it was this." She sucked in a breath, then blew it out. "However, if I was to be completely honest, I'd have to admit that as hurt as I am, the truth is you made the right decision. A year ago, I was not in a good place. If I'd known about your diagnosis back then, it would've really messed me up.

"I'd completely failed as a wife. There was nothing wrong with my marriage that a little time and attention wouldn't've fixed. But I was so focused on Bliss that I took Ralph for granted. I thought he'd always be there, you know? But apparently, everyone has their breaking point, and a year ago he found his. I was in a very dark place after that. If I'd found out then what you just told me now, I'm pretty sure it would've pushed me over the edge."

Lydia swallowed. "You have no idea how glad I am to hear that I didn't add to your distress."

Dinah looked intensely at Lydia. "But you're okay, right? You really are doing better and not just telling me that so I won't worry?"

"I really am doing okay."

"Promise you'll keep me updated. I want to know about every appointment, every visit, every meeting, every consult—"

"I get it." Lydia laughed.

"I mean like, *every* single one."

Lydia nodded.

Dinah extended the little finger on her right hand. "Pinky

promise?"

Lydia wrapped her pinky finger around Dinah's. "Promise."

"And now," Dinah leaned her head back and shook it. "I guess I'm ready for part two."

"Are you sure?" Lydia separated their fingers and rubbed the back of her neck. "Because this one's a doozy."

Dinah nodded. "I'm ready. I've been waiting a long time to know the name of my father."

Lydia picked up the lid to her tea and stared at it. "Your father's name is Philip."

Dinah wrapped her hands around her coffee cup. "Philip. That's a good name. A nice name. Sounds like he'd be a nice guy." She took another sip of her coffee. "Do you know his last name? Or the last place he may have lived? I've been told even something as simple as a birthdate would be helpful in my search."

"I know all of those things. But you won't need to search for him. He lives right here in Habakkuk."

Dinah's eyes widened. "He's still alive then?"

"Oh, yeah."

"Are you … in contact with him?"

"Kinda, sorta."

Dinah smiled and her eyes grew wider. "So you have information? Current information? Like, where he lives, where he works, if he's married, if I have any other siblings? If he knows about me …?"

"I know all of that, yes." Lydia placed the lid back on her cup and took a sip. She savored the tea for a moment, then put the cup down.

"There's something else, isn't it?" Dinah narrowed her

eyes. "Something not good."

Lydia tightened her lips and nodded.

"Is he like a serial killer or something?"

If killing the hopes and dreams of everyone you came in contact with was a crime, then yes. He was. "It's just that you already know him. You've met him. You know his wife." Lydia fought back tears. "There are no children."

Dinah furrowed her brow and looked down at the table. Lydia couldn't see her eyes but thought for sure she'd heard wheels turning.

"I've met him. I know his wife. They have no children. His name is Philip." She scratched her head and continued to stare at the table. "I'm sorry, Mom. My mind's coming up blank."

Lydia rubbed the back of her neck again. She hated to do this. She *really* hated to do this. Dinah's entire life was about to change. And not for the better.

"Mom?"

"His last name is Stockton. Eve's husband. Your biological father is Philip Stockton."

Dinah raised her head and stared at Lydia. She didn't blink, and the muscles in her face didn't move. Not even the ones around her mouth. It looked like she'd stopped breathing.

"Dinah, are you okay?"

"Philip *Stockton* is my father?"

"Yes."

"I … I don't understand."

"Years ago, when we were young, before he married Eve, Philip and I had, oh, how should I put it?"

"A relationship?"

"No. It wasn't that. But nevertheless, whatever we had, it resulted in you. Philip Stockton is your father."

"Wait. That would've been shortly after you left high-school. You were on drugs, right?"

"I was."

"Huh." Dinah ran her fingers through her hair again. "Does Eve know?"

"She suspected it. Ever since you were little. She never said anything because she didn't know for sure. But yes, she knows now."

"Does he?"

"I haven't told him, and neither has Eve. We figured we'd let you decide what the next step should be. If he ever suspected it, we have no idea."

The right side of Dinah's face twitched. "I do not like that man, Mom. I'm being respectful of you sitting here, in phrasing it that way. If you weren't here, those are not the words I'd use to express how I really feel about him."

"I'm so sorry, Dinah. I wish I had better news for you. I really do."

"And you're sure it's Philip?"

"I am. However, Eve said she's on board if you'd like to prove it with a DNA test. Just tell her what you need, and she'll get it. They're going through a divorce, but she said there's still enough of his items—clothing, toothbrushes, combs, etc.—at their house for her to pull his DNA from."

Dinah nodded slowly. "Yeah. I'd like to know for certain before I make any decisions. Will that be okay?"

"Absolutely."

She scooted her chair back and stood. "My flight leaves in a few hours. How fast do you think Eve will be able to get me a sample?"

"I don't know. They're meeting today with their lawyers."

"Good." Dinah chuckled. "She deserves so much better."

"Well, don't congratulate her just yet. Philip's had a recent change of heart, and Eve's fallen for his acts before. But she seems stronger this time, so maybe she'll go through with it."

"I hope so." She picked up her coffee cup. "I don't feel comfortable enough to call her just yet. Would you mind asking her for the sample?"

"Not at all."

"Thanks. If she can get me a sample before three o'clock, I'll be able to drop both of our samples off at a lab, before my flight. I'd like to know as soon as possible. Otherwise, I'll drive myself crazy."

"I'll call her."

"Love you, Mom." She reached across the table and gave Lydia a hug. "I still have lots of questions about your health, but since you've made it clear you're not going to answer them, I'll be having several conversations with my sisters. I'll make them fill in the blanks."

"And if I ask you not to do that?"

"I'm not going to listen."

"That's what I figured."

Dinah gave her another quick hug, followed by a kiss on the cheek. "Talk to you later, okay?"

"Okay." Lydia followed her to the door. "And let me know when you get on the plane, and when you land, and when you get on the other plane, and when you arrive at the hotel—"

Dinah laughed. "Okay, I get it." Then she paused and turned toward Lydia. "Remember when I asked to see your phone the other day?"

"Yes."

"I installed an app that'll let you see where I am at any given moment. It also keeps track of Ada, Bethany, and Claudia. Let me see it again."

Lydia gave her the phone. Dinah pointed to an icon on the main screen. "You see this? Just tap it and another screen will pop-up. Then you'll see colorful little dots all in different places. I've labeled each one. When you want to see where we are, tap on a name like this," She tapped the yellow dot labeled Claudia. "See? Right now, Claudia's at Abe's Hardware. She can't tell a screwdriver from a hammer, so I have no idea why she's there, but there she is. My color is red. Just tap that one and you'll be able to see where I'm at in real-time."

"I've never seen anything like this."

"Well, just play around with it a little and you'll get the hang of it. I really do have to go, though. Call me."

"I will."

Lydia closed the door and stared at the phone. What a neat idea. Was she really able to keep track of her family on this? Not only were her daughters on there, but their spouses and her grandchildren were too. Ralph was even on there.

She clicked the screen off and dialed Eve. If only the rest of her life could be like those colorful little circles—where she could see everything at once and be aware of all the moving parts as they were happening.

Eve picked up on the second ring and Lydia told her about Dinah's request. They agreed to meet in the lobby of

Bliss at one o'clock.

Lydia hoped she was wrong. That somehow, someway, Philip was not Dinah's father. But the more she thought about that time in her life, the more she couldn't hold on to that hope. The test would definitely come back positive.

Things ended great with Dinah. Could be because she hoped the DNA would prove her father was someone else. Once that doubt was removed, what would her relationship with her daughter look like then? Dinah *hated* Philip. Would she end up hating her mom, too? For putting her in this situation? For ruining her life? Because that's exactly what Philip would do if he ever found out that Dinah was his daughter.

Lydia tossed her phone on the bed. Would her life ever stop being a mess? Would her past ever stop coming back to haunt her? The doctors said it'd be hard to draw a direct correlation between her history of drug abuse and the tumor, but she wouldn't be surprised if they were connected.

She was okay with her past mistakes only hurting her.

But they weren't.

If only she'd known back then that her loved ones would also have to pay a price. If only she'd listened to the godly wisdom and guidance of her parents instead of resenting them for it. If only she'd taken church and the advice of her youth counselors as seriously as she'd taken the boys and the drugs who'd pursued her.

If only.

But she couldn't do anything about that now. She had to focus on Dinah, because if she didn't handle this situation carefully, it could cause Dinah a lot more harm than good.

And Lydia wasn't about to let that happen.

Chapter Thirty-Nine

Eve sat in one of the over-stuffed brown leather chairs near the elevators and texted Lydia that she was in the lobby. She'd texted earlier to let her know she was on her way with the sample, but Lydia hadn't responded. Odd. Lydia usually responded to messages rather quickly.

If she didn't hear from her soon, she'd make her way up to her suite. Or better yet, she'd ask the lady at the welcome desk to take her to Dinah's office. Dinah had a flight to catch, but Eve wanted to talk with her about Philip before she left the country.

The elevators dinged. Lydia stepped out and rushed toward Eve. "I lost track of the time. Hope you weren't waiting long."

"Just arrived. I'd texted earlier, but you didn't respond."

Lydia sighed. "I turned my phone off. I was deep in prayer for my daughter. I didn't want to be interrupted."

"Dinah?"

"Yeah."

"I thought you said everything went well."

"Oh, it did. I just … wanted to make sure I covered her in prayer. Moving forward knowing that Philip is her dad will not be easy for her."

"I know."

Lydia sat in the chair across from her. "Is that the sample?"

"Yes. And I was able to get a good one, too. Our insurance policies are being renewed so they sent someone out to do testing and lab work. When they swabbed the inside of our cheeks, I asked them to get an extra swab from Philip. They did it with no questions asked." She glanced around the lobby. "Is Dinah here? I don't want there to be any tension between her and me, so I'd like to speak with her before she leaves."

"We can double-check with the front desk, but I don't think she's here. I checked her red dot on the app thingy she downloaded to my phone, and it says she's at the bank."

"My mom has something similar on her phone. Only she uses it to keep track of her new boyfriend."

"Kay has a new boyfriend?"

"I know. Can you believe it?"

Lydia grinned. "And how are things with you and Roger?"

Eve's cheeks warmed. "There's nothing going on with Roger and me, but I am on my way to the studio. We're wrapping up the project we're working on. Can you believe you may actually hear one of my songs on Christian radio one day?"

Lydia's countenance brightened. "We should throw a launch party! I'll plan it. It'll be wonderful."

"No. Not yet, anyway. Roger thinks it's good enough to

launch. I'm not so sure. But I'll let you know when we've given it the final thumbs up."

"Good, because I've already mentally started the party planning."

Eve laughed and handed Lydia a small glass container. "The sample is in there. Tell Dinah I'm sorry I missed her."

Lydia took the container and stood. "You're leaving already? I was hoping we'd spend some time together this afternoon. Maybe walk around the lake for a bit?"

"I can't. I really should get going. I'm trying to avoid staying late at the studio." She furrowed her brow. "Especially since some people have been getting the wrong idea."

"Fine, I deserve that. But I stand by my warning. You may not have any feelings toward Roger, but he definitely has them toward you."

"We're only there to work."

"Of course."

Eve stood. "Take you up on that walk tomorrow?"

"Sure. Call me?"

"Will do." She hugged Lydia and headed for the exit. She turned to wave good-bye, but Lydia had already stepped onto the elevator.

Eve sighed. Lydia had no idea what she'd just started. Ever since the get together at Kite's, all Eve could think of was what they'd said about Roger—which made her think about him. A lot.

When Lydia had called to ask about getting samples, Eve focused on that and was able to have a morning free from Roger-thoughts.

Then Lydia just *had* to mention his name.

To make matters worse, Roger knew something was wrong. He'd asked her several times if everything was okay. She'd tried her best to act normal. When he didn't buy it, she'd started distancing herself. Which had been hard, because it used to be normal for them to stand shoulder-to-shoulder while they went over her recordings and while she wrote songs. Heavens, he'd even helped her find the right words when she wrote songs about her and Philip.

Now that closeness had become awkward.

Eve started her car. The last couple of weeks, singing, writing, and recording had been her refuge. Instead of fretting over Philip and the divorce, she'd poured her heart into her work. Going to the studio had been a blessing. A place to unwind. A place to talk and laugh and get work done at the same time. It'd been a breath of much-needed fresh air. But now that air had become thick with tension.

She turned onto the expressway and tried to steady her hands. Even her body knew what she needed to do next. She needed to talk with Roger. She'd didn't want to admit it, but there may have been some truth to what the girls had said. But where would that put her and Roger's working relationship? It would change everything, and she didn't want that to happen. She craved the same easy, friendly, and relaxed working relationship they'd always had. Just two old friends, working together, like they'd done many times in the past.

She took the exit that led to the studio. Her initial plan had been to put aside all of that nonsense and go about her sessions with Roger as if her world hadn't been rocked by the news that he had feelings for her. But that plan had failed. It wasn't fair to keep him in the dark, especially since he'd started apologizing like he'd done something wrong.

She tightened her lips as sweat gathered around her temples and her stomach bubbled. What if she brought it up, and he looked at her like she'd lost her mind? What if he laughed in her face? What if the girls were wrong?

What if they were right?

She parked in the space directly in front of the studio door and yanked her keys out of the ignition. Her purse and tote bag hung off of the passenger seat. She'd leave them. If the conversation went as badly as she thought it would, she wanted to be able to make a quick exit.

She looked at the keys. It'd be an even quicker exit if she left the keys in the ignition. Dropping or fumbling with them would be the last thing she'd want Roger or anyone else in the studio to see. She wanted a quick exit, but also a dignified one.

She got out of the car and slammed the door. No more waiting. The torment was driving her insane. The not knowing. The uncertainty. The what-ifs ...

"Eve, are you all right?"

She stopped in her tracks. How long had Roger been standing there?

"Eve ... ?"

She swallowed but didn't answer. Roger pushed the glass studio doors open and walked toward her.

"Eve, please tell me what's going on. You know you can trust me. I want to—"

"Are you in love with me?"

He stopped in front of her. "What?"

"Do you have feelings for me?"

He looked to his left. Several musicians had made their

way to the parking lot. A couple of them piled into a car and took off. Another loaded instruments into a van.

"Eve—"

"Yes or no?"

He rubbed the back of his neck and opened her car door. "Can we finish this conversation inside the car?" He motioned to the young man who was sliding a keyboard into the van.

Eve nodded and plopped into the driver's seat. Roger got in on the passenger's side. He locked the doors before facing her. "Where is this coming from?"

"A simple yes or—"

"Where is this coming from?"

She lowered her gaze. "Lydia and the girls seem to think that you have feelings for me. And have had them for quite a while. Since college."

He chuckled. "I thought I'd done a better job at hiding it than that."

She shot forward. "It's true?"

He nodded.

"Roger, I—"

He gently touched her wrist. "This is not the way I wanted you to find out. As long as you were married to Philip, I vowed to never make my feelings known. But I planned on telling you how I felt when the divorce papers were signed."

She tried to close her mouth, but her facial muscles apparently were just as shocked as she was. Words flew around her brain, daring her to catch them. One. She just needed to grab ahold of one of them, before Roger realized he had feelings for a complete and utter fool. "Philip."

Roger pressed his lips together and nodded. "He knows."

The words in her brain had stopped flying and started buzzing. She shook her head to make the noise stop, but the sound increased. She reached for the door handle. She needed to get out of the car. Needed to get some air.

Roger held on to her wrist and used his other hand to start the ignition and open the windows. "Don't go. There's a nice breeze coming through." He let go of her wrist and turned her face toward him. He inhaled a deep breath and slowly released it. "Do that with me." He took in another deep breath.

Eve followed his lead. Her heart rate slowed, but it took several more before the words stopped buzzing.

He smiled as her breaths became more even. "Better?"

The tenderness in his eyes brought tears to hers. As if she weren't embarrassed enough already. She blinked them away.

He popped open the glove box and handed her a few tissues from a packet he found inside. "It's okay. I'm right here, Eve. I'm not going anywhere."

She managed to stop a sob before it escaped her throat. "Roger, we can't do this."

He nodded. "I know."

She blew her nose and balled the tissue into her hand. "I don't understand. I've always seen you as a friend. A really good friend. And Philip knew you had feelings for me? He said nothing to me about that. Not one word."

"He wouldn't."

"But why would you tell him and not me?"

"I didn't tell him. He came to me before he asked you to marry him. Said he knew how I felt about you but wanted to know if I was okay with him taking it to the next level." He groaned. "I said yes because I'd tried everything I could think of to make you notice me as more than just a friend. And I knew from our conversations how excited you were at the prospect of becoming Mrs. Philip Stockton. I'd wanted to ask you to consider becoming Mrs. Roarke instead, but I had nothing to offer you. I was failing most of my classes and going to school on government loans that I had no idea how I was going to pay back. I had no family. No job. No money. No prospects. Philip had all of it. Family. Career. Opportunities. Money. I honestly thought you'd be better off with him. If I'd known then how he'd treat you …"

Eve dabbed at her eyes with the tissue. "Wouldn't have mattered. I would've chosen Philip, regardless."

He turned his head and looked out the passenger window.

She touched his arm and held it until he faced her again.

"I was under Philip's spell. You could've dangled the stars in front of me and promised me the moon. I still would've scurried after Philip."

"I never understood the pull he had on you."

She let out a ragged breath. "Neither did I."

Roger leaned in closer. "And that's how I know that we'll never have a shot at being together. Philip is your world, and I've learned to respect that. But now that it's out in the open, I want you to know that I love you, Eve. Always have. When you and Philip got married, I tried to find that same type of love with others. Five times I've tried. Five times I've failed." He shrugged his shoulders. "No wife number six for me. It's you or no one."

He reached for the door handle. "I'll understand if you

want to find another producer. I know of several who'd love to work with you."

She shook her head. "I'd like to finish what we've started."

"I would, too." He smiled then, stared at her as it faded. "I'll continue to keep it professional."

"As long as I'm Philip's wife?"

He nodded.

"And when I'm not?"

"Then I'll look forward to creating more than just beautiful music together." He winked and stepped out of the car. "You coming inside?"

"Tomorrow maybe. I have some things I need to think about."

He closed the door. She watched as he walked into the building. Had his stride always been that relaxed? That … confident?

She retrieved her cell from her purse and dialed Philip.

He let out a long sigh before he spoke. "What is it?"

She turned the car on and backed out of the parking space. "Have you signed the divorce papers yet?"

He mumbled something, then cleared his throat. "I told you I'm having second thoughts about signing them. I've thought about what you said about counseling. I'm open to it. If that means meeting with the pastor at your church, then … I guess I'm open to that as well."

Eve pulled onto the main thoroughfare, then took a sharp left into the first fast-food restaurant she spotted. She parked at an open space near the dumpster.

"Why are you doing this, Philip? You're the one who started this process and now you don't want to end it? You're playing games with me. With my heart. You always have. I don't know what I've ever done to you to deserve this, but now I'm ready for it to end. Sign the papers. You don't love me. You never have. Set me free, Philip. Please."

"What makes you think I don't love you?"

Her mind flashed back to her conversation with Roger and how easily he'd expressed his love for her. "Because you've never said it, Philip. Not once. Not ever."

She waited for his response. For an excuse. For him to spout off some meaningless diatribe and then blame her for him not loving her. When he didn't answer, she gritted her teeth. "Sign the papers, Philip."

"I've always wanted to tell you. I just didn't know how."

"Didn't know how to do what?"

"Tell you how much I loved you. I'd treated you so badly, for so long, I didn't think you'd believe me when I said it. But I do love you." He paused a few seconds, then continued, his voice thick. "And I'm sorry for everything I've done. I'm sorry for every time I laughed at you, mocked you, and abused you. And for all the times I've blamed you for my own shortcomings. It's me that I hate, not you. It was never you."

Eve stared at the dumpster in front of her.

He cleared his throat again. "I don't expect you to believe me, but being without you has made me realize that I really don't like who I've become, and that's why I've decided to go to counseling. I don't know if it'll work, but I want to try. For me. For us. For you, Eve."

"I don't believe you, Philip. If you want to change, it's going to take a lot more than just words. And even then, it may be too late."

"What do you mean?"

"I mean, I'm ready to move on, with or without you."

"I'm hoping you choose with me. All I ask for is time. A few months. If you're still not happy, then I'll sign the papers. I'll even have our lawyers draw up a document saying if I don't meet the criteria you've set in place, that you can have everything. Including what I've inherited from my grandfather. I'll walk away with nothing but the clothes on my back. I need to earn back your trust, Eve, and maybe even your love. Will you give me a chance to do that?"

"If you truly loved me, you'd let me go."

He paused again, then let out a soft whoosh of air. "I can't, Eve." The pitch of his voice was higher. "I just can't. Not yet. Give me another chance, please."

Eve clicked off the phone and smacked her hand against the steering wheel. She frowned at the oily odor of rotting garbage that had made its way through the air vents. She placed her hand over her mouth. She wanted to puke. And not just at the odor.

Her stomach roiled as she entertained Philip's offer. He was slicker and rottener than anything in that dumpster, yet she thought about taking him back.

He'd talked about how it wasn't Eve who he'd hated, but himself.

What about her? Did she hate herself? Did she secretly loathe the person that she'd become? She had to, because why else would she consider taking back someone who'd admitted to abusing her?

She couldn't do it.

She had to do it.

Despite the happiness she'd be able to find with Roger—

a happiness she deserved after all the painful years of being with Philip—she'd never be able to enjoy it. Philip acknowledging what he'd put her through, apologizing for it, and asking for help were proof that her decades-long prayers had been answered.

Her soul wanted to rejoice in the steps that he was taking, but she couldn't do it. She wasn't joyful. No matter how hard she tried, she couldn't help but feel like she was the garbage in the dumpster and that Philip was the flies.

She owed it to God to continue to try to save her marriage.

She owed it to herself to be truly loved by another human being. To live a life full of purpose and passion. A reset with Roger. She wanted more. Needed more. Craved more.

No more trying to please a man who would never be pleased.

She started the car and wiped away the tears and dreams of what could've been. She clasped her hands to her mouth and tried to muffle the battle cries that erupted from it as her flesh warred with the truth. The cruel truth.

Her heart had room for only one man in her life.

Philip.

It would always be Philip.

Chapter Forty

Mary wrapped her arms around Christianna as they walked out of Agent Rudd's office. "Thanks for coming today. It helped a lot."

Christianna rubbed Mary's shoulder. "Anytime."

Ethan pulled up in front of them when they stepped outside and unlocked the car doors.

"Oooh!" Christianna said as she climbed into the backseat. "You got me the triple-decker from Rosco's."

Ethan grinned. "There was a twenty-five-minute wait for the patty melt. I've seen you gobble down triple-deckers before, so I got that instead."

"Good choice. Oh! And you got extra bacon. Mary, I'm loving my new-to-me brother-in-law more and more. You picked a winner."

Mary settled into the passenger seat. "Yeah. I think I'll keep him."

Ethan placed a large Styrofoam container on Mary's lap. "Here's your extra-large fries. I don't know why you had me order them since you're not going to eat them all."

"Watch me."

Mary opened the container on her lap. Ethan had salted and peppered them just the way she liked. She pulled a fry from the heap and took a bite. "Forget the burgers. I loved their fries when I was a kid. Can't believe they taste the same."

Ethan popped one in his mouth and pulled away from the building. "How'd it go? When I left, there were only a handful of photos that still needed to be identified."

"I identified a few more. The rest of the girls I didn't recognize. Agent Rudd and his team tried cross-referencing their photos with what remained of Miss Autry's files. They didn't have much luck. Not even with the missing children database. So far, it appears they were never reported missing."

Ethan rubbed her thigh. "I'm sorry, babe. How many were there?"

"Three."

"Agent Rudd has a remarkable team." He pulled onto the highway. "They've located or reunited a lot of those girls with their families. They're not going to give up."

"I know. It just breaks my heart that no one, not one single person, reported those girls missing. They look to be between the ages of seven and nine. How could they have gone missing and no one noticed?"

"I wish I had the answer, but crazy as it may sound, maybe it was a good thing they landed with Miss Autry. So far, it appears that most of the girls were adopted by good families. Maybe those remaining three ended up with people who actually cared about them."

Mary pulled his right hand away from the steering wheel

and kissed it. "You always know how to make me feel better."

"Can you two please stop with the lovey-dovey stuff? You're ruining my meal."

Mary faced Christianna. "Don't you have a burger to eat?"

"I'm trying to eat it, but all that sweet-talk and kissing is distracting. We're five minutes from my place. Can't you control yourselves until then?"

Mary kissed Ethan three times on the cheek. She turned and stuck her tongue out at Christianna.

Christianna took a large bite of her burger, chewed it, then opened her mouth wide at Mary.

Mary laughed.

"Girls," Ethan tried to mimic their father's stern look. "If you don't behave, they'll be no dessert."

"Dessert?" Christianna rifled through the white bags in the seat next to her.

Ethan pulled into Christianna's driveway. "Yeah. Mary told me about their award-winning cookies."

Christianna tossed the rest of her burger into the bag with the cookies and stepped out of the car. Mary grabbed her arm. "Thanks again for coming this morning. I couldn't have done it without you."

"You could've, it just wouldn't have been as much fun." She blew Mary a kiss, then jogged to her front door. When Brad answered, Ethan backed out of the driveway.

"Brad didn't go to work today?"

"No. Chrissy said they both took the day off. They wanted some time alone before the girls got home from school."

He smiled. "And she wants to make fun of us?"

"I know, right?"

"I bet they're glad to be back in their own home. Everyone staying at your parent's place after the attack was nice, but now that Michael and most of his family are behind bars, we should start making our way back home as well."

Mary shoved several fries into her mouth.

"It's time, babe. You know that."

She blinked away tears. She missed her kids. She missed getting up in the wee hours of the morning to take Levi to swim practice, and she missed staying late into the evening at the ballet studio with Israela. She missed their chaotic Sunday mornings, lingering lunches, and lazy Sunday afternoons with her adoptive parents. But that life was in Delaware, this was Missouri. Her birthplace, her hometown. Where her roots were. Where her biological parents, siblings, and childhood friends were.

Ethan reached for her hand. "You okay?"

Mary looked out the window. They'd already arrived at the hotel they'd temporarily moved back into. She'd loved the past few weeks they'd spent at her parent's home. It'd been cramped with both Christianna and Paul's families there, but Mary had loved every minute of it. She'd had constant access to her nieces and nephews, and she and Christianna would talk late into the night. She'd had coffee before sunrise with her brother and her dad and long walks at sunset with her mom.

But Ethan was right. They'd prolonged their stay after Brad and the girls were attacked, but the Kildare's were no longer a threat and her family was trying to get back to their lives. She needed to get back to hers as well. She lowered her eyes. "I don't know what to do, Ethan. I know we need to leave, but I just don't think I'm ready."

"Will you ever be ready?"

She shook her head.

"That's my point. You're never going to be *ready* to leave. You've spent thirty years trying to reunite with your family. But this isn't like before. The last time you were *taken* from them, and you didn't know if you'd ever see them again. This time, they'll know where you are. They'll know that you're alive and that you're safe. They're also coming to visit soon, and we'll return to visit them—with kids in tow. You're not missing anymore." He lifted her chin toward him. "It's not an ending. It's a new beginning. We're moving on so that we can fully integrate both families together."

She pulled away from his hand. "I can't say good-bye to them. I just can't."

"You don't have to. That's what I'm trying to tell you. It's not good-bye. It's 'see you soon.'"

"Doesn't matter. To me, it feels the same."

Ethan opened the door and got out. Mary hurried after him. She reached for his hand as they made their way up to their room. "Don't be mad at me."

He pulled the key card from his pocket and placed it in front of the panel. When it beeped, she grabbed his arm. "Ethan."

He stepped inside and turned to her. "I'm not mad. But we are leaving. It's time for you to let everyone know."

Mary plopped down on the bed. "How long do I have?"

"Your parents, my sister, and the kids'll arrive back in the States a week from today. I'd like for us to be there to greet them."

The timing wasn't perfect, but it would give her the rest of the week and the weekend. "Fine. I'll let everyone know. Being here on Saturday is important. Kite's throwing a surprise party for Jack. Everyone's going to be there. That'll give me a chance to have some fun with the girls before we fly out Sunday."

"Sounds like a plan." He kissed her on the forehead. "I forgot to bring my laptop in from the car. Need anything while I'm down there?"

"My purse."

He nodded. When she heard the door click, she fell backward onto the bed. He may have forgotten his laptop, but that wasn't why he'd left. He was letting her know that there would be no further discussion on the matter.

Raising the topic again when he returned would be pointless. Heading home now was not only the right decision, it was a much needed one. Her balking about when to return home was not only taking a toll on Ethan, it was taking a toll on their kids. The last few conversations with her seven-year-old had not only ended in tears, it ended with Israela needing to be comforted by her grandfather. Not only was she missing her mom, but she'd had the lead role in a performance and had received accolades from an instructor who rarely gave them. And she was angry that her mom hadn't been there to see it.

Levi used to keep her and Ethan up all night on video calls, excitedly sharing everything that was happening in his life. But lately, the calls had been short. Sweet, but short. Something was bothering her fifteen-year-old. He needed his parents.

And she needed hers. Both sets. Biological and adoptive.

The longer she stayed, the longer it was going to take to start that new life Ethan was talking about. But she needed to reconnect with her kids first before introducing them to the rest of the family.

She picked up the hotel room phone and dialed Kite's phone number.

"Hey, Mary."

She frowned at the frustration in Kite's voice. "Everything okay? You sound upset."

"I am, but it's not at you. Has to do with Windy. What's going on?"

"Was wondering what time Jack's party is on Saturday?"

"J.S. will bring him here around five that evening. I'd like everyone else to show up at least an hour before then."

"Need help with anything? If so, I can come earlier."

"Oh, please do if you can. I'm so far behind on getting things ready for this party."

"I can be there at noon."

"Seven would be better."

Mary chuckled. "Oh, you really *do* need extra hands."

"You have no idea."

"Count on Chrissy and me to be there bright and early."

"Thank you."

"But there's something I'd like for you to know before then."

"Okay. What is it?"

Mary fiddled with the phone cord. She didn't want to say the words. Speaking them made her leaving … real. Imminent. "The next day, Ethan and I are leaving. We're flying back to Delaware."

Kite gasped. "Oh, Mary. I knew you guys had to head

back soon, but I had no idea you'd be leaving this weekend."

Mary swallowed a sob. "I'd originally told my family I'd only be gone for thirty days. That turned into six weeks. Then two months. Then three. My kids were patient at first, but now, not so much."

"I'm sorry, Mary. I should've realized."

"Nothing to apologize for. To me, after being away for forty years, leaving after three months seems too soon. To them—"

"I get it. They need you. I'm going to miss you, but I understand. How's your family here taking it?"

"They don't know yet."

"Not even Chrissy?"

"No. Ethan and I just made the decision a few minutes ago. I'll stop by my parents place tomorrow and tell them then. That'll give me a few hours to cry my eyes out."

"You're not there, now?"

"No. Ethan and I are back at the hotel. I'm glad you answered my call, though. I needed to share that news with someone before I told them, or it would've driven me insane. Wanting to be in two places at the same time."

"There's not much left for me to do here at the office. I can stop by if you'd like."

"No, I'm fine. Ethan stepped out. But he'll be back in a bit."

"Yeah, but Ethan's a guy. Sometimes you just need your girlfriend and a gallon of ice cream."

Mary laughed. "You're right. I may take you up on that offer after I talk with my parents. They hoped that I'd be able to stay a while longer."

"Won't they be flying out soon after?"

"Not yet. Since we've been away so long, I'd like for Ethan and me to have some time alone with Levi and Issie first. But I can't wait for my children to meet their grandparents, aunt, uncle, and cousins for the first time."

"That's going to be wonderful, Mary."

"After that, hopefully you and the girls will come for a visit. You've seen pictures, but when you see Issie in person, you'd be amazed at how much she looks and acts like Christianna."

"That's funny. One of the first things I noticed when I saw you again was how much you looked like Christianna's daughter Rose. She also has the same peaceful demeanor."

"Mom says that Chrissy takes after our grandfather and that my personality aligned more with my grandmother. Amazing how all of that works."

"I know. I regret not agreeing to have kids earlier in my marriage with Neth. He'd wanted to, but I always figured we'd have plenty of time to start a family. Now I often find myself wondering what our kids might've looked like. Would they have had his dark eyes and smile? My wild brown mane? Or both? Would we have had twins? What a blessing it would've been to have someone who shared his DNA and his legacy. He was a great man, Mary. You would've liked him."

"And I'm sure he would've been an awesome dad."

"He would've loved it."

"I wish I could've gotten to know him, Kite."

"He got a chance to know you, though. I'd told him countless stories of the silly things we did as girls, like the time we tried to put make-up on your aunt's cat."

"I remember. Did he believe you when you told him?"

"He did. Not sure what that said about me, but he did."

They laughed before Mary cleared her throat. "Thanks for taking the time to talk with me, Kite. You made me laugh, and that means a lot."

"You'd do the same for me. Love you."

The door clicked open. "Love you, too."

Mary placed the phone on the receiver and looked up at Ethan. "Just so you know, I'm still mad at you."

"I figured as much." He sat on the bed next to her. "But when I was in the hall, I heard laughing, so I figured it was safe for me to return."

"I was on the phone with Kite."

"Did you—?"

"Yes. I told her about us leaving. I haven't talked with my family yet. I'll wait and tell them in person."

"We are leaving on Sunday, Mary. No more ifs, ands, or buts."

She jumped off the bed. "I know that, okay? I thought a lot about it while you were gone. I agree with you. We're going back. I'll be on that plane. But that doesn't change the fact that this is hard for me."

"Mary—"

"Habakkuk isn't the town that I remembered." She paced the floor. "I haven't felt at home here since I've been back. But now that I'm getting ready to leave, that's exactly what it feels like. I didn't realize until now just how much I've loved walking into my mom's arms every morning and getting to know my family again to the point where it doesn't feel like four decades were stolen from us. It's hard, Ethan. It's just …. hard."

He grasped her hand and gently pulled her down onto his

lap. "I know, sweetie." He wiped her tears with his thumb and kissed her cheek. "If I could trade places with you, I would. It kills me knowing how much pain you're going through."

She smiled. "You would take my place, wouldn't you?"

"In a heartbeat."

She placed her head on his shoulder. "The thought of leaving again gives me chills."

He slowly ran his hand along her arm and her muscles loosened from the warmth. When he continued the motion along her neck, shoulders, and back, her breathing slowed and matched his. She was being lulled to sleep.

Working with Agent Rudd this morning and knowing she had to say good-bye to her loved one's tomorrow had left her an emotional wreck.

But right now, she had this.

She'd trust God with the rest.

Chapter Forty-One

Jack Eagle.

No doubt about it—she loved him.

Kite slid a pan of cake batter into the oven and yanked off the oven mitt. She had to get a grip. Relief, happiness, and gratefulness were not the same as love. She was *grateful* that Jack was able to get Windy out of Miss Lauren A-D-A's clutches, and she was *relieved* he made sure she'd never be able to use Windy as blackmail bait again.

But that wasn't love. Not romantic love. What she felt for him at this moment was a lot more than appreciation.

"There she goes, staring off into space again." Windy cracked an egg against the counter and added it to another bowl of batter.

Christianna sliced an apple at rapid speed, then added the pieces to a bowl. "And she has that same grin, too."

Kite leaned against the kitchen counter. "I'm just thinking, that's all."

"About Jack?" They spoke in unison, then laughed.

"Of course, I'm thinking about Jack. We're throwing

him a surprise party today. Why wouldn't I be thinking about him?"

"That's not all you're thinking about." Windy wiped the counter with a towel. "You're also thinking about how he got you out of a sticky situation the other day. Now you're having all kinds of … gooey feelings about him."

"Excuse me. *I* wasn't the one in a sticky situation. *You* were the one Lauren was threatening to throw in jail."

Windy chuckled. "There was no way I was going to let that woman put me in prison. Even *she* knew that. She could've put pressure on me to get you to create that bogus file, but she didn't. She went to you instead. She knew that *you* were the weaker twin."

"Well, pardon me for not wanting to see my look-alike in an orange jumpsuit." Kite shrugged. "The whole thing is moot now. Jack saved the day."

"Saved the day? He walked behind your desk, opened a cabinet, and showed you recording equipment. You've worked there for two years. I don't understand how you didn't know your office was being recorded."

Kite threw her hands in the air. "I've never had to use that cabinet. My files are always with me, and my camera equipment is always locked in the car. Investigating is not a desk job. I was in the field ninety percent of the time."

Windy turned on the hand mixer.

As much as Kite hated to admit it, her sister was right. She was an investigator who'd had no idea what was going on in her own office.

Jack never mentioned that the offices at Eagle Eye were monitored. Apparently, he'd had several shady characters ask him to do some very questionable investigations. To protect his business, he'd had recording equipment installed. Cameras were hidden in the light fixtures, and audio turned on automatically at eight o'clock each morning.

It wasn't until she'd told Jack about her encounter with Lauren that he'd told her about the hidden equipment.

Windy may never see the inside of a jail cell, but Lauren might. Jack turned the tapes over to the DA's office the next morning.

Kite pointed to the mixer. "I asked you to mix it, not beat it. Jack's cake needs to be perfect."

She slid the bowl across the counter. "Then you do it, and I'll tackle the sandwiches. How many should I make?"

"Around two hundred."

The knife slipped from Christianna's hand and clanged to the floor. "Two hundred? How many people are coming to this party?"

"I don't know. I lost count days ago."

Windy held up her hand. "Kite, this event should've been catered."

"I didn't want it catered. I wanted to do as much as we could ourselves. Jack has done a lot for his friends. This is a nice way to show our appreciation."

"Okay, so where's the list of who's bringing what?"

"What do you mean?"

"I'm sure you asked everyone who *appreciates* Jack to bring something."

Kite stared at her and blinked.

"Seriously, Kite?" ·

Heat filled her cheeks. "Okay. My party planning skills need help. But we can still do this. The party is at seven o'clock, and it's barely after nine."

"Let me call Anthony. He caters events all the time. If he can't do it, he'll find somebody who can. He's filled in for plenty of them at the last minute. They'll be glad to help out."

When did Windy become so knowledgeable about Anthony? When Kite had mentioned to her before about possibly dating him, she did everything but throw daggers her way. Now she knew him well enough to know the businesses he worked with?

Kite shook her head. "Invite Anthony, but it's a no to the caterers. I'd still like to do most of it ourselves. I haven't completely dropped the ball. Pastor Greene, Mr. Melson, Barry, Philip, and Ethan have agreed to grill and Paul, J.S. and Ram are putting the finishing touches on the stage in the backyard.

"Pris, Liz, and Lola are in charge of decorating. Lydia and her girls are running last minute errands, and Mary's the official party manager. There's still a lot to do, but if we hustle, we can get everything done with time to spare."

Doubt was clear on both of their faces.

"We can salvage this."

Windy threw up her hands. "Fine. While Chrissy works on the desserts, I'll start on the sandwiches. Paul has tables set-up in the back yard. I'll use those to get an assembly line going."

Kite grabbed several sticks of butter from the refrigerator. "Eve's in the den making phone calls. She may be done by now. Ask her to help with the sandwiches."

Windy mumbled something as she made her way out to the yard. Christianna handed Kite a pie, and she slid it into the oven.

Lola walked into the kitchen. She wore a pair of blue denim overalls with a lacey pink tank underneath. She was barefoot and didn't have on an ounce of make-up, yet beauty radiated from her. Life so wasn't fair.

She nodded at the bouquet of balloons she was holding. "You wanted us to decorate with the firecracker red and pearl-white ones, but we're running low. I can substitute with one of these if you'd like."

Kite glanced at the candy apple red and grayish-white balloons she held. "Those colors don't stand out like the others. Stay with the original color scheme. I'll give Lydia a call. Hopefully, she'll be able to grab some more."

"I'll tell Pris and Liz."

When she left the kitchen, Christianna sniffed the air. "An hour ago, she smelled like strawberries. Now she smells like mango. Likely a mixture of the lotions and creams that she uses, but whatever it is, it drives my poor nephew nuts."

"Luke David? What is he now, sixteen?"

"Yes. And he's in love with Lola. I told him that she's twenty-years older than he is and that she's happily married, but that hasn't stopped him from grinning like an idiot whenever she's around."

"Is he here?"

"Yeah, helping the guys prepare the grills. Paul's trying to keep him distracted."

Kite laughed. "Good luck with that. I remember my first crush. When someone grabs your attention the way Lola does, it's hard to keep them off your radar."

"You're right. The first time I saw Brad, I knew he was the man I was going to marry. He was only thirteen at the time, and I was ten. But the heart wants what the heart wants."

"Hmm." Kite poured more batter into a pan and wiped the rim. Their hearts may know what they want, but do they know what's best? Her heart never stopped crying for what she had with Nethaniah, and for what could've been. It longed to be reunited with him.

But her heart also wanted her to make peace with his passing. To do that, she'd have to accept the fact that he'll never be able to come back to her.

Christianna placed her hand over Kite's. "You okay?"

She wiped at a tear. "No. And especially not now since Jack's cake is going to be flavored with my tears."

"I don't think he'll mind." She handed her a mitt, and Kite pulled the baking cake out before inserting another one. When she turned, she saw the backyard decorations through the kitchen window and smacked her forehead. "I forgot to text Lydia about the balloons."

She typed out a text and, as it *whooshed* from her phone, she made her way to the den.

Eve placed a finger to her lips and pointed to the phone in her hand when she entered. She was at Kite's desk, so she collapsed on the settee and waited. When Eve hung up, she turned toward Kite. "Windy asked for help with the sandwiches, I'll be done here in a few."

"I'll help her with those. I just wanted to make sure that we're going to have a band tonight. I apologize for asking at the last minute."

"Three-Sixteen's available. Of course, they're a Christian rock band and not your typical party music, so I'm not sure how Jack's friends will react, but the key word there is *rock*. The music is definitely upbeat and loud enough to keep a party going." She rolled her eyes. "However, I doubt anyone'll be able to understand the lyrics. But if they do, then maybe they were supposed to."

Kite nodded. "I'm stoked that we have a Christian band playing for the party. You never know what'll come of that."

"Exactly."

"You're still going to lead the singing of *Happy Birthday*, though, right?"

"Absolutely."

Kite debated on getting up from the settee. She'd awoken before dawn to start on the party prep. After not falling asleep until after midnight, she now realized she should've stayed in bed a couple more hours.

Eve laughed. "Need help getting up?"

"No, but I am tempted to close my eyes for a bit."

"Go ahead. You've been going nonstop the past few days. Mary's on top of things. Minutes before you showed up, she'd already popped in asking about the music."

"I'd love to, but I wouldn't be able to rest knowing that everybody else was working so hard."

"Everybody else probably got a full night's sleep. Windy said she didn't think you'd slept at all last night. Sometimes a body just needs to rest."

Kite looked closer at Eve. Her eyes were as bright as her smile, so it was clear she'd gotten plenty of rest. Her cheeks were also a slight rose color. Was that blush? Or something else? She raised a brow. "You definitely look well-rested. I take it Philip signed the divorce papers?"

"No. He asked that I give him a second chance."

Both of her brows raised.

"The only reason I think he might be serious is because

he's attended several counseling sessions with me. He's receiving one-on-one counseling as well."

Philip agreed to go to counseling? And he actually went? It all sounded good, but still …

Eve leaned on the desk. "I know what you're thinking. That this is just another one of his ploys and that he's going to continue to string me along." She lifted a shoulder. "And that may be the case. Time'll tell. I desperately wanted to move on and put the Philip years behind me, but I had to give him the chance he'd asked for. If he blows it again, it's over once and for all, and he knows that."

"Eve, you know I've never liked Philip, but I'm glad to hear that you agreed to another attempt, especially since he's going to counseling. But I also know everything that he's put you through, so please stay prayerful about it."

"Trust me. I am."

Kite smiled. "You look so happy that I have to confess— I thought the color in your cheeks was because of Roger, not Philip."

"You thought I'd moved on with Roger?"

"I did."

She tossed her head back and laughed. "That came very close to happening, actually. But after our getaway—"

"With Philip?"

"No, Roger."

Kite straightened.

Eve tilted her head. "You know I'm not the type who'd take part in any kind of hanky-panky while I'm married, so don't look at me like that." She giggled and leaned back into her chair. "I went to the lake and rented a cabin. I needed that time away to figure out what *I* wanted, not what Philip wanted. But I also needed to talk with Roger.

"He came to visit, and we talked. In the end, we decided not to pursue a relationship, even if I divorced Philip. Roger wanted me to not only be legally free of Philip, but emotionally free of him as well. I couldn't make that promise. Philip left a lot of scars. But I also wanted a future free of him. I didn't know what to do, but I had to make a decision and stick with it. After Roger left, I canoed on the lake. That time alone helped clear my mind."

"And you chose your husband."

"I chose the man Philip showed me when we were dating. The man he'd promised to be in our wedding vows. And the man he said he would be when he asked for a second chance."

"Do you think you'll get him?"

She sucked in a breath, then blew it out. "I don't know. I hope I do. If the past week is any indication, then I think I just might." She smiled, and the pink in her cheeks turned pinker. "We've been having a bit of fun while trying to figure it all out."

"But what about Roger? Are you two still working together?"

"I asked Philip how he felt about that and—"

"Philip knows?"

"Yes. He's known for quite some time."

Kite couldn't believe it. "He never said anything?"

"As long as it was one-sided he didn't care. But now that he knows that it had the potential of becoming a lot more, he doesn't want us spending time together. We're finishing up my first album, so that would've been a problem, except Philip said he didn't want to take that away from me. So

Roger and I will see the project through—with Philip in tow, of course. After that, if my music finds an audience and there's more music to create, Roger will make arrangements for me to work with another producer."

"But what about the Philip and Dinah situation?"

She pursed her lips. "The last thing I wanted was to start our second chance with a secret, but I decided to honor Dinah's wishes and let her take the lead on when to approach Philip about it. The DNA was conclusive—no surprise there. But she's not ready for him to know that he's her father."

Kite nodded, even though she didn't agree with her decision. Dinah deserved her right to privacy, but didn't Philip also deserve to know that he had a daughter? He was going to be livid when he found out that Eve kept that information from him. Right now everything was rosy in their relationship. But Kite had personally witnessed how Philip could go from romantic to monstrous in a matter of seconds. And then where would their marriage be?

But Eve didn't look worried. Not even in the slightest. Before, if she even *thought* Philip was going to be mad at her, she'd dive into panic mode.

The Eve in front of her now looked like she didn't have a care in the world.

Did she truly not fear his reaction? Or was it the potential relationship with Roger that had given her confidence? If her marriage failed, Roger would give her a safe place to land, but … that didn't sound like Eve. More than likely, she'd made peace with the situation, regardless of the outcome.

Kite rounded the desk and wrapped her friend in a hug. She'd struggled so long to find peace when it came to Philip. It was nice to see that she'd finally found it.

She gave her a squeeze. "I love you."

Eve patted her forearm. "Love you, too."

"Well, right now, I'm finding it hard to love either one of you."

Windy stood in the doorway and dramatically pointed at her watch. "The clock is ticking. We don't have time for this love fest. We have things to do." She clapped loudly. "Come on, ladies. Get moving. Chop-chop."

They giggled their way to the backyard and stopped at the table with the sandwiches. Eve and Kite couldn't believe it. Windy had outdone herself. She'd wrapped each of the sandwiches, then beautifully decorated the table with a bright red cloth and attached note cards from some of Jack's friends. She'd asked them to write down their favorite memory, then displayed them across the table.

She pointed to a large, wooden frame with a dark blue matte inside the glass. It leaned against the corner of the table. "I've asked J.S. to take a picture of everyone before Jack arrives. After he does that, I'll print it out in your office then place the photograph in the center of that frame, surrounded by the memory cards. Then you can present it to Jack as a present."

"Windy, he's going to love it, but I can't take credit for this. You're the one who did all the work. You should present it to him."

Windy rolled her eyes. "Fine. But only if I can't find someone else."

Eve glanced at the table. "Windy, I'm sorry I didn't make it out in time to help. I have a couple hours until the band gets here. Anything else I can help with?"

"Anthony De Santis will be here in a few minutes. He's

asked for as much help as he can get in the kitchen."

Eve nodded. "I can do that."

Kite looked at Windy. "Have you seen Mary?"

She pointed over Kite's shoulder. "Mary's over there with Pris and Liz."

Kite turned and saw the three of them near the edge of the yard, staring at her wooden fence, while a much shorter lady stood on a ladder and arranged a string of balloons.

"Is that who I think it is?"

"Yes." Windy cleared her throat. "That's Miss Mabel. She's been re-doing what they've done for the past hour."

What on earth? Kite jogged across the yard and stood between the ladies and Miss Mabel. "Why are you letting her stand on a ladder like that?" She frowned at Priscilla and Liz. "Please step down, Miss Mabel."

"I will, just as soon as I show these girls how to properly decorate a fence."

"Miss Mabel. I have no doubt that you're showing them the correct way to do it, but could you please come down?" Kite covered her mouth as Mabel stood on her toes to reach a string that had been tied to the top of the fence. "You're making me nervous."

Priscilla crossed her arms. "Save your breath. She's not going to come down until she's ready."

"She could fall."

"I know that, and she knows that. And if she falls, it'll be her own blazing fault."

"Priscilla—"

"Kite, there's nothing you can do. Liz and I were doing just fine, but Mama here said we were doing it all wrong. And because she has a takeover spirit, we're standing here while she shows us how to string balloons on a fence."

"Watch your mouth, Miss Prissy. I don't have no takeover spirit hounding me. You girls was doing it wrong. That's all there is to it."

Priscilla threw her hands in the air.

Kite stepped closer to the ladder. "Mabel, for my own peace of mind, will you please come down off of that ladder?"

"Kite, you have a party to throw. Isn't there somewhere else you need to be?"

Kite took a step back. Was she just … dismissed?

Mary and Liz struggled to hold in their laughter, but Priscilla let out an exaggerated breath and whispered in her ear. "She's not even supposed to be here. I told her we were coming early to help set things up, and we'd pick her up in time for the party. But she wasn't having it. I tried to talk her out of it, but"—she motioned toward her mother—"you see who won the argument."

"I love how your mom wants to help, but I can't have her on that ladder. If she falls—"

"The reason Liz and I are still standing here like idiots is because we're going to make sure that doesn't happen. Otherwise, we would've left her to her madness and helped Lola decorate the inside."

Kite was about to protest when Priscilla held up a hand. "Kite, I promise you. I will not let anything happen to my mama."

She let out a breath and looked around the rest of the yard. Thanks to Mary's dad, the bushes and trees were trimmed and well-manicured. Tables and chairs had already been set up and decorated, and so had the lighting. Two of the three grills had been started.

Mary walked to stand next to Kite. "It's all coming along."

Kite looked at her watch. It was after one o'clock. "Everything needs to be wrapped up by five so we'll have time to get dressed for the party. Did you bring a change of clothes?"

She nodded. "I put them in your bedroom."

"Good. Half of the ladies will get ready in my room, the other half in Windy's. There's an extra bedroom and bathroom upstairs for the men if they need it."

"Got it."

"Thanks, Mary."

Her plan was to have a birthday party for Jack that he'd never forget. It was shaping up to be just that.

~

Kite carefully placed her edge of the cake on the table, and Mary followed her movements. When it was centered, they took a step back and wiped theirs foreheads.

"If I'd known that was gonna cause this much perspiration, I would've done it before I applied my make-up."

Mary grabbed a napkin from a nearby table and wiped frosting from her hands. "I'm just glad we made it down the steps and through the yard without dropping it."

Kite smiled. Everything was perfect. The sun had dipped behind a cloud and the weather had cooled. The deep green of the lawn and the brown of the sugar maples contrasted perfectly with the red and white décor.

The lamp posts and the lights strung along the fencing created a soft ambiance. And the smoke from the grills made her mouth water.

The band had arrived and had already performed their first sound check. The first song they'd played was so loud it shook the newly built stage, but the one they played now reminded her of a lullaby her mom used to sing.

Mary had brushed her brown hair into a neat little ponytail at the nape of her neck. She had on a pair of capris, a white shirt, and matching sandals. She placed her hands on her hips. "I still can't believe we pulled this off."

Kite chuckled. "No way I could've done this without your help."

Mary nodded. "Anything for Jack."

Anthony opened the back door, and Windy and Christianna walked down the steps. Windy had parted her hair straight down the middle, and the dark waves cascaded across her shoulders and down her back. She wore a soft yellow peasant blouse that hung off of her shoulder and a pair of white shorts that were too short for Kite's taste and borderline inappropriate. But Kite knew she didn't wear them for her. She wore them to entice Anthony. And from the way he looked at her as she walked down the steps, she'd succeeded.

Christianna placed two dishes on the table. Windy poked a thumb toward the house. "Guests are arriving."

Kite checked her watch. They had twenty minutes.

Mary turned toward her. "Has J.S. left to pick up Jack?"

"Jack's mom and sister are going to bring him instead. But Windy's right. We need to get moving."

Eve and Philip walked down the steps as they headed toward the house. Philip was smiling, holding Eve's hand, and whispering something in her ear. They heard her giggle as they walked past them and toward the stage.

Christianna furrowed her brow. "That guy that Eve is with looks like Philip. But it couldn't be Philip because that guy is smiling."

Mary gave her sister a playful shove. "Be nice."

Kite's phone dinged before they made it to the door. She flipped it open and read it. "Oh my. Rhoda said they're less than ten minutes away."

Mary, Christianna, Windy, and Anthony quickly organized an assembly line of the guests and ushered them outside.

Kite maneuvered her way through them and made a mad dash to her bedroom. She shut the door and stood in front of the full-length mirror. The day had been warm and humid, so she'd gathered her hair into a messy bun for the party, instead of wearing it down. It had somehow now become messier than she'd intended. She gave it another spritz of hairspray, and re-applied a shade of her favorite red lipstick, interestingly named Ignited. It matched perfectly with the red and white plaid swing dress she wore and the siren red peep toe wedges. She twirled to get a better view of the back of her dress and smiled as the skirt floated gracefully around her knees.

There was a knock at the door. She smoothed out her dress and opened it. Mary grabbed her hand. "Quick, I've already positioned everyone for the group photo. The only one missing is you." She pulled her down the hallway, through the kitchen, and into the yard where she placed her right in the center of the group. She then went to stand by Ethan and the rest of her family. J.S. steadied the tripod, pushed a few buttons, then ran to the left side of the group, to stand with the other Eagle Eye employees.

The camera snapped several photos right before Rhoda, Jack, and their mom entered the yard. Rhoda quickly untied his blindfold. How in the world did they get him to wear that?

"Surprise!"

Jack stepped backward and almost knocked over his sister.

He spread his arms wide like he was going to make a speech, but he said nothing. Finally, his arms fell to the side, and he uttered a hoarse, "Thank you."

The band played an upbeat version of the happy birthday song as Eve made her way to the stage. Her curly, dull, and usually lifeless brown hair was now straight, shiny, full of bounce, and had been styled to lay across her left shoulder. She wore a long white summer dress that moved along with the breeze. She stepped to the microphone and smiled. She was stunning and she possessed an air of confidence. When she opened her mouth and sang the first few choruses of the birthday song, Kite knew why. No one had a voice like Eve. She'd made a simple song sound fun, eloquent, and poetic at the same time.

When the song started again, everyone joined in. Kite smiled when Jack's cheeks burned as red as her sandals. He rubbed at the back of his neck. She knew he was uncomfortable with the attention, but he deserved it. His mom nudged him, and he lifted his head and smiled.

People surrounded him when the song was over. She watched as they greeted him and planted kisses on his cheek.

She felt a hand on her shoulder and turned around. Lydia smiled. "Everything is so beautiful, Kite. You ladies did a wonderful job."

"I couldn't have done it if you hadn't run those last minute errands for me. When did you guys arrive?"

"Not too long ago. Everyone was getting dressed about that time."

"Where are your girls?"

"Over there with the Melson's. Except for Dinah. She's about to greet Jack."

Kite looked at the circle surrounding Jack again. He hugged Dinah, and they started chatting. "Does Dinah know that Philip is here?"

Lydia nodded. "She plans to keep her distance."

The band started up again. The lead singer, Gabby, sang a song that encouraged hand clapping and feet tapping. Lydia let out a quick breath. "Well, I guess it's time for us to mingle."

She made her way to the small crowd near the stage while Kite visited each table and asked if she could get them anything. Most of them had already stopped by the buffet tables and several more, mostly men—since the only female she saw was Diamond Liz—were in the game area where a spirited game of corn hole was underway.

She was about to greet the guests playing the game when she saw Jack trying to get her attention. He stood next to an attractive couple with two kids.

As she drew closer, he reached for her hand and pulled her to his side. "Kite, I'd like for you to finally meet Ted." He hugged his friend as Ted extended his hand to shake hers.

Jack talked about his college buddy all the time and their many exploits. After college, Ted joined the ministry and eventually became a pastor. He no longer lived in Missouri, but Kite had extended an invitation for him and his family to come to Jack's birthday party. She shook his hand. "Ted, it's good to finally meet you. I've heard so much about you from Jack. So glad you and your family could make it to the party."

Ted laughed. "I wouldn't have missed it for the world." He turned to his right and wrapped his arms around the shy-looking woman next to him. "This is my wife, January, but everyone calls her Jan. Standing next to her is our son Adam, who is twelve and our darling girl, Laynee. She's eight."

Kite shook his wife's hand then knelt in front of Adam and Laynee. They both had piercing dark eyes and hair to match. Laynee had on a bright yellow sundress, and her hair was braided in two long braids that extended down her back, with yellow ribbons tied to the end of each of them.

"Thank you guys for coming to the party. Hope you're having fun."

Laynee's eyes lit up. "I am! I've played ring toss and hopscotch. And I had some taffy."

Kite laughed and mischievously tilted her head toward her. "Would you like some cotton candy too?"

"Yes!"

Jan looked down at her daughter. "Only after you eat some real food, Laynee."

Laynee's gaze dropped to the ground then shot back up toward Kite. "Do you have hot dogs?"

"We do."

She let out a tiny squeal. She was way too adorable and reminded Kite of a doll she'd had when she was little. She wrapped her arms around her middle to keep them from reaching out and trying to play with her.

Kite looked at her mom. Her daughter was a spitting image of her. "How long will you be in town?"

"About a week."

"Will you be staying with Jack?"

"No. We don't get to vacation often as a family, so we splurged on a nice hotel nearby."

"Oh, we should do a dinner date then." Kite stiffened and resisted the urge to slap her hand over her mouth. Did she just invite Jack on a date? How did that happen? She'd repeatedly told him she wasn't ready to date. And that was true. At least she thought it was.

She tossed a casual look his way. His eyes told her that he was just as shocked as she was that she'd made that invitation. But his ear-to-ear smile told her that he was glad that she did.

"That would be wonderful. Jack's told us so much about you. I'm looking forward to it."

Jack cleared his throat. "My mom asks about these two all the time. I know she'd love to babysit."

Kite stood. "Great. It's a date then." She said good-bye to Ted and Jan and waved at Adam and Laynee. "Don't forget about the cotton candy."

Laynee practically dragged her mom through the maze of people. Ted and Adam followed, stopping to talk with Jack's family along the way.

Jack wrapped his arms around Kite's waist. She wanted to step back as she'd done many times before, but since she'd already invited the man on a date, she didn't see the point of it now.

He stared into her eyes. "I don't know how you did it, but ..." He looked around him. "You've managed to surprise me. I didn't see this coming. I'm having a great time. Seeing Ted and his family again was great. Thank you."

She placed her hand on his chest and raised a brow. "Are you sure? Because earlier, you looked really uncomfortable."

He chuckled. "Yeah, I've gotten over that. To know that the people I see every day cared enough about me to help pull this off, it's … humbling."

"How did you—?"

"Windy. After everyone yelled surprise, she told me everything."

"Windy and that blazing mouth of hers. However, speaking of Windy …" Kite pulled him closer and looked up at him. "I have something for you."

"Oh, yeah? What's that?"

She wrapped her arms around his neck, then planted friendly kisses across his cheeks, nose, and forehead. And she ended the gift with a peck on his lips.

His body tensed and his eyes changed from amused to serious. "What was that for?"

She loosened her arms. "That was my way of saying thank you for what you did for Windy."

He furrowed his brow. "I didn't do anything except show you where the recording equipment was."

"But having that equipment there made a difference. You have no idea how stressed I was after Lauren left. And then you walked in and just like that," she snapped her finger, "problem solved. You were my hero in that moment, and I just wanted to let you know how much I appreciated it."

"Your hero, huh?" The humor returned to his eyes. "Well, that means you owe me another set of kisses."

She leaned back. "What makes you think that?"

"You and Windy are twins. I helped her which helped you, so I should get double the kisses for all my hard work."

"Hard work? All you did was come in and unlock a cabinet."

"Yeah. Like I said, hard work."

She laughed and wrapped her arms around his neck again, and repeated the same kissing pattern as before, but this time she ended it with a double peck on the lips. "You're right. You deserve double the gratitude. Sorry I missed that before. Is there anything else I can do for you?"

His eyes went from humorous to gleaming. "Yes." He placed a finger under her chin and tilted her head up. When his lips were a breath away from hers, he paused, gazed into her eyes, and whispered. "Kite, if you're going to stop me, I need you to do it now."

When she didn't respond, he leaned in until their lips touched. When she still didn't protest, he gripped her waist and pulled her to him until the warmth of his body melded with hers. When their lips touched, he kissed her deeply. Intimately. She hadn't felt passion like that since—

Applause and whistles interrupted her thoughts. She tried to pull away but Jack gently pulled her back in, and they looked out at the crowd. They'd had an audience.

When the crowd resumed what they were doing before the interruption, Kite wiped at a tear. The only man she'd ever kissed was Neth. And she'd just broken that sacredness by allowing herself to indulge in a public display of affection with Jack. She'd betrayed her husband. And some of the people she cared about the most had just witnessed it.

Jack cupped her face and held it until she looked up at

him. "Are you going to tell me what's wrong?"

"I can't do this, Jack. I thought I could, but I can't."

He looked down at her and smiled. "This is about Neth, isn't it?"

She swallowed a small cry. How could she have been so weak?

"Hey, hey, hey." Jack pulled a handkerchief from his pocket and dabbed at her eyes. "It's okay. I understand."

That was the problem. He understood. Which was why all of this was so difficult. Or was she the one making things difficult? She shook her head. She'd never stop loving Neth. But if she didn't make peace with his passing, she'd never be able to lead the life that God had planned for her. Whether or not that life included Jack, she had no idea. But she needed to take the first step. She needed to live. Neth would be disappointed if he knew she was continuing to grieve over something that couldn't be changed. Until they saw each other again, he'd want her to embrace the life God's given her. She just needed to want the same thing.

"I apologize Jack. A lot of emotions came at me all at once."

He nodded.

Her voice shook, but she needed to do this. "I want you to know that I like you, Jack. A lot. I'd be lying if I told you I was ready to date again, but I think it's time that I tried. But that's all I can offer you right now."

"Then that's all I'll ask of you." His fingers smoothed a strand of tear dampened hair. "We'll take it day by day."

"There could be some long days ahead of us, Jack."

"I can be patient."

"Good, because you'll need to be."

"Hey, lady. Are you going to date me or not?"

She wrapped her arms around his neck again. "Yes."

He kissed her, then laid his forehead against hers. She turned to see if they still had an audience. They did, but it wasn't the same as before. It was Windy, who was locked into an embrace with Anthony. It was Priscilla and Barry, who danced to a tune that was a lot slower than the one the band played. It was Lydia and her daughters as they looked over at them and smiled. It was Eve, who'd tossed her head back and laughed as Philip snuggled behind her. It was Mary and Ethan, both of whom were looking at them with tears in their eyes.

Ethan whispered in her ear, then Mary slowly approached the stage. When Gabby handed her the microphone, she cleared her throat. "Hi, everyone. For those of you who don't know me, my name is Mary Rabin. Mary Melson Isaac Rabin. I know this is Jack's birthday party, but he's graciously given me permission to extend an invitation to some friends." She pressed her hand against her throat and continued. "Almost forty years ago, I lived next door to two fun, bright, and witty girls. Twins. One morning, one of them asked if I'd like to jump rope with them later that day and I said yes. Unfortunately, we never got that chance." She looked down for a second before resuming. "Before I leave my friends again, I'd like to honor my word. So I'd like to ask Kite Tanner and Windy Jordan to help me restore what was stolen from us so long ago." She extended an arm toward the far right side of the yard. "Kite and Windy, will you jump rope with me?"

Kite followed her gaze. Standing on one side of her patio was Christianna, and directly across from her was her oldest daughter, Sarah. A long, corded rope extended between them. As they turned it, Mary bounded down the stage steps and across the yard. She jumped into the rope without hesitation and they swung the rope faster.

She laughed, and the guests cheered her on as she hopped on one foot, and then the other. She waved her arms toward Kite and Windy.

Windy dashed across the lawn and jumped in with Mary. She hopped at first, but then switched to holding on to one leg and twirling in circles.

Jack gave Kite a slight nudge. "What are you waiting for?"

She shook her head. "I haven't jumped rope in years."

He placed a hand on her back and led her toward the patio. "That doesn't seem to be stopping them."

"That's because Mary's a former dancer and Windy's a show-off."

The closer they got, the more the guests chanted her name. She turned toward them. "I don't know if I can."

Lydia and Eve met them at the patio. Eve removed her sandals and Lydia shoved her inside the rope. Instinct kicked in and she marveled at how easily it all came back.

She laughed, jumped, hopped, and crossed her legs back and forth. Mary jumped her way between her and Windy and grabbed their hands. Lights flashed. Ethan had started taking pictures, and so had everyone else.

Eve and the guests chanted a jump rope rhyme that Kite remembered from childhood. Then she and Lydia jumped rope for a bit, then hopped out so that Priscilla and Diamond Liz could join in on the fun. By then, Kite was completely out of breath and Mary hopped out when she did.

Then Miss Mabel and Lola took their turns and showed everyone how it was really supposed to be done. Kite stood in awe and watched as they held on to each other and did things with their feet inside the rope she'd never seen before.

An hour later, another rope was added so the guests could jump double-dutch. Priscilla, Lola, Miss Mabel, and Windy really showed off their skills then. By the end of the night, almost everyone at the party had their turn inside the ropes, including the band members.

As the party wrapped up, Kite sank into one of the hard, plastic chairs they'd rented from the party company. No doubt she was going to have to buy this one. There was no way she was going to be able to get out of it.

Priscilla and Lydia plopped down next to her. "Barry said he'd never seen me laugh so hard." Priscilla's arms flopped down on the plastic table in front of them. She laid her head on top of them. "I know I'm going to pay for this tomorrow. What was I thinking?"

Lydia let out a chuckle. "You? What about your Mom?"

Priscilla moved her head from side to side. "Mabel's going to be fine. She does jazzercise, water aerobics, and cycling every morning at the senior center. Aaargh." She lifted her head and frowned. "That means she's going to be up and at 'em tomorrow morning while I'll be inching about like a snail. She's going to give me a hard time about that, I just know it."

Lydia yawned then gave her back a good stretch. "I'm thinking that maybe we ought to join her in some of those classes."

Kite rubbed her foot as the muscles inside twitched. "I told you ladies we weren't in the best shape to do this." Her foot fell back to the ground. "But I wouldn't have wanted to end this party any other way. That was a blast."

Jack came up behind her and rubbed her shoulders.

She patted his hand. Windy walked toward the table, followed by Eve and Mary. She carried the large picture frame she'd shown them earlier. She looked at Jack and smiled. "Everyone who was invited wrote out a special memory that they'd shared with you, and in the center is a photo of everyone at the party. Happy birthday, Jack."

He took hold of the frame and studied it. "Wow. Just … I don't know what to say."

Kite grasped his fingers. "It was Windy's idea to make that collage. She's also the one who put it all together."

"That's not all she did." Mary stepped forward and placed three eight-by-ten picture frames on the table. She slid one in front of Kite, and the other two in front of Priscilla and Lydia.

Inside each frame were dolls made of paper. Five of them. They'd obviously been drawn and cut a long time ago. Some were frayed around the edges, and others looked to have been torn at least once or twice during their lifetime.

"Eve and I drew these dolls and played with them repeatedly when we were younger," Mary said. "After I disappeared, she held on to them. She brought them to the party tonight so I'd be able to take a few home with me in the morning. But when Windy saw how fragile they were, she displayed them in these beautiful frames for us. That's when we came up with the idea to make doll frames for everyone."

Kite picked up her frame and stared at it. "Eve, I can't believe you still have these dolls after all these years."

"They've been buried the past couple of decades. That's why a few of them look like they've been through some rough times. But who knew that one day they'd see daylight again?"

Kite glanced at the ladies surrounding her and reached for Jack's hand and squeezed it. Who would have thought that any of them would have seen daylight again?

A few months ago, she wouldn't have thought it was possible.

But somehow, the five of them had made their way above ground.

And the future looked bright.

Really bright.

- THE END -

Kara Hunt enjoys both fiction and non-fiction and has been a contributing author to the devotional, Marriage Matters. Kara, an evangelical minister, hosts the Cheer UP! Podcast. She is a member of the Advanced Writers and Speakers Association (AWSA), the National Association of Christian Ministers, and American Christian Fiction Writers. She has garnered finalist and semi-finalist recognition in the ACFW Genesis Awards in the Mystery/Thriller/Suspense and Women's Fiction categories. Her personal testimony and Christian journey have given her a depth of knowledge from which to draw as she writes, shares, and helps women who have faced similar circumstances. Kara and her husband reside in rural Missouri.

Social Media: Facebook: https://www.facebook.com/kara.hunt.31

Twitter: https://twitter.com/KaraRHunt2022

Website: https://kararhunt.com/

Pinterest: https://www.pinterest.com/AuthorKaraRHunt/_saved/

Goodreads: https://www.goodreads.com/user/show/2610898-kara-r-hunt

Linked: https://www.linkedin.com/in/kara-hunt-23b4a1220/